# NIGHT OF THE LIVING THREAD

This Large Print Book carries the
Seal of Approval of N.A.V.H.

A THREADVILLE MYSTERY

# NIGHT OF THE LIVING THREAD

## JANET BOLIN

**WHEELER PUBLISHING**
*A part of Gale, Cengage Learning*

GALE
CENGAGE Learning·

Farmington Hills, Mich • San Francisco • New York • Waterville, Maine
Meriden, Conn • Mason, Ohio • Chicago

## GALE
### CENGAGE Learning®

**LIBRARY OF CONGRESS CATALOGING-IN-PUBLICATION DATA**

Bolin, Janet.
   Night of the living thread / by Janet Bolin. — Large print edition.
      pages ; cm. — (Wheeler Publishing large print cozy mystery) (A threadville mystery)
      ISBN 978-1-4104-7379-0 (softcover) — ISBN 1-4104-7379-1 (softcover)
   1. Murder—Investigation—Fiction. 2. Large type books. I. Title.
PS3602.O6534N54 2015
813'.6—dc23                                        2014039414

Published in 2015 by arrangement with The Berkley Publishing Group, a member of Penguin Group (USA) LLC, a Penguin Random House Company

Printed in the United States of America
1 2 3 4 5 6 7 19 18 17 16 15

*To everyone who lovingly creates
one-of-a-kind wedding gowns for
themselves, their friends,
or their family members*

# ACKNOWLEDGMENTS

Welcome back to Threadville again, and thank you for returning!

Many thanks to Krista Davis and Daryl Wood Gerber, who also writes as Avery Aames, for the friendship and support dating all the way back to when all three of us were unpublished but hopeful — and stubborn. Oops, I mean *determined.* Special thanks to Daryl, the punning title guru, who came up with the title *Night of the Living Thread.* And thanks to all my mystery writer friends. You are some of the most helpful people around.

Again, many thanks to my friend Sergeant Michael Boothby, Toronto Police (retired), for his excellent comments and suggestions. I'm afraid that my characters do not always follow Mike's advice . . .

Jessica Faust of BookEnds, LLC, continues to be my dream agent.

Berkley Prime Crime is a wonderful publisher. Thanks especially to my editor, Faith Black, and to the department that comes up with cover ideas. Robin Moline's paintings of Threadville are fabulous. If I didn't already "live" in Threadville — I often feel I do, anyway — I'd want to dive into her paintings.

Many members of the Berkley Prime Crime team help turn my manuscripts into books and put them onto the shelves of stores and libraries, and I thank all of them. Annette Fiore DeFex created the cover design, and Tiffany Estreicher designed the interior text.

Thanks to Threadologist Gail Heller Robertson for an entertaining and educational day with thread.

I had a wonderful time at needlework retreats at Brentwood on the Beach, hosted by the incomparable Joan and Peter Karsten. I loved the camaraderie of the other attendees. We laughed a lot. It was sort of like being a Threadville tourist. Besides, the other "tourists" were fabulous listeners to my readings.

I also greatly enjoyed reading at the Bony Blithe Gun Club & Quilting Bee Gala Award Reception and at the Scene of the Crime Mystery Festival, where they also let me babble about one of my favorite subjects, writing. Thank you to the organizers of both of those events.

Thanks to all of my friends, the new ones I've made during this writing and publishing journey, and those who have stuck by me through all my years of being stubborn. I mean determined.

Most of all, many thanks to my readers for returning with me to Threadville. Welcome back.

# 1

"Gord?" a woman's heartfelt plea fluted through the misty night.

Who was calling Threadville's favorite doctor in that flirtatious tone? In less than a week, Gord was marrying Edna.

That voice was not Edna's.

Dropping to a crouch behind the branches of a weeping willow, I put my arms around my two dogs, a brother-and-sister pair who were part border collie. Taking their cues from me, they remained silent, but they tensed against me.

"Gord!" The second plea was still bell-like, but now it was a command.

Mist drifted away, and the fairy lights in the gazebo-like bandstand on the hill above us were bright enough for me to see the woman on the riverbank.

I had never met her, but I knew who she was. She called herself Isis. Like many others, she was in Elderberry Bay for the

Threadville Get Ready for Halloween Craft Fair. Halloween was just over four weeks away, and Threadville tourists and customers were keen to create costumes and decorations.

Isis bound books by hand, books she titled *The New Book of the Dead,* which, she claimed, tied her craft to Halloween. To me, it seemed like a bit of a stretch.

Was Isis in costume? Despite the evening's foggy chill, she wore a sleeveless white gown with a gold cord tied around the empire waistline. She raised both hands, palms up, toward the sky. I squinted, but the fog kept me from figuring out what those small objects on her palms were.

I could have gone closer and introduced myself as Willow, one of the craft fair organizers, and also the owner of In Stitches, Threadville's machine embroidery boutique. However, I was curious about Isis's weird behavior. Okay, maybe I was just plain snoopy. I stayed hidden with my dogs, where we could watch without being seen.

Isis glided down the concrete boat launch ramp until water had to be lapping at the toes of her sandals. She stooped, placed the object from her right hand on the surface of the river, and intoned, "When your time comes, you will go to the afterlife I have chosen for you. I will join you there, eventually." Then she raised her voice and called out in raspy, doom-filled tones, "Edna!"

As far as I could tell in the wispy mist, Edna was nowhere near. I held my breath. Quivering in my embrace, my dogs stared toward Isis.

She thrust the object from her left hand onto the water, pushed it down, and held it underwater. "Go," she ordered, "to the deepest, darkest river! Go to the bowels of the Earth. Fall apart. Scatter. Go where you will never rise!"

The fog thickened, hiding Isis and enveloping the dogs and me in a cold gray cocoon that would keep Isis from seeing us. I shuddered. The little scene had turned nasty.

Hanging on to their leashes, I let the dogs pull me away from Isis and toward the dark trail that would take us along the river to our hillside apartment underneath In Stitches.

Isis's voice rang out again. "Who's there?"

I thought Sally-Forth and Tally-Ho might bark and give us away, but they only lowered their plume-like tails and increased their pace. No one answered Isis, but I heard footsteps, as if someone were running up the wooden access ramp leading to the bandstand, up the hill from me. I stopped the dogs and turned around. Distorted in the foggy glow, an elongated shadow flew through the mist in the bandstand. Isis, or someone else?

Farther away, down toward the beach, the fog parted, revealing a figure walking with a jerky gait, his arms held stiffly in front of his body, wrists bent, and palms down. He shambled up the hill toward where I'd seen Isis. He wore a dark suit with a 1930s silhouette, broad at the shoulders, narrow at the waist and hips, and lots of fabric in the pant legs. I couldn't make out details of his black hair or whiter-than-white face, other than he appeared to have a large wound near his chin.

For the past couple of days, zombies had been booking into the Elderberry Bay Lodge for what they called a zombie retreat.

The zombies were . . . unusual.

They weren't half as creepy as Isis.

Seeming totally freaked out, Sally-Forth and Tally-Ho tugged me to our apartment underneath my shop. The building was on a steep slope, so the apartment was mostly aboveground.

I gave the dogs extra treats, praised them, and, with Sally's help, gave my half-grown black-and-white tuxedo kittens, Mustache and Bow-Tie, an outing in the backyard. Sally had taught the kittens from an early age to stay close to her when outside. She supervised them while they did their duties, and then herded them to the patio door.

For once, I was too worried to relax, wind down, and play with my four pets.

Isis had just threatened Edna, who was one of my favorite people.

And Isis was Edna's houseguest.

# 2

Maybe I was being irrational, but for my own peace of mind, I needed to warn Edna about possible threats from her guest. I forced myself outside again, into the sinister, foggy night, and ran up through my sloping side yard.

My friends' Threadville shops and apartments were in a row of stores on the ground floor of a Victorian building on the other side of Lake Street. Under the streetlights, the building's red bricks looked almost black.

Like the other shops, Edna's notions boutique had large front windows. Edna's lights were on, and I could see her inside Buttons and Bows. Gord was there, also, on a ladder, apparently helping his fiancée arrange reels of trims on upper shelves, packing them together upright like books in a library. I ran across the street and opened the door, setting off Edna's *Buttons and*

*Beaux* tune, an old vaudeville one that had, I'd been told, slightly risqué lyrics. As always, Edna's shop dazzled, with buttons totally covering one wall, ribbons, braids, lace, and fringe covering the other, and an aisle down the middle between glass display cases.

From high on his ladder, Gord waved a bolt of purple ball fringe at me. "Hi, Willow! I'm having a ball up here."

Edna hugged me. She was a cute little birdlike person, short compared to my height of almost six feet. She was barely over fifty, and though her hair was still naturally brown, she had colored it silver for her wedding. Not the silver of graying hair, but metallic silver. She'd grown it to a shoulder-length bob. At the moment, she'd added nothing sparkly to it besides the color, but I was sure that on the day itself, she would be a vision of crystal, an ice princess in October. She asked. "Did you come to help us, Willow?"

"In a way." I felt my forehead crease. "I just saw something disturbing."

Gord took a step down the ladder toward me. "What's wrong, Willow?" I half expected him to whip out a stethoscope and rush the rest of the way down the ladder to check my heartbeat.

In Edna's cheerful shop, my story sounded a little silly, and I couldn't blame Edna and Gord for their skepticism.

Still on his ladder, Gord peered toward Edna's front windows. "Fog?"

Our section of Lake Street was high and free of fog at the moment. I mumbled, "There's plenty of it down by the river."

He felt his way down another step. "Yes, some evenings are like that. Romantic, right, my little chickadee?"

Edna beamed up at him. "Right. And I'm not worried."

Gord inched down to the next step. "I'm not, either, but thanks for your concern, Willow."

Edna's *Buttons and Beaux* tune played again. Isis dashed into the store, pulled the door shut faster than it wanted to go, and stood panting, her back to us and her palms on the door frame as if she were trying to prevent a wild animal from coming inside with her.

I couldn't see anything on the other side of the door.

She turned around. She was older than I'd first believed, in her late fifties. Maybe she only looked older because the corners of her mouth were turned down and her pupils were dilated. "Gord!" she shrieked.

"I just had the most unspeakable fright!" Her gown was made from a light nylon knit, as if she'd taken a nightgown and dressed it up with a scratchy gold cord tied around the empire waistline.

Again the picture of concern, Gord took another step down the ladder. "What happened?"

Isis took a deep shuddering breath and clutched at her throat. "A zombie attacked me." Apparently, the fright hadn't been entirely unspeakable.

Gord put his left hand up to his ear and hung on to the ladder with only his right, which, considering that I was standing below him, was about to give *me* an unspeakable fright. Not that Isis's sinister curses on the riverbank hadn't already scared me enough.

Gord asked her, "Did you say a zombie? Attacked you? Want us to call the police?"

She trilled a little laugh that seemed incongruous after her *unspeakable* fright. "He didn't attack me physically, but he had some notion that I might be casting a spell on him, and he told me to stop it or he would . . . I'm not sure what, but he looked violent."

I should find this zombie as a possible ally to help me convince Gord and Edna to be wary of Isis. Maybe the zombie was the big-shouldered one I'd seen in the dark suit. Or had zombies been all over the park while Isis was shouting into the fog, and I hadn't seen the others? While the dogs and I were fleeing Isis and her curses, someone else, apparently not the zombie in the 1930s suit, had run through the bandstand and away from the park.

Gord reassured Isis, "The zombies visiting Elderberry Bay aren't real."

"I know that," she said seriously. "But this guy's threat was."

Gord asked her again if he should call the police.

"No, I guess I was just being a big silly-pie." Her coy smile showed off a dimple in her cheek. "What are you doing up there on that ladder, Gord?"

"Coming down."

She cooed, "That ladder doesn't look safe." I could have sworn she batted her eyelashes at him.

He patted his belly. "You mean I'm too portly."

Her "silly-pie" laughter put my teeth on edge. "I mean that ladder looks flimsy." The woman was an accomplished simperer.

I felt ill.

Edna was obviously miffed. "It's a perfectly good ladder."

Isis shaded her eyes against the shop's sparkling beads, buttons, sequins, and crystals. "Oh, hullo."

Maybe Isis hadn't seen me, either, beside Edna on the other side of Gord's ladder. I stepped into the center of the aisle. "Hi, I'm Willow. I own the machine embroidery boutique across the street, In Stitches."

Isis covered her mouth and tittered. Where had she learned these old-fashioned mannerisms? "Willow! What an apt name for such a beanpole. Do you weep, too?"

I was about to . . . Or hurl.

Edna stepped closer to me. "Willow is lovely and slender."

Isis eyed me up and down. "Yes. I see. Is she another of your 'daughters'?" She made air quotes with her fingers.

Edna smiled. "She does look a bit like Haylee, doesn't she — tall, slender, and beautiful? But no, my girlfriends and I didn't raise Willow, though we'd gladly take credit for her."

I flashed Edna a smile.

Gord said, "In Threadville, they're all like family."

Edna's chin came up. "They?"

He let out his warm boom of a laugh. "We. I guess we're done here, Edna, and we should let you and your guest get some sleep. C'mon, Willow, I'll walk you home."

His message was clear. I wasn't supposed to confront Isis about what the zombie, whoever he was, and I had seen. I wasn't sure what it meant, anyway, and I wasn't about to embarrass Gord and Edna by starting an argument. In a way, Isis was the guest of all of Threadville, and as the owner of one of Threadville's shops, I should be hospitable.

But I still wanted to hurl.

The little tune started when Gord opened the door for me. I thought I heard Isis ask something like, *Didn't she say her shop was only across the street?*

After the door closed and we were in the middle of Lake Street, I turned to Gord. "She was flirting with you!"

He stopped walking. Luckily, no traffic was around. "Was she?"

"You didn't notice? Being flirted with must be an occupational hazard for doctors."

"I suppose so."

It had to be a hazard for Gord, anyway. He was genuinely thoughtful, and couldn't help being charming. And almost grandfatherly toward both Haylee and me. He was considerably older than Edna.

"She *was*," I insisted.

"The woman barely knows me. She had dinner with us last night. She was in Edna's apartment when I picked Edna up, so I invited her, and she came. The woman spent one entire evening in my company — hardly enough time for anyone to work up a proper crush."

I teased, "You're fishing for compliments."

He staggered playfully, hand over heart. "You've wounded me."

Laughing, I pulled him to the safety of the sidewalk in front of my shop. "You'll be responsible for *all* of your injuries if your dramatics get you run over."

"Good thing I'm a doctor."

"You're incorrigible."

He pointed. "Your shop looks great." Trying to distract me, no doubt.

He succeeded, at least for a moment. I loved In Stitches. Night-lights inside the shop drew my gaze away from the building's classic Arts and Crafts architecture and through the windows to the merchandise inside — sewing machines and their embroidery attachments, natural fabrics, racks of embroidery thread, and all the other supplies and accessories needed for machine embroidery. Still, I made one last attempt to sway Gord. "I'm worried about Edna alone with that woman."

He patted my shoulder. "My little chicka-dee is one of the strongest people I know."

"Yes, but . . ." I spoke the rest of the sentence in a rush. "What if that woman thinks she can harm Edna and have you for herself?"

"She can't."

"She may not know that."

"Willow." The kindness in his voice softened the rebuke I suspected was coming. "Isis, or whatever her name is, can go to the river in the fog and mutter all the curses she wants. None of them can harm Edna or anyone else. Besides, some zombie obviously thought that Isis was casting a spell on him, not on Edna or me."

So much for the zombie, whoever he was, helping me convince Gord that he and Edna could be in danger from Isis and her incantations. "I suppose you're right. But I'll be glad when you're married and that woman is gone from town."

His smile outshined the streetlight above us. "I'll be glad when Edna and I are married, too. You have a good night, now."

"You, too."

He strode down the street. As he passed Edna's shop, he raised his head and sang toward the windows of her second-floor apartment. Gord loved opera and had an amazing voice.

I hoped that Isis didn't think his love song was aimed at her.

If it hadn't been late, I might have let myself into my shop and spent a few hours playing with software, thread, and fabric. Instead, I opened the gate and walked down the hill toward my apartment door.

Below my apartment, Blueberry Cottage, a curlicued Victorian gem painted dusty teal, brooded in the darkness. The cottage had been moved up the hill from its original 1890s position, which had been too close to the river. Now that it was finally safe from possible floods, I could rent it to tourists as soon as the renovations were done. The interior had been taken down to the bare studs.

Farther down the slope, my yard disappeared in low-lying mist. I couldn't see my back gate, or the riverside trail leading to the park where Isis and an unknown number of zombies had been, or the Elderberry River, or the backdrop of the state forest rising on the opposite bank.

My pets greeted me with their usual zeal. Settling the two dogs for the night was easy. They'd spent the day upstairs in their pen in the rear section of In Stitches, where they'd watched everyone browsing and learning. The two kittens, however, must have snoozed most of the day in my apartment. After I got into bed, they tussled with each other and pounced on my head.

But that wasn't all that kept me from falling asleep. Unease drifted through my mind like the swathes of fog down by the river. What was Isis up to? How could anyone dislike Edna or want to harm her? And why had a zombie taken Isis's curses personally? Had the zombie really threatened her, or had she only been flirting with Gord?

Eventually, I managed to sleep. And then the sharp ringing of my phone startled me. A phone call in the early morning usually meant I needed to respond to an emergency with the village's other volunteer firefighters. But the siren on the fire station's roof was silent.

Who was calling me? The clock beside the bed said six thirty. I could have slept another hour and still had plenty of time to shower, dress, walk the dogs, have breakfast, and open In Stitches for the day. Mentally muttering, I fumbled for the phone.

"Willow?" My mother. Why was she phoning me at this hour?

Was something wrong? My breath caught. Was my dad okay? He was quiet and uncomplaining, but I always feared he would hurt himself in his workshop way out in their woods, and no one would realize for hours that he was missing.

My mother purred, "I need a favor."

I'd learned not to grant my mother a favor before asking questions. Whenever she was in the midst of a political campaign, she seemed to forget that I couldn't abandon In Stitches and run home to arrange a dinner party or fund-raiser.

"What?" Between my caution and grogginess, my question undoubtedly came out sounding surly or peeved.

"I need you to let someone stay with you this week."

"Here?"

"Where else?" She sounded amused.

"This week is, um, kind of busy. Our village is putting on a pre-Halloween craft show, and helping friends with their wedding."

My mother's Southern accent became as thick and sweet as corn syrup. "I don't ask much of you, Willow, honey, now do I?"

Well, she did, but I'd had to decline, again and again. I clutched the phone tighter and gulped. "No."

"And you've often told me that you have a guest room where you could put your

27

father and me up."

"I do, but —"

"Brianna Shrevedale is coming to see you, and she needs a place to stay, so you'll want to be her hostess," my mother said.

"Who is Brianna Shrevedale and why is she coming to see me?"

My mother was good at patient encouragement. "Brianna's a thread distributor."

I pointed out, "Sales representatives aren't usually the houseguests of shopkeepers." In my early years, my mother had drilled Southern hospitality into me, so of course I felt guilty. Apparently, I'd lost some of those old Southern attitudes, along with most of my accent, while living in New York City, and I hadn't regained them up here in northwestern Pennsylvania.

"Don't you follow my career even the itsy-bitsiest bit?"

I could tell she was trying to hide her disappointment in her only child, which made me feel worse, but I managed to defend myself, more or less. "I know you're in the South Carolina House of Representatives and that you're running for the state senate."

"And can you guess who has been instrumental in my success so far and, with luck, will help me get into the senate, and possibly beyond?"

Not me, I feared. "Brianna Shrevedale?"

"Her father. Todd Shrevedale is my biggest financial supporter. He's done so much for me! We can pay some of that back now by giving his daughter a hand up. She can start her business by selling her threads to you and your customers. You'll want to buy lots to help her out."

I repeated, "It's busy here right now. The Threadville Get Ready for Halloween Craft Fair starts Saturday, and —"

"How perfect is *that*? Brianna can have a table at your fair and sell her threads for people up there to use in their costumes. You'll like her. She's a nice kid."

I could tell that as far as my mother was concerned, the matter was settled, but I went on with my fruitless objections. "And Edna's wedding is Monday, and —"

"Who's Edna?"

"A friend. All of us in Threadville are helping with her wedding."

"Threadville? That's not really the name of the village where you've set up shop, is it?" I heard her mouse click. "Aha. Found it. Your address is Elderberry Bay."

"Threadville is a nickname because of all the textile arts shops here." I was sure I'd already mentioned this in e-mails and phone calls.

"How *adorable*. And it's so perfect! Brianna would probably *love* to help you with the wedding. It will be a good way for you two girls to bond."

Girls? I was over thirty. However, I didn't exactly come across as mature when I tried one more time to avoid hosting a guest during this extra-busy week. "The wedding's being held at the Elderberry Bay Lodge. It's a wonderful hotel. Brianna could stay there."

"It's full. They're having some sort of weird convention — werewolves or something."

"A zombie retreat."

"Whatever. It's solidly booked."

That wasn't surprising. The restored Victorian lodge was beautiful inside and out, but it wasn't huge, and in addition to the zombie in the park the night before, I'd already encountered lots of zombies wandering the streets and beaches. Some of them had even rented tables at the craft fair. I wasn't certain that I looked forward to finding out what their crafts might be, but I'd been assured that it was all harmless fun.

Because the lodge was small, many of the

Threadville shopkeepers besides Edna had opened their homes to people renting tables at the craft fair, but no one had been keen on staying in a two-bedroom apartment with two largish dogs and a pair of adolescent kittens.

I relented, not that I had a choice. "If Brianna's not allergic to dogs or cats, I suppose she can stay with me." I added in somewhat warmer tones, "When's she coming?" Surely, she wouldn't stay long and wouldn't expect me to entertain her. My co-conspirators and I had a lot to do to finish Edna's wedding gown — the one that Edna didn't know about.

My mother gave her politician's tinkle of a laugh. "She's parked outside your store as we speak."

## 3

The guest my mother wanted me to host was outside In Stitches this very minute? Couldn't my mother have warned me sooner?

She asked, "Your store is called In Stitches, right?"

"Right." The way I drew the word out, I almost sounded like I was reverting to my Southern accent.

"Go outside, Willow, honey. She could use your help unpacking and moving in."

*Moving in?*

Before I could say anything else, my mother, State Congresswoman Wanda Vanderling, MD, disconnected the call.

I threw on a bathrobe, slid my feet into slippers, and took the stairs two at a time. All four of my pets rumbled up the stairs as fast as their legs could take them, and they all, except Bow-Tie, who stopped to bat at something that only he could see, reached the top before I did.

The mischievous kittens would have to mellow a little before I could give them the run of my boutique. Undoubtedly, they would view spools of embroidery thread as rows of kitty toys that should be removed from their racks and chased all over my vintage walnut floor. I managed to let the dogs into the shop and close the door before the kittens could join us.

I shut the dogs into their large pen in the back of the store, then trotted past sewing machines with samples of embroidery displayed in hoops in their embroidery attachments. I rounded my cutting table without bumping into a corner, rushed between bolts of beautiful fabrics, unlocked the front door, and stepped out onto my porch.

Out on Lake Street, a small blonde dragged a heavy sales case out of the trunk of an old, dull red sedan. The October morning sun must have been in the woman's eyes. She squinted toward me as if at a loss about what to say.

Who could blame her?

My mother, who tried to be kind but often came across as overbearing, may have forced the woman to barge in on me at this peculiar time of the morning. Taking pity on the obviously embarrassed woman and hoping that none of my friends would look out their windows or drive past and see me wandering around in my fuzzy pink robe and slippers, I ran down the porch steps.

Up close, I understood why my mother had referred to Brianna Shrevedale as a "girl." Brianna must have been barely out of college. She had that pulled-an-all-nighter look, with her makeup flaking, her lipstick mostly chewed-off, and her single braid losing wisps of hair.

I asked her, "Are you Brianna?"

"Yes."

"Can I help you carry anything?"

She pointed at the sales case at her feet. "Your mother said you'd like to see my thread samples."

"She was right. Come on in. My guest room is ready for you." Fortunately, I kept it neat most of the time, unless I was working on a sewing project. At the moment, I was, but not in my apartment. I couldn't help a fleeting grin at the thought of how Edna would react when she saw the surprise wedding gown we were creating for her.

Brianna hesitated. "Is there a place to park near your apartment?"

I offered her an apologetic smile. "I'm afraid this is as close as you can get. My apartment is beneath In Stitches."

I followed her glance to the front of my shop. I loved the deep, wide front porch, invitingly sheltered under a roof. These early October days were still warm, and I had not yet put away my rocking chairs, tables, books, magazines, and potted flowers. I'd chosen deep red mums for autumn and had added cornstalks, pumpkins, and strangely shaped gourds to the décor.

Brianna frowned.

I picked up the case. "I'll show you how to go downstairs from my shop to my apartment, and then you can settle in while I get ready for work."

Usually, when sales reps first saw the inside of In Stitches, they made appreciative comments. Brianna didn't say anything until we got to the racks of embroidery threads — almost every color imaginable in silk, rayon, cotton, nylon, and polyester. "You already have thread." Her voice was so flat that I couldn't tell if she was disappointed or happy. She could have even been angry. Or scared.

I turned to look at her. The top of her head barely came past my elbow. "I should hope so! But I love thread and trying new kinds and colors." I set her sample case beside my racks of threads and headed for the dogs' pen. "I hope you don't mind dogs."

"Do they bite?"

Who could look at Sally and Tally's sweet faces and possibly think the little charmers would bite? At the moment they were whimpering and clamoring for attention, and their tails were wagging at about a hundred miles an hour. "No. The black-and-white one is Sally-Forth and the brindle-and-white one is Tally-Ho. They're brother and sister. I adopted them from a rescue organization when they were about a year old. They're very friendly." I opened the gate and told the dogs to sit. They did, but their tails swished across the floor, and their mouths hung open in happy grins.

Brianna hunched her shoulders and pulled her fists to her collar. "They have a lot of teeth."

I showed her how to let the dogs sniff the backs of her hands, but she wouldn't try.

Sally closed her mouth, leaving the tip of her tongue out, a particularly endearing pose. She tilted her head, obviously bewildered. Usually, people wanted to stroke her glossy fur. I rubbed both dogs behind their ears so they'd know that I still loved them, even if Brianna was less than impressed.

Yowling and scratching erupted from the

stairs leading down to my apartment.

Brianna jerked her head around to stare at the apartment's closed door. "What's that?"

"My kittens. They're almost full-grown."

"How many cats?" She sounded wary.

No wonder. They were making a terrible ruckus. "Only two."

"Two dogs and two cats for one apartment?"

I wondered what, if anything, Brianna actually liked. Her threads, I hoped. "The apartment has two bedroom and bathroom suites," I countered. "You get your own. The pets will stay out of it."

She didn't look convinced.

"Tell you what," I said. "I need to shower, dress for work, and have breakfast. How about if I show you the outside way to the apartment? I'll shut my pets into the master suite with me, and you can carry your stuff inside without tripping over animals."

She yawned. "Okay."

Leaving the dogs where they were for the moment, I led her out through the shop's front door. She yawned again.

I asked, "Where did you stay last night? You got here very early." It had to be somewhere nearby. Maybe the Elderberry Bay Lodge wasn't quite overflowing with zombies yet.

She mumbled, "I drove all night."

"You poor thing!" That could explain her lack of enthusiasm. "Let's get you settled. Maybe you'd like a nap before you show me your threads."

"Okay." Still no sign of interest.

At her car, I couldn't help staring in concern. She had brought a surprising amount of luggage. Her trunk and her back-seat were crammed to the top.

*Moving in,* my mother had said . . .

Carrying a garment bag and an overnight case, I led the way down the sidewalk to my gate. Behind me, Brianna rolled a large wheeled suitcase. She grunted when she had to pick it up on the grassy hill outside my bedroom windows. My guest suite, the one that would be hers, looked out on the other side yard, but I didn't have a gate on that side, and the sliding glass patio door was in the middle of the rear of the building, any-way.

My serene backyard should help my young guest feel refreshed after her all-night drive. Below Blueberry Cottage, my newly seeded lawn and flower gardens sloped down to my back fence and the riverside trail beyond it. Tall cedars on both sides of my yard had bushed out, and almost hid the chain links.

Maples above us were turning gold and red. A puffy blanket of early-morning fog on the river gave the entire vista a dramatic and mysterious feel. I took a deep breath of contentment. Autumn even smelled good.

Brianna yawned.

I led her to my patio. The wheels of her suitcase rattled across the flagstones. At the sliding glass door, Mustache and Bow-Tie stood on their hind feet and pawed at the glass. I made certain the garment bag and overnight bag wouldn't fall over. "I'll imprison the cats," I told Brianna, "so we won't have to worry about them escaping if you want to bring in more." Between the two of us, we'd hauled enough luggage from her car in one trip for at least a two-week stay.

Brianna didn't exclaim over my kittens' cuteness as I scooped up the warm little squirmers. I shut them inside the master suite, returned to the patio, and brought Brianna and her luggage into my great room.

My kitchen and dining area took up the left half of the great room, and a comfy seating area was on the right. Behind us, the patio door was centered in a wall of glass that made the room bright and airy. Again, most people told me the apartment was lovely with its white walls and upholstery and its touches of colorful machine embroidery.

Brianna didn't say a thing, maybe because of the racket the kittens were making on the other side of my bedroom door.

My suite was ahead and to the right. The laundry room door was straight ahead. The door to the left of the laundry room opened to the hallway leading into the guest suite. Brianna would have her own bedroom, bathroom, and a large walk-in closet, but most of the guest closet was taken up with sewing supplies. I tried not to let my stash grow too much, but although I sewed a lot, I always seemed to purchase ahead of what I could finish that week. Or that month. Or that season . . .

The stairway to In Stitches was to the left of my guest suite, between it and the kitchen area. I thought my apartment was perfect for one person and the occasional guest.

Brianna must have been really tired. She didn't speak when I ushered her into the guest suite with its white furnishings, including a duvet cover I'd embroidered. Maybe Brianna didn't care for ruffles, even the restrained, tailored ones I'd added to the bedding and curtains.

As we left her suite, I pointed to the

stairway. "When you feel like showing off your thread samples, go up to In Stitches. People come to Threadville every day by bus, car, and on foot. All of the Threadville store owners give workshops. I'll have one this morning and another after lunch. Besides, other customers come and go all day. I'm sure the women attending my workshops would love to see your samples."

"Okay." How could a thread distributor sound so bored about thread? "I'll go out for another load," she said in her monotone, "then crash for a while."

"Want breakfast? I can scramble eggs and make toast and coffee. Or there's cereal."

"Maybe when I wake up."

"I don't have much food on hand." I would have, though, if my mother had told me in time that Brianna was coming. "For lunch, I usually grab a peanut butter or grilled cheese sandwich and some carrots and an apple, and there's plenty of that for you, too. If that's not enough, go north on Lake Street — that's down the hill toward the beach — and you'll find a couple of restaurants. The Threadville tour ladies who don't bring their lunches usually eat at Pier 42."

"Okay." She yawned, turned around, headed into her suite, and closed the door.

Maybe she'd be more companionable after her nap.

I collected the dogs from upstairs, showered, and dressed in jeans, an orange T-shirt, and a jean jacket I'd embellished with machine-embroidered pumpkins and fall leaves.

Brianna didn't come out of her bedroom or join me for breakfast. After a brief outing, the kittens went back into my suite and the dogs and I trotted upstairs to In Stitches.

We'd left one of Brianna's heavy cases in the shop. I carried it to the storeroom, turned the embroidered *Come Back Later* sign in my glass front door to *Welcome,* filled the dogs' water dishes, and petted the dogs until the Threadville tour buses arrived and my morning students crowded into In Stitches.

I wasn't actually teaching classes that day. I was helping with a project that Rosemary, who drove the bus from Erie, had suggested. "Everyone loves Edna," she had said, "so why don't we make a wedding quilt for her?"

Naturally, everybody associated with Threadville, except Edna, who didn't know about it, loved the idea. At In Stitches, we had embroidered blocks for the quilt.

The women in my shop helped themselves to cider and cookies and then commandeered embroidery machines.

I glanced out my big front windows. Other Threadville tourists were inside Buttons and Bows, learning how to decorate everything they made with every possible trim. Little did Edna know that some of the decorations she'd sold to my students had been brought to In Stitches to be added to a quilt for her.

To the left of Edna's shop was Tell a Yarn, where quilt blocks were being knit and crocheted for Edna.

Many of the fabrics and some of the embellishing techniques and yet more quilt blocks came from Haylee's fabric shop, The Stash, at the far left end of the row of Threadville shops.

To the right of Edna's shop was Batty About Quilts, where the blocks would be sewn together, the quilt top would be stitched to the batting and the backing, and the entire quilt would be bound.

Threadville was a wonderful place. Everyone gave everyone else moral support. Besides, if I ran out of anything, one of my friends in the other stores was sure to have what I needed, or know who did.

Edna loved bright colors, sparkle, and glitter, and all the women in my shop were going wild.

Using water-soluble stabilizer and my embroidery software and machines, I had made 3-D lace bride and groom dolls, like wedding cake toppers, to attach to my block. I had even used silver metallic embroidery thread for the bride's hair.

For the 3-D effect, I had made an almost-circular skirt for the bride, which would fasten in back with loops and tabs that I'd built into the embroidery design. The groom, with his cylindrical pant legs and tuxedo, was a little more complex.

I'd soaked the figures in warm water to dissolve the stabilizer, then, without rinsing all the dissolved stabilizer out because I wanted it to remain as starch in the lace, I'd assembled both the bride and groom, complete with a tab on his hand and a loop on hers so they could hold hands, and had hung them to dry on a doll-sized clothesline I'd set up on the low wall surrounding my front porch. By now they should be dry enough to take apart, iron, and put back together. I crossed my fingers that by letting them dry while assembled, I'd kept the loops and tabs in the right places, and her skirt wouldn't be hiked up, and his legs would be close to the same length.

Eager to see how the cute couple had fared, I went out to the front porch to get them.

The little clothesline was where I'd left it, tucked behind one of my rocking chairs.

The bride and groom dolls were gone.

# 4

The tiny clothespins were still clipped to the line. Could the miniature bride and groom have blown away? I hadn't noticed anything resembling a strong wind since the afternoon before, when I'd hung my free-standing lace creations. I ran down the porch steps and around to the side.

The bride and groom weren't among the hostas and mums in the flower bed below the porch, either.

Trudging up the steps, I shivered, even though it was a warm morning for October.

Last night, Isis had put a couple of objects into the river and called out Edna's and Gord's names. Surely, she wouldn't have stolen the lace dolls as part of a curse against Threadville's favorite bride and groom.

However, there was a bright side to missing crafts — the need to make replacements. I could show a different group how to make

3-D lace with machine embroidery.

I went inside and invited all who were interested — which turned out to be everyone in the shop — to gather around my computer monitor to see how I'd drawn the original design. "Basically," I told them, "you have to make certain that each element of the design is attached to other elements with enough stitches that the design won't change shape after you rinse out the stabilizer." If I hadn't done that, my bride and groom could have stretched to long, thin, unrecognizable shapes.

Two women who had already finished their quilt blocks volunteered to make the new bride and groom dolls. They transferred my designs to sewing machines with embroidery attachments, stitched new bride and groom dolls, and soaked them in a basin of hot water to partially dissolve the stabilizer. We hung the cute little bridal pair up to dry — in the restroom, this time.

We were so busy that I forgot I had a houseguest until Rosemary took over for me at lunchtime.

Sally-Forth, Tally-Ho, and I clattered downstairs to our apartment. Discordant music reverberated from the guest suite through the closed door. Not to be outdone, Mustache and Bow-Tie created their own clashing harmonies from my bedroom. An opened jar of grape jelly with a knife sticking out of it, a plate of toast crumbs, and a glass containing about an inch of orange juice were on the counter near the sink.

I let the kittens into the great room. They rubbed against me and the dogs while Sally-Forth sniffed them all over. She looked up at me, then pointedly at the glass door, her signal that it was time for all four animals to go out. As usual, Sally curtailed any exploring tendencies the kittens showed, and wasn't ready to play with Tally until after I took the kittens inside again. I tidied away the remains of Brianna's breakfast, made my lunch, shut the kittens into my suite, and ate at the picnic table on the patio while the dogs wrestled and explored.

After my lunch, music still blasted from Brianna's room, but she didn't emerge. I took my hair dryer and the dogs upstairs to the shop.

While I blow-dried and pressed the lace dolls my students had made in the morning, the after-lunch group completed their quilt blocks. It was late in the afternoon when, with lots of admiring noises, we arranged the blocks on the cutting table. The 3-D lace bride and groom, standing and holding hands in a machine-embroidered garden, made everyone smile.

Resembling a lost soul, Brianna straggled into the shop through the front door. I introduced her to everyone. Rosemary proudly showed her the quilt blocks we'd made for Edna's quilt.

"Won't it be small?" Brianna asked.

Rosemary gave her a once-over, like a mother checking to see if a child had washed her face and combed her hair before school. "They're making blocks in the fabric store, the yarn store, and the quilt store, too. It may end up humongous."

"Nice," Brianna said in her flat voice.

I brought her case out of the storeroom. She opened it and showed us the thread she could sell us. She still didn't become enthused.

The rest of us did. She had exciting new threads to show us, in many different colors, weights, and sheens.

I picked up a box marked *Glow-in-the-Dark Thread.* The thread was white. "What color is this when it glows in the dark?" I asked her.

"Kind of a yellowish-greenish white, like fireflies. They're designing different colors every day." She showed us a card with pictures of brighter green, blue, yellow, orange, and pink spools of thread. "These are the ones I can order now, but there will be more."

I didn't need the oohs and aahs of my students to tell me to order some of each color available now, and others later.

Luckily, Brianna had lots of the whitish glow-in-the-dark thread. Customers wanted to buy them from her, but she pointed at me. "It's her store. *She* can buy them and sell them to you."

I bought lots of thread, including three dozen spools of glow-in-the-dark thread, many of which I sold to Threadville tourists who wanted to help make trick-or-treaters safer.

Brianna stayed in the shop, fiddling with her threads and answering questions in a very offhand fashion while Rosemary and some of her friends carefully carried the quilt blocks off to Batty About Quilts.

They returned with a pair of zombies.

In a stiff-legged walk with their arms angled ahead of them, the zombies stumbled toward the cash desk.

Some of the women gasped and a few backed away, but most of us smiled. No one ran outside screaming, or even *not* screaming. In their pen, Sally and Tally stood up, stretched, sniffed, and wagged their tails.

Both zombies were tall, with whiter-than-white skin — quite a makeup feat for the one wearing nothing besides wildly flowered surfer shorts, flip-flops, and a beach towel. He was about my age, and the clothing, or lack of it, showed off a physique that any man, undead or alive, might want to achieve. His white-blond hair lay flat against his head. I wanted to touch it to see if it was wet or merely heavily gelled.

The other zombie's ultra-white face was marred by a red gash running from one corner of his mouth to his chin. Red dribbled down the jacket of his disheveled black 1930s suit and smeared the tops of his black leather dress shoes. All of the "blood" looked fresh and wet. The man could have been in his early forties, but it was hard to be sure. Was he the zombie I'd seen in the park the night before, the one who had allegedly confronted Isis? Maybe lots of the zombies in the retreat resembled this one. I wasn't about to interrogate him in my crowded shop, however. I'd watch for a chance to talk to him alone.

Actually, I wasn't very fond of that idea, either.

I asked, "How can I help you two?"

Rosemary nudged me and murmured, "Maybe you shouldn't ask."

Disheveled suit displayed his teeth.

Surfer shorts tramped closer. A rope with a sliced-off end trailed from a loop tied around one ankle. "Any fresh meat?"

I managed not to laugh. "Sorry, no, but would you like supplies for machine embroidery? A top-of-the-line embroidery machine, perhaps?" I could always hope.

Surfer shorts said, "We hear you have glow-in-the-dark thread. We live underground with only glowworms for light. Sell us some of your glow-in-the-dark thread and we won't insist on raw meat."

The guy could probably see in the dark by the twinkles in his eyes. Zombies wandering around Threadville could be fun.

He pulled a wallet from a pocket sewn to the underside of his beach towel.

Disheveled suit made a derogatory sound in his throat. "You should check the expiry date on his credit card. Surfer boy here drowned off the coast of California in 1975."

The surfer was a man, not a boy. The first name on his credit card was Lenny. The expiry date was in the future. Grinning at him, I ran the card through my reader.

Disheveled suit handed me a ball of crumpled bills. Straightening them, I hid a shudder. Surely, those weren't blood stains on the bills . . .

"Floyd's the name, liquor's the game," he told me.

I stared pointedly at the red-rimmed "bullet" holes in the front of his jacket. "I can introduce you guys to a good tailor."

Lenny cracked a smile. Floyd stared at me coldly. Lenny handed me a stack of flyers. The two zombies stowed their wallets and spools of thread in their pockets, turned, and walked, if I could call it that, outside.

The door closed behind them. My beach glass chimes were still jingling when everyone in the store except Brianna burst out laughing. Brianna bent over her display case, shut it, snapped the latch, and carried it out the front door.

Rosemary picked up one of the flyers Lenny had left us. "This could be fun." She read in a doleful voice, "Haunted Graveyard. Come to the Elderberry Bay Lodge Graveyard on Saturday night for an experience you'll remember for the rest of your short life."

## 5

We all agreed that a convention of zombies might put on quite a show at a haunted graveyard.

I pointed out, "There's no such thing as the Elderberry Bay Lodge Graveyard."

Rosemary asked, "Wasn't someone buried on the grounds, though?"

I hid a shudder. "A former owner of the lodge. But he wasn't *supposed* to be there, and his remains have been placed elsewhere." Not keen on reliving the events surrounding the discovery of the former innkeeper's remains, I changed the subject back to 3-D lace machine embroidery.

After Rosemary and her group left for the evening, I closed the shop, followed Sally and Tally downstairs, took all four animals outside, and made one of my favorite bare-cupboard suppers, macaroni and cheese.

Music boomed from my guest room. The aroma of melting cheddar filled the apartment. Rubbing her eyes as if she'd had another nap, Brianna emerged from my guest suite. I offered her macaroni and cheese.

"Okay." We sat on stools at my kitchen island. Staring out the back windows, she asked, "Why is there a house in your backyard?"

"It was one of the village's original homes. It became a rental cottage after the house we're in was built. When I bought this property, the cottage was much closer to the river. Every few years, the river floods, so I had the cottage moved up the hill."

"I could stay there instead of in here with all these animals."

I clenched my teeth, nearly breaking them on my fork. Ordinarily, "all these animals" had the run of the apartment. For Brianna's sake, they were in my suite, behind a closed door. I extricated my fork from between my teeth, but sounded terse. "Blueberry Cottage is not ready for guests. It's been gutted."

"Your animals could stay out there."

She wasn't only "moving in" — she was also planning to take over? Although my mother had said something about Brianna helping with Edna's wedding, I hoped Brianna wouldn't be around that long. This was Thursday. The craft fair was Saturday and Sunday. The wedding would be Monday afternoon.

In any case, I wasn't about to let Brianna decide where my pets could live. "No. Animals would be in the way of the workers in Blueberry Cottage, and besides, someone might let them out."

"So?"

"They wouldn't be safe. I have to watch them carefully, especially the kittens, or they might scramble over or under my fence." The dogs had never been unsupervised in my yard long enough to consider tunneling out, though to my horror, someone had once let them out.

Brianna shrugged. Maybe she'd never had or loved pets. She ate glumly for a while, then demanded, "Is there anything to *do* around here?"

"A bunch of us are going out tonight, only around the corner, to work on a surprise for a friend who's getting married. Lots of Threadville people will be there, including shop owners, so you're welcome to come along."

"Okay."

Not very gracious, but, as my mother would have observed, neither was my invitation.

I tried to sound more welcoming. "You'll meet Haylee, who owns the fabric store, and Naomi, who has the quilt shop. You'll want to show them your thread before you go on to your next stop." Okay, that hint was blatant. My mother would have been appalled.

She yawned. "When are we going?"

"After I clear supper away and give the animals another outing. About ten minutes."

"Okay." She shoved her plate forward, edged off the stool, shuffled into her suite, and shut the door.

She was young, I told myself, that's why she didn't clean up after herself.

Or look me in the eye. I didn't think she'd done it even once since she'd arrived early in the morning.

And she avoided my gaze after I let my pets out, brought them back inside, and fed them. She was looking at the animals instead, as if afraid that if she didn't watch them every second, they'd decide that *she* should be their dinner.

I locked the sweet little critters inside the apartment and led Brianna up through my side yard and then down the street past my friends' shops.

I explained that Haylee's store, The Stash, had been the first textile arts shop in Elderberry Bay, and that she'd encouraged her three mothers join her.

Brianna didn't react when I said that Haylee had three mothers, but I explained anyway. "Haylee was raised by three women — Opal, who owns the yarn store, and Opal's friends, Naomi and Edna, who own the quilting and notions stores." I didn't tell Brianna that Opal had been only seventeen when she'd given birth to Haylee, and that each of Haylee's three mothers were now barely over fifty. I added, "Opal, Naomi, and Edna have always called themselves The Three Weird Sisters, from *Macbeth,* you know?"

"Oh."

I went on, "So Haylee calls them The Three Weird Mothers."

People usually laughed or commented, but Brianna remained silent.

After we were far enough from Edna's shop and apartment that she wouldn't hear us even if her windows were open, I confided, "We've all been helping Edna with her actual wedding gown, and it may be the most decorated wedding gown in history." Remembering the one we were about to finish, I corrected myself. "Well, maybe the *second* most decorated gown. She even embedded tiny flashing lights in the one she's making. She wanted sound effects, too, but we convinced her not to." I paused.

"Oh."

Maybe it was all the encouragement I was going to get. I continued, "Tonight, we're going to finish the alternative wedding gown we're making to surprise her, the really decorated one. On this one, we've added everything she asked for on her real gown, and more, as a Threadville joke."

"Oh."

Brianna sounded so disinterested that I was surprised she stayed with me all the way to the fire station. The big garage doors were open. Light and laughter came from inside, toward the back. It was, I thought, very inviting.

"Fire station?" she asked.

I led her inside between our two big red trucks. "That's where we're putting the gown together. It won't fit through an ordinary door."

Dragging her feet, Brianna followed me to the workshop in the back of the garage.

The gown was really only an overskirt that Edna would be able to wear over her real gown. When I caught sight of the enormous skirt, I had to smile.

It was a thing of awesome beauty. Wider than it was tall, the skirt was decorated with almost every embellishment the denizens of Threadville had imagined — ruffles, pleats, crocheted and machine-embroidered lace, knit and quilted panels, flounces, sequins, crystals, and beads.

And sticking out all over it like rhinestones on steroids . . . twenty-watt incandescent lightbulbs.

Just as we'd planned, the skirt was totally over the top.

It wasn't plugged in at the moment, though, so the lighting and sound displays were dark and silent.

However, even when not lit, those bulbs looked huge on the skirt. Some might call our creation ridiculous. We called it whimsical.

Brianna asked, "Is that it?"

"Yes." What else could that vision of spangled, ruffled tulle be?

"It's ugly," she said flatly.

"Edna will laugh."

"Lotta work for a joke."

It was my turn to shrug. How could I explain Threadville and how we all went out of our way to have fun and ensure that everyone around us enjoyed life, too?

Haylee wasn't there. I led Brianna to Opal. Tall, thin, and blond, like Haylee, Opal wore a long, dove-gray, hand-crocheted dress. Brianna ignored Opal's outstretched hand. Opal introduced us to the studious-looking woman beside her as her houseguest, Patricia. "She's a sewing machine historian, and has come to participate in our craft fair."

A sewing machine historian? Trying not to show my skepticism over a craft that sounded even less like Halloween than Isis's handmade books, I smiled and welcomed Patricia to Threadville.

She blushed and looked down at her feet.

Why the shyness? She looked about Haylee's and my age, and our height, but even thinner.

Brianna yawned.

Edna wasn't there, of course, and Brianna barely managed to cover another yawn as I introduced her to Haylee's third mother, Naomi, who owned the quilt shop and would undoubtedly be interested in Brianna's threads.

Slender and pretty in a jacket and skirt she'd pieced and quilted, Naomi patted the arm of a woman wearing a long skirt made of gathered tiers of orange, turquoise, and red, each tier trimmed in white lace. Her ruffled peasant blouse matched her skirt. "This is Madame Juliette," Naomi told us. "She's staying with me during the craft fair."

*Madame?* What an odd thing for someone in her early thirties to call herself.

Brianna didn't bother covering more yawns. I ran the names of Haylee's mothers' guests through my mind to keep them straight. Isis, the woman fond of issuing midnight curses, was staying with Edna, and neither of them was in the fire station. Opal's houseguest was the shy sewing machine historian named Patricia, and Haylee's third mother, Naomi, had this very flamboyant Madame Juliette staying with her.

I asked the woman, "Will you be selling outfits like the one you're wearing at the craft fair, Madame Juliette? It's very pretty." Maybe she'd like to learn how to add touches of machine embroidery.

Madame Juliette was almost as tall as I was, with long brown curly hair highlighted in auburn and blond. "Just call me Juliette. And thank you, I do sew, but I didn't make my outfit. My table at the craft fair will be for telling people's fortunes."

I tried not to look clueless.

"It's a good thing to know your fortune around Halloween, don't you think?" she pressed.

I didn't know what to say.

Luckily, Juliette didn't wait for me to

answer. She explained, "I conduct séances, too."

Since Juliette had said she could sew and Brianna sold thread, I asked both of them if they'd help add some of my recently purchased glow-in-the-dark thread to a frill I'd embroidered and attached to the enormous hoopskirt.

Brianna blanched and shook her head.

Juliette and I approached the magnificent creation.

"What's it made of?" she asked. "Hula hoops?"

I tapped the hip area of the skirt. The skirt swayed. "Good guess. We did tie one hula hoop to the underside near the top. The entire skirt is built on a wheeled frame."

She tilted her head. "How is your friend supposed to wear it?"

I handed her the spool of thread, a packet of needles, and my small, tweezerlike thread nippers, and then lifted the tulle draperies at the back of the skirt. "You crawl into the back and step over the brace between the frame's two back legs. Like this."

I crouched and maneuvered myself into the thing. Clay Fraser had contributed an old steel jigsaw stand as the skirt's frame. He had also made the inside of the skirt a work of art. Cords, speakers, and batteries were neatly arranged on a shelf in the front, and a thick orange extension cord in a huge black plastic reel hung from one side.

I battled my way up through the waistband and stood. Clay had cut the jigsaw stand's legs short enough so that after he added casters, the top of the stand should be at Edna's waist. We weren't positive about that, though, since we were keeping the bizarre overskirt a secret from her.

I could hardly wait to see her face when we revealed it.

Taller than Edna, I had to cinch the drawstring around my hips. I grabbed flounces above the hula hoop, took a few dancelike steps, and moved the gown back and forth on its casters. They worked beautifully.

Behind me, a woman snarled, "You can't do that."

I whirled the giant skirt around.

Isis, again in that flowing, gold-trimmed, white nylon jersey gown that looked for all the world like a nightie, glared up at me. "It's not ordained that you should wear someone else's wedding gown."

Not ordained? What could she mean?

Stunned speechless for the second time in about as many minutes, I managed, "It's not finished." Staring down at her, I tried to come up with a polite way of asking her if she had removed my lace bride and groom dolls from my front porch.

I couldn't think of one.

Scowling, she backed away from me.

"Stay there, Willow," Opal ordered. She plugged the overskirt's cord into an outlet. Lights came on all over the skirt.

Some of them shined up onto my face, probably turning me into a specter rivaling any of the zombies at the zombie retreat.

And that was when Clay walked in.

Clay always looked good, but tonight he was especially hot in jeans and a blue chambray shirt with *Fraser Construction* embroidered in red over the pocket. He had commissioned me to embroider shirts for him and his staff.

Clay and Fraser Construction had done many of the renovations in Threadville, and had moved Blueberry Cottage up the hill for me. Between building entire housing developments, Clay and his employees were renovating Blueberry Cottage.

However, no matter what Haylee might have hoped or believed, Clay and I each worked incredibly long hours, and hardly ever saw each other. Although we'd shared a few romantic moments in the past that may have given me some hopes and dreams,

65

Clay and I were still only friends.

Remembering those romantic moments, I felt my face heat and redden. I hoped he didn't think I was wearing the wedding skirt as a hint.

I ducked out of the skirt. Brianna watched me with scorn on her face. She wasn't the world's greatest houseguest, and she wasn't much fun, either.

Behind me, Isis shrieked, "You!"

# 6

Her incongruous nylon gown billowing, her hands at shoulder height, and her fingers curled outward, Isis raced toward Clay as if she were going to claw into him. She dashed around him, though, and confronted a man in the shadows behind him.

The other man was dressed in black — slacks, turtleneck, blazer, loafers. He was tall and trim like Clay, although not as muscular, and his hair was a darker shade of brown.

Clay's eyes could warm a room. The other man stepped into the light and gave Isis a look that should have turned her to ice.

Undaunted, she screeched, "How dare you!"

He smirked. "How *dare* I what?" An amused undertone lurked in his deep voice.

"Call your book *The Book of the Dead.*"

He remained calm. "I'll call my book whatever I want."

"But *my* book is *The Book of the Dead.*"
The last word was especially loud.

He drawled, "Last I knew, the Book of the Dead was not a book at all, but a collection of curses written in places like the inner walls of pharaohs' tombs in ancient Egypt. You don't look quite *that* old."

Isis ignored the insult. "And that's why my complete title is *The* New *Book of the Dead.*"

He demanded, "So what's your problem?"

She continued to hold her hands like claws in front of her. "Your thriller is cutting into sales of my book."

"I've never heard of your book," he said.

"See what I mean? You're overshadowing everyone and everything."

He tossed a lock of hair off his forehead. "Can I help it if I'm a bestselling author?"

Now I knew why Isis had recognized him. I also understood his ironic emphasis of the word "dare." I'd seen his handsome face on posters in bookstores and in ads in Sunday supplements.

Dare Drayton, the darling of booksellers everywhere, was with us in Elderberry Bay's fire station.

He looked down his hawklike nose at Isis. "No one's going to confuse your psychic gobbledygook with literature."

68

I'd been wrong that Opal's houseguest, Patricia, was timid. She walked right up to Isis and glowered down at the shorter woman. "I'm writing *The Book of the Treadle*. I suppose *that* will cut into your sales, also?" Patricia's voice was harsh and trembling.

With rage? Why? Was she trying to protect Dare? He seemed capable of looking after himself.

Isis stared at Patricia blankly at first, and then her eyes widened. "You! You're nothing but a copycat."

A patchy flush rose up Patricia's neck and face. Clamping her lips together, she pushed her wide-rimmed glasses up her nose and backed away, into Juliette.

Isis caught sight of Juliette. "A fortune-teller," she scoffed. "You make things up!"

Juliette challenged, "And you don't?"

Isis raised her chin. "The original Book of the Dead is older than time."

Dare laughed in a scornful way.

For some reason, which I hoped had nothing to do with a desire to chomp on any of us, Floyd, the 1930s zombie, had come into the fire station. Leaning against a wall just inside the workroom, he appeared to be watching the drama. How did he manage that lackluster, dead look in his eyes — with

69

contact lenses?

Brianna surprised me by slouching up to Isis and announcing, "I'll write a book and call it *The Book of the Thread*."

Isis taunted, "Copycat! You're all a bunch of copycats without an original thought in your heads."

Brianna shrugged and slunk away, out into the garage where the fire trucks were.

Floyd shambled toward us and sneered at Isis. "And I'm writing *The Book of the Living Dead*. It's about zombies."

Slinging an almost triumphant glance my way, Isis brushed a hand against her throat. "Stop following me around. I can be dangerous. You knew that last night when you accused me of casting spells on you. My spells are potent." Her previous night's fright seemed to become more speakable by the moment.

At his sides, Floyd's hands became fists. "Then stop cursing people, alive or undead."

Isis taunted him, "I'll do as I please. I have powers that none of you can guess at. Besides, zombies don't exist. I know. I have studied the curses that usher the dead into the afterlife, and I have contributed new ones, also, and the available afterlives don't involve zombies."

A pulse throbbed at Floyd's whitened temple. "Then what am I doing here?" The streak of "blood" on his chin glistened wetly in the fire station's bright lighting. "Zombies are real." Baring his teeth, he lurched toward her.

Isis stomped out of the workroom and into the garage. "You're a fake," she called over her shoulder. "You're all fakes and copycats. Don't underestimate what I can do to all of you."

Dare Drayton called after her, "Be careful, or I'll kill you in my next book!"

But she must have kept going. I heard her sandals patter past the fire trucks.

A strangely rueful look on his face, Clay came over to me and murmured, "Is the skirt ready? My cousin came to help roll it to the park."

I stepped closer to him so I could whisper, "Your cousin? Floyd the zombie?"

His teasing smile was almost enough to melt me. "I don't know if I'm related to any zombies. Come meet Dare." One hand on my elbow, he guided me to Dare Drayton and introduced us.

I stammered something vaguely friendly. The appropriate thing to say might have been, "I love your books." But I couldn't — I hadn't read even part of one.

Dare looked past me. "What *is* that monstrosity?" He turned to Clay. "Is that the thing I'm supposed to help move?"

Someone had unplugged the skirt, so it was no longer merrily flashing lights, but it was still a glaring white. Opal and Naomi crawled around it, weaving glow-in-the-dark thread through the lace and frills on the gown.

The warmth left Clay's face. "You don't have to help," he told Dare.

"How reassuring. I'll go see what other excitement your little world has to offer. See you at your *truck.*" The way he emphasized "truck" made it obvious that he thought riding in a pickup truck was beneath him. "I knew I should have driven over here from your place." Heels hitting the concrete floor, he strode out.

"Sorry about that," Clay said.

"Your place," I repeated. "Is he staying with you?"

"Yes. My mom said I had to put up with him. She and his mother are cousins, and have always spent lots of time together. My mother always drummed into me that I have to be nice to Dare because he had a difficult childhood. My childhood was difficult, too, when *he* visited us, which wasn't every day, or I'd be a *fiend.*" His grin was anything but scary. "So now, I not only have to put up with him, I have to put him up while he does research for his next book, *Terror on Lake Erie,* or something like that."

I laughed. "Our mothers must be alike. Wait until you meet the person my mom foisted on me."

"Someone's staying with you, too?"

"Brianna. She was here in the fire station, but she left."

"The scared one in the glasses? Supposedly writing *The Book of the Treadle?*"

I glanced around the room. Patricia was gone, too. "No, that was Patricia, Opal's guest."

I didn't see Patricia out in the garage, but Juliette's bright skirt, presumably with her still inside it, swished past a tanker truck and disappeared toward the street.

Apparently, none of our houseguests were eager to push a bright white hoopskirt through the streets of Threadville. Or maybe the women were chasing Dare Drayton for autographs. Or they wanted to talk to Floyd the zombie. He was gone, too.

I answered Clay's question. "Brianna is the petite blonde. She threatened to write *The Book of the Thread.*"

Clay frowned. "That girl is staying with you?" He put both hands on my shoulders.

"I caught her giving you a nasty look, as if she didn't like you." He squeezed my shoulders. "Hard to believe."

"She's young."

"I didn't like the way she looked at you." His concern nearly unhinged me.

I tilted my face up toward his. "Was it worse than the way Dare talks to you?"

"Dare has always been like that. Do you think they really are writing all those books?"

"Not Brianna," I guessed. "And I suspect that some of the others were jumping into the fray, also, having fun making Isis angrier."

Why? Her original rage had been directed at Dare, though he claimed he'd never heard of her. And Floyd the zombie obviously had a bone to pick with Isis. But why had Patricia, Juliette, and Brianna decided to annoy her? Although their crafts seemed a little farfetched for our Get Ready for Halloween Craft Fair, Isis, Patricia, and Juliette had all come to Threadville to participate in it. Isis knew that Juliette was a fortune-teller, as if she might have met her before. Patricia's and Isis's reactions to each other had made me wonder if they had met before, too. But what about Brianna?

Troubled, I looked up at Clay. "They

ganged up on Isis. Like bullies."

His mouth was grim. "I thought Dare had outgrown that."

"Isis did attack him first," I pointed out. "But the others seemed to revel in making her angrier."

"He was always good at manipulating others to do his bullying for him."

"I'll bet you never let him make *you* do that."

Clay brushed the side of my face with his fingertips. "Thanks for the vote of confidence. I learned to ignore him."

"And that made him try harder?"

"Eventually, he had to give up."

I had to look away for fear Clay would see how much I admired his toughness. And his tenderness.

Luckily, Opal provided a distraction. "Come check out our finished masterpiece, Willow!" She snipped glow-in-the-dark thread from its spool.

I joined Opal and Naomi beside the overskirt. "Edna will love it! It's perfect."

Naomi leaned forward and studied one of the big lightbulbs. "Not quite. Do we have time to scrape the lettering off the lightbulbs?"

Opal slapped at her. "No. Tiny signs like 'twenty double-u' add to the mystique.

Besides, we'd better get this art installation in place so Gord won't have to keep finding ways to prevent Edna from looking toward the park."

Naomi, Opal, Clay, and I wheeled the ungainly skirt toward the garage in the front section of the fire station. I kicked something that rolled away from me.

It was my spool of thread. I set it on a ledge with my thread nippers and packet of needles. I'd walk the dogs later, pick up my sewing supplies, and lock the fire station. At the moment, my hands were full of tulle and satin. I tried to clutch the jigsaw stand beneath all the fabric without harming our glorious creation or breaking any of its many lightbulbs.

Outside, Floyd, Juliette, Dare, and Patricia had all disappeared, but underneath the streetlight near the driveway, Brianna wrote in a small book like a checkbook, tore out a page, and handed it to Isis.

Opal called to them, "Want to join the fun?" Her voice brimmed over with smiles.

Barely glancing at us, Brianna and Isis refused. They walked quickly toward Lake Street.

The wedding skirt's casters rumbled along, bumping over the sidewalk seams in a beat that made us laugh. At Lake Street, I couldn't see Isis, but Brianna turned toward the gate leading to my side yard. Carefully, we eased the mammoth skirt off the curb.

Something slithered against the leg of my jeans and over the toe of my sneakers.

Opal gasped. "Is that a snake?"

Clay apologized. "It's my extension cord." The cord had been unwinding from the reel inside the skirt. Clay jogged back, unsnared the plug from the base of a utility pole, and returned, holding the plug in his hand like a trophy.

"Why is that cord so long?" Opal asked him.

"That's what I had. Short extension cords aren't very useful at construction sites. And this one is rated for outdoors."

Clay and I rewound the cord on its reel until only the plug dangled outside the skirt.

Figuring that if we tried to push the skirt over the lawn, the casters would ensnare themselves in the grass or dig trenches in the earth, we guided the overdecorated wheeled jigsaw stand the long way around, down the road leading to the concrete boat launch ramp, and from there along the accessibility boardwalk zigzagging up the hill to the bandstand.

Yelping, Opal whipped her right hand from our ruffled concoction.

We all asked her what was wrong.

"We must have left a pin somewhere in that skirt. Something pricked my right thumb." A sly grin crossed her face. " 'By the pricking of my thumbs . . .' " She poked at one of the skirt's many flounces. " '. . . something wicked this way comes.' "

Naomi laughed. "I think you mean 'something *stitched* this way comes.' " She gave "stitched" two syllables so that it almost rhymed with "wicked."

With great drama, Opal made the universal bad-pun groan. "That's not what the second Weird Sister says in *Macbeth,* and you know it."

Naomi gave the skirt a push. "Lead on, Macduff!"

Opal muttered, "Macbeth said, '*lay* on.' "

Naomi rationalized the misquote. "No one in this century says 'lay on.' "

Joking and teasing each other, we shoved the ridiculous overskirt up the hill as quickly as it would go. The skirt shimmied whenever its wheels hit another plank. By the time the casters clattered into the bandstand, Opal, Naomi, and I were howling with laughter at the dress's lifelike antics, and Clay was grinning.

The only lights in the bandstand were the twinkly fairy lights, but it was easy to see

Dare leaning against one of the white-painted pillars.

He asked Clay, "Are you chasing me with that thing, cuz? You realize that I'm at your mercy to take me back to my laptop and the book I'm working on." He stared straight at me, but there was no warmth in his eyes. "It's my twelfth, and will be a best-seller like the others."

"Nice," I said.

Naomi clapped her hands. "You must be *very* talented."

Opal agreed. To someone who didn't know them, they probably sounded completely sincere.

Clay told Dare, "I'll be ready to go in a few minutes. I want to see Edna's face when she catches sight of this."

Dare scowled at him. "Meet you at your truck."

"It's unlocked," Clay told his departing back. I threw Clay a sympathetic look. Frowning, he watched his cousin stroll up the grassy hill toward the sidewalk.

Naomi threaded a white ribbon through loops on a quilted satin label and tied the ribbon around the top of the skirt. She made a pretty bow and adjusted the label so that anyone coming down the sloping lawn from Lake Street could read the words that my machines had embroidered in pewter-colored metallic embroidery thread: *Edna's Wedding Skirt.*

Opal pulled a phone from her pocket, fingered its screen, and said, "Okay, Gord. We're ready. Bring her to the bandstand."

## 7

From our perch in the bandstand, Naomi squinted down toward the river. Wisps of mist inched toward us. She shivered. "I don't know why people think fog is romantic. They even create it with machines at wedding receptions! Fog is cold and wet. Anything could be hiding in it."

Opal stuck her right thumb up. It wasn't noticeably bleeding. "Let's hope it rises this far. From up on Lake Street, Edna won't know what she's seeing."

Haylee arrived first, in a black suit she'd tailored for herself. She shortened her strides to accommodate the tiny woman by her side. "This is Mrs. Battersby," she told Clay and me. "She's Edna's mother." Haylee had always called all three of her mothers by their first names. Opal and Naomi, who must have known Edna's mother since the Three Weird Mothers were little girls, greeted Mrs. Battersby warmly, but, it seemed to me, cautiously.

Mrs. Battersby's eyes were dark and alert, reminding me strongly of Edna's. She darted glances behind Naomi, Opal, Clay, and me. We were doing our best to block the overskirt from view until Edna arrived.

Opal got her wish about the rising mist. Fog enveloped us. Two forms walked carefully down from the street. Gord was in a suit. Edna wore a long silver gown trimmed with gold spangles.

Clay plugged in the enormous hoopskirt. The twenty-watt lightbulbs came on. He flicked a switch at the back of the waist, and Mendelssohn's "Wedding March" began playing. The skirt's lights flashed, appearing to dance over the skirt in time to the music

Edna let out peal after peal of laughter. The rest of us joined her.

But not Mrs. Battersby. Her voice cut through our merriment. "No wonder she wouldn't let me see her gown. That thing is atrocious." If Mrs. Battersby was always this critical, I understood why Opal and Naomi had been cautious when greeting her.

I almost giggled. Mrs. Battersby's fashion sense might not be as acute as she seemed to think. Her beige pantsuit was vintage, possibly an outfit she'd inherited from her own mother, and the elastic knit into the polyester fabric known as "double knit" had given out here and there, making the suit strangely warty.

Edna said softly to her mother, "I'm wearing a less elaborate gown to the ceremony, but this is perfect for me to put on over my gown for the reception."

Mrs. Battersby argued, "You wouldn't."

Now I also understood why Haylee had insisted that Edna's mother had to stay with her instead of with Edna during the week leading up to Edna's big day.

Gord put an arm around Edna and pulled her closer. "Everyone, come back to my place to toast my little bride and all of her wedding gowns." He kissed the top of her head.

I'd given Brianna a key to my patio door, but wasn't happy about leaving my animals alone in the apartment with her. "I'd better walk my dogs."

Smiling into my eyes, Clay started to say something. That he'd come with me?

I imagined a stroll along the dark riverside trail with him, and maybe a long walk with my two dogs. My heart rate sped up.

However, about a block away, a horn started honking, taps and blasts likely to awaken the zombies a mile away at the

Elderberry Bay Lodge. Clay jumped off the bandstand steps and loped up the hill. He called over his shoulder, "I'll make him stop." He turned around and added more genially, "I'll lock the fire station while I'm at it."

Gord asked me, "You're sure you won't come with us?"

Although disappointed that Clay couldn't stick around, I smiled at Gord. "I'm sure. Another time."

Edna gazed dreamily at the white over-skirt. "I guess it's all right to leave that fantastic creation here."

I pointed above it to the banner strung between the bandstand's pillars. *Threadville Get Ready for Halloween Craft Fair.* "It's advertising. The police chief said she'd keep an eye on the overskirt during her regular patrols."

Mrs. Battersby suggested, "Maybe she could use it as target practice. She could shoot that car horn while she's at it." She sniffed. "I hope she arrests whoever's making that racket."

Maybe she had, or Clay had caught up with whoever had been pounding on the horn. The noise stopped.

Mrs. Battersby placed a hand on her forehead. "That thing gave me a headache.

Haylee, take me back to your place so I can lie down."

"I'd love to come with you, Gord," Opal said, "but Naomi and I have to go to the classroom in Haylee's shop. Haylee's helping us with our bridesmaids' dresses." They started up the hill. Gord and Edna followed. Haylee straggled behind them with Mrs. Battersby, who was grousing about people who didn't know enough not to wake the dead.

I jogged down the hill to the riverside trail.

Mist parted near the river, showing a petite woman in a long white gown. Isis? She reached up among branches drooping from a weeping willow. Something silver glinted in her hand. The woman had chosen an odd time to prune willow trees.

Fog shrouded her again and I shrugged. I suspected that I could try for years to understand Isis, but never succeed.

I felt my way along the dark trail until my backyard appeared out of the mist. Opening the gate, I winced at the cold, dewy metal.

I ran up the hill. Blueberry Cottage was dark, but my apartment was brightly lit. I unlocked the sliding glass door and let my pets out of my bedroom suite. Again, music crashed behind Brianna's closed door, but between drumbeats, I heard her voice. A light on the phone showed that she was using the cordless receiver I kept in the guest suite.

It was nearly nine thirty. I encouraged the dogs and kittens outside. Mustache and Bow-Tie dug in my flower garden, then puffed themselves up and skittered sideways through the open door and into my apartment. I shut them into the master suite and let the dogs play in my fenced backyard.

Watching Sally-Forth and Tally-Ho, I almost missed the blur sneaking toward the lake along the mist-covered riverside trail. It was a tall person, walking softly as if he or she didn't want to be seen or heard, and wearing dark slacks and jacket.

It couldn't have been Haylee. She wouldn't have avoided the dogs and me. I was almost certain the person was a man, maybe Floyd the zombie or Dare the thriller author.

Fog closed around him. Staring at where he'd been, my dogs raised their noses to test the air. Who had that been, and why had he been creeping around? I dashed up the hill to my patio, opened the sliding door, and grabbed a flashlight and the dogs' leashes. Brianna's music blared. The light on my phone showed she was still on the line. I didn't hear her voice.

I went outside. Unnerved by that furtive person in the mist, I locked the door. My usually adventurous dogs had, for once, followed me up the hill. Had the person inching along the trail alarmed them? I snapped leashes onto their collars.

Pulling my strangely unwilling dogs behind me, I ran down the hill and out the gate to the trail. I couldn't see anyone in the thick fog.

The river made eerie noises like monsters gulping and swallowing. My flashlight was almost useless in the white air, but when I aimed it down the middle of the trail, something near my fence caught my eye — a greenish strand undulating as if it were alive. The world's longest glowworm? The dogs ignored the thing, but I went closer. I shined my light on it, and it went gray, but when I took the light away, the thing glowed again.

Glow-in-the-dark thread.

Slowly, I turned around. I caught glimpses of it near the fence going both up the river and down, the direction the slinking person had taken. I hadn't noticed the thread ten minutes earlier when I'd been on my way home, but maybe its glow had worn out, and I'd regenerated it just now with my flashlight.

A scream pierced the fog.

A woman? I started downstream toward the sound, but my dogs were reluctant to do anything besides weave their leashes around my legs.

The woman screamed again.

With some confusion and not much help from Sally and Tally, I sorted us all out and we trotted down the trail toward the park.

In the fog ahead, a wavering glow separated itself from a larger, steadier glow on the hill and wobbled down the slope toward the river.

Sally and Tally became determined to investigate the steep riverbank. Pulling me with them, they veered off the trail and into the mud.

I planted my feet on the slippery slope and whispered their names. They charged up the bank. Tails down, they tried to lead me home.

Again, I untangled their leashes and forced them toward the park.

The smaller glow had gained speed on the downward slope. Metal wheels like casters clattered on concrete. The boat launch and the road to it were the only pavement in that part of the park.

Again, the dogs tried to take me home, but I gave them the hand signal for "stay."

Panting nervously, they leaned against my legs.

What was I seeing? The glowing thing on casters would have to be Edna's wedding skirt. Could it be traveling downhill by itself? I ran, pulling my reluctant dogs with me.

The woman shrieked again. "Don't push me! Don't —"

The scream was bitten off.

The dogs instantly straightened their legs, an effective way of putting on their brakes, and mine, also. Whimpering, Tally-Ho again tried to lead us all home. "Sh," I cautioned. Holding my breath, I listened.

Metal casters rattled. I heard Mendelssohn's "Wedding March," tinny and distorted by distance, and then a splash and a series of pops.

Both the large glow on the hill and the one that had been heading toward the river dissolved into darkness. The music stopped, also.

The dogs and I were alone in swirling fog.

My flashlight accomplished little besides making the fog appear denser. I crept forward.

It seemed like hours, but was probably only a minute, before I managed to bring my dogs out of the shelter of trees and into the grassy park. I turned off my light. The strand of thread led up the hill toward the now-dark bandstand.

The screams and splashing had been ahead of me.

The dogs' leashes firmly in one hand and my flashlight in the other, I eased past willows lining the riverbank. My toes found the edge of the boardwalk, and I stepped up onto it. The dogs' claws clicked on planks.

I called out, "Hello? Is anyone there?"

The dogs panted. Ripples lapped at the riverbank.

Hard soles slapped against pavement up the hill near Lake Street. I yelled, "Come back and help!" The person was quickly putting distance between himself and me.

I couldn't take time to chase him or her. A woman had screamed, and then I'd heard a splash.

If the woman had fallen into the river, someone needed to rescue her.

Now that the screaming had ended, the dogs were braver. Sniffing, they pulled me to the concrete boat ramp. I turned on my flashlight and swept its beam in front of me.

Clay's orange extension cord led up the hill toward the bandstand, but at the foot of the hill where the dogs and I were, the cord went to the base of the boat launch and disappeared underwater.

The unsewn end of a frill trimmed with lace floated next to the cord. I snapped off my flashlight. Bits of glow-in-the-dark thread showed up. I turned the light on again and aimed it farther out.

A whitish blur rolled downriver in sluggish underwater currents.

# 8

The extravagant overskirt we had constructed for Edna was now near the bottom
of the river, and it couldn't have gotten
there by itself.

Someone must have pushed it out of the
bandstand and started it down the ramp.
And the wheeled skirt couldn't have zigzagged down the switchbacking ramp to the
boardwalk and from there to the boat
launch by itself, either. It would have
scooted off the ramp and tipped over.

Someone had guided it down the hill at
least as far as the straight, sloping concrete
boat launch.

I wanted to believe that pranksters had
shoved the skirt into the water, and that no
one had been hurt, but the terrified scream
kept echoing through my mind. *Don't push
me!* A woman's voice, but panic had re-
shaped it, and I hadn't recognized it.

Had Edna returned and tried on the huge

overskirt? Had someone pushed it, with her inside it, down the slope and into the river? If so, had she scrambled out before the skirt sank?

Remembering how the woman's voice had carried through the damp air, I again called, "Is anyone there? Help!" I shined my flashlight on the misty river. Bubbles broke on the surface above the white blur, still rolling downriver.

I stooped and yanked at Clay's extension cord. I managed to lift it a couple of inches from the water, and I seemed to pull it toward me, but its reel had turned easily earlier in the evening, and I was probably merely unwinding the extension cord, not hauling the heavy skirt in.

Tally-Ho and Sally-Forth sniffed the boat ramp. I shined my light on partial footprints. Had someone run away from the river and up the hill, perhaps on tiptoe?

Tally raised his head, stared toward the dark bandstand, and whimpered.

Was someone up there? The woman who had screamed?

Hoping she was, I again shouted for help.

No answer.

Taking shortcuts by leaping over parts of the switch-backing plank ramp, I rocketed up the hill. The dogs ran as fast as their leashes would let them. They arrived at the now-dark bandstand a second before I did.

The bandstand was empty except for a half-full spool of glow-in-the-dark thread, the quilted label that said *Edna's Wedding Skirt,* and a handful of ten-inch-long willow wands, lined up as if someone had placed them there carefully.

And Clay's extension cord, still plugged in.

I'd seen a flash and heard the popping and tinkling of glass, and I was almost positive that the hot bulbs would have exploded when they hit the cold water, which would probably have caused the electrical circuit to short out. The bandstand's fairy lights were dark, but I unplugged the cord anyway, in case a circuit might still be live.

Knowing I was calling in a possibly false alarm, I dialed 911 and babbled to the dispatcher that someone might have fallen into the river. She told me to stay on the line.

"I . . . I have to call someone." I wanted to be certain that Edna had *not* been inside that skirt when it rolled — or was pushed — into the river.

Sternly, she contradicted me. "I need you to stay on the line. I'm sending police, fire, and ambulance. Don't go into the water by yourself, and let me know of any developments."

I agreed. The dogs and I ran down the hill to the foot of the boat launch.

The siren on the fire station's roof wailed. Haylee would have to leave Mrs. Battersby and run to the fire station. Maybe Clay, driving his cousin home, would hear the alarm and turn back. Others among our firefighting colleagues would be here soon. I wouldn't have to cope with this situation — whatever it was — alone.

Impatient for the emergency workers to arrive, I squeezed my hand more tightly around my phone.

I needed to call Edna. *Was she all right?*

Tally-Ho growled low in his throat at someone approaching from the direction of the lake.

With his arms angled out in front of his body, Floyd, the zombie in the torn 1930s suit, clomped toward us. In the fire station, Isis had said that Floyd had accused her of casting spells on him, and he hadn't denied it. I wasn't frightened, either speakably or unspeakably, but I was glad that I still had the dispatcher on the line.

When Floyd was close, he shouted over the siren, "What's wrong?"

I shined my light at the river. I could no

longer see the white blur and the end of the frill, but the extension cord was still heading underwater. "Someone may have fallen in."

The dispatcher asked, "Who are you talking to, Willow?"

"A . . ." I stopped myself from telling her I was talking to a zombie. She'd be certain I'd made a crank call. "A passerby."

"Don't go into the water even with one other person there," she ordered.

Floyd grabbed the flashlight from my hand. "Maybe they swam to shore." He shined the beam up and down the river. He probably didn't notice that he licked his lips.

I couldn't see anyone on the opposite bank, and the near one was steep and hidden by weeping willows.

Floyd handed me the light. "No one's there, but go ahead and dive in for a better look. I'll hold your dogs for you."

Until that moment, I'd found the zombies around Threadville amusing, but with his dripping blood, shot-up suit, hungry smacking of lips, and cold eyes, Floyd was beginning to give me a fright. I hadn't appreciated the way he'd grabbed my flashlight, and I didn't trust him with my pets or anything else. Besides, his hard-soled dress shoes could have been the ones I'd heard pounding up Lake Street. He could have circled down to the beach in hopes that I wouldn't guess that he had run away from this spot only minutes ago, after he pushed that giant skirt — with someone in it — into the river.

Usually, I felt safer when my dogs were with me, but they were obviously wary of Floyd and were again trying to tug me home. I desperately wanted to let them do it.

But I couldn't leave until I was certain that no one was in trouble in the river. Behind my back, I made the hand signal for "speak." Sally let out a volley of barks so loud and abrupt that Floyd stepped back. Maybe Sally's bark was worse than Floyd's bite. How reassuring.

The siren continued blaring. Tally-Ho let out that one woof that said someone else was coming.

Lenny, the surfer zombie, sprinted up from the beach. I told him that someone may have tumbled into the river. He threw his towel down on the concrete ramp and stepped out of his flip-flops. The frayed rope tied around his ankle seemed realistically hideous in the foggy darkness. He waded into the river and grabbed the extension cord.

I yelled, "Wait. Help is coming."

Naturally, the dispatcher wanted to know what was going on.

"Another passerby," I said.

In the dim light, Lenny's whitewashed face looked both wan and determined. "I'm a lifeguard. I know what I'm doing. There's a life ring on a post right behind you. Toss it to me?"

Holding one end of the rope attached to the life ring, I tossed the ring to Lenny.

He clamped it under one arm. With his other hand on the extension cord, he walked down the ramp and then floated, kicking his feet, out onto the river. I was not going to let Lenny out of my sight. Or the rope out of my hands.

Floyd called to him, "You'll ruin your makeup!" To me, he muttered, "That guy can't stay in character."

I snapped, "It's an emergency."

Floyd's voice sounded almost as lifeless as the zombie he was portraying. "You told me someone *may* have fallen in. So you don't know if it's an emergency or not."

"We have to treat it like it is."

I let my flashlight's beam rake the top of Floyd's black leather shoes before aiming it down the ramp and, from there, across the mist-covered water to Lenny.

During the fleeting moment I'd looked away from Lenny, I'd made out water droplets dotting the streaks of fake blood on the toes of Floyd's polished black leather shoes. If he had pushed the wedding skirt into the river, water could have splashed his shoes. And was all of that red stuff smeared on Floyd fake, or could some of it have been real blood, acquired only minutes ago?

But Floyd might not be the only one with wet toes . . .

I slipped my phone into a pocket and the dogs' leashes over my wrist. Holding my flashlight and the rope attached to the life ring in one hand, I casually stooped and felt around with my other hand for Lenny's flip-flops.

The toes felt wet.

Without glancing away from Lenny, I straightened his flip-flops beside his towel. Maybe Floyd wouldn't catch on that I was snooping. He might merely think that I liked order.

Either of the zombies could have left damp spots on the concrete. Both of them had come from near the lake, though, which could have explained why their shoes were wet. I straightened and placed my phone against my ear again.

*Where was Edna, and was she all right?*

# 9

As long as I had to keep the 911 dispatcher on the line, I couldn't phone Edna. I pictured her answering in her chirpy little voice that she was fine, why wouldn't she be?

I asked Floyd, "Do you have a phone with you?"

He demanded coldly, "How could I?" I might have known he'd act like he'd died in 1934 and had never heard of phones that weren't attached to cords.

Meanwhile, Lenny floated downriver. His flowered surfer shorts ballooned on the water's surface. He came up for air. "I can't see anyone," he called. "Only that ghostly blob."

The fire siren stopped. The station was only a block away, so it was easy for me to hear one of our big engines start, and then the blat of the truck's big, loud horn.

I turned to ask Floyd to please run to Gord's house and pound on the door and ask Edna to come down here where I could see her.

But as if he'd vaporized in the mist, Floyd was gone. Why? I could only guess that he didn't want to be here when the emergency responders arrived.

Cowering against me, the dogs stared into the fog at the beginning of the trail leading upriver. Maybe Floyd had gone that way. No wonder the dogs had stopped trying to lead me home.

The fire truck raced into view at the top of the hill and stopped, its mist-filtered spotlight on me and the surrounding area. Clay jumped out of the driver's seat. The dogs stood straighter, wagged their tails, and faced up the hill as Clay, Haylee, and the other volunteer firefighters thundered down it. Apparently, Sally-Forth thought this was an excellent opportunity to practice obeying the "speak" command, even though I wasn't giving it.

The 911 dispatcher let me go. Juggling dog leashes and the rope attached to Lenny's life ring, I phoned Edna. No answer. I left her a breathless message to return my call.

Clay reached me first and steadied me with one warm hand on my shoulder. "What's wrong, Willow?"

I pointed at Lenny and told Clay and the other firefighters what had happened.

As we'd practiced, in the absence of the fire chief and his deputy, Clay directed the rescue operation. Two members who were divers began putting on their gear. The rest of the crew spread out to search the river-banks.

I grabbed Haylee's arm. "Do you know where Edna is?" I asked. "She didn't answer her phone."

Her eyes opened wide with fear that matched mine. "She should be at Gord's. I'll try him." She fingered her phone screen. Her hands were shaking as much as I was.

Out on the river, Lenny hung on to both the life ring and the skirt's extension cord as currents carried him toward the lake. He lifted his head to breathe, then continued his underwater search.

Haylee left a message for Gord to have Edna call her or me immediately. She pocketed her phone and bit her lip. "No answer. I'll go help Clay search the banks."

I'd have gone, too, but I needed to focus on Lenny.

Our two divers plodded down the boat ramp and into the water. When they reached Lenny, he handed one of them the exten-sion cord.

I beckoned to the surfer-boy lifeguard zombie. Still gripping the life ring, he swam to the base of the boat ramp and waded out of the water. No vestiges were left of his zombie makeup, and he had turned into a rather stunning man, though not nearly as stunning as Clay, nearby on the riverbank in his jeans and chambray shirt.

I handed Lenny his towel and pulled my dogs away in case he wouldn't understand Sally-Forth and her nurturing ways and wouldn't want her holding him down with her paws and attempting to lick him dry.

Clay strode to us, pulled a packaged survival blanket from a pocket, and tore open the packet. "Wrap up in this," Clay ordered, "and please wait here for the ambulance. The techs will check you out and give you a warm drink."

Lenny's teeth were chattering. Mine were, also, although except for the toes of my sneakers, I hadn't been in the water.

Clay and I both thanked Lenny and asked him if he'd like to join our volunteer fire department.

"I would," he said, "but I live down near Slippery Rock."

Clay slung an arm around my shoulders and pulled me close. "When did you hear that splash?"

"About ten to ten."

His jaw tightened. "Over fifteen minutes ago. If someone was trapped in that dress this long, only a pocket of air could have saved her. Do you think that fabric would hold enough air?"

"I hope so." I grasped the dogs' leashes more tightly. I could barely speak. I managed a halting, "What if it's Edna?"

"She's probably safe and sound at Gord's." His voice was comforting, but I could tell he was worried, too.

I leaned into him. "She didn't answer her phone. Haylee and I both left messages."

"Maybe no one is in that skirt," he said. "Maybe kids pushed it in."

"I hope so. I did hear someone running away, up Lake Street. And they left wet footprints."

"You're shivering." Clay locked both arms around me. "We've got a good crew here. I hope it will turn out that we're only doing a water rescue drill in a realistic setting. I wish I'd made the base of that skirt from wood though, instead of steel."

"We had no idea this would happen." I clung to him. "I thought you were driving your cousin home."

"He wasn't at the truck when I got there. I waited for him, but he didn't show up, so

I was about to look for you and your dogs when the emergency call came in. I was outside the fire station, so when a few of the others arrived, I drove the fire truck here."

"Did you hear or see anything unusual while you were waiting for Dare?"

"No."

I clamped my lips shut. I wasn't about to tell him that I may have seen Dare, in his black slacks and jacket, on the trail shortly before I heard the woman shout, *Don't push me!*

Another siren came closer. Elderberry Bay's police cruiser sped down Lake Street and slammed to a halt.

Leaving her car's spotlight trained on the riverbank, Police Chief Vicki Smallwood ran down the hill. Her uniform was tidy, and she wore her neatly combed ponytail low to accommodate her police hat. She always looked younger than she was. Once, it had seemed to bother her that she was shorter than Haylee and I were, but she must have realized that we respected her abilities and authority as Elderberry Bay's only police officer.

She asked me, "You called this in, Willow?"

I nodded.

She asked Clay, "Do you need me at the moment, or can I have a few minutes to talk to Willow?"

He didn't remove his gaze from the divers. "We've got it under control, I hope, but thanks for coming. I'll whistle if we need you." His arms dropped from me, leaving me colder than ever. Back straight, sleeves rolled up, he walked downriver toward the divers. I wished I could go with him.

Lenny edged away as if guessing that Vicki wanted to talk to me alone, but before he got very far, she asked him if he was okay and if he wanted to warm up in her car.

He gave her a very nice smile. "I'm fine. I'm more concerned about those divers. I'm trained to watch other rescuers." He turned the smile on me. "Like she does. Thanks, by the way."

"You're welcome." I thanked him for helping.

Vicki told him to let us know if he needed anything.

Lenny nodded, pulled his shiny blanket around himself, and ambled like a person, not a zombie, to the riverbank.

Vicki opened her notebook. "Okay, Willow, let's hear it."

I told her about the screams, the sound like wheels clattering on the boat launch, the pops and flashes, the lights going out, the enormous skirt settling near the bottom of the river, the wet marks like partial footprints heading up the ramp and disappearing in the grass, and the sound of hard-soled shoes as someone ran up Lake Street, away from the scene.

She held up a hand to halt my breathless monologue. "This sounds potentially serious. I'm going to call the state police for backup. Wait here, and I'll get all the details from you in a minute." She frowned up toward the bandstand. "We're not sure that a crime has been committed or that anyone has been injured, but I'll tape off the scene anyway." Talking into her radio, Vicki jogged to the boat ramp, examined it with her flashlight, and then returned to her cruiser.

I took the dogs down the hill to where Lenny stood watching the divers.

Keeping Lenny, the dogs, and me outside her taped area, Vicki tied yellow tape to a weeping willow on the riverbank and strung the tape around the uphill side of the bandstand, then back down the hill to a tree downriver from the divers' current position, already way beyond the boat ramp.

Stubbornly, my phone refused to ring. Why didn't Edna return our messages? My mouth was drier than cotton.

An ambulance barreled to a stop outside the tape on the road to the boat ramp. Clay directed the two technicians to Lenny. They checked him quickly and agreed with him that he was fine, then he went with the technicians toward the ambulance, where all three of them would be closer to the action. I stayed where I was with my dogs lying at my feet.

The divers took turns holding the extension cord and disappearing under the water. Each dive began nearer the mouth of the river, and seemed to take forever.

I hoped the divers were discovering that the fabric-wrapped jigsaw stand had gone into the water by itself.

One diver came up, said something to the other diver, and signaled to Clay.

I recognized the signal.

The divers were asking for the rescue stretcher that firefighters on the riverbank had been keeping near the divers. Clay and Haylee helped move the stretcher to the water's edge.

My knees might have given way underneath me if I hadn't been focusing on the safety of the divers.

Both of them disappeared under the water. Like the rest of my firefighting colleagues on shore, I concentrated on where they'd been.

The divers surfaced and paddled toward shore. From where I was, far up the river, it looked like they were bringing out a bundle of pale fabric. Because I still had my dogs with me, I stayed where I was.

Clay, Haylee, and other volunteer firefighters steadied the stretcher on the water. The divers placed their burden on it.

Slipping on the slope, six rescuers carried the stretcher up to flat ground and laid it on the grass. I couldn't be certain because of the mist and the distance, but I guessed that the victim was a woman wearing pale clothing.

*Edna had been wearing a long silver dress.*

# 10

I chewed on my knuckles. *The woman on the stretcher couldn't be Edna.*

Whoever she was, she'd spent about a half hour in the depths. As far as I could tell, she wasn't moving.

*Not Edna. No, not Edna . . .*

Although all three emergency vehicles had spotlights, the night was still foggy, and people cast misty, wavering shadows around the stretcher. Clay, Haylee, the firefighters, and Lenny in his silver cape hovered over Vicki Smallwood and the ambulance crew kneeling beside the victim. The medical technicians appeared to attempt CPR.

I imagined all sorts of hope and luck. Maybe the large skirt had trapped a bubble of air. Maybe the woman had survived and was merely unconscious. They would revive her . . .

Edna had worn a silver dress. Her mother's pantsuit had been beige. The only other person I remembered seeing in a pale outfit that evening had been Isis.

Isis had been near the river, possibly pruning willows, when I'd gone home to take my animals out. Pieces of willow had been on the bandstand floor after the skirt disappeared underneath the water.

Tally scrambled to his feet and whimpered. Sally tilted her head and looked up at me with concern in her doggie eyes.

The two divers returned to the river with a large package and what looked like an aerosol can. With other volunteer firefighters, I had attended lectures about underwater recovery. The divers were about to use the can of compressed air to inflate a lift bag. The air-filled bag should help raise the enormous wedding skirt and its jigsaw stand from the bottom of the river.

On the far side of the group around the stretcher, Clay stared toward me. I knew he was trying to tell me something, but he was far away, and I couldn't see his eyes, let alone figure out what he wanted to say. His posture showed defeat and disappointment.

Standing beside him, Haylee waved as if to make sure she had my attention, then pointed up the hill.

Edna, Gord, and Mrs. Battersby were taking a shortcut from the sidewalk onto the grassy slope above us.

I sank down on the dewy grass and hugged my dogs. Edna was fine.

Gord left the other two and strode toward the emergency workers. Edna helped her mother down the steep hill.

I jumped up and threw my arms around Edna.

Mrs. Battersby gasped. At my show of affection?

Edna patted my dogs. "What happened, Willow?"

"Someone must have rolled down the ramp in that wedding skirt we made for you, and ended up in the river. I guess she got trapped and couldn't swim out."

"Who?" Edna's voice was sharp with worry.

Mrs. Battersby grumbled, "That so-called gown was the stupidest thing I've ever seen. The bottom of the river is the best place for it."

"Mother!" I'd never heard Edna sound that exasperated before. "Someone may have drowned."

Mrs. Battersby retorted, "All so *you* could parade around in a tacky piece of junk."

I stepped in. "Edna didn't know about that gown at all until this evening." And now she would never wear it.

Mrs. Battersby raised her chin. "She won't let me — her own *mother* — see the gown she is going to wear to her wedding. So many of today's wedding gowns look like someone wrapped bandages around the bride from the armpits down. Why would any bride want to look like a half-naked ancient Egyptian mummy?"

Busily trying *not* to picture a half-naked ancient Egyptian mummy, I couldn't figure out how to answer that question, and Edna didn't come up with a reply, either.

Mrs. Battersby went on, "My daughter might make a spectacle of herself in something completely unsuitable. You're supposed to hide your gown from your bridegroom, but not from your own *mother*. Mothers could be the only thing between brides and disasters." She stared toward the group around the stretcher. "What's your intended think he's doing over there with the police and emergency personnel, anyway?"

Edna explained patiently, "He's a doctor."

Mrs. Battersby grunted. "The victim looks past anyone's help to me, not that I'm a *doctor.*"

I put an arm around Edna again. "Gord assists the county coroner."

Mrs. Battersby flinched, putting more

distance between herself and her daughter. "A coroner? And you think you're marrying him?"

Edna could raise her chin as high as her mother could. "I don't just think it. I *am.*"

"You always did have a morbid streak. I live in constant fear that you'll come to some bad end."

"Gord is the love of my life."

I added, "Gord is wonderful." And maybe he'd work a miracle. He was taking a turn at giving the woman CPR.

Again, Edna asked me, "Who's the victim?"

"I don't know, but he or she seems to be wearing something pale and flowing —"

Edna seemed to shrink. "Not . . . Isis? What was she doing in my wedding overskirt in the dark of night?"

"I don't know." I didn't mention the person sneaking past my yard or the footsteps I'd heard on Lake Street. Edna could keep important details to herself, but her mother didn't strike me as someone who thought before she spoke. I was certain that Vicki Smallwood wouldn't want me blabbing about the case and starting rumors.

Gord stopped working on the victim, stood, and shook his head.

Haylee ducked out underneath the police

crime scene tape and ran up the hill, around the bandstand, and down to us. She hugged Edna. "I'm sorry to tell you this, Edna, but Isis seems to have drowned."

*Isis . . .*

Floyd the zombie could have been the person I'd seen sneaking along the riverside trail. He had frightened Isis the night before, and then tonight in the fire station, he'd told her to stop casting spells. He'd also lurched threateningly toward her. Later, he'd arrived here only minutes after I'd heard Isis screaming at someone to stop pushing her. Floyd's shoes could have been the hard-soled ones I'd heard running away, and they'd been spattered with water droplets as if he'd been too close to the river when something fell splashing into it.

Edna straightened her shoulders and looked up at Haylee. "How did it happen?"

Haylee cupped one side of Edna's face in a gentle hand. "We don't know, but they found her trapped in that skirt we made you."

Mrs. Battersby frowned, tapped her foot, and nodded.

Haylee looked down at her. "Is your head better?"

Mrs. Battersby patted her forehead. "No, and those sirens didn't help, and now this!"

115

Edna explained to Haylee, "Mom phoned me when she heard the siren. She wanted to see what was going on. Then Gord was called to attend the scene."

Mrs. Battersby complained to Haylee, "And your door locked automatically when I left. I can't go back to bed."

Haylee apologized for the door. "I can't take you back now. As I scribbled on the note I left for you, I'm a volunteer fire-fighter. I need to stick around until we're done here." She pulled keys from her pocket. "Here, take these."

Mrs. Battersby made no move to accept the keys. "A real granddaughter, which I don't have, would walk me home." She glanced toward the blanketed form on the ground. "This village is not safe."

"I'll walk you home," Edna offered.

"Not to *your* home, you won't," Mrs. Battersby grumbled. "*You* didn't invite me to stay in *your* home. You invited that strange woman, instead, who ended up dead." She didn't seem to notice the rhyme she'd made. "You put me with this woman you call your daughter when she's no more your daughter than the man in the moon."

Haylee managed to maintain her poise. "As far as I'm concerned, Edna, Naomi, and Opal are all my mothers. They all

116

showered me with love." She turned to Edna. "I suspect the police will want to search Isis's things, though, so even if they let you stay in your apartment tonight, you wouldn't be able to sleep. You can stay with me and your mom."

Mrs. Battersby mumbled, "Great. One big happy family."

Edna beamed at Haylee. "Thank you, darling daughter, I will."

Haylee slipped an arm around Mrs. Battersby's shoulders, which seemed to disgruntle the woman even more.

Edna nodded toward the group around the stretcher. "Do they need me to identify the body?"

Haylee said gently, "Gord only knew her first name, and they haven't found her ID. Vicki called the state police. They'll search your apartment and Isis's car for her real name and next of kin. Gord pronounced her dead and will sign the death certificate."

Edna sighed. "That poor dear." She placed a hand on her mother's back. "C'mon, Mother, I'll take you to Haylee's."

Haylee gave Edna the keys and a resounding kiss on the cheek. "Help yourself to whatever you need. Your mother has the bedroom next to mine. You can have the next one down the hall."

Mrs. Battersby commented to the air beside her, "I never saw such a big apartment for only one person."

Haylee held her hands out like she couldn't do anything about it. She owned the largest store in Threadville, and the apartment above it was huge. "Most of my guest rooms are full of sewing projects." She turned to Edna. "You can ransack my dresser drawers for a nightgown."

Mrs. Battersby contributed helpfully, "Haylee's nightgowns will be miles too long for you. You'll trip and break your neck. Right before your wedding."

"I'll try not to trip and break my neck," Edna promised. "Are you coming?"

Mrs. Battersby took a deep breath, started up the slope, and warned, "We'll have to stop and rest a hundred times on this hill. Why do you folks live in such a difficult place?"

Edna said mildly, "The exercise will do us good."

Muttering, Mrs. Battersby went with her.

When they were out of earshot, I said to Haylee, "How are you managing not to talk back to your reluctant grandmother?"

Haylee's eyes twinkled in the light from the emergency vehicles. "You can see why Edna didn't want her hanging around all

118

week before the wedding! She'll have to put up with her mother's criticizing now, though, with all of us in my apartment. I try to think of Mrs. Battersby the way Edna and my other mothers do — as entertainment. Besides, she'll go home after the wedding."

"And she'll enjoy staying with you so much that she'll come back every weekend forevermore," I predicted darkly.

Haylee let out a breath that was halfway between a sigh and a laugh.

Tally-Ho turned his head toward the dark, wooded entrance to the riverside trail and gave a tentative, warning woof.

Someone had to be on that trail.

# 11

A strident voice came from the foggy trail. "What's going on?" A flashlight shined on the bottom half of a long, swishing skirt, and I recognized the voice.

Juliette, the fortune-teller who had helped me add glow-in-the-dark thread to Edna's wedding skirt, aimed her light toward Haylee, the dogs, and me.

Patricia, the sewing machine historian, was a half step ahead of her on the riverside trail.

I beckoned to them. When they were close, I pointed toward the group near Isis's body. "I'm afraid Isis, the woman with the handmade books she calls *The New Book of the Dead,* has drowned."

Both women gasped, covered their mouths, and backed a step away.

Juliette waved the beam of her flashlight toward the solemn people inside the crime scene tape, but as if afraid of seeing what was actually there, she turned off the flashlight. "What happened? Did she go for a midnight swim?" She scratched at her throat and tucked in a tag that had popped out at the ruffled neckline of her turquoise, red, and orange peasant blouse.

She was wearing the blouse backward.

Had it been like that at the fire station, too? Or had she changed into dark pants and jacket and then back into her dress?

*And I would suspect everyone?*

Haylee answered, "She must have tried on the overskirt we made. It had casters. It rolled into the river."

Patricia stared at the fog-layered dark river. "How?"

"Why did she try on Edna's skirt?" Juliette asked. "Anybody else's skirt? That doesn't make sense."

I shook my head. "I don't understand, either." Isis must have gotten into the overskirt willingly. Donning it involved crouching and stepping over a steel brace. Forcing someone into it would have been difficult, if not impossible.

But Isis had told me it was not "ordained" for me to wear someone else's skirt. Had she thought *she* was ordained to wear it? I tried not to tremble.

Juliette peered back toward the dark,

misty trail. "Here comes Dare Drayton." Her voice was warm with appreciation. "He'll know what to do."

It seemed to me that the emergency responders were already doing everything possible.

In his black jeans, turtleneck, jacket, and loafers, Dare sauntered into the park and waved toward the crime scene tape, the people clustered near the form on the stretcher, and the drenched white wedding skirt now lying in a sodden mass on the riverbank. "What's all this?"

Where had Dare been when Clay was waiting for him in his truck? And when Isis was being pushed into the river?

*Yes, I would definitely suspect everyone.*

"Someone drowned," Juliette answered.

"That Isis person," Patricia added.

Dare shook his head. "Why am I not surprised? She wasn't the brightest incantation in the book."

Juliette scolded, "You should speak nicely of the dead."

He stuck his hands in his pockets. "Why? She wasn't nice when she was alive." He seemed to focus on the group around Isis. "What's my cousin up to now, playing fire chief and undertaker's assistant, too? That guy is starved for attention. I wouldn't be surprised if he pushed her in just so he could strut around —"

I interrupted him. "Well, *I* would!"

Dare only looked amused. "My cousin has a loyal supporter? Someone actually has a crush on him? How quaint."

Haylee said evenly, "Clay Fraser has many admirers."

Battling the desire to say what I thought of Dare and his conjectures and judgments, I looked down to conceal my heated face.

And to check out Dare's loafers.

They appeared to have hard soles. Like Floyd's, Dare's shoes could have been the ones I'd heard hitting the pavement. Juliette had turned off her flashlight, but in the uncertain light from the emergency vehicles, I saw spots of mud on their toes. Had the mud splashed onto his shoes because he'd pushed that overskirt — with Isis inside it and screaming at him — into the river?

As long as I was studying feet, I glanced at Patricia's and Juliette's. A light-colored, sequined slipper stuck out beneath the hem of Juliette's floor-length tiered skirt. Patricia wore jeans, a jean jacket, and sneakers. Juliette and Patricia had also come from the trail, but if any mud stained their shoes, I couldn't see it.

Either of the two women could have

changed their shoes after pushing Isis in, but Dare's callous boorishness and his mud-spattered shoes made me wonder if he had murdered Isis. Why would he, though? Why would anyone?

As she left the fire station, Isis had warned everyone that she had unusual powers, which I took to mean she planned to curse anyone who teased her or made fun of her book. Dare hadn't seemed concerned.

Floyd the zombie, however, had appeared determined to prevent Isis from casting spells on him.

*Suspecting everyone would be cautious and sensible. And a good defense, besides . . .*

Lights flashing, a state police cruiser joined the other emergency vehicles on Lake Street. Dare stifled a yawn that looked totally fake. "Well, ex*cuse* me! It looks like my well-admired cousin's about to enjoy more adventure. I'll leave you small-town folks to your small-town excitement and go wait for my cousin to finally drive me home. I could have walked there by now."

*Why hadn't he?*

He turned and strolled up the hill, right next to the crime scene tape.

Like a couple of girls stalking a teen idol, Patricia and Juliette followed several paces behind him.

I glanced farther up the hill and nudged Haylee. "Your reluctant grandmother is still here."

Haylee grinned up toward Mrs. Battersby, sitting on a bench beside Edna at the top of the hill. "She did predict that she'd need to rest during her climb to Lake Street."

A uniformed state trooper and a man in a suit got out of the state police car, marched down toward the river, and joined Chief Vicki Smallwood beside Isis's body. The trooper and the other man bent over the stretcher.

Our police chief left them, ran up the hill, passed the bandstand, and, much to my dogs' delight, came all the way down to the riverbank and rubbed their ears. She straightened and gave me an earnest look. "Willow, in a few minutes, I'm going to let a trooper guard the scene until the rest of the investigative team comes, and then Detective Neffting and I will talk to you about what you witnessed." She gave Tally-Ho one last pat, took a step away from us up the hill, and then turned around and warned us, "Oh, and by the way, it would be better if you two and your friends don't call me 'Vicki' around Detective Neffting. He's a stickler for protocol and formality."

Guessing that warning had been her entire

reason for coming to talk to us, I saluted. "Yes, ma'am."

Vicki flapped a hand at me. "No need to go overboard, either."

Haylee smiled at Vicki. "Too bad we didn't get our usual detective."

Vicki adjusted her hat, a clever way of hiding her face at the mention of the state trooper who had once been her work partner. When Toby Gartener was promoted, Vicki left the state police to become Elderberry Bay's police chief. She tried to pretend that she and Detective Gartener were not romantically involved, but she didn't fool me. She lowered her ringless left hand. "He's not on duty tonight. Neffting is good." Her tone lacked conviction. She ran up the hill, passing Clay on his way down.

The dogs were even more ecstatic at being with Clay again. We ended up in a group hug, Haylee, Clay, and me, with the dogs in the middle. We humans asked each other if we were all right, and we all said that we were. Our sympathy was with Isis and her family and friends, whoever they were.

"I hate losing anyone," Clay said.

"She'd been dead when she came out of the water, hadn't she?" Haylee asked.

"Yes. In her attempts to get out of that skirt, she must have tangled a piece of it around her neck. It seemed too late, but we tried to revive her."

"A piece of the skirt," I repeated. "A frill was trailing from the overskirt when I first saw it underwater."

Haylee studied my face. "We sewed that skirt together securely."

I grabbed the leashes more tightly. "Someone must have used a lot of force to undo our stitches." Shuddering, I peered up at the bandstand, now only slightly obscured by mist. "Remember the quilted label that said *Edna's Wedding Skirt*? Naomi draped it on the overskirt just before we called Edna."

Haylee and Clay both nodded.

I went on, "After I saw the skirt underwater, I ran up to the bandstand and unplugged Clay's extension cord. That label was lying on the floor, but Naomi had strung it on a ribbon and I don't think the ribbon was with the label." I focused on Clay's face. "Could Isis have been tangled in that ribbon? It was white satin."

"How wide was it?" he asked.

I held my thumb and finger about an inch apart.

"No," he said decisively. "The thing I saw was more like two or three inches wide, and it had lots of stuff on it."

I prompted, "Embroidery, crocheted lace,

glow-in-the-dark thread?"

"Could be," he answered. "And ruffles — or is it tucks? And those shiny things that Edna loves."

Vicki led the detective lower down the riverbank to the drenched white thing that had been Edna's joke wedding skirt. They examined it for a few seconds, and then Vicki raised her head and called, "Willow! Haylee! Can you both come here, please?"

# 12

Vicki swept her hand to point to us, then to the bandstand, and then back to the tape tied to a tree near her. She didn't need to gesture to Haylee and me to stay out of the taped scene. Even under these stressful circumstances, we'd have remembered.

"I'll hold the dogs," Clay offered.

I handed him Sally's and Tally's leashes. His fingers brushed mine. I wanted to cling to his hand, but Vicki — Chief Smallwood — was waiting.

Haylee and I ran up the hill and waved at Edna and Mrs. Battersby. Edna waved back. I hesitated at the uphill side of the band-stand long enough to shine my flashlight on the bandstand's floor. Clay's extension cord was gone, and the only things left were the sheaf of willow wands, the half-full spool of thread, and the white satin rectangle that I had embroidered and Naomi had quilted.

"No ribbon," Haylee summarized.

We ran down the hill on the other side of the crime scene tape. In a sort of salute and farewell, I glanced toward Isis's covered body. She had upset me, but she couldn't have harmed Edna or anyone else with her curses, and she hadn't deserved this horrible death.

Vicki lifted the crime scene tape so we could scoot underneath it and meet the man in the suit. She introduced him as Detective Neffting.

His paunch was too round for his thin body. His head, bulky at the sparsely haired crown and narrow at the chin, seemed to balance precariously on his long neck. He stared down at what was left of Edna's once-fabulous wedding skirt, now a wet and sorry-looking thing lying on its side, its lightbulbs smashed and its wet flounces drooping over electrical wires, a hula hoop, and a cut-down jigsaw stand. Detective Neffting's face was completely unreadable. "Chief Smallwood said you two could explain what this thing is." His voice was high and nasal, making him sound boyish, though I guessed he was over forty.

We attempted to explain why and how we'd made the gigantic wedding overskirt, but I suspected he was having trouble understanding it all. Building a skirt on a jigsaw stand would seem a bit odd, along with wiring the skirt for sound and lights and attaching casters so that the person wearing it could move it around easily.

He kept referring to our creation as "this death trap." He and Chief Smallwood scribbled notes. Finally, he scratched the baldest part of his head, peered at me, and said, "Now let's see if I've got this straight. You two and a couple of other women — people you refer to as your mothers, Haylee — got together and made this rather . . . er . . . strange object as a prank."

Haylee nodded.

"For the wedding of another one of your mothers, Haylee?"

She nodded again.

"How many mothers do you have?"

"Three."

He scratched his head again and muttered, "Last I knew, most of us have only one or two." He raised his voice to a conversational tone again. "Okay, so you made this death contraption and then you forced someone to get inside it —"

I broke in, "We didn't force anyone to do anything."

"Okay, so then the victim, for reasons unknown, got inside the death contraption and wheeled herself down into the river."

131

"I think she was pushed," I said. "I heard a woman yelling, 'Don't push me!' "

"A woman . . ." His words hung in the air, not quite a question.

I answered, "I wasn't sure who it was. She sounded terrified, but the voice was definitely a woman's."

"So it could have been the victim being pushed or someone being pushed *by* the victim, or someone else entirely, who had nothing to do with this death contraption?"

"All of the above," I agreed. I aimed my light at the frill that had come loose from the dress and now trailed across the grass. "We sewed that piece of fabric firmly to the skirt. It couldn't have come undone by itself. Someone took it apart."

"How?" Neffting asked. "Was it torn, frayed, cut, or what?"

I studied the end of the frill. "It appears to have been cut off in a hurry, but I can't tell if it was cut by a knife or scissors. Can you, Haylee?"

She examined the end. "No."

Detective Neffting nodded in a smug way. "For your information, the very end of it, the part you were examining so closely, was cut by a knife wielded by one of the divers, to free the victim so they could raise her to the surface in hopes of reviving her."

"What about farther back?" I shined my light down the length of the now ungathered frill so that Haylee and I could get a good look at it. "That was cut, also," I concluded. "The stitching's still there, attaching the gathered part of it to the skirt. The rest was cut. But I can't tell you with what. Could be a knife or scissors."

"Or a razor blade," Haylee contributed.

"Even a rotary cutter," I said.

"What's that?" Detective Neffting asked.

"A circular, rotating blade in a handle — quilters use them, but so do picture framers, for cutting mats —"

Neffting half closed his eyes and nodded. "Okay. Got it." He opened his eyes to their widest, which made them seem to bulge in an intimidating way. "You really think it could have been one of those — rotary cutters, I think you said?"

I shook my head. "No, for a rotary cutter to work, you need to press against something hard. The skirt would have been too soft."

But Haylee disagreed. "Some rotary cutters, the ones that don't automatically retract, can slash. I've seen people injure themselves and each other with them."

Neffting merely stared at her.

Haylee added, "Accidentally."

133

Vicki Smallwood asked, "What about manicure scissors? See the curved and jagged edges where it was cut?"

I explained, "That would be because the fabric was gathered before it was sewn to the skirt." I shined my light along the fabric. "See? The part closest to the seam is still here, and the cuts along the seam are straighter than manicure scissors would do, but because the fabric was bunched up, the top of the part that was cut off is uneven."

Neffting asked, "How can one side be straight and the other uneven?"

I answered. "The part next to the seam only looks straight. If we undid the threads holding it to the skirt, the edge would be as ragged as the part that was cut off."

He nodded. "And the two ragged edges would fit together?"

"You got it," Haylee told him.

I added, "Either scissors or a knife could have made the cuts. I'm guessing it was scissors."

"Why?" Neffting asked.

Haylee answered for me. "I don't see any nicks in the fabric below where it was cut. It would have been hard to be that neat with a knife. Or with a razor blade or rotary cutter."

I added, "Especially if someone was in a hurry."

Neffting demanded, "What makes you keep saying they were in a hurry?"

I answered with a question of my own. "Aren't attacks usually done in a hurry?"

He tilted his garlic-shaped head on his stalklike neck. "It's not a hard and fast rule."

Did he expect us to laugh? I glanced at Vicki. She frowned and gave her head a slight shake.

Considering that we were discussing a death, I had no problem keeping a straight face. "In this case, I think the attack was done in a hurry," I said. "Shortly before I heard the woman screaming, I saw someone slink along the riverside trail."

Neffting seemed to peer into my brain. "When did you see this person? And where were you?"

"It was after nine thirty, probably close to nine forty." I nodded toward where the trail disappeared between trees. "I was in my backyard with my dogs, about a half block away."

He glanced toward the end of the trail and wrote in his notebook. "Chief Smallwood tells me you were the first one on the scene. What made you leave your yard and come here?"

"First, I was merely curious about why the person I saw on the trail was acting furtive, so I ran up to my apartment, grabbed my flashlight and the dogs' leashes, and ran back to the trail."

He scribbled some more. "How long did that take?"

"Two or three minutes. I had to encourage the dogs to come with me, plus untangle my legs from their leashes, which delayed things. We didn't make fast progress on the trail, either. The dogs seemed spooked and kept wanting to drag me home."

Vicki was writing, but I saw the ghost of a grin cross her face. She knew my dogs and their skittishness — or, perhaps, their common sense.

I continued, "We'd probably been on the trail for a couple of minutes when I heard a scream and saw a largish glow that must have been the skirt moving down the hill in the fog."

"How far away were you?" he asked.

"Close enough to hear the wheels on the concrete boat launch. They're metal and made quite a racket. But between the fog and the low-hanging weeping willow branches, I couldn't see much. It must have been about nine forty-five when the woman yelled 'Don't push me! Don't —' That

136

scream ended suddenly, and then I heard a splash and what I thought were lightbulbs exploding."

He didn't look up from his notebook. "What did you do?"

"I came out from behind the willows and felt my way through the fog to the boat launch. I called for help. No one answered, but I heard someone run south on Lake Street. Whoever it was, his shoes made a slapping noise, like hard-soled shoes, and he didn't come to help. I didn't have time to chase him, though. I was more worried about the woman who had screamed." I shuddered. "And then I saw the skirt underwater. It was a whitish blur, slowly drifting downstream."

Detective Neffting wasn't as tall as I was, but he had maneuvered himself to stand higher on the slope. "You didn't attempt to rescue the victim?"

I looked up into his eyes. "I tugged at the extension cord attached to the skirt, but I thought I was only unwinding it, turning the reel it was on. Maybe I should have waded in, but I didn't want to believe that anyone would be trapped inside that skirt, and Tally — my dog — acted like someone might be in the bandstand, so we dashed up there."

Vicki asked, "Who did you find?"

I shook my head. "No one."

She shoved her hat up off her forehead. "What time did you last see the wedding overskirt in the bandstand?"

How long had it taken me to get home from the park? About five minutes? "It would have been around nine twenty-five."

She asked, "And when did you hear that first scream?"

I thought of everything I'd done after I'd let the dogs and kittens out around nine thirty. "I didn't check the time. Do you know when I phoned 911?"

Neffting stated definitively, "Nine fifty-eight."

"I'm guessing I heard that first scream around nine forty-five."

Nodding, Vicki wrote in her notebook.

Neffting asked, "And the last scream?"

"About five minutes later."

He took a step closer to me. "And you didn't call emergency for at least eight more minutes?"

I resisted the urge to back away from him. "It took me a couple of minutes to get from the trail to where the scream had come from, and then a few more minutes to assess the situation. Even then I thought, hoped, that I might be phoning in a false alarm."

Seeming to accept that, Neffting paged back in his notebook. "Earlier, you said you saw someone slinking along the trail near your yard. Can you give me a description?"

"I thought it was a man, but I couldn't be certain in the dark and the fog. He or she wore dark clothes, slacks, and a jacket, it looked like. The person could have been Floyd, a guy who's wandering around this evening wearing zombie makeup and a 1930s black suit —"

Neffting nodded. "Aha. Yes. The zombie retreat."

I told them about the night before, and Isis saying that a zombie had frightened her with his accusations about her spells. "Her description matched Floyd, the first person to join me at the boat ramp after the skirt went into the water. And earlier this evening in the fire station, Isis mentioned that Floyd had accosted her the night before, and he didn't deny it. She warned him, and everyone else in the fire station, that her spells were potent. No one besides Floyd seemed to take her threats very seriously."

Vicki had been watching me closely. "Could the person you saw sneaking along the trail have been anyone besides this

Floyd character, Willow?"

I glanced uneasily toward Clay. His cousin had been in the vicinity and was distinctly unpleasant, but he was Clay's cousin, and I hated to cast suspicion on the man.

# 13

"Willow?" Vicki prodded. She knew me too well. She probably guessed I didn't want to cast suspicion on a certain person, and may have read my glance toward Clay correctly — or worse, incorrectly. Clay was wearing jeans and a blue shirt, no jacket, but what if Vicki or Detective Neffting thought I suspected Clay of pushing Isis into the river?

I muttered, "It could have been Clay's cousin. Actually, I think he's his second cousin — Dare Drayton."

"Not Dare Drayton, the author." Neffting clearly didn't believe me. "A guy who wrote a ton of bestselling thrillers wouldn't be anywhere near here, much less pushing people into rivers."

What an annoying man. What an annoying *detective*. I answered quickly, "Clay's cousin said he was the author. He's in town doing research for his next book."

Neffting became animated. "You've got to

be kidding! I have all of his books. I'll have to get him to autograph them. He would never risk his career by getting involved in something like this."

Just what we needed, a detective who refused to be objective. I didn't want Dare to be a murderer, because he was related to Clay, and Clay and his family could be affected, but Detective Neffting was dismissing a possible suspect without first weighing all the evidence.

Vicki did not look impressed, not favorably, anyway, but she did untighten her lips enough to ask me, "Did you see or hear anything else, Willow?"

I scrunched up my face, trying to put all the events in order. "Floyd the zombie showed up a few minutes after I heard that person running south on Lake Street. Floyd came from the north, from near the beach, but he could have circled from the bandstand and then behind the shops on the other side of Lake Street, if he'd sprinted the whole distance."

Vicki didn't look up from her notebook. "Didn't you say you saw wet footprints on the concrete boat ramp?"

"Partial footprints led from the river up the ramp and toward the grass. They've probably dried by now."

Vicki corroborated, "They were nearly gone when I looked for them."

If Neffting leaned farther toward me on that slope, he'd topple over. He asked me, "What size shoes, approximately?"

"They weren't entire footprints. I'm guessing they were from the toes of someone's shoes."

"Not heels?" he asked.

"I figured that someone pushing someone else into the river would be more likely to get his toes than his heels wet."

Neffting pointed his pen at Vicki. "Let's go take a look." The pen swung around to aim at Haylee and me. "You two stay here."

He and Vicki strode to the boat ramp and shined their lights on it. Vicki's camera flashed several times.

They returned to us. "No footprints now," he said. "A few bits of glass —"

"Thin, like from broken lightbulbs?" I asked.

Behind Neffting, Vicki nodded decisively.

Neffting only hedged. "Could be." He looked at Vicki. "Let's go see that bandstand."

He lifted the yellow tape and marched uphill outside the crime scene. His long legs moved jerkily, reminding me of Floyd.

I had recognized Floyd by his zombie gait,

and Floyd had criticized Lenny for not staying in character. However, if Floyd had wanted to commit a crime, he could have disguised himself by moving normally. He could have slunk toward his victim before the crime and then run away afterward.

Vicki hurried to catch up with Neffting. They hadn't told Haylee and me to stay behind, so we followed.

Edna and Mrs. Battersby must have become tired of watching, or they'd been unable to see through the fog. Or maybe they'd gotten cold. I hadn't dressed for the damp chill of midnight in early October, and had to fight involuntary tremors.

Without going inside the crime scene tape, Haylee and I joined Vicki and Detective Neffting on the uphill side of the bandstand. I aimed my light at the quilted white satin label on the bandstand's plank floor. We could easily read the embroidered words: *Edna's Wedding Skirt.* I explained, "A ribbon was strung through the loops on that label and tied in a bow around the top of the skirt."

The two police officers only looked at each other. What did that mean?

I moved my light to the handful of willow wands. "Those sticks are all about the same length and look like someone placed them here very carefully. They weren't here when we installed the big overskirt. As I left afterward, I saw Isis down by the river. I thought she was pruning a willow tree."

Neffting frowned as if perplexed.

Vicki photographed the sticks and the label. After her camera flashed, the bandstand seemed darker than ever, except for the spool of glow-in-the-dark thread.

"What's that weird, bright spool thing?" Neffting asked.

"Glow-in-the-dark thread," I told him.

He beamed his flashlight on it, and the thread looked dull white, but when he shut off his light, the spool resembled a convention of fireflies. "Whatever is it for?"

Haylee explained, "We don't need a reason for owning different types of thread, but this is great to use on kids' Halloween costumes to make them more visible in the dark."

"Thread," he repeated. "How's a driver going to see a *thread,* especially if it's a dark and stormy night?" His eyes gleamed, probably from the thrill of reciting the clichéd first line of mysteries.

He probably didn't want to listen to an entire lecture about machine embroidery. I condensed it to, "We can mass it together, like in embroidery, and it shows up."

He muttered, "I should have known to

145

stay away from *Thread*ville."

Again ignoring what might have been another wisecrack, Vicki asked Haylee and me, "Does either of you sell this kind of thread in your shops?"

"I do," I answered, "as of today." It was past midnight, already Friday. "I mean yesterday. And I've sold a lot of it to other people, too."

Vicki rubbed her forehead with her wrist. "Who bought it?"

"Some of my regular customers, plus two zombies, Floyd and Lenny, the lifeguard who went into the river to search for the victim and hung around afterward." I glanced around the park. Lenny was gone.

Neffting stared expectantly at Vicki.

"I got his statement, and then a volunteer fireman drove him back to the Elderberry Bay Lodge so he could change and warm up," Vicki told Neffting. "At the time, he was carrying a towel, but as far as I could tell, he was wearing only bathing trunks underneath his emergency blanket. What about when he arrived, Willow? Was he wearing dark slacks and a jacket?"

I shook my head. "Only surfer shorts, flip-flops, and his towel." And that horrid, frayed rope around his ankle. "He keeps his wallet in a pocket sewn to the inside of the towel."

Vicki laughed. "I saw that when I asked for his ID. Nothing like a well-prepared zombie. He'll be at the lodge all weekend, but I got his home address, also. Did anyone else buy the thread, Willow?"

"I did, both for the store and for myself. The woman who sells it is staying with me."

Vicki looked surprised. I hadn't seen her in the past couple of weeks except when she drove past in her cruiser, so she didn't know which of the Threadville shopkeepers were housing guests, or who our guests were.

Neffting asked, "Was some of that glow-in-the-dark thread on that death contraption?"

Haylee answered, "Yes."

I pointed out the glowing strand snaking from the spool to the edge of the bandstand floor. "I suspect this thread didn't come off the wedding skirt, though. It's probably connected to the thread I saw going up the riverside trail past my place, just after the person skulked along the trail."

"Skulked," Neffting repeated. "That's a good one. Dare Drayton uses words like that." He shook his head in apparent wonder. "*Dare Drayton* is visiting this area."

Vicki paid no attention to the detective's google-eyed awe. "Where on the trail did you see the thread?" she asked me.

"Some of it went upriver from my place, and it came this direction, too. I didn't pay much attention to it, because of the woman yelling." Imagining Isis's last minutes and hoping that she hadn't suffered long, I couldn't help rubbing my own throat.

Neffting nodded toward the end of the trail. "Let's have a look."

Although we avoided the taped crime scene, we saw the strand of pale, glowing thread snaking down the hill nearby.

When we reached Clay and my dogs, Vicki told him and Haylee, "We're done with you two for tonight, but we may need to talk to you tomorrow."

The other volunteer firefighters had walked back to the fire station, leaving the big red fire truck behind.

"Race you to drive it back," Haylee teased Clay.

She got a head start while Clay gently looped the handles of my dogs' leashes over my wrist. Even though she was tall and fast, I was sure he could have made it to the top of the hill first if he had really tried. I wished I could go with them instead of hanging out with a police chief and a detective.

I moved my light around where we'd seen the strand of thread, then snapped the flashlight off. In the sudden darkness, it was easy to pick out the glowing thread draped across the lawn and trembling whenever a breeze snagged a leaf or a blade of grass.

"Ugh," Vicki exclaimed. "It's like it's pulsating."

"Pulsating," Neffting repeated. "You two must have been around Dare Drayton a lot."

"Never met the man." Vicki continued to stare at the thread. "It looks like a long worm, maybe a slimy one."

I laughed. "It's only thread."

She shuddered. "As if zombies weren't bad enough."

I knew her well enough to tell she was exaggerating.

Apparently, Neffting didn't. "Zombies aren't *real*," he informed her in a know-it-all way that irritated me. I was cold, tired, and verging on cranky.

Vicki folded her arms. "If they go around scaring babies and little old ladies, I'll . . . I'll make them go back underground."

*And if they go around murdering people, too,* I thought, picturing Floyd and his apparent fear of Isis and her powers.

Neffting put out a hand to keep us from approaching the thread leading down the riverside trail. "We'll have to close off this as part of the scene, also." He stuck two fingers in his mouth and let out a whistle.

I jumped about two feet into the air. Sally and Tally yelped.

Neffting yelled to a state trooper, "Bring me another roll of that tape!"

"We can move what I already strung up," Vicki said. She detached the tape from the nearby willow tree. We all walked uphill a few feet. Vicki retied the tape to a bush above the trail, blocking the entrance to the trail.

Neffting turned to me. "Can you take us to see the other end of the thread?"

"I don't know where it is," I said, "but it must be upriver from my place." I gestured toward the yellow tape. "Since this end of the trail is now part of the crime scene, and I saw the thread south of my place, we'll have to go up Lake Street and around to the other end of the trail."

Vicki nodded.

"Walking or driving?" Neffting asked.

"It's not far," Vicki said. "And I have a radio."

A trooper pelted down the hill with a roll of crime scene tape. Neffting only stared at him as if wondering what he was doing. Vicki held out her hand, took the roll of tape, and thanked the man. He sprinted back toward the people surrounding the stretcher.

Vicki and I led Neffting up to Lake Street, then south to where the trail came out near the highway bridge.

Although I shined my light around in an attempt to fire up the thread's glow, we couldn't spot any.

We walked slowly north, shining our lights on both sides of the trail and glancing off into the darkness beyond our flashlight's beams.

We didn't catch sight of the thread until we were behind my fence.

The thread came from the direction of the park and ended underneath my gate in a glow-in-the-dark tangle.

# 14

I burst out, "Someone moved that thread into my yard!"

Detective Neffting and Chief Smallwood only looked at me as if the glow-in-the-dark thread might be sprouting from my head.

I pointed to the section of the trail south of us, where we'd been searching for the thread. "When I left with my dogs around nine this evening, the thread was coming from upriver."

My dogs strained toward the closed gate. They probably knew who had wadded up the thread and pushed it underneath my gate. Wishing they could tell us, I held them back.

Vicki tied a piece of crime scene tape from my fence to a silver maple on the riverbank, blocking off the trail behind the downriver half of my property. The crime scene already covered most of the riverside park. Now it encompassed the trail from the park all the way past my gate.

Neffting stared down at the heaped-up thread. "You won't be able to use your backyard tonight. We'll have a look by daylight, and will probably be able to clear it for your use again quickly."

I thanked him absentmindedly. When I shined my light on the thread, it looked dull and gray, but underneath it, I glimpsed a silvery glint. Without touching anything I wasn't supposed to, I moved my flashlight back and forth while I bobbed my head up and down. "There's something else with that thread," I told the officers. "It looks like the thread nippers I left in the fire station with a spool of glow-in-the-dark thread and a packet of needles."

"Next thing you know we'll be looking for needles in haystacks," Neffting deadpanned.

I was beginning to believe the man did have a sense of humor, but I took my cue from Vicki, who acted like she hadn't heard him.

She looked up at me. "If those are your thread nippers, could the spool of thread we saw in the bandstand, which may be attached to this mess, be yours, too?"

I nodded. "I wasn't the only one with a spool of thread like that, but yes, that spool could be the one I left in the fire station with the other things."

Vicki asked, "Who has access to the fire station besides firefighters?"

I admitted, "Clay and I left the fire station unlocked for about ten minutes this evening while we rolled the wedding skirt down to the bandstand."

Vicki demanded, "Why? Trying to make extra work for me? What if someone vandalized the fire trucks or disabled them, and they couldn't get to an emergency? You have garage door openers. And closers. You should learn to use them." She hadn't lost her sarcastic touch.

My excuse wasn't great. "We were eager to get that wedding skirt in place so we could surprise Edna. And we were near the fire station."

She echoed my thoughts. "Not near enough."

"Who's 'we'?" Neffting asked.

He'd met Clay briefly. I explained to him that Naomi and Opal were two of Haylee's mothers. He had me spell their names.

Vicki must have seen me shiver. She asked me, "Can you get into your apartment through your shop?"

I felt in my pocket for my keys. "Yes."

Keeping to one side of the trail and examining it by flashlight, we retraced our steps up the trail. Near the bridge, Tally lunged toward what looked like a scrap of paper in tall grass. I pulled him to me.

Vicki and Detective Neffting focused their lights on the thing. It was a tiny envelope with a windowed front. Silver metal gleamed inside the square opening.

As if finding sewing needles beside a hiking trail were a common occurrence, I said, "That's probably my packet of needles."

"In tall grass. *Almost* in a haystack." Neffting shook his head as if in admiration, but I didn't think he was admiring Tally and me for sniffing out this piece of evidence, or whatever. "Did you leave it there yourself?" he asked.

"No. Last I knew, it was at the fire station."

"One package of needles might look like any other," Neffting cautioned. "Just like one spool of thread and one pair of nippers could look like any other."

I nodded. "Yes, but it would be quite a coincidence for an identical trio of sewing supplies to show up somewhere besides the fire station tonight. I wonder if that man I saw skulking along the trail dropped all three things."

I couldn't blame Vicki and Neffting for looking skeptical.

"Accidentally," I added. "Maybe he didn't realize the thread was unwinding?"

Vicki frowned. "How could that happen, Willow? Thread should be too light to unreel from a spool by itself. If you guessed that the *spool* was caught in the bandstand, which it didn't seem to be, and that the thread had unwound itself while someone unknowingly carried one end of it all the way from the bandstand to your gate, I could almost believe it."

Quickly, I came up with a theory. "Maybe the thread had become tangled in my nippers, and the nippers fell out of his pocket and acted like a sort of anchor, and the thread started unwinding."

"Describe those little nippers," Neffting ordered. "They were too buried in thread for me to comprehend what they were."

"They're forged from one thick strip of steel, shaped in a U with the two legs flattened and sharpened into blades."

"So your little nippers are what cut the ruffle partially off the death contraption." He stated it as if it were fact, but he didn't look at me. Was he trying to put words in my mouth, or fishing for information?

Whichever it was, I took the bait. "Thread nippers don't offer enough leverage to cut through that many layers of fabric —"

He interrupted me. "Only one."

I repeated what I'd told him before. "The fabric was gathered, that is, bunched up closely, before it was cut. And even if someone had enough strength to make those nippers cut through all that fabric at once, the blades are short. That frill had been hacked off messily, but not as messily as if it had been done by short blades."

Vicki asked Neffting, "The lab will be able to tell all that, don't you think?"

"Could be." Without looking up from his writing, he asked me, "And how would those little nippers and that mass of thread have ended up in your yard?"

I stared out over the river, flowing past in the dark like black silk. "What if the man was oblivious to the thread unspooling, like it was in the pocket of that loose jacket, as he walked —"

"Skulked," Neffting corrected me in a murmur.

I went on, "— and the thread unwound all the way to the bandstand, and when he got there, Isis fought with him, causing the spool to come out of his pocket. Maybe he realized then that he might have left a trail of thread leading to him in the bandstand, but he was too busy pushing Isis toward the river to pick up the spool and go back for all of the thread."

"You're coming up with some wild and tangled explanations," Neffting complained. "So why didn't your bad guy simply pick up the spool of thread in the bandstand after he pushed the woman into the river, and then come here from there, grabbing his errant thread as he went?" He waved his hand to take in the entire area between the lake, the river, the bridge, and Lake Street. "Why did he go out of his way, all around the block, to get to the other end of the thread?"

I guessed, "By then, I was shouting, and in his way on the riverside trail. He wouldn't have dared retrace his steps for fear I would see him."

Neffting persisted. "So even if he did come from the other end of the trail, why didn't he keep going past your gate, picking up his thread all the way back to the band-stand? Why did the thread end up under-neath your gate?"

"Maybe he was afraid I was still on the trail or coming back? Or he didn't dare go to the park for fear of being seen and con-nected with his crime? So he shoved the thread he'd collected underneath my gate, turned around, and fled back toward the bridge."

Neffting shook his head. "Whoa, there. You're stringing things together that maybe don't belong in the same thread."

Well, he had asked. I gave him a weak smile, but he stared at me coldly. "He didn't have to leave the thread and nippers in your yard. He could have used those little nippers to cut the thread. Then he could have gone off, taking the wadded-up thread and nippers with him. You said you and the dogs got tangled in leashes on the way to the park. Are you sure you weren't tangled in thread?"

"Yes."

Not quite looking at me, Neffting continued his interrogation. "And you're sure it was a man you saw on the trail?"

"No, but I thought it was. Or a tall woman."

"Hard to tell when they're *skulking.*"

I had a feeling I was going to hear that word from him many more times before this case was solved, if it ever was. Vicki snapped pictures of the needle packet and its surroundings. Her lens zoomed in and out. She was taking close-ups of the packet as well as photos showing the entire scene.

Sniffing, Tally-Ho pulled me toward a spot near the needle packet. He whimpered. Both dogs edged their noses toward the ground. I shined my flashlight, but the dogs were in my way. Vicki took their leashes and pulled them back.

I bent closer to what they'd been trying to investigate.

Two small slashes in the ground were about the same distance apart as the blades on my thread nippers.

# 15

Vicki was still holding my dogs. I asked Neffting to have a look at the two small holes in the earth.

First, he had trouble seeing them, and when he did, he made a sound between a laugh and a grunt. "Chief Smallwood thought she saw worms, so maybe you've found the front and back doors of an earthworm's den."

Was he serious?

Afraid he'd step on the holes and accidentally fill them, I stood in his way. "The gashes appear to have been made by something sharp and flat, like blades."

Staying between him and the two tiny holes in the ground, I took my dogs' leashes and let Vicki inspect the holes.

She moved her flashlight across them at several angles. Muttering that the photos might not turn out, she aimed her camera at them.

I pointed out that the holes were about eighteen inches from the packet of needles. "If someone crouched down to push the nippers into the soil, the package of needles could have fallen from his pocket."

Neffting asked, "Why would someone stab your little nippers into the ground?"

I was tempted to suggest that they were attacking earthworms. "We were wondering how the loose end of thread would get so stuck that the thread could come unwound as someone walked. What if they *meant* to make a trail of thread? What if they tied one end to the curve between the blades and stuck the nippers down into the dirt like a big staple? As long as they didn't tug on the thread, the nippers would stay in place, and they could make the sort of trail of thread we found."

"But why would anyone do such a thing?" Neffting asked.

I admitted that I didn't have a clue. "Your investigators could measure the thread that's under my gate, and see if it's long enough that the end could have been here. And while they're at it, they could see if the thread was tied to the nippers or only tangled around them."

By flashlight, Vicki's grin was mischievous. "Are you feeling okay, Willow?"

I smiled back. "Probably. I guess that the person who carefully laid a trail of thread can't be the person who pushed Isis into the river, though, because who would leave such an obvious trail to a crime?" I answered my own question. "Someone who didn't plan the crime, but committed it on impulse. And then came back later to pick up the telltale thread."

Vicki scowled. "At this point, we won't rule anything out. But remind me, Willow, who investigates homicides?"

"Possible homicides," Neffting corrected her.

She ignored him. "Who, Willow? Police or civilians?"

"Police," I answered quickly. "Don't worry. I'll keep out of it. I'm only trying to figure out what could have happened with a bunch of sewing things and how they might tie into the . . . *possible* homicide."

The way Neffting seemed to scrutinize me without looking at my eyes made me fidgety. Fortunately, holding the leashes of two curious dogs gave me the perfect excuse for not standing still.

Finally, Neffting shifted his attention from the side of my head. He radioed a request for a state trooper to come guard the end of the trail where we were.

163

The dogs and I went a few steps away while Neffting and Vicki put the packet of needles into an evidence envelope, left an orange marker where the needles had been, and covered the two gashes with another marker. Then they started unrolling yellow tape. When they were done stringing it between trees, the taped-off crime scene extended along the entire riverside trail from where we were near the bridge and included most of the park at the mouth of the river.

Neffting asked me, "Can you get us into the fire station to see if your thread, nippers, and needles might be there, and not scattered about the countryside?"

The man's flare for drama and exaggeration might be a good trait in a detective. Or not.

"Sure." Sally and Tally wouldn't mind a longer walk.

Vicki reached for Sally-Forth's leash. The dogs helped pull us up to Lake Street.

A state police cruiser pulled up beside the curb. A male trooper got out.

"Don't go into the fire station without me," Neffting ordered.

Vicki, the dogs, and I waited while he talked to the trooper, pointed him toward the crime scene down the hill near the bridge, and gave him what was left of the roll of tape.

After Neffting rejoined us, the three of us could almost have resembled friends walking two dogs, except that our slow pace was not really a companionable stroll. I wasn't sure about the two officers, but I was still in evidence-searching mode, and Sally and Tally persisted in following possible clues.

"I wish I had a nose like a dog," Vicki said.

I laughed. "Yours suits you better."

Neffting ignored us.

In front of In Stitches, Vicki stopped and cocked her head. "Is that noise coming from your place, Willow?"

"I'm afraid so."

"That's not like you." Her statement implied a question.

"It's my guest, Brianna."

Neffting eyed In Stitches, but didn't say anything and continued walking down the street. Vicki, the dogs, and I caught up.

Several state police vehicles were now at the park, along with ominous-looking windowless vans. A noisy, smelly diesel generator supplied electricity to portable lights that haloed everything in mist. Investigators in white hooded coveralls swarmed lawns.

Maybe if the zombies caught sight of all this, they'd come back next fall, bring similar white coveralls, and stage an aliens-from-outer-space retreat.

We turned the corner. The fire station's big garage doors were pulled down to the pavement. Clay and Haylee had locked them and the people-sized door. I pressed buttons on a keypad, opened the door, and switched on the lights. Tally-Ho and I led Vicki, Sally-Forth, and Detective Neffting through the garage, past the fire trucks, into the back room, and to the ledge where I'd last seen my thread nippers, spool of glow-in-the-dark thread, and pack of needles.

None of them were there.

We searched, including shining flashlights underneath fire trucks. The dogs seemed to think this was a wonderful game.

"And you're not the one who moved them?" Neffting asked me.

"I left them here," I repeated. "After we showed Edna her skirt in the bandstand, I went home for the dogs. I planned to come back here, pick up my things, and lock up again, but I got distracted."

Neffting asked me, "Who else may have seen the things you say you left on that ledge?"

"Everyone who was in the fire station at the time could have seen them. Opal, Naomi, and a woman who calls herself

'Madame Juliette' used them when they sewed some of the thread to the skirt. Brianna, the thread distributor who is staying with me, was here, too, and so was a woman named Patricia who says she's a sewing machine historian. The other people here besides Isis were Clay Fraser, Dare Drayton, and the zombie calling himself Floyd."

"Anyone else?" Neffting prompted.

I couldn't think of anyone else.

"You," he said. "*You* were here."

"Of course." *Or I wouldn't have been able to tell you about the others.* What an odd detective.

He underlined something in his notebook, snapped it closed, and led the way out.

Still wondering why he'd made such a pointless point about my not stating the obvious, I checked the door. It had locked itself behind us.

Striding ahead of us and my investigating dogs toward the park, Neffting asked me over one shoulder, "Does anyone lock the fire station when the trucks are out on a call, like a fire or other emergency?"

Vicki gave me a sour look. "They do when they remember to use their door closers. One garage door was standing open when I arrived on the scene tonight."

I excused my fellow volunteer firefighters. "We often leave it open so that late-coming volunteers can run in and read the chalkboard for the location of the emergency. It speeds up our response to the emergency, but I'll mention the subject at our next firefighters' meeting."

"You'd better," Vicki said.

Neffting let us catch up. "So," he concluded, "the fire station could have been left unlocked and unoccupied twice this evening. First, when you took that death con*trap*tion to the park, and second, during the water rescue call. Your sewing things could have disappeared either time."

"The nippers and needles, yes," I agreed. "But if the thread strung along the trail was from the spool I left here, it was taken during the first time the fire station was left unlocked."

"How can you be certain?" he prodded.

Hadn't I explained all of this? Was he trying to trip me up on minor details? "I saw the thread on the trail before I heard the screams, before I called for emergency help." Picturing Isis trapped and being wheeled down the ramp toward the river, I scolded myself for not using the woman's name. "Before I heard *Isis's* screams."

He returned to a different question. "Are

you sure it was Isis who screamed and not someone else?"

I repeated that I hadn't been able to figure out whose voice I'd heard. "But it was a woman. She yelled, 'Don't push me!' And Isis was the one stuck in the wheeled —" I fumbled for a word other than "contraption."

Neffting had no such qualms. He supplied, "Death con*trap*tion." He licked his lips as if savoring the phrase he'd coined for our once-lovely work of art.

Thanks to the portable lights, the bandstand in the park was even more brightly lit than when the skirt had been flashing its lights and playing the "Wedding March."

It was all tragic and unnecessary. Why had Isis clambered into that skirt? Had someone known she was going to wear it? Had that person come along to "help"? Or had the person arrived from the trail, found Isis wearing the skirt, and taken advantage of the situation?

*Floyd, so afraid of Isis's curses that he put a permanent end to them?*

I expected Neffting and Vicki to join the investigators in the park, but they continued up the street with the dogs and me.

# 16

Maybe Vicki was merely enjoying walking the dogs, but why did Neffting accompany us up Lake Street instead of joining the investigation in the park? He made me nervous.

He stayed with us all the way to the sidewalk in front of In Stitches, then asked me, "This Brianna that you said is playing the music that we can hear all the way out here — didn't you tell us she sold you thread like we found under your gate? And you sold it to others? Did she still have some after you bought it?"

I nodded.

Vicki asked, "Could she have left thread along the trail *before* you saw the skulker?"

And the thread had nothing to do with Isis's murder? Proving that my sewing supplies were not connected to a murder might be a good thing.

"Anyone could have," I answered. "I

didn't notice that spool on the floor of the bandstand when we took that skirt there, but I could have missed it." And the willow wands, too? "About a half hour later, when I went home for the dogs, the night was so foggy I could barely see where I was going, and someone could have been unwinding thread or doing nearly anything else on the trail ahead of me. I doubt that it would have been Brianna, though. I heard her voice as soon as I went into my apartment."

Neffting stood with his head tilted to one side, as if waiting for something.

"Want to come inside?" I offered. "If Brianna's still awake, you can talk to her."

Vicki laughed. "How could she sleep with all that noise?"

I groaned. "She had it on all day while she napped."

Vicki asked, "As loud as that?"

"Almost. It's a shock. The only other guest I've ever hosted was perfect."

Neffting wasn't looking at Vicki. She shot me a scowl.

Grinning at her, I amended my praise to, "*Nearly* perfect. I didn't expect her, either."

Vicki looked pained. Maybe it wasn't fair to remind her of the rough time she'd had that night.

Ordinarily, I would have unleashed the

dogs the moment the door of In Stitches closed behind us, but we were heading for my apartment, where Brianna, who seemed frightened of the little darlings, could be wandering around. As always, Vicki was observant. Taking her cue from the way I hung on to Tally's leash, she didn't let go of Sally's.

I turned on enough lights for us to negotiate the aisles of In Stitches. Neffting seemed to memorize everything. He even managed to zero in on my quickly arranged display of glow-in-the-dark thread. "Any spools missing?" he asked.

I did a quick count. Nineteen. "No."

He demanded, "How can you be sure?"

I dragged Tally to my desk in the dogs' pen, fished out my records, and showed that I'd bought thirty-six spools and had sold seventeen, including the one I'd sold to myself and taken to the fire station, which left nineteen in my inventory.

Neffting thanked me and wrote in his notebook.

*What did he write? "Willow told the truth about at least one thing"?*

"Okay," he said, "let's go talk to this Brianna person."

I opened the apartment door. We went downstairs, which wasn't easy with two dogs, one police chief, and one state police detective all vying to be first.

We stopped at the foot of the stairs. I tightened my hand on Tally's leash. Vicki handed me Sally's. Both dogs wagged their tails happily.

Looking half awake and wearing a rumpled pink sweat suit, Brianna sat slumped on my couch with the cordless phone that was usually in the guest room next to her ear. The guest suite door was open, and music blasted from her room. "Oops, gotta go," she hollered into the phone. "Miss you." She made kissy noises, clicked the phone off, set it on an end table, rose slowly, and folded her arms. Her expression was stony and closed.

I shut the guest suite door so we could hear each other over her music, then introduced her to Detective Neffting and Chief Smallwood. Was it my imagination, or did Neffting become still and watchful when I said Brianna's last name was Shrevedale?

Brianna challenged, "You officers are here without a search warrant?"

I answered for them. "They're here with my permission, and they're not searching for anything. Can you tell them who all we sold your glow-in-the-dark thread to?"

"Why?"

I said in a mild voice. "Long story." Maybe I was a little abrupt.

"I sold a bunch of it to you." Her tone was as flat as usual, but her mouth twisted scornfully, undoubtedly showing the officers what she thought of me. "*You* sold it to the others."

Neffting asked, "Do you remember who she sold it to?"

"Two guys made up like zombies."

"Floyd and Lenny," I translated for the officers. I asked Brianna, "Anyone else?"

"A bunch of women. How would I know who they were? That's your job."

I listed the women I could remember and added, "I'll get their last names for you tomorrow."

Neffting cleared his throat. "We can find that out." He turned back to Brianna. "Did you see or hear anything unusual tonight?"

Brianna lifted one shoulder in a gesture of dismissal. "No. Only . . ." She pointed at me. ". . . *she* wasn't here, but maybe that's common. I don't know when and where she goes."

Vicki asked her, "Did you see anyone in Willow's backyard or down on the trail?"

"No. I was in my room until a few minutes ago. I was on the phone."

Neffting asked her mildly, "Did you go

174

outside at all?"

She gave him the look that bullies give kids on playgrounds. "No. Didn't you hear what I said? I was in *that* room." She made a speedy backhand gesture toward the door I'd shut.

Vicki and Detective Neffting studied her as if wondering why she was showing so much attitude.

I pointed to the dishes on the kitchen counter, which I'd left tidy after our supper. "You must have come out of your room long enough to fix yourself a snack."

"So? Is eating a crime? It was dark outside. How would I see anyone out there?"

Vicki pointed out, "You said you'd been in your room the whole time until a few minutes ago."

Brianna let out an exasperated sigh. "All but what, five minutes? And I've been on the phone ever since I came back from helping *her* at the fire station." She stared boldly at Detective Neffting. "You can check her phone records."

What a convenient alibi, I thought. And glib, too, as if she'd rehearsed it. And would it hurt her to call me "Willow" instead of "she"?

My phone records might show that the phone had been in constant use, but that wouldn't prove that Brianna had actually been inside or on the phone.

Vicki must have been thinking similar things. "Some people take cordless phones outside while they're talking."

Brianna said, "Well, I'm not *some* people, and I didn't. I never stepped foot outside. You got that?"

Neffting took out his notebook and wrote.

Brianna glared at him. "Listen here, you. I know my rights. You can't come barging in here asking me questions."

I held up both hands in a "halt" gesture. The loops on the dogs' leashes slid down toward my elbow. "Brianna, I invited them in, and you're right that you don't have to answer their questions, but someone drowned tonight, and they'd like to know if you saw anyone outside. That's all. No need to get on the defens—"

Brianna stared boldly at me. "Did you get yourself involved in *another* murder?"

Vicki began, " 'Involved' isn't quite the right word —"

A smirk played around Brianna's mouth. "Yeah, well, lots of people might like to know what the right word is."

Vicki asked Brianna, "Are you sure you didn't go outside and . . . maybe move some thread around?"

Brianna made an outraged face. "Why would I do that? And why are you asking me all these stupid questions? I was on the phone. Got that? On the *phone.*"

What *I* got was that her repetition about being on the phone sounded more and more like a preplanned alibi. And I'd only said that someone had drowned. Why had Brianna immediately labeled the death a murder? Neffting and Vicki had avoided calling it that in my hearing.

Vicki stared at the sliding glass door to the patio. "Willow, I thought you always kept that door closed so your animals wouldn't get out."

As Vicki had learned, the dogs could wedge the door open with their noses. "I do." I frowned at the teeny gap between the door and the jamb. "I'm sure I closed it and locked it when I went out around nine forty." I started toward the door for a closer look.

Vicki yelped, "Don't touch that, Willow. We'll have to fingerprint it."

Brianna paled. "Well, maybe I did open it, but I just stuck my head out to see if it was raining. My boyfriend asked me what the weather was like. I didn't go out." She flicked a challenging glance at me. "That door was already unlocked."

Vicki asked me, "You say you locked it?"

I nodded.

Brianna sneered. "If she locked it, then maybe someone else came in after she went out. One of her friends. Or an intruder."

She embellished the last word with sarcasm. Trying to make Neffting and Vicki doubt me and suspect me of anything and everything, including murder?

Vicki persisted. "Who else has a key, Willow?"

"No one, as far as I know, besides Brianna. I lent one to her." I hoped Brianna heard my tiny emphasis on the word "lent."

Neffting asked me, "May I borrow a knife?"

What a strange request from a detective. I opened my mouth, closed it, and finally managed, "What kind of knife?"

"A dinner knife. Or a fork." He gestured at my patio door. "I don't want anyone touching that door, but I also don't want to leave it open tonight."

I quickly got him a knife *and* a fork. With the knife barely touching the door and the lever, he closed the door and locked it. "I'll get a fingerprint guy to have a look at that first thing in the morning to check for any intruders. Meanwhile, keep everyone out of your backyard tonight."

Turning to put the knife and fork away, I kicked one of the clogs I kept underneath a bench by the door. My animals had been known to move those clogs, but Sally and Tally had been on leashes ever since we came inside, and the kittens were still shut inside the master suite.

I squatted and picked up one of the clogs. Damp earth filled part of the treads.

I hadn't worn those shoes for at least a week.

## 17

Maybe I shouldn't have touched the clog. I might have obliterated someone's fingerprints. I nudged it and its mate underneath the bench where I usually kept them, then stood and stared at Brianna. "Someone borrowed my gardening clogs."

Vicki and Detective Neffting didn't say a thing.

Brianna challenged, "How would you know that?"

"The dirt on the soles is damp," I answered, "and I haven't worn those for a week."

"Or you don't remember," Brianna accused.

"I remember." I sounded almost as menacing as I felt.

Vicki put on plastic gloves. "I'll remove these for fingerprinting."

Neffting handed her a large paper bag.

Brianna picked up one of my embroidered

pillows from the couch and threw it, hard, back where it had been. "Maybe I did borrow your shoes without asking," she admitted. "Is that a crime? You weren't here to ask. I put them back."

I reminded her, "You said you only stuck your nose out the door."

"I did." She pointed at her bare feet. She probably didn't mean to call attention to her chipped black toenail polish. "I didn't want to get my feet all muddy and track on your pristine white floors."

They were tile, easy to clean. When Haylee had designed the place with me in mind, and without telling me what she was up to, she'd foreseen that I would want to adopt dogs within days of moving in.

Our police chief glanced toward the glass doors, but it was dark outside, so she wouldn't be able to see anything besides our pallid reflections. But she'd spent more time than she probably wanted to remember in my backyard and knew what it was like. "Willow has a stone patio. Where did the mud on the shoes come from?"

Brianna turned the corners of her mouth down in a surly way. "Her patio must not be as pristine as her floors."

"My patio is not muddy, and neither is my yard." Ignoring Vicki's warning glance, I went on, "The first place you'd get into mud would be the trail beside the river-bank."

Brianna came back with a swift, "Well, in that case, you're the one who got mud on your shoes. I didn't even know there *was* a river. Don't you have flower beds out there? Like, right beside the patio? I must have stepped in one." She made a grimace that verged on a gloat.

Vicki looked at Neffting. "Can the finger-print guy look for shoe prints out there in the morning?"

Neffting nodded, putting that top-heavy head and his thin neck at risk. "He sure can."

Brianna lost the rest of her smug expression and indicated me with a slight tilt of her head. "I don't know why you're making such a fuss about me setting one foot outside, when she's the one who was probably out murdering people."

There it was again — "murder." What did Brianna know that we didn't?

Vicki stood up tall and said in a louder-than-usual voice, "Ms. Shrevedale —"

She couldn't finish whatever she was about to say. Mustache and Bow-Tie yowled in unison from my bedroom. They were particularly fond of our police chief.

Vicki gazed at my bedroom door. "Those kittens of yours seem to have gained adult voices, Willow."

Brianna griped, "They never shut up."

So she drowned out their voices with her music? I told Vicki, "They've grown a lot. Want to see them?"

Detective Neffting sneezed.

"Allergic to cats?" she asked him.

His eyes were watering, but he didn't answer her question. "I think we're done here. Let's head back to the park."

I put the dogs in my bedroom with the kittens, then escorted Neffting and Vicki upstairs, through In Stitches, and out the front door.

On the porch, Vicki asked me quietly, "What's with that girl?"

I shrugged. "I guess she doesn't like the law."

Vicki moved her hat back and blew at strands of hair on her forehead. "I don't think she likes *you* much, either. Maybe you should boot her out."

"I can't. My mother would disown me. She told Brianna to come stay with me. Brianna's father is one of my mother's most important financial backers."

Neffting peered at me. "You said her name is Shrevedale — is she one of Todd

Shrevedale's family?"

"His daughter."

Neffting glanced at Vicki. "That guy wields a lot of power." He raised an eyebrow, as if telling Vicki they'd have to tread carefully around Brianna Shrevedale. He handed me his business card. "Don't hesitate to call one of us if you think of anything else." He turned to Vicki. "Do you have a card you can give Willow?"

I admitted, "I have her number on speed dial."

That startled him. "What? Oh, I get it. I should have figured it out when that Shrevedale kid said Willow kept getting involved in murders. Willow's the one who —"

Vicki nodded. "Keeps *solving* murders. Yes."

I backed away. "Not by myself. Chief Smallwood and detectives did most of it. I just happened to be in the right place at the right time."

Vicki corrected me. "Or the *wrong* time."

I asked both of them, "How does Brianna know that Isis was murdered?"

Neffting answered, "I don't think she did. She was jumping to a conclusion based on your reputation."

"For solving murders," Vicki reminded

184

him. "Don't forget to lock up, Willow. And call us if you need us."

"I will. Meanwhile, feel free to check my phone records, although she probably *was* on my line for hours. But that doesn't prove she was inside the entire time."

Neffting only shook his head. "Kids are always on the phone or texting. Don't let it worry you. My instincts are good. That girl's not a murderer."

So he was calling it murder now, too? Hoping that his good instincts would lead him to the actual murderer and not to an innocent person, I went inside. Vicki watched through the glass until I locked the door, then she trotted down the porch steps after Detective Neffting.

So far, Neffting seemed to have ruled out Dare Drayton as a possible murderer because Dare was a celebrity. And now he was excluding Brianna because her father was powerful and wealthy.

I supposed it was natural to ignore certain people as suspects because we didn't want to believe they could be murderers. I did it, too. But *I* wasn't a detective. I plodded grumpily down to my apartment.

Brianna and the phone from her room were nowhere to be seen, but music boomed behind her closed door. I put her dishes into the dishwasher, then joined my animals in my bedroom. A few years before, when I was working in New York, Haylee had decided to tempt me to move to Threadville and open the shop I'd always dreamed of owning. She had enlisted Clay to renovate the building in a way she knew I'd love. A practical and thinking man, he'd been very thorough, and had put locking doorknobs on each of the suites. I locked my door and fell into bed.

Isis's horrific death and Brianna's incessant music invaded my dreams, and when the phone awakened me shortly before time to get up, I was gritty-eyed and grouchy. It seemed to me that Brianna had played her music most of the night, and had sometimes sung — or shouted — along with it, but now her room was silent. Maybe she'd gone home?

A state trooper was on the phone. He told me he was on the front porch of In Stitches, ready to fingerprint my patio door.

Apparently, I was destined to be seen day after day in my pink fuzzy bathrobe and matching slippers. Someone was probably about to create a TV show called *Desperate Housecoats* and cast me in the starring role. I left my pets shut in my suite.

Upstairs in my shop with its big front

windows, I lost all hope that silence from Brianna's room meant that she'd packed up and left. Her car was still parked in front of In Stitches.

The trooper was a big bear of a man, gray-haired and old enough to be my father, so I wasn't as embarrassed about my garb as I could have been around a younger trooper.

I ushered him downstairs to my apartment. He dusted for fingerprints, then asked to see my hands. "Yep," he said, "your fingerprints were on the shoe that was taken for evidence last night, and they're on the door, the handle, and the locking mechanism, and so are someone else's. I got good prints of that person's thumb and forefinger."

"Were her fingerprints on the shoes?"

"I didn't see any besides some that I'm sure are yours. Couldn't someone slip in and out of those shoes without touching them with their hands?"

"Yes. But if she stuck her bare feet into them . . . ?"

He nodded. "She could have left toe prints. And since this is a murder investigation —"

"Murder?" I squeaked. "For sure?" Neffting had finally used the word during the night, but I hadn't been certain that he meant it.

He hedged, "Since this is *potentially* a murder investigation, we may have to cut the shoes apart for toe prints. I hope you weren't in love with those shoes. Even if we don't take them apart, you won't have them back for a while."

I made my best mournful expression. "I guess I'll just have to order the cute ones I saw online."

I noticed that he very carefully did not allow his gaze to dip toward my pink fuzzy slippers.

I asked him, "Want to see a drinking glass my guest used?"

"Yep, might as well rule her out as last night's alleged intruder, too, the one who supposedly left your door unlocked."

*That could depend on your definition of "intruder."* I opened the dishwasher and pointed. The trooper applied black dust to a couple of the glasses, and then grunted in satisfaction. "I'll check the prints I lifted from the door and from these more carefully, but I'm about ninety percent certain that no one else has come into your apartment besides you and your guest." He opened the door. "I was told we're supposed to look for footprints outside."

He and I searched all of the borders near

the patio. We found doggie footprints, but we didn't see even one print of a human foot or a shoe, and we didn't see any footprints in the flower gardens near the front porch, either. The trooper left, and I put on jeans and an embroidered sweater for work.

The kittens would have to use the litter box in my en suite bathroom until we were allowed in our backyard again. I gave them a quick cuddle, shut them into the master suite, and took the dogs out through In Stitches to the street. Naturally, I was curious about the crime scene in the park.

White-garbed people combed the grass and the switch-backing boardwalk between the bandstand and the boat launch ramp. Sally and Tally were quite happy to bypass those scary-looking aliens and run to the sandy beach instead.

Wind must have come from the north during the night, pushing the waves high on the strip of sand, but they'd subsided, and the dogs and I were able to jog across a wide strip of hard sand between the water and the curved ridges of foam, sticks, shells, and other flotsam the biggest waves had left behind.

One piece of flotsam was larger than the rest. Reining in my dogs, I walked carefully to the thing and stooped for a better look.

It was a boat-shaped basket, crudely woven from willow wands that were still hanging on to a few torn and storm-tossed leaves.

The boat was small. It could have been held in the palm of one hand.

A 3-D machine-embroidered lace groom had been tied into it.

# 18

I recognized the lace groom doll in the boat. I'd made it for Edna's quilt and hadn't seen it since I'd hung it on my front porch to dry.

The groom, now unstarched and limp, lounged on a bed of blood-red chrysanthemums, the exact color of the mums that had been in urns beside the doll-sized clothesline.

I didn't touch the little willow-wand boat.

I stood and surveyed the high-water marks farther down the beach.

At first glance, the spot of white several yards away could have been foam, but it was bigger than the other bits. Leaving the tiny boat and its passenger behind, I ran with the dogs to the white thing.

The lace bride doll I'd created for Edna's wedding quilt was in this boat.

The roaring in my head wasn't only from the waves and the wind. The small makeshift boat nauseated me.

Not only did the bride have no bed of flowers matching the groom's; she was lashed in place with her head down and her feet up.

Bias tape had been used to fasten the dolls to the boats. The groom's had been black, matching his 3-D lace tuxedo. The bride's bias tape had originally been white, but was now, like the bride doll, wet and speckled with sand.

Isis had been staying in Edna's apartment. To get to it, she'd had to go through Buttons and Bows, where Edna sold bias tape.

I had no doubt that these tiny basketlike boats were the objects I'd seen Isis place in the water on Wednesday night. She had called Gord's name, urged him toward an afterlife where she would meet him, and let something float away from her. But when she'd called Edna's name, she'd held an object underwater. The symbolism was plain. The groom was supposed to sail on a bed of flowers. The bride was supposed to drown.

Feeling even sicker, I didn't touch the thing or let the dogs go near it. They were quite pleased to run back down the beach and up the sidewalk.

Standing beside the yellow tape defining

the crime scene, the dogs and I caught an investigator's attention. White outfit flapping, Detective Neffting loped to me.

I babbled that a pair of little boats that Isis had put in the river had washed up on the shore of the lake.

"Why would the deceased put little boats into the river?"

"I think it was part of her curses." I explained about the bride and groom dolls. "I heard her call out Edna and Gord's names as she placed what I think were those boats on the river. She let the one representing Gord float, but when she cursed Edna, she held the object underwater."

"Edna?" he repeated.

"Edna Battersby." I pointed to her shop. "She owns Buttons and Bows. Isis had been staying with her in the second-story apartment."

"Aha. Yes. That Edna. We'll be questioning her about her recent guest. Do you think Edna knew about these curses?"

"I told her about them."

"How well do you know this Edna?"

Pulling my inquisitive dogs closer, I stood up tall. "Very well. She's a wonderful person, very upbeat. She and Gord laughed about the spells. Edna wouldn't kill anyone, especially over a curse she didn't believe in."

"And the groom is . . . Gord?" He tilted his white-hooded head.

"Gord Wrinklesides, a local doctor. He assists the county coroner. You probably talked to him last night. He and Edna were at Gord's house when Isis was pushed into the river."

I didn't like the knowing look on Neffting's face.

I added, "I saw them go off together before the murder, and I saw them come back to the park after the rescuers got here."

"Back to the park." He repeated my tones precisely. "They'd been in the park at the time of the murder?"

"No. A half hour before, when Gord brought Edna to see the dress we created for her."

He let one side of his mouth go up slightly. "The death con*trap*tion, yes. Didn't you tell us that someone else accused the deceased of casting spells against him?"

"Floyd the zombie."

He asked, "And did you actually see the deceased cast spells against this man?"

"No, but I did see him tell Isis to stop casting spells against everyone — living or undead, I think he put it."

"So it's only hearsay that she cast any spells on the zombie."

I guessed it was the job of a detective to be difficult. I pointed out, "I'm not sure it matters, as long as Floyd *believed* Isis was casting spells on him. Last night it was clear that he did."

"And now, this morning, you're telling me you actually observed the deceased uttering curses against two other people. Why didn't you tell us about the those two people last night?"

"Because I *know* Edna and Gord. Neither of them would hurt anyone. Besides, when I told them about Isis's curses, they laughed them off. They didn't care. And both of them are too short to have been the skulker I saw."

"Who may not have been the murderer. Did you find any little boats with miniature lace zombies riding around in them?"

"No. I wouldn't expect to. Someone stole the little lace bride and groom I made. I didn't make any 3-D lace zombies." And although it was a cute idea, I didn't think I would make any freestanding lace zombies until long after this case was settled.

Turning, Neffting snapped his fingers at a uniformed trooper. The trooper ran to us.

Neffting asked him, "You have evidence bags?"

The trooper was a hunk with an engaging smile. "Yes, sir."

"Go with this lady. She may have found some evidence that washed up on shore." Looking at me, he tilted his head for confirmation.

I nodded.

He turned back to the trooper. "See if we need to extend the search area. If it appears to you that the objects merely washed up from the lake, bring them back. We can't tape off the whole lake. Take pictures of the site." Neffting stalked toward the bandstand.

Giving me the full force of the smile, the trooper let the dogs sniff his hand, then offered to take one leash. "I've been standing around half the night," he explained. "Mind if I run ahead?"

I handed him Tally's leash. "He loves to be first, and we'll be right behind you."

The trooper only jogged, and Sally and I had no trouble keeping up with him and Tally.

At the first boat, the one with the groom and the chrysanthemums, I told the trooper about Isis and her curses — the ones I'd seen her make, and the spells that she'd said a zombie had accused her of casting.

"Weird," he said. "But I'm sure you're right that this washed up. See the curving pattern of dried foam over everything, including this basket with the figure in it?" He gave me Tally's leash, took photos, and placed the tiny groom and his boat into an evidence bag. We all raced to the second boat, where he took more photos and loaded the boat containing the upside-down bride into another bag. "Did you see anything else unusual, like maybe a boat related to the spells she allegedly cast against the zombie?" He smiled.

I pulled Tally closer. "Not here, but last night after the victim was pushed into the river, I saw a fistful of willow wands like the ones used to make those boats. They were in the bandstand, arranged as if they'd been placed carefully on the floor. Maybe she planned to make another boat for the zombie." And when the investigators searched Isis's room, they'd find a tiny 1930s zombie constructed of bias tape or other trims from Edna's notions boutique?

The trooper studied my face, then seemed to decide to trust me. "I saw them, too. The sticks were sort of mashed at the cuts like the ones in these boats, as if someone's pruning shears were dull." Widening his stance in the deep sand, he held up his evidence bag. "Did you see the victim make these boats?"

"No, but shortly before she was killed, she appeared to be pruning a willow tree beside the river."

He gazed toward waves lapping the beach. "People do strange things."

I couldn't deny that. After all, I had helped make the bizarre wedding skirt that had ended up killing Isis. I told him I'd be at In Stitches if anyone needed to talk to me, and then the dogs and I left him to continue searching the high-water mark.

It was almost time to open In Stitches. The dogs and I ran past the investigators in the crime scene, past Brianna's car, into my shop, and downstairs to my apartment.

I stroked the kitties, gulped down my breakfast, and signaled to the dogs, who undoubtedly knew it was time to go upstairs and greet our customers. Carrying a carafe of hot coffee up the stairs, I heard absolutely no noises from my guest suite.

My students and I spent the morning creating and stitching Halloween designs with embroidery software and machines. Laughing and chatting, we incorporated glow-in-the-dark thread in a ghost, the features in jack-o'-lanterns, the faces of zombies, the moon behind a witch on a broomstick, and the web of a scary spider. Everyone's designs were different and original, and quite spectacular. We were all hyped with success and camaraderie. And caffeine.

And then Vicki Smallwood walked in.

She admired our work before drawing me aside and commenting quietly, "Too bad someone wasted so much of that thread by spreading it around on the trail and in the park."

I agreed.

"One of the guys untangled it and measured it, and guess what?" She didn't wait for me to answer. "It could have gone past your property, as you said it did, and ended just about where we found those two little slashes in the ground." A smile flickered across her face. "The end of the thread was *tied* to the thread nippers."

"Tied," I repeated.

She nodded. "Yep. And the pointed ends of the blades were crusted in dirt. You guessed that someone could have used the nippers like a big staple to anchor one end of the thread to the ground. That guess could have been right."

Great. Detective Neffting would think that I had done all of that, and then had "solved" how it was done. I pointed out, "That thread may have nothing to do with the murder."

"I would agree with you — except for one thing."

# 19

I asked Vicki what made her suspect that the thread nippers could have been connected with Isis's death.

"Those steel thread nippers should have had fingerprints on them. They didn't. Not one. Someone had wiped them off."

Hadn't she said that the blades had been crusted with dirt? I suggested, "They wiped the nippers without knocking the dirt off the tips of the blades?"

"You got it."

"They could have been afraid they'd cut themselves." I tilted my head and raised my eyebrows. "Maybe they did."

She wrote in her notebook. "We'll look for anyone with cuts in their fingers."

I held my hands out. As usual, I had a few little nicks and scrapes. Sewing could be dangerous. "I can guess why someone wouldn't want it known that they went around stringing glow-in-the-dark thread through the grass on dark, foggy nights," I said. "But I can't figure out why they'd make a trail of thread in the first place."

She didn't bother checking my hands. "You're the thread expert."

"No, she's downstairs."

"She cause you any trouble?"

"Not unless you count playing music and shouting along to it part of the night."

Vicki screwed up her face in disgust. "It wasn't even nice music."

"The state trooper who took fingerprints this morning thought he saw hers on my door."

"I heard that, too."

"Why would she lie about going outside? It looks to me like she set up an alibi *before* Isis was murdered."

Vicki repeated, "Alibi?"

"She was on the phone. Supposedly."

"Oh, that. Neffting thinks she was merely embarrassed because she'd borrowed your shoes without asking."

"The fingerprint trooper and I looked for prints in my flower borders that would show where those shoes picked up the mud. We didn't find any."

Vicki thinned her lips and stared beyond me. I recognized that expression. Vicki was trying hard not to tell me something.

I made a stab at it. "Did they find prints that matched my gardening clogs on the trail down by the river?"

She managed to avoid exactly confirming my theory. "The prints didn't follow the trail, which isn't very muddy, so we couldn't be certain."

I guessed, "They headed down the bank?"

"Only a little bit, then back toward your gate. So depending on how far your cordless phone service works, she could have been telling the truth about talking on the phone and telling her boyfriend about the weather."

"Right beside a river that she claimed she didn't know existed." I couldn't help sounding sarcastic. "Detective Neffting doesn't want to believe that Brianna *Shrevedale* murdered Isis."

"You heard Brianna on the phone shortly before you went outside around nine thirty last night, right?"

"Yes."

"And you told us you heard Isis scream about fifteen minutes later."

"Give or take a few. But it was enough time for Brianna to put on my clogs, run up through my side yard, dash to the park, and start pushing Isis toward the river."

"How would she have known Isis would

be at the park trying on someone else's overskirt?"

"When Clay, Naomi, Opal, and I left the fire station with that skirt, Brianna and Isis were on the sidewalk, talking to each other. Maybe Isis told Brianna she was going to try on that skirt after all of us were gone."

"How would Isis know that the skirt was on its way to the park?"

"We asked Isis and Brianna if they wanted to help take it there. They declined. But then Brianna tore a page out of something that looked like a checkbook and handed it to Isis."

"Interesting," Vicki mumbled, writing in her notebook. She raised her head. "When you and your dogs were in your backyard after you heard Brianna on the phone, wouldn't you or the dogs have noticed her coming out your patio door and running up through your side yard?"

"Probably. But she could have run through my shop instead. Or waited until we were on the trail, following that skulker."

"Which would have given her even less time to commit the murder. You told us you heard someone running away after the skirt was pushed into the river. Did you hear anyone running on Lake Street toward the park *before* you heard the first scream? Like from your shop down the street?"

"No, and I was extra alert because of that skulker, so I probably would have heard those shoes slapping on concrete. I also didn't notice hearing any vehicles, by the way."

"Neffting has already theorized that the murderer could have arrived at the scene — and fled it — by car. Or pickup truck. However, your skulker headed toward the park right before the screams, didn't stick around to rescue the victim, and didn't come back after you yelled for help, so who would you focus on, a vehicle that no one heard or saw, Brianna and her phone call, or the person you saw heading toward what turned out to be a homicide?"

I gave her a lopsided grin. "At this point, all of the above. Maybe the person I heard running away was racing toward a phone to call 911."

"But no one called besides you." Her eyes became serious. "Detective Neffting picked up a hint that you don't like Brianna Shrevedale."

"She's not the most likable person I've ever met. But she does sell nice thread."

"Brianna's about the same size as Edna, wouldn't you say?"

"Close." I stared helplessly at her. "Oh,

no, don't tell me Detective Neffting suspects that Edna killed Isis, and that I'm trying to divert suspicion from Edna by accusing someone who Edna could have passed for in the dark and the fog?"

Vicki didn't say anything.

"No one could seriously suspect Edna! She was with Gord at the time."

Vicki tapped her notebook with her pen. "Neffting might say it wouldn't be the first time a man has lied for his woman."

"Not Gord. Not Edna. He wouldn't lie, and she wouldn't murder, especially over something as silly as a curse."

"Neffting might ask, 'But what if she truly believed that Isis could steal Gord from her?' "

I guessed that Neffting had already proposed these theories in Vicki's presence. "Edna wouldn't believe that. Didn't believe it. She laughed at me when I told her about it. Is Neffting really considering that Edna could have murdered Isis?"

"He's not ruling anyone out. Including, I might add, the first person on the scene."

"Me? What motive would I have had? I barely knew the woman."

"Maybe you wanted to protect Edna? Especially since Edna didn't believe you that the victim might steal Gord?"

"I was one of the few people that Isis *didn't* yell at when we were all in the fire station."

"Who did she yell at?"

"She ran toward Dare Drayton with her hands curled like claws, like she was about to scratch his eyes out."

"That sounds extreme."

I didn't blame Vicki for doubting it. "I'm not exaggerating. Then she told him he couldn't call his latest book *The Book of the Dead.*"

"Did he seem angry or upset about it?"

"He seemed amused."

"Exactly."

"He always seems amused. But with a cruel streak."

"Hunches, hunches."

"I know," I admitted. "Dare threatened to kill Isis."

*"What?"*

"In one of his books."

She gave me an overly dramatic scowl. "No wonder you didn't report that to me before."

"He could have been semi-serious," I pointed out.

"But you said that Isis yelled at lots of people. Who else?"

"She called Patricia, the sewing machine historian who's staying with Opal, a copycat.

Said it in a mean way. She claimed that the fortune-teller, Madame Juliette, who is Naomi's houseguest, 'made things up.' "

"Did anyone besides Dare threaten her?"

"Floyd said he would — I don't know what — bite her and turn her into a zombie?"

Vicki snickered.

I added, "Brianna also irritated Isis, for the fun of it, I thought. As I told you and Detective Neffting before, when Isis left the room where we were putting the skirt together, she appeared to threaten that she would cast spells on all of them."

Vicki turned pages back in her notebook. "Didn't Isis scold you, too?"

I couldn't think of anything. "No." I lengthened the word, showing my uncertainty. Vicki read aloud from her notebook, " 'Isis told Willow she couldn't wear someone else's wedding gown.' "

"Oh, that. She yelled at the other people, but she didn't raise her voice at me. And she didn't word it quite like that. She said something weird, like it wasn't 'ordained' for me to wear someone else's wedding gown. I thought maybe she meant it was bad luck. Ironic, isn't it? Maybe she thought it was 'ordained' that she should wear it, but that turned into truly bad luck for her."

Vicki removed her hat and placed it on the cutting table. "So you see why you're not in the clear? You were the first on the scene after she was killed, and for all Detective Neffting knows, you may have tried to turn the tables on Isis, to show her who would have bad luck wearing that skirt . . ."

"You don't believe I would do such a thing, do you?" I asked.

She plunked her hat on her head. "No, but you're definitely more hotheaded than your friend Edna."

I opened and closed my mouth.

"Don't worry," she consoled me. "I'm going to keep poking my nose into Neffting's investigation."

I tried a smile. "Thank you. Do you know where Dare Drayton was at the time of the murder?"

"Just walking around, he said, waiting for Clay to take him home. So where was Clay?" she asked.

"Sitting in his truck outside the fire station, waiting for Dare."

"You said you were in your yard and on your trail. You couldn't have seen Clay sitting in his truck."

"He said he was. I believe him."

"How do you know that Clay wasn't your skulker?"

I nearly choked. "Clay wouldn't skulk past my yard when the dogs were out. He'd have joined us." I twirled a pair of scissors on the cutting table. They spun like a top, balancing on the bolt holding the blades together.

Vicki bit her lip.

I demanded, "You were pushing my buttons, weren't you?"

"It can be easy. But you have to see everything the way Detective Neffting might. All of you in this village could be suspects. Detective Neffting didn't actually see Clay's concern last night before and after the body was brought ashore, like I did. That guy's a catch, you know."

I pretended shock. "Detective Neffting?"

"Clay."

I spun the scissors. "I know."

"So catch him."

"Easier said than done, when neither of us has time outside of work."

She groaned. "Tell me about it. Never be a police officer dating another one. We're nearly always on different shifts." She put her hand down flat on the scissors, ending their mad whirl. "Didn't your parents tell you not to play with scissors?"

"No. They encouraged me. My mother wanted me to be a surgeon. My father uses sharp blades, and everything else, to invent things. Speaking of scissors, did you find whatever was used to cut that frill off the skirt?"

"You guessed right. Scissors. We found them in the grass near the bandstand."

"Whose?"

Vicki stared up into my eyes. "Are you sure you want to know?"

# 20

Uh-oh. Maybe I didn't want to know whose scissors had been found in the grass near the bandstand. One of my pairs? Last Christmas, Naomi had given us all scissors engraved with our names. I kept mine downstairs with my personal sewing things, in the closet in my guest room. Had Brianna "borrowed" them and left them in the park?

Around us, sewing machines whirred. People talked and laughed. Threadville tourists always helped each other with their projects.

Holding the scissors on the cutting table still as if they were about to run off by themselves, I asked in a small voice, "Whose scissors did they find?"

"Edna's," Vicki told me. "Her name is engraved on one of the blades. Not the sharp part."

"So, let me guess." My mouth tasted bitter. "Between the curses against Edna and the scissors found at the scene, Detective Neffting is *sure* that Edna murdered Isis?"

"He's a good detective. He's keeping an open mind."

I didn't remind her that he'd already closed his mind to suspecting either Brianna or Dare. "Isis must have taken Edna's scissors to the park. What was she planning to do, try on the skirt, and then cut it into tiny pieces?"

Vicki searched through her notes. "Maybe. A snipped-off piece of that frill was tucked down inside one of her gown's pockets."

"Why?"

"Good question. It does make Detective Neffting wonder if one of the skirt's creators saw the deceased hacking at the skirt and, as he put it, 'overreacted.' "

"Great. Now he suspects Haylee, Opal, and Naomi."

"And who else?"

"Me." I frowned at her. "Remind me never to be first on the scene. If I hear anyone scream, I'll run the other way."

She laughed. "That would make you look suspicious for sure. But you could try a little harder not to snoop around things that don't concern you."

My frown turned into a glower. "Even if I weren't a volunteer firefighter and trained to rescue people, I couldn't ignore screams. Or screams followed by splashes."

My outrage only seemed to amuse Vicki.

I thought about the curses and the little boats. And Isis had cut off a piece of the wedding skirt and pocketed it? What other strange things had she done? I asked, "Could Isis have committed suicide? Maybe she yelled at someone to stop pushing her *away* from the water?" I drew invisible circles with my fingernails on the table's smooth surface. "Clay said one of the frills had been around her neck. Do people who want to kill themselves often try hanging and drowning at the same time?"

"Self-strangulation isn't a sure bet, so maybe drowning was her back-up plan. We'll know more after the autopsy, but Gord thought a ribbon had been tied around her neck and held there, which would have been hard for her to do by herself."

"I thought Clay said a frill was around her neck, and you're saying it was a ribbon."

"The frill hid the ribbon."

"Let me guess," I said. "The ribbon was white satin, and about an inch wide."

"How come I'm not surprised you knew that?"

"I mentioned it to you last night. Naomi

had hung a label from it, the one I showed you that was on the bandstand floor."

Nodding, Vicki scribbled.

"So Isis didn't drown?"

Vicki closed her notebook and spoke softly. "We don't know for sure, but Gord thought she was dead before she went into the water."

I breathed a sigh of relief. "So she didn't suffer as long as I keep imagining."

"She couldn't have been conscious for very long after someone looped that ribbon around her neck."

I stared down at the end of a bolt of linen. When had I clutched the cloth, and why was I gripping it tightly enough to crease it? "I guess I'll still always feel terrible that I didn't get there soon enough to prevent it. Or to at least see who the culprit was."

"You're safer not knowing," she reminded me. "Unless the culprit *thinks* you saw him or her." She gave me a piercing look. "Be extra vigilant. Call if you need help. If you think that *any*thing, no matter how small or seemingly insignificant, should be checked out, call us and let us do it."

I asked when I would be allowed in my backyard again.

"Now. We're done with it. We're sure the thread only went past it, except for right inside your gate, but they've searched that area and didn't find a thing. We're not done with the trail behind your place, though, so don't go out there. There are footprints on it in addition to the ones your gardening clogs made to the riverbank and back to your gate. You were wearing sneakers last night, right?"

"Yes. And Juliette, Patricia, and Dare all walked on that trail after I did. Dare had on loafers, Patricia wore sneakers, and Juliette was in party flats."

"Most of the trail wasn't muddy, though, so the investigators only got a few smidges of their footprints and the prints of everyone else who's been on the trail since Monday's rain. I suspect that they found your prints, and Sally's and Tally's, too, where your dogs pulled you down toward the river a couple of times." After again telling me to be careful, she left In Stitches.

I returned to our glow-in-the-dark ghosts and goblins. *Footprints,* I thought. If they had found some that matched my gardening clogs near the boat launch where Isis and the skirt had rolled into the river, would Vicki have told me? Maybe Brianna really had put on my gardening clogs, walked quickly but quietly down Lake Street to the park, pushed Isis into the river, and then run back. It wasn't entirely believable, but neither were my other theories, including a skulker carefully laying down a trail of glow-in-the-dark thread on his way to murder Isis.

Rosemary took over for my lunch hour, and the dogs and I went downstairs to our apartment. While I was foraging for bread, peanut butter, and jelly, Brianna came out of her room. She wore her wrinkled, faded pink sweat suit. The long braid down her back was coming apart. Yawning, she padded to the patio door. "Ugh, what's all this dirt on the handle?"

"Fingerprint powder."

"Whose prints did they find?"

I didn't know for certain whose the other person's were, so I answered only, "Mine."

Looking smug, she returned to the eat-in counter. "What's for breakfast?"

"Whatever you'd like and can find. I'm grabbing a quick sandwich for lunch, then I'll take the dogs out. We're allowed in my backyard again, by the way."

"Why would I want to go out there?" It was one of the longest and most animated responses I'd yet received from her. Maybe we were making progress in the bonding my mother hoped we'd do. She added, "No, thanks."

It wasn't the most polite use of the word "thanks" that I'd ever heard, but I got the point. She had no interest in my backyard, and therefore, had never gone out there.

I didn't believe her.

In addition to the supposed bonding, my mother had told me to let Brianna sell her threads at our craft fair.

I took a deep breath and plunged in. "The Threadville Get Ready for Halloween Craft Fair starts tomorrow morning —"

Looking bored, she shook her head.

I went on anyway. "If you'd like to show and sell your threads, you can have a table. The fair's in the community center."

She clamped her lips together in the middle of a yawn. "A table? How much will that cost?"

I told her it was a small percentage of her sales.

"Who's keeping track?"

"You."

She shrugged, went into her room, and closed the door. What a definitive answer. What a fun houseguest, too.

I took all four animals outside. After their incarceration in my bedroom, the kittens wanted to frisk toward tree trunks, and I had to help Sally herd them to the door, something she could usually do by herself.

Carrying the roguish kitties inside and shutting them into my room again, I mentally designed zippered vests for them, with loops where I could attach leashes, all of it embroidered.

Outside again, I ate while the dogs played. When my lunch hour was about over, we all trooped inside. The door to Brianna's room was still closed, and everything was quiet.

We went upstairs. I shut the dogs into their pen and started the afternoon workshoppers on glow-in-the-dark Halloween characters. We settled into our usual routine of designing, creating, and enjoying each other's company. Rosemary called to me and I went to her machine.

Suddenly, the door to my apartment stairway banged back against the wall. The dogs barked. Brianna threw herself across their pen and did a scissors-style high jump over the railing.

Everyone's heads popped up to watch her. She was still in the sweat suit, and most of her hair had finished tumbling out of the braid.

She marched to me and slammed one of my drinking glasses onto the table next to Rosemary's sewing machine.

"Explain this," Brianna demanded. Her

eyes were bloodshot with anger or lack of sleep or both.

## 21

Hoping to calm my obviously upset house-guest, I asked quietly, "Explain what?"

Brianna pointed to the glass. "This black stuff all over one of the glasses from the dishwasher — that's fingerprint powder, right?"

So she did know what a dishwasher was. "Yes."

Her forehead wrinkled and frown lines appeared beside her mouth, not a great look on her otherwise pretty and girlish face. "You had them fingerprint your door, and also one of the glasses I used?"

"I —"

"Don't you know I have the right to privacy?"

I gestured with my head toward the apartment door. "Let's go downstairs to discuss this, just the two of us."

She sneered. "So your customers won't know what you're really like? Investigating murders. Maybe even causing —"

"That's enough!" Rosemary barked.

I flashed Rosemary an appreciative smile before raising my head again to speak seriously to Brianna. "You told the police last night that someone may have come into the apartment. The fingerprint guy needed your prints to distinguish them from mine and from those of possible intruders. That's all."

Leaving the glass behind, she turned around. "I still don't think you have any right."

She headed toward Sally and Tally's pen. They came to the railing and wagged their plume-like tails.

Brianna stopped about a half yard away from them. "How do you expect me to get back to my room with them in the way?"

Georgina, a regular customer who lived within walking distance of the Threadville stores, marched to the gate, opened it, grabbed both dogs by their collars, and led them to the far corner of the pen. She smiled at Brianna — with her mouth only, not her eyes. "Here you go. But they don't bite." Georgina wore mauve slacks and a matching tunic. She'd made the outfit in Haylee's classes after embroidering the fabric with mauve hearts and curlicues at In Stitches.

Brianna only sniffed, stalked to the stairs, and pulled the door shut behind her.

Rosemary murmured to me, "Why are you letting her stay with you?"

I grinned. "Mother's orders."

Rosemary waggled her eyebrows. "That explains everything. Not." She glanced at my racks of thread. "But she does have nice thread for sale."

"Here's the good news," I told her. "I think she'll be selling them at the craft fair, too."

"Good," Rosemary said. "That should keep her out of your hair."

Georgina often helped in the store and was going to work at the In Stitches table at the fair. She came close, bent toward Rosemary, and whispered, "But maybe not out of mischief." Georgina straightened and patted my shoulder. "Don't worry, Willow, I'll be watching her at the craft show."

A light on my phone showed that someone was using my landline. No one in the shop was on the phone.

Shortly after the light went out, my shop phone rang. I answered.

"Willow? It's Mother."

"I'm at work."

She let out a little laugh that her constituents might think was empathetic. I recognized a certain knifelike edge to it. "I know. That's why I called your store. I'll make it short."

I clutched the receiver more tightly.

"What are you doing up there, Willow?"

"Waiting on customers."

"You know what I mean. You've gotten yourself mixed up in another murder, haven't you." It wasn't a question.

"No." I peered toward the closed apartment door as if I could see through it. "What gave you that idea?"

"It's all over the news."

"What do people in South Carolina care about what goes on in the northwestern corner of Pennsylvania?"

"Your last name, honey. Vanderling. Are you trying to sabotage my campaign?"

I shook my head even though she couldn't see me. "There was a death. It barely made the news in Erie. I doubt that anyone in Pittsburgh or Cleveland has heard about it."

"Well, it could harm my campaign if we weren't working hard down here on damage control."

Had Brianna's father sent Brianna to spy on me? "What's Brianna been saying?" Too bad I couldn't make an allegation sound like a compliment the way my mother could.

"That you've involved yourself in a murder and have been accusing her."

"First, I'm not involved in a murder. I may have heard the victim scream, and I was first on the scene."

My mother gasped. "Whatever for? You should stay away from situations like that. They're dangerous, in more ways than one. You could be hurt. You could be suspected of committing crimes."

"Mother, someone *screamed.* How could any decent person not want to help?"

"You could have called emergency."

"I did. I'm also one of our first responders, so I needed to attend the emergency anyway."

"That's very admirable of you, Willow, honey, as long as you stay out of trouble."

"I do." I plowed on, answering one of her earlier statements. "And, despite what Brianna may have reported, I have not accused her of anything. If her father's worried about her, maybe he should tell her to come home."

"She's an adult, Willow."

She didn't act like one. But I didn't want to say that and prolong an argument that might cause an unmendable rift between my mother and me. She always wanted to run everything, but she loved me and meant well, and I was learning to bite my tongue. And to change the subject. "She sells excellent threads," I managed. "Everyone wants some. I've told her she can have a table at our craft fair."

My mother's voice warmed. "That's wonderful, Willow, honey. This should help her get her business off the ground."

"She hasn't accepted."

"You need to act like you really want her to. Don't put her off or frighten her. She's young, only twenty-two." Very sweetly, she said she wouldn't keep me any longer and ended the call.

I slowly replaced the receiver in the charging station. *Danger averted,* I told myself. *For now . . .*

It wasn't very hospitable of me, but I looked forward to the day that Brianna packed up and went home, whenever that might be.

As usual, my students cheered me up, and by the time they left, I was in a good mood again.

I took the dogs and the black-powdered drinking glass downstairs to the apartment underneath In Stitches. Brianna's room was quiet. I put the glass into the dishwasher again, gave all four animals an outing, then shut them into my room so they wouldn't bother Brianna if she came out of her suite while I went shopping with Haylee.

Outside, Brianna's car was gone. It was probably too much to hope that she'd left for home.

Haylee was waiting beside my car in the lot behind her three mothers' shops. She frowned. "You look exhausted. Are you sure you want to drive?"

I opened the driver's door. "Sure."

Buckling her seat belt, she gave me a worried look. "Did you sleep at all?"

"Enough." I pulled out onto Lake Street. "How are you doing? And how are Edna and Mrs. Battersby?"

"We're all fine. Gord's taking Edna and her mother out to dinner tonight."

"He'll win Mrs. Battersby over yet."

Haylee grinned. "Yep. What happened after you left with Chief Smallwood and that detective last night?"

I told her all about my activities with the two police officers during the night, the initial confrontation with Brianna, my disturbing discoveries on the beach during my morning dog walk, the additional information that Vicki had given me before lunch, and the latest confrontation with Brianna after lunch.

Haylee agreed that the person I'd seen on

the trail had to have been the murderer or have witnessed the murder, and the fact that he — or she — hadn't come forward as a witness made him highly suspect. "And that zombie, Floyd, was enraged about those curses."

"He's my prime suspect," I said. "But there are others besides him and Dare. You weren't with me when Juliette and Patricia came off the riverside trail. Patricia was in jeans and a matching jacket, an outfit like the skulker wore. Juliette was wearing a long skirt and blouse. She had her blouse on backward."

Haylee snorted. "That must have looked good."

"A peasant blouse is easier to wear backward than some blouses. I don't know if she had been wearing it like that all evening, and the tag chose that moment to slip out, or if she'd changed out of it into a pantsuit and then back into the skirt and peasant blouse in a rush."

We cautioned each other about staying a safe distance from Dare, Floyd, Patricia, and Juliette.

"That Brianna sounds like a real horror," Haylee added. "Wearing your shoes outside and then pretending she had never borrowed them! Acting like you owe her privacy in your apartment! Even if she hasn't killed anyone, she's hiding something. Don't trust her."

"I don't."

"And anyone, including Brianna, could have helped themselves to your thread, needles, and thread nippers when the fire station was unlocked."

"What worries me most," I said, "is the way Detective Neffting seems to have decided that Edna is the most likely culprit. Or Gord."

Haylee sighed. "And their alibis are only from each other. We'll have to prove Detective Neffting wrong."

I reminded her, "Vicki doesn't want us sleuthing."

"I don't want Edna to go to prison."

"We'll be careful with our snooping, then, so Vicki won't know."

"We always are," Haylee said.

I pulled into the grocery store parking lot. "And Vicki always seems to find out."

"She won't this time."

I wished I had Haylee's confidence. But one thing was certain. Neither Edna nor Gord would have harmed Isis, or anyone else.

I stocked up on foods like frozen pizzas that Brianna might be able to prepare if she wanted a meal when I wasn't around to fix it. I also bought everything I would need the next night for the barbecue, when Haylee, Clay, and the local innkeeper, Ben, were coming to help me decide how to finish the interior of Blueberry Cottage.

With Clay as his contractor, Ben had done a fabulous job of restoring the Elderberry Bay Lodge, the previously boarded-up Victorian inn that he'd bought. Haylee and I had worked with Ben to choose which of the old photos he'd found in the lodge to display, so Ben felt he owed me. He didn't. Haylee and I had loved sorting through photos dating from the 1890s to the 1980s.

Haylee thought Ben was just about perfect, but Ben had been widowed a couple of years before and was still grieving his wife, and Haylee was afraid he would never be interested in another woman. I suspected that he would, eventually, and I didn't mind giving him little pushes toward Haylee. I also didn't mind that Clay had the same goal, since that could mean something resembling double dates, and I'd see more of Clay. Finally, tomorrow night, the four of us could have dinner together. The Haunted Graveyard was later in the evening. Maybe we could all go.

Meanwhile, I bought plenty of food for

the barbecue. I wouldn't be as gracious as my mother would expect me to be, but if Brianna was around when I was cooking and serving the meal, not inviting her would be more awkward than inviting her.

In a way, I was hoping to win the young woman over. She'd seemed to dislike me from the moment she'd met me. Somehow, I doubted that my pink fuzzy bathrobe and slippers had caused her attitude. But what had? Maybe by being as nice as my mother urged, I could undo the damage.

Brianna's car was still gone when I parked in front of my gate. Haylee and I agreed to meet again in about an hour at the storytelling event that Opal held most Friday nights at Tell a Yarn. I quickly put away my groceries, cooked one of the frozen pizzas, made a Caesar salad, and set two places at my eat-in counter, but Brianna didn't return before I left for Opal's.

Tired as I was, I looked forward to a comfortable evening surrounded by friends.

Friends?

Maybe not.

I should have guessed that Opal would invite Patricia and Juliette, two of the people that Haylee and I had just cautioned each other about possibly being murderers.

# 22

Opal's dining room was as lovely as usual. Fall flowers in vases decorated the mantel and the center of her large oval table. Opal's cat purred on the hearth near a blazing fire.

Unfortunately, however, storytelling night couldn't possibly be as relaxing as I'd hoped, not with Juliette and Patricia there. If one of them was a murderer and I showed even the teeniest suspicion, I could endanger myself and my friends.

In a hand-knit white turtleneck sweater, Patricia seemed to shrink behind her thick-rimmed glasses. She didn't seem to notice that she was scrunching up one of Opal's hand-crocheted place mats.

Juliette sat beside Patricia. She'd knit only about two rows so far, so I couldn't guess what her project might be. I complimented her on her yarn's pretty shade of midnight blue. The ends of her needles kept snagging the voluminous sleeves of her metallic gold, red, and purple gown.

Beside Juliette, Naomi used a pencil and ruler to draw quilt blocks on paper.

Edna and Mrs. Battersby were already back from their dinner with Gord. Apparently, Mrs. Battersby didn't need to look down at the tiny sweater she was knitting, maybe because no one could focus on fingers and needles that were flying that quickly. Edna stopped beading a length of white satin and smiled at me.

Between Edna and Mrs. Battersby, Haylee waved her knitting needle, complete with knitting, at me.

Opal was handing around plates heaped with date bars, lemon bars, meringues, and gingersnaps. I loved them all, but Opal's date bars were my downfall.

The only other people in the room were Elderberry Bay's librarian, our postmistress, and Georgina. Everyone had a bone china cup and saucer and a silver spoon.

Handcrafts could wait. We ate gooey treats and drank tea, then trooped off to Opal's restroom to wash our hands. Finally, we were ready to return to our knitting, crocheting, sewing, mending, and whatever else we'd brought to keep our hands busy during one of Tell a Yarn's storytelling nights.

Opal put on a pair of white gloves. Except

for the handknit slacks and crocheted apron, she could have passed for someone at a 1940s tea party. She lifted a large book from the top of her buffet and laid it gently on the table, then sat in the empty seat beside me. The book was handmade, its birch bark covers laced together with thin strips of rawhide.

The book's title had been scribed into the birch bark with a wood burning tool.

*The New Book of the Dead.*

Edna leaped out of her seat and leaned over the table. "That's one of Isis's books! She had a dozen or so of them in my apartment so she could sell them at the craft fair, but that detective took them all for evidence."

Haylee's eyes danced with merriment. "How did you get that book, Opal? Steal it out from under the detective's pointy nose?"

Opal stroked the birch bark. "Haylee! Of course not. Isis was supposed to tell stories about ancient Egypt tonight. She dropped the book off with me last week. She didn't come near it afterward, so I don't see how any detective, with or without a pointy nose, can claim it's evidence. I thought that as a tribute to Isis, we could read from it tonight, and *then* I'll offer it to him. Or to Chief Smallwood, instead, since she's more approachable." She patted the book. "Wait until you hear what Isis wrote!"

I looked at my knitting to hide a smile. Haylee's three mothers could be as naughty as Haylee and I were at rationalizing a tiny bit of sleuthing that might possibly upset the police. But how could this handmade book that Isis had dropped off several days before her death offer the police any real clues about who her murderer was? The police already had similar books that they'd found in Edna's apartment.

Isis's murderer could be in the room with us while we learned more about Isis and her book. Was that helpful, or could we be putting ourselves in peril? Hoping it was the former, I didn't say anything, and leaned forward to listen to Opal. My knitting had improved since I'd moved to Threadville, but I was still making simple scarves, and whenever one of the evening's tales became scary, my knitting loosened and I dropped stitches. Opal had taught me how to go down the ladder of stitches and retrieve them with a crochet hook, but I wasn't good at it, and I hoped that Opal wasn't about to read anything too frightening.

First, she gave us background information about ancient Egyptian beliefs and legends, which had evolved over centuries. She told us that Isis — the original one — was one of the most important Egyptian goddesses. Isis symbolized motherhood, and also protected the dead. And, in some myths, she protected sailors.

Thinking of those tiny boats and the upside-down bride doll, I tried not to shudder.

Finally, Opal opened the massive tome. "Isis seems to have retold ancient legends and added touches of her own. Maybe a lot more than *touches* . . . As Dare Drayton said the other night in the fire station, the original Book of the Dead wasn't a book. It was a collection of spells for ushering people into the afterlife. Many were written in tombs." She elbowed me. "Carved in stone."

I made suitable groaning noises.

Opal held the book up for everyone to see. "Isis's incantations are written in ink." The calligraphy appeared to be flawless.

Opal set the book down and turned pages. Almost all of them featured at least one pen-and-ink sketch. Opal stopped at an illustration of boats floating, one after the other, down a dark river. The title on the page was *Guide to an Afterlife with the Sun and in the Company of the Person Issuing the Spell.*

I asked, "Can you read that page to us, Opal?"

She read, "Weave a willow-wand boat by moonlight, and in the boat, tie an amulet representing the person with whom you wish to spend eternity on the sun. The amulet must lie on cushions of flowers and face the sky. On a dark night, launch the boat on a flowing river close to where it enters a larger body of water. Chant these words to the sky." Opal murmured a bunch of syllables in a spooky voice. I thought I heard the name of the Egyptian sun god, Ra, several times. She marked the words with her finger and looked up at us. "And here's Isis's English version: 'Using my magic, you and I will reincarnate ourselves, and we'll cross the sky together every day in our own blaze of glory. Go, now, to the afterlife where I will join you.' "

Edna asked, "Joining the sun in the sky was considered a *good* afterlife in Egyptian mythology?"

Haylee laughed. "The ancient Egyptians must not have understood how hot the sun actually is."

Opal lifted pages and turned them with loving care. "There's more."

We all commented on Isis's artistic talent. One picture showed a mummy case and a bunch of crockery urns. "What's that one about?" I asked.

Opal scanned the article. "The dead had to be able to put all their body parts back together, and to do that, they had to be mummified, while specific organs were placed in specific jars."

Juliette piped up, "Ugh! Wouldn't it have made life, I mean death, easier for the dead people if they'd left the organs where they were in the first place?"

Winding yarn around the tip of her needle, Patricia shivered as if she were cold. But how could she be? She was closer than any of us to the fire, and she was wearing that heavy turtleneck sweater, besides.

Opal answered, "They believed the organs had to be preserved differently from the rest of the body, and if they couldn't reassemble themselves, they wouldn't be able to go to any sort of afterlife. In ancient Egypt, mummification was for the upper classes." She read silently for a moment, and then summarized, "Isis makes a point that her book is for everyone. We can all, she claims, cast spells for ourselves and for others."

She read a few incantations, both in English and in phonetically spelled translations of authentic-looking hieroglyphs.

Opal came to another illustration of boats

on a river.

I asked her, "Would you read that one, too?"

She said, "Isis seemed particularly fond of tailoring other people's afterlives for them. This incantation is for sending someone to an afterlife different than your own, for people you don't want to spend eternity with."

Mrs. Battersby turned her little sweater to start a new row. "That's the best idea that woman has come up with yet."

Naomi looked wide-eyed at her. Haylee and I exchanged grins.

Opal went on as if Mrs. Battersby hadn't interrupted. "She says to craft a willow-wand boat by moonlight, tie an amulet representing the unfavored person head down in a boat, call out that person's name, launch the boat into a stream or river near where it flows into a larger body of water, and hold it underwater while reciting the spell."

Remembering Isis on the riverbank Wednesday night in the mist, I felt a little seasick. Maybe I shouldn't have been paying such close attention to my moving knitting needles.

Opal read a bunch of other syllables in a ghostly voice. This time, I heard the sun god's name, Ra, only once. And then, in a flatter voice devoid of her usual humor, Opal read the English translation. "Go to the deepest, darkest river! Go to the bowels of the earth. Fall apart. Scatter. Go where you will never rise!"

I set my knitting down, or I'd have dropped stitches for sure. I'd heard Isis shouting parts of this spell. And I'd found the boat with the upside-down amulet representing Edna. The groom doll had been tied facing the sky, as if Isis had planned to spend eternity with Gord, maybe the two of them blazing across the sky with the sun.

Edna must have recognized the horror on my face. "It means nothing, Willow," she said.

Opal gave a grim laugh. "Isis even included 'Helpful Hints' in sidebars for some of the curses and spells. The Helpful Hint for the upside-down amulet curse says, 'For best results in taking someone else's place in an afterlife of your choosing and consigning them to a different one, wear or carry something belonging to that person.' "

I grabbed the edges of my chair seat to keep myself from toppling onto the floor. Isis must have followed her own advice and put on Edna's super-decorated, heavy wed-

240

ding skirt. And Vicki had told me that Isis had been found with a piece of one of the skirt's frills in her pocket.

Isis had to be the person who had carried Edna's scissors to the bandstand.

" 'What goes around comes around,' " Patricia quoted.

Mouth dropping open, I stared at her, but only for a second. I didn't want her guessing that I had detected a note of satisfaction in her voice. What did Patricia know about Isis's threats against Edna? Or was she merely making guesses based on Isis's having been inside that giant skirt?

Opal plucked a printed sheet of paper from inside the back cover of the book. "A price list. Wow, she was charging several hundred dollars for each of her books."

"The books are worth that," Georgina guessed, "to people who collect handmade books like this."

Edna commented in a soft voice, "Her work was amazing."

"What?" Haylee teased. "I don't see any crystals glued to the book."

Edna tapped Haylee's arm. "I'm sure she would have added crystals if she'd had time. She could have bought perfect ones from me. I'd even have given her a discount."

I picked up the price list. "She was selling

more than books. She has individual prices for personally casting her curses, incantations, and spells." I checked the numbers. "She charged twice as much for 'everlasting damnation among the palace slaves' as she did for 'gentle escort into a pharaoh's afterlife.' " Had she been serious? At a hundred dollars per spell, even the "gentle escort" prices were steep.

Mrs. Battersby flung the tiny sweater, already completed, down on top of an equally tiny pom-pom cap. "What a bunch of hooey." She began casting on another project.

"What are you making?" Juliette asked her.

"Sweaters and caps for premature babies. *Some*one has to do it."

Opal picked one up. "They're beautiful, Mrs. Battersby. I remember watching you knit when I was a child, and that's what got me started, but in all the years since, I've never seen anyone else knit so well so quickly. Do you have a pattern for the sweaters and caps? An address where we could send any that we knit?"

"I've made so many of the things I no longer need a pattern, but I can find you the website with the information."

We all agreed that we wanted that website

address, and maybe it was my imagination, but Mrs. Battersby's frown may have softened.

Patricia looked at her watch, gasped, and pushed her chair back.

Looking startled, Juliette asked her, "Is it time to go?"

Patricia nodded. "We'd better hurry."

The rest of us looked mystified.

Juliette rose from the table. "Dare Drayton is giving a reading at the Elderberry Bay Lodge at nine."

"Isn't that rather late?" Mrs. Battersby asked.

Georgina stood. "Is it open to the public?"

Juliette said it was, and that Dare was hoping someone besides zombies and his cousin would show up.

Clay was going? I shoved my knitting into my bag.

The librarian and postmistress decided to go to the reading with Patricia, Juliette, and Georgina.

Haylee and her three mothers began tossing each other meaningful looks.

I knew these women pretty well. They were not leaving.

And then I understood. Now was our chance to snoop around Opal's guest room, where Patricia was staying, and around

Naomi's guest room, where Juliette was staying. I sat back and let Patricia, Juliette, the postmistress, Georgina, and the librarian go without me. I'd see Clay the next night anyway.

Edna cast a sideways glance at her mother. I read that look, also.

Edna and her friends did not want to include Mrs. Battersby in their sleuthing.

## 23

Mrs. Battersby seemed to be completely ensconced in her chair, however, and not about to stop her rapid-fire casting-on.

Edna looked at her watch and said with a great show of reluctance. "I guess it's time to adjourn the meeting."

"Why?" Mrs. Battersby started her first row. "You said we'd go on until nine or after. I finished the sweater, and planned to make a cap, and I've only begun the cap."

"Everyone left," Naomi tried.

Mrs. Battersby retorted, "*We're* still here. Or aren't we important?"

Opal yawned. "And Willow, weren't you up very late last night?"

"Yes, but don't stop on my account."

"I should think not," Mrs. Battersby agreed. "Willow can go home if she's that tired."

"I'm okay." I would have been happy to drop into bed, but who was going to guarantee that Brianna wouldn't play loud music and keep me awake? I asked Naomi, "Did you have something you wanted to show Haylee and me? Maybe we should go do that before I keel over."

"You might as well run along," Mrs. Battersby informed me. "You stopped knitting. You're just wasting time sitting around like that. Life's too short."

Haylee stood and patted Mrs. Battersby's shoulder. "Will you be okay here, or would you like me to take you back to my apartment before I go with Willow and Naomi?"

Mrs. Battersby moved the marker on her knitting. "I'll be fine as long as my hostess stays here and acts like a real hostess, right, Opal?"

"I'm staying up as long as you are. We have more squares to eat." Opal didn't look overjoyed. She undoubtedly wanted to go upstairs and comb through the room where Patricia was staying.

"I'll stay with you two, too," Edna said. "It'll just be the three of us. Very cozy." She scooted back in her seat and managed to appear to like the idea. "And I've got your key, Haylee, if my mother does decide she wants to go back to her room."

Mrs. Battersby snapped, "I don't. Why are you all so suddenly anxious for me to go to

Haylee's apartment? It's not like she's my real granddaughter."

Haylee gave her a smile that should fill any grandmother, if she were looking, with pride. "See you later, then." Carrying her knitting, she started toward the front door. Naomi scooped up the quilt templates she'd been drawing. I grabbed my embroidered bag.

We left sedately, but as soon as Opal's door closed behind us, we ran past Edna's Buttons and Bows to Naomi's quilt shop.

The front room of Batty About Quilts was a gallery of beautiful quilted objects. Without slowing to admire them, we continued through the sales rooms, one chock-full of quilting fabrics plus the latest in long-arm quilters, and the other displaying huge rolls of different types of batting.

At the back of that room, one door led to the parking lot, and another led to the stairs up to Naomi's apartment. We climbed quietly. At the top, Naomi eased her apartment door open, peeked around the jamb, and gestured for us to follow her.

Nearly everything in Naomi's apartment was quilted — upholstery, drapes, and sofa pillows. Even the tablecloth in her dining room and the tea towels hanging in the adjoining kitchen had been pieced together from lightweight linen.

Naomi led us down the hall leading to bedrooms and bathrooms. She knocked on a closed door. "Juliette?" No answer. She opened the door and whispered to us, "While you're in there, I'll go call Opal and tell her I need information from her apartment. That should allow her to get away from Mrs. Battersby for a few minutes." She headed back toward her living room.

Haylee seldom looked shocked, but the state of Juliette's room must have gotten to her. "What a mess!" she said. "How will we find anything? Especially when we have no idea what we should be looking for?"

Stepping over clothes on the floor, we tried to see everything without moving anything.

Haylee stared at the night table. "What's this?" She pointed down at a sheet of paper that had been cut more or less in half.

Someone — Juliette, I guessed — had printed a series of fortunes on the paper.

One read, *Peace and prosperity will be yours.*

The next one was *You will delight in your many grandchildren.*

I giggled. "That one must be for Mrs. Battersby."

Haylee groaned. "Isn't she a stitch?" She

pointed at another one. " 'Beauteous happiness.' "

I asked, "Who says 'beauteous'? Maybe Juliette was copying fortunes from somewhere else."

"I've never heard anyone say it." She read another fortune aloud. " 'A gift of apples.' " She laughed. "She started getting specific."

The last fortune read, *Despite everything,* and then the paper had been cut off.

I ran out to the living room. Standing guard at the top of her stairs, Naomi was still on the phone. She placed her hand over the mouthpiece. "I'm listening to Opal rustle around in Patricia's room. She left Edna and Mrs. Battersby downstairs, so she'll have to hurry back to them before Mrs. Battersby takes a notion to trot around and find out what Opal's up to."

I grinned. "Poor Edna! She loves snooping."

"Opal said to go over there after you're done here. She said to look at what's on Patricia's computer screen. Meanwhile, she'll think of some reason why you need to go up into her apartment without her."

"The whatever-it-is you're showing us needs to be taken to her apartment?"

Naomi touched my hand. "Good idea. I'll tell her to go into her shop where she can't see her back door. Then you and Haylee can smuggle some fabric through the back door. On your way in, whisper to Mrs. Battersby that you have to sneak up to Opal's living room to see if the fabric matches Opal's couch because we're making sofa pillows as a surprise for Opal. You'll have to tell Mrs. Battersby that it's up to her to keep Opal from following you or even knowing you're there. That'll keep Mrs. Battersby out of the investigations."

I held up one thumb. "Perfect." Then I remembered why I'd come barreling out of Juliette's room. "Do you have a camera? I'd like to photograph some fortunes that Juliette must have written, in case they hold a clue we can figure out later."

She nodded. "Guard the door."

A few seconds later, she handed me a small camera. I carried it into Juliette's room. Kneeling on the floor beside an open suitcase, Haylee was using one of her knitting needles to poke among wrinkled clothing. "I haven't found anything interesting," she reported. "Except I don't think much of her packing methods."

I photographed the half page of fortunes.

Heaped clothing on the closet floor prevented the door from closing. The heel of one of Juliette's sequined party shoes stuck out underneath the hem of the long skirt she'd worn the evening before. I lifted the skirt off a pair of black jeans and found a matching black denim blazer.

Haylee commented, "A black denim pant-suit? That doesn't seem like Juliette's style."

I agreed. "It's similar to the one Patricia was wearing last night, except Patricia's jacket was a traditional jean jacket. The jacket on the person I saw sneaking toward the park was more like this blazer, and I think it was unbuttoned."

Haylee frowned down at the jumble of clothing. "Patricia and Juliette are about as tall as Dare and Floyd."

"And Dare was wearing an unbuttoned blazer, but Floyd had on his suit. Double-breasted and buttoned up. Maybe he unbuttoned his suit jacket while unspooling thread."

She laughed. "Isn't that what everyone does? Was Patricia wearing her jacket open or fastened?"

"Open." I snapped photos, then bent for a better look at the bottom hems of Juliette's jeans.

A tiny bit of mud smudged one of them.

# 24

Afraid that Juliette might somehow bypass Naomi guarding the door to the apartment and catch me gawking at the mud smeared on her pant leg, I whispered to Haylee, "Let's get out of here!" Besides, we needed time to search Patricia's room. "Opal said we were to check out the screen of Patricia's computer."

I photographed the mud on the jeans and repositioned the skirt on top of the jeans, jacket, and shoes. The mess of clothes on the floor of the closet looked similar to the way we'd found it — Juliette should never be able to guess that we had tampered with her things. We slipped out of the room.

With a mischievous smile on her face and a bulging quilted drawstring bag in her hands, Naomi waited for us in her living room.

I handed her the camera. "Can you e-mail me the photos I just took?"

"Sure."

I also asked her, "Do you know where Juliette was and what she was doing last night after we showed Edna her wedding skirt?"

The light went out of Naomi's eyes. "No, sorry, I don't. Opal and I were working on our bridesmaid dresses in Haylee's workroom. So Opal won't know where Patricia was, either."

Haylee added to me, "I was going to help Opal and Naomi after I settled Mrs. Battersby and her headache into a nice dark room, but the siren on the roof of the fire station went off and I had to leave."

Naomi handed me the bag. "Here. Smuggle this into Opal's apartment."

"Huh?" Haylee asked.

"I'll explain on the way," I told her, gripping Naomi's bag and my embroidered knitting bag. "You're sure you don't want to come along, Naomi?"

She grinned. "I'd better not. Mrs. Battersby would be sure she was invited up into Patricia's room. You two have a good time."

"And you be careful," Haylee said. "I don't like you staying here alone with Juliette. Come over to my apartment for a sleepover with Edna and her mother. You, too, Willow. Everything you've told me about that Brianna person gives me the willies."

"Patricia could have been the one to murder Isis," I said, remembering how satisfied the shy sewing machine historian had looked when apparently thinking about Isis's final fate. "Opal should join us."

Naomi objected, "They can't *all* be murderers."

"Great," Haylee said, "we're gambling that *none* of them are. I have only Edna and Mrs. Battersby, but the rest of you could be harboring desperate houseguests!"

I laughed. "I am gambling that none of *our* houseguests are murderers. Good night, Naomi!" Racing down the stairs, I reminded Haylee, "Floyd the zombie scared Isis. And they threatened each other. Most of all, Floyd acted guilty last night. He arrived at the scene almost as soon as I did, but after the fire engine started, he made himself scarce, as if he feared emergency workers and police. And he was definitely wearing a dark suit right after Isis was pushed underwater. His jacket was buttoned, but he could have skulked along the trail with it loose and flapping, and then buttoned it before walking like a zombie again."

"So Ben may be harboring a dangerous guest at the Elderberry Bay Lodge." Haylee opened the door to the parking lot. "I should go warn him, right now!"

"I'll come, too! Clay's supposed to be at the lodge, listening to Dare read."

We were both tempted to give up our sleuthing mission and hop into Haylee's pickup truck — which was almost beside us — to go find Clay and Ben.

But when would we have a chance to search Patricia's room?

Haylee asked, "What are we going to do if Mrs. Battersby still refuses to go back to my apartment?"

I pulled her to a stop, pointed at the quilted bag Naomi had lent me, and whispered, "Naomi told Opal to go into her shop where she can't see her back door. You go in first and tell Mrs. Battersby that you and I have to match some fabrics to Opal's couch because we plan to surprise her with a new pillow, and Mrs. Battersby is not, under any circumstances, to let Opal follow us. I'll sneak this into Opal's kitchen, and go upstairs."

Haylee giggled. "That should be fun! Mrs. Battersby will probably send Opal up to join us!"

"All the better," I said.

"Unless Mrs. Battersby comes, too. I can just imagine her telling Vicki Smallwood that we've been snooping where we shouldn't be."

I groaned. "Even though the mud on Juliette's jeans may not have anything to do with Isis's death, how are we going to convince Vicki to search Juliette's room and find the jeans?"

In the flower garden behind Opal's dining room, I stepped between plants and peeked through the window. Mrs. Battersby had her back to me, but I could see the side of Edna's face. Opal was nowhere in sight.

Haylee opened the door, tiptoed to Mrs. Battersby, and whispered in her ear. Mrs. Battersby craned her neck around and stared up at Haylee with something like amazement.

Edna glanced toward the window where I stood. Surreptitiously, she gave me a thumbs-up. Opal must have managed to caution her to stay put and keep Mrs. Battersby entertained, which wouldn't be too difficult as long as Mrs. Battersby had not yet finished the cap she intended to knit that night.

I tiptoed into Opal's dining room. Finger to lips, I caught Mrs. Battersby's eye, then scooted into the kitchen and up the stairs to the rest of Opal's apartment, a huge liv-

ing room and several bedrooms and bathrooms.

Haylee was right behind me.

We found Patricia's guest room on the
second try. It was much neater than Juliette's had been. Haylee reached the computer first. "Look at this. Patricia really is
writing *The Book of the Treadle.* Here's the
manuscript. '*The Book of the Treadle: A
Historian's View of Treadle Sewing Machines*
by Patricia Alayna Aiken.' " She scrolled
down. "She has a file of pictures she intends
to include, too."

One by one, Haylee highlighted the names
of Patricia's folders. Near the bottom was a
folder titled *Isis Crabbe.* Haylee sat up
straighter and clicked on it.

I held my breath.

Haylee clicked on a subfolder labeled *Photos.* A bunch of thumbnail images came up.
The first one was a woman's face. Haylee
clicked on it, but she didn't need to enlarge
it. I'd recognized the woman from the tiny
photo.

Patricia knew Isis's last name and had
been collecting photos of her.

Haylee and I stared at each other in
amazement.

I said, "At the fire station, Patricia and
Isis seemed to have met each other before,

and to already dislike each other."

Haylee clicked back up the chain. The folder labeled *Isis Crabbe* had not been revised since a month before either woman arrived in Threadville. "Patricia definitely knew who Isis was before they came here," Haylee concluded.

Now I needed to see if the hems of Patricia's jeans were muddy. Her jean jacket was in her closet, but I couldn't find the jeans. "Was Patricia wearing blue jeans tonight?" I asked Haylee. "With her beautiful white turtleneck?"

"Probably."

Voices sounded on the stairs. "Those girls are up to something, I tell you!"

Mrs. Battersby.

Leaving Haylee madly clicking the mouse to return Patricia's computer screen to the way we'd found it, I dashed out to the living room, leaned over Opal's couch, and pulled a bit of a fabric out of the bag. The bright orange batik was a little startling among Opal's blue and gray furnishings.

Grinning, Opal came into the room first, followed by a red-faced Mrs. Battersby and a slightly worried-looking Edna.

I made a show of punching the fabric into it the bag.

Opal managed to sound stern. "I didn't

see you come upstairs, Willow."

I plunked onto the couch and hugged the bag to my chest. "I came with Haylee. We —" I waved my hand vaguely toward the other part of the apartment.

Edna loudly finished the sentence for me. "Wanted to wash their hands before we all tidied up your kitchen."

Haylee must have heard Edna's explanation. She came down the hallway rubbing her hands together as if she hadn't quite finished drying them.

Mrs. Battersby detained me at the foot of the stairs while the others went on into the kitchen. "That neon orange won't do for Opal's couch," she whispered. "If you want a pop of color to go with that grayish blue, try something more subdued, like burgundy or purple. Or maybe pale yellow."

I thanked her, agreed that the colors she suggested would look much better with Opal's things, and opened the door to the kitchen. Mrs. Battersby went into the dining room with the others. I was about to follow her, but Edna carried a tray from the dining room into the kitchen.

I quickly asked, "Edna, is it possible that you could have been the intended victim when Isis drowned?"

Grinning, she ran her fingers through her

metallic-looking hair. "No way. Isis's hair was mousy brown. No one could have mistaken that woman for me!" She became serious. "Willow, *you* could be in danger if the killer thinks you could identify him. Come stay at Haylee's with my mother and me until that thread distributor leaves."

I laughed. "I'm not keen on letting Brianna roam around my apartment by herself. You might try getting Opal and Naomi to join you at Haylee's, though. We found things in both of their guest rooms that worried us."

"What?"

The others came in with loaded trays.

I murmured to Edna, "Ask Haylee when you get a chance."

I washed Opal's beautifully gleaming bone china cups and saucers while the others rinsed, dried, and put them away.

Haylee and Mrs. Battersby were the first to leave. Edna and I said good night to Opal and dawdled near tempting yarns and patterns in Tell a Yarn. "I've got to try these beaded yarns," Edna crowed.

I admired skeins of hand-dyed yarns in scrumptious color combinations.

Out on the sidewalk, Haylee was grilling Mrs. Battersby about the needs of preemies. Haylee was an expert tailor. Imagining extra-tiny newborns in tuxedos, I grinned. I guessed that many of us were about to switch from our previous knitting projects to knitting sweaters and caps for preemies. They were a little beyond my ability, but I'd learn.

Edna, Haylee, and Mrs. Battersby headed to The Stash, and I started across the street.

Down toward the lake, the park was no longer lit by temporary lights, and no police vehicles were visible. Yellow tape fluttered, rustling in the wind.

Brianna's car was parked in front of In Stitches, and music boomed from my apartment.

Grumbling to myself, I strode down the hill and went inside through my patio door. I let my pets out of my room and into the backyard for a few minutes, then shooed them all inside and locked the door.

Shut inside her suite, Brianna laughed and talked over the sound of her music. A light on the phone showed she was on my landline.

My mother's election, I reminded myself. Considering that I wasn't very helpful in my mother's campaigns — wasn't helpful at all, in fact — and never went back to South Carolina to arrange fund-raisers and dinners as she asked, the least I could do was try to be polite to her supporter's daughter.

Brianna wouldn't stay much longer, would she? She hadn't made her sales pitch to Haylee yet, and I doubted that she'd approached Naomi, but surely she would soon, and in only two days, after the craft fair ended, Brianna would surely move on.

And I would be gracious, no matter how much gritting of teeth would be involved, until I could finally bid Brianna good-bye, except for ordering thread from her. From a distance, preferably.

I wanted to learn more about Patricia Alayna Aiken and the late Isis Crabbe, but I was exhausted. Besides, Haylee and I had found out Isis's last name rather easily. If we could, detectives from the Pennsylvania State Police could, also, and probably had. If there was a connection between Isis and Patricia, investigators had probably found that, too.

I couldn't very well tell Vicki about the mud-specked jeans we'd found in Juliette's room, either. Vicki would scold me for interfering.

Brianna had eaten and left her dirty dishes on the counter. I put them in the dishwasher, turned off the light above the stove, and locked my menagerie into my suite with me. The dogs and I went to bed while the kittens conspired to keep us awake.

I fell asleep anyway, and it wasn't the kittens who startled me out of sleep. It was one sharp bark from Tally-Ho, a bark that usually meant he'd heard something and wanted Sally-Forth and me to help him investigate.

Shivering in the dark, I listened. Bass notes still pounded from Brianna's suite, but she wasn't talking. The piece of music ended, and I detected the sound of my patio door sliding closed.

I had locked that door when I came in.

## 25

More loud and jarring music began in Brianna's room, but between pieces, I had definitely heard the patio door close.

Who had closed it? Brianna? Had she been going out or returning?

Or had someone else come in?

I pressed the back of my hand against my mouth, which did nothing to slow my racing pulse. I wanted to lie in the dark under my warm comforter and not think about intruders, but Tally-Ho was whining at my bedroom door.

Was someone on the other side?

"Speak," I whispered to Sally-Forth, but she didn't. I pushed the comforter aside, fumbled for my pink fuzzy slippers and robe, and staggered to my bedroom door. I halted the onslaught of pets with one hand while easing the door open with the other.

The light above the stove was on again. I had turned it off.

Leaving my pets shut in my bedroom suite, I slipped through the great room to the patio door. Someone had unlocked it.

I was tempted to lock it in case Brianna had gone out without her key, but if someone else was inside, I wouldn't want to slow his or her exit.

My phone's light showed that the line was in use, but I didn't hear Brianna's voice.

I put my nose almost on the glass and shielded both sides of my face to block out the light above the stove, but I didn't see anyone outside. Had someone gone up through the side yard to the street?

About the only complaint I had about my apartment, other than my current house-guest, was that I couldn't see the street from it.

I crept upstairs and opened the door a crack. In Stitches seemed to be the way I'd left it, with one night-light burning. If intruders were inside my shop, I couldn't see or hear them, though for me to hear intruders over Brianna's music, they'd have to stomp, shout, and throw things.

I tiptoed between rows of fabrics to a front window.

Brianna was on the other side of Lake Street.

Her hand on the doorknob of Edna's front

265

door, she was peering through the glass.

I was all set to traipse across the street in my pink fuzzy robe and slippers and ask her what she wanted in Edna's shop, which had closed for the night long ago, but Brianna turned around, trotted to the sidewalk, and hurried down Lake Street toward the beach.

If she wasn't going to listen to her music, I shouldn't have to, either. I ran downstairs and knocked on her door. I didn't know who I thought might answer. No one did.

I opened the door. Every light was on. I strode down the hallway into the bedroom. Aghast, I stopped in my tracks. She was worse than Juliette. How could anyone create such a mess in less than forty-eight hours? She'd thrown candy papers and torn-off crusts from buttered toast on the carpet. No wonder she'd fled even though it was the middle of the night.

Groggily rubbing my eyes, I stepped over and around clothes, shoes, CDs, and cases of thread. I wanted to turn the music off, but she'd only turn it on again, so I lowered the volume to a level that might not sound loud in my suite.

My phone was on the night table. I picked it up. Someone was reciting the weather forecast for Sydney.

*Sydney?*

Australia, I guessed, judging by the accent. Was this Brianna's method of creating alibis for herself? Dial a number that would stay on the line for hours, and then go out and do whatever she wanted? Glad I had a toll-free long-distance plan, I set the cordless phone down without disconnecting it. She would discover I'd been in her room and had turned her music down, but she didn't need to know I'd listened to her call.

I was about to sneak out when I saw a checkbook.

Okay, that was really snooping, but about an hour before Isis was pushed into the river, I'd seen Brianna hand her something that could have been a check.

Nervously listening, wishing I had locked the patio door, I opened the checkbook. It was the kind that created carbon copies of checks.

The most recent check had been made out to Isis Crabbe for two hundred dollars. In the portion marked *Memo,* Brianna had written, *Curse against WV.*

"WV" could have meant lots of things, but those were my initials. My mother's, too.

Feeling angry, violated, and hurt, I no longer wanted Brianna to take the hint about the loud stereo. I didn't want her to know I'd been in her suite, not that she couldn't have guessed I might enter it whenever I wanted. I turned the volume up, but not quite to the ear-splitting levels where she'd left it.

What if she was on her way back? She could be near the patio door. She would see me leave her suite.

I skedaddled as quickly as my pink-slippered feet and the mounds of her belongings on the floor let me.

Leaving the light on above the stove, I dashed into my suite, locked the door, sank down on the carpet with my back against my bed, and cuddled Sally-Forth and Tally-Ho. Mustache and Bow-Tie jumped around on the bed and swatted at my hair.

Why had Brianna paid Isis two hundred dollars to write or utter a curse, possibly against me or my mother? The two-hundred-dollar curses on Isis's price list had been the bad ones. Earlier, I'd guessed that the pieces of willow that Isis had cut might be for a boat to "drown" a toy zombie, but maybe she'd planned to cast spells against me. Or against both Floyd and me.

Brianna had disliked me from the moment I went outside to help her unpack her car. I hadn't treated her like a long-lost best friend, but I'd given her a place to stay, had provided meals and snacks, and had cleaned up after her. I'd invited her to sell thread at our craft fair. It wasn't that I needed to be liked, but I didn't understand why she would want to harm me or my mother.

I wanted to go out into my great room, put the bar across the patio door, and let Brianna in only if she promised to pack her things and drive far, far away.

But I could imagine what my mother would say.

The longer I huddled on the floor with my warm pets, the sillier I felt for being upset over a curse. If Isis had been as powerful as she'd seemed to think she was, she could have prevented her own death. She couldn't have hurt me or my mother. Or Edna or Gord or Floyd the zombie.

The dogs fell asleep with their heads on my lap, and the kittens gave up attacking hair that barely attacked them back. Purring, they sat at my shoulders like sphinxes guarding a pharaoh's tomb.

I gently crawled out from under my slumbering dogs and climbed into bed. Brianna's music thumped on the other side of the wall. I listened for her to come in, but if she did, I didn't hear her.

I didn't know how long I'd slept when my smartphone rang.

Apparently, Vicki was on duty. In a businesslike voice, she identified herself as Chief Smallwood. "Your landline's busy," she said.

"Brianna must be talking to her boyfriend again." I tried not to sound half-asleep, but was sure I didn't succeed.

"Brianna's with me. Where are you, Willow?"

"At home. In bed. It's . . ." I checked the time. "After one." I didn't mean to be rude and abrupt.

Vicki laughed. "That hasn't stopped you from wandering around before."

I had to smile. "I must be getting old."

Her voice became serious again. "I need to come over and talk to you."

"Um, okay. The patio door should be unlocked."

"Put a kettle on."

## 26

Vicki disconnected the call, leaving me staring at my phone in disbelief.

She'd asked me to put a kettle on. At one fifteen in the morning. What an odd time for her to come to tea.

At least she liked my animals. I let them into the great room and started heating water.

Maybe pink and fuzzy wasn't quite the right look for when a police chief came calling. I ran into my bedroom and threw on jeans and a sweatshirt. However, the dogs barked, someone rapped on the frame of the patio door, and I thrust my feet into the pink fuzzy slippers and shuffled out to the great room.

Before I could reach the door, Brianna shoved it open. She appeared to be drenched, hair, shoes, and everything between. Her eyes looked bruised and angry. She clutched a thin, silvery survival blanket at her neck. It rattled as she walked.

Behind her, Vicki ordered, "Wait!"

"I live here," Brianna snarled. "I can come and go whenever I want." She marched toward her suite.

In my slippers, I skated past her to help Vicki round up my animals before they could wander outside on their own.

Vicki was doing a fine job of it by herself. Yipping with excitement, Sally and Tally licked her hands and wagged their tails. The kittens launched themselves toward her pant legs. By the time Vicki and I had convinced all four animals to stay inside, Brianna was about to shut herself in her suite.

Vicki called out, "Brianna, hang on a second."

Brianna turned around and glared.

"Take a hot shower, put on dry clothes, then come out here and warm up with some tea."

"I don't want tea." Brianna's eyes glittered with brittle fury. What was wrong with her?

"Then come out here after you've showered, anyway," Vicki demanded. "We've got to straighten this thing out."

"What's to straighten?" Brianna demanded. "You just do your job. Don't tell me what to do."

By straightening her back only slightly and

272

thinning her lips, Vicki became amazingly formidable. "Part of my job is looking after people, and that includes you. If you won't follow my advice and warm yourself up, I'll have to call an ambulance."

Brianna only glowered and slammed herself into her guest suite.

Realizing I was gaping at where she'd last been, I closed my mouth and turned toward Vicki. "What's happening?" I didn't feel quite awake yet, which didn't help me understand it, whatever *it* was.

The music in the guest suite stopped.

Vicki eased onto one of the stools at the counter and massaged her forehead.

I grabbed a plastic bag of homemade molasses cookies from the freezer. "You need cookies."

"I need more than cookies." She fished her digital camera out of a pocket. "Turn your face so you're looking at your fridge again," she said.

"What?" But I did it.

She took a couple of pictures.

I put the cookies on an ovenproof platter and turned on the oven. "What's going on?"

She backed toward the sitting area of my great room. "Stay there. I want a picture of you in that outfit, complete with bedroom slippers."

I put my hands on my hips. "Are you taking up blackmail?"

She snapped more photos. "Nope. I'm looking after people. You, this time."

"Why?"

She lowered the camera. "To prove my case."

"*Your* case? I'm beginning to think it's mine."

She squinched her mouth to one side and nodded. "Don't worry. It's her word against yours, and I don't think she's telling the truth."

I slid the platter of cookies into the oven. "That doesn't surprise me."

Vicki took her place on the stool again. "Why not?"

"For one thing, she waffled the other night about whether she'd gone outside, and only admitted it after you said you were going to have the door fingerprinted." I held up a jar of dried chamomile. "Is this all right, or would you prefer something to keep you awake?"

"Chamomile's fine. I'm supposed to go off duty soon. Any other ways she seemed dishonest?"

"At first, she said she didn't wear my shoes, but then she retracted that, too." I lowered a tea infuser into the pot. "And I

274

just found out about another possible lie. Remember she said that she was on the phone with her boyfriend when Isis was killed?"

Examining my face, Vicki nodded.

I filled the teapot with boiling water. "After I went to bed this evening, Brianna's music went quiet for a second, and I heard the patio door close." I gestured to indicate my great room. "No one was in here, and my landline was in use. I couldn't see anyone in my backyard, either, so I went upstairs to look out the front windows. Brianna was at the door of Edna's shop, and she had her hand on the doorknob and her face almost against the glass, like someone trying the door to see if it was unlocked, or at least checking out the inside."

Vicki got out her notebook and began writing in it. "Did she enter Edna's shop?"

"No. She turned around and hurried down Lake Street toward the beach. So I thought it was my chance to turn down her music. While I was in her room, I picked up the phone and listened. A woman was droning on and on about the weather in Sydney. The woman had an Australian accent."

Vicki gazed toward Blueberry Cottage, dark in my backyard. "Mm-hm."

"Did you get my phone records from last

night?" I asked.

"The state police did. They didn't warn you?"

I shook my head.

She frowned. "I'm sorry. I should have told you to lock up your phone. The so-called boyfriend was actually a number in Sydney, the number people call for a recorded weather report. That call lasted for over four hours."

I waved away her concern. "My number's toll-free worldwide, incoming and outgoing calls."

She blew out a relieved breath. "Glad to hear that. Sorry none of us said anything about it to you."

"No problem. I saw something else odd in Brianna's room, though. She had a checkbook, and I'm afraid I opened it."

Vicki tilted her head and pursed her lips.

"I know, I shouldn't have snooped. But as I told you, I'd seen her tear a page out of something that looked like a checkbook and hand it to Isis shortly before Isis was murdered. And now I'm sure that it was a check. Brianna's checkbook is the kind that makes copies. She'd written a check for two hundred dollars to Isis Crabbe. Down at the bottom where you're supposed to write a memo to yourself about what the check is for, she wrote, 'Curse against WV.' If those are initials, they could stand for me or for my mother."

Vicki was silent for a second, pondering her notebook. She raised her head and gave me the full force of her honest blue eyes. "We found that check among Isis's belongings in Edna's apartment."

"So that's Isis's last name? 'Crabbe,' with two *b*s and an *e*?"

She nodded. "Her wallet was in her room, too, and that was the name on her driver's license."

I turned from Vicki, both to pour the tea and to hide my gratification. Haylee and I wouldn't have to confess that we'd searched Patricia's computer and discovered Isis's last name.

My face in control, I hoped, I faced Vicki again and shoved a mug of tea toward her. "Are you going to tell me what this wee-hours visit is about?" Water was running in my guest suite.

She shook her head. "Brianna will. In about two minutes. Even if we have to haul her out of the shower ourselves."

"We wouldn't dare."

Vicki grinned, but it was a toothy, humor-less grin that reminded me again that she was a tough police chief. "Yeah, you're right. *We* wouldn't." She checked her wristwatch. "But if she doesn't get out here pretty soon, I'm going in after her."

Maybe the smell of warm cookies would tempt Brianna into the kitchen. I removed the plate from the oven and set it on the counter in front of Vicki, then poured myself a mug of tea. I loved the flavor and the comfort of chamomile, but it often made me sleepy. With any luck, the evening's festivities, such as they were, would end before my head fell face-first into the plate of cookies.

We didn't have to haul Brianna out of the shower. Her lower lip protruding in defiance and her hair even wetter than when she'd marched into my apartment claiming that she *lived* here, she slouched out of my guest suite, closed the door, and stood at the end of the counter, where she could see Vicki's face.

"Well?" Brianna demanded. She was wearing one of the warm fleece bathrobes I'd embroidered for potential guests. White, not pink.

I poured another mug of tea and placed it in front of Brianna.

"Well, what?" Vicki asked. She could be very cold, almost accusing, but I was used to the official police side of her personality, and I didn't feel threatened.

Without looking my way, Brianna snapped at Vicki, "Are you going to sit there having a tea party, or are you going to do your job and arrest her?"

## 27

I nearly spewed my tea. "Arrest me?" I repeated.

Her mouth tightening, Vicki shot me a quick glance and gave her head a nearly imperceptible shake.

Okay, I got it. I was supposed to let her handle this. I clutched my hot mug against my chest.

"Drink your tea and warm up," Vicki told Brianna in a calm voice. "And tell me why you want me to arrest Willow."

The corners of Brianna's mouth turned down. "I already told you." Like a petulant child, she still didn't look at me. She also didn't touch the tea.

Vicki shoved the plate of cookies toward her. "Humor me, okay? Tell me again why you want me to arrest Willow."

Arms tight against her sides, Brianna muttered, "She pushed me into the lake."

I managed not to sputter, but my eyes

opened rather wide for that time of the night — morning — whatever.

Vicki asked, still in a deceptively sympathetic voice, "Do you have proof, Brianna?"

Brianna exploded, "Proof? You saw me. I was soaking wet. I could have drowned."

"Willow says she was asleep."

"Well, she's not going to confess, is she?" Brianna still avoided looking my way. I hoped that meant she was ashamed of lying. "She's not going to admit she goes around trying to drown people. She's probably the one who pushed that other woman in."

Dangerous sparks lit Vicki's eyes. "Who says that other woman was pushed?"

"Everybody. Anyone could figure that out."

"That woman was tangled in a heavy, um, contraption. You weren't. She ended up in the river, which gets deep dangerously quickly. You told me you were on the beach when someone pushed you. The slope at the beach is gradual. If someone pushed you, you'd get your feet wet, but you wouldn't be all wet like you were when you flagged me down. Did you resist your assailant?"

Finally, Brianna did look at me, for less than a second, with frightening rage. "Okay,

I get it. All you hayseeds stick together. She goes around murdering people and blaming others and you stick up for her. *Your* cases are solved and *she* stays out of jail. Nice little game you two have going."

"Just tell me the truth, Brianna," Vicki demanded.

"I am."

"Okay. Tell me where you were and who you saw and what happened." Vicki's exaggerated patience should have frightened Brianna.

But Brianna only sulked. "I told you."

"Tell me again. With details."

Brianna heaved a dramatic sigh. "I was standing on the beach looking out at the lake, and she suddenly ran up behind me. I couldn't hear her coming on the sand, and I didn't know she was there until she shoved me into the water. I went right down on my face. If my head had hit a rock or something, I'd be dead now, thanks to your friend there."

How did I luck out with this houseguest? Even though she gave no sign of wanting to touch the plate of cookies, I wanted to yank it away from her.

Vicki asked, "What part of your body did she shove?"

Brianna scowled. "I don't know. It happened fast, you know? My back, my shoulders, I guess."

Vicki didn't raise her eyes from her notebook. "We'll have a doctor examine your back and shoulders for bruises."

Pouting, Brianna picked at the edge of my counter.

Vicki asked, "And your knees? Did they get skinned?"

"You saw me. I was wearing jeans."

Vicki gazed at her face. "Show me the palms of your hands."

Brianna averted her eyes and slid her hands into the armpits of the bathrobe. "I don't have to."

"Okay, fine." Vicki was being extra agreeable, another danger sign that Brianna probably didn't recognize. "Look at Willow's face."

Brianna didn't. Instead, she complained, "Why should I look at her after what she did to me?"

Vicki answered easily, "You don't have to, but when we first got here, she had a crease on her cheek."

I clapped my hands to my cheeks, but couldn't feel any creases. Not that being Brianna's hostess wasn't enough to give anyone wrinkles. My hair was probably going gray that very minute.

Brianna stood a little straighter, slumping less. "So maybe I did get a swing in at her. It was self-defense."

Vicki shook her head. "No, it's the kind of crease she'd have gotten from sleeping in one position for a while." She tapped her pen on the counter. "So you didn't see the person who pushed you, but you *know* it was Willow. How?"

Brianna stared at her hands. "She was following me down Lake Street."

This was too much. "What was I wearing?" I asked.

Vicki frowned at me but didn't object.

Brianna continued to speak as if I weren't there. "What she has on."

"I guess you didn't splash her when you fell in." By this time, Vicki's polite and encouraging tone barely masked a challenge.

Brianna's face turned red. "How would I know? I had my back to her. She probably jumped out of the way. You're not going to arrest her, are you." It was an accusation, not a question.

Vicki maintained her calm equilibrium. "Not tonight," she said.

I said to Brianna, "What were you doing at Edna's shop, Buttons and Bows? Trying to enter?"

Vicki cautioned, "Willow . . ."

Brianna glared at me. "Nothing." She turned to Vicki. "See? She was following me."

I retorted, "I was looking out the window of In Stitches."

Vicki reworded my question to Brianna, "Why were you peeking into Edna's store at that time of night? Had you, perhaps, given Isis something that you wanted back?"

Brianna answered with an abrupt, "No."

"That's good," Vicki went on, "since the police have taken away everything that was Isis's, including a check you wrote her." Vicki shook her head as if to clear it. "For a *curse,* of all things?"

Brianna mumbled, "Not a real one."

Vicki pressed her, "A fake curse that cost two hundred dollars?"

Brianna changed the subject. "I guess I did look into that store for a moment. To see if she sold thread."

"You could have asked," I pointed out.

Brianna only shrugged.

Vicki said slowly and clearly, "In the morning, I'll get the surveillance tapes from the bank down the street, and we'll see where all you went and who was following you."

Brianna's face turned redder. "She started

following me later, way past the bank. I think she came along the hiking trail."

Vicki grabbed a cookie and stood. "And *I* think your story keeps changing. I don't know who pushed you, if anyone, but I'm almost certain it wasn't Willow. But after accusing her, you probably don't want to stay here, so I'll tell you what I'll do for you. I'll wait for you to pack up your things. I don't think you need an ambulance, so I'll take you to Emergency myself and you can be examined for signs of an assault."

"I have a car," Brianna said.

"I'll take you, or a state trooper will. It's policy."

"I don't need to go to any hospital."

"I'm not charging anyone with assault without evidence of an assault or a witness to the assault."

Finally, Brianna must have recognized the steel hidden in Vicki's exaggerated politeness. Brianna pointed at me. "She did it! You're letting her get away with murder!"

Vicki took a step toward her. "Do you need help packing?"

Instead of answering, Brianna swore, flung herself into my guest suite and slammed the door.

Vicki sat again and bit into the cookie. "These are delicious. Don't worry, Willow,

I'm not leaving here until she does, and then I'm telling the state trooper who takes over after my shift to swing past on Lake Street often after Brianna leaves the hospital. That is one angry young woman."

I grasped my mug by its handle. "I don't know why, either. I've tried to be a good hostess, and she's been like this — well almost like this but not quite as bad as tonight — ever since my mother foisted her on me."

"Maybe she feels like your mother foisted you on her?"

"Well, she can just get herself unfoisted. I've had enough."

"So even if she comes out here all contrite and retracts her accusation, and I have no real reason to drive her to the hospital, you'd still like her to leave?"

"I would, but my mother would disown me, so no, I guess I'd have to say she could stay here until the end of the craft fair. But after that, she's going."

"I'd feel better if she left now," Vicki said.

"Yes, well . . ." Sipping at my tea, I glanced at the phone. "Look at that little light. She's on the phone again."

"She must need to talk to that boyfriend in Australia."

Why did people keep saying outrageous or

funny things when I was drinking my tea? I nearly snorted tea out my nose. As soon as I could speak, I said, "It's going to take her hours to pack. You wouldn't believe the mess."

With a strange look on her face, Vicki slipped off her stool. "I'd better go help." She tried the door to my guest suite.

Brianna had locked it.

Vicki sorted through the gadgets hanging from her belt, stuck one of them into the hole in the doorknob, opened the door, and walked into my guest suite.

I stayed in the kitchen, which didn't prevent me from hearing Brianna's startled protest. "You can't come in here without a search warrant." The light on my phone turned off.

Vicki hollered, "Willow, do I have permission to go into your guest suite?"

"Be my guest!" I yelled.

My phone rang. Maybe it was the weather station in Australia.

Of course it wasn't.

"Willow . . ." I cringed at the honeyed-over disappointment in my mother's voice. "What are you doing *now*?"

# 28

Not sure I wanted to answer my mother's restrained question, I managed, "It's the middle of the night."

"Exactly. Why are you kicking Todd Shrevedale's daughter out at this hour?" The disappointment turned to hurt empathy. For me or for Brianna?

"I'm not." I squeezed my hand around the receiver so tightly that my fingernails stabbed into the heel of my hand.

"That's not what I heard."

"What did you hear?" I might as well find out what lies Brianna was spreading. She'd certainly lost no time.

"That you called the police to kick her out of your apartment. In the middle of the night."

"Um, that's not how it happened. She went to the police with some ugly allegations, and the police brought her here to confront me. Her story didn't hold water."

Uh-oh. Bad choice of words.

"Why kick her out? It's nearly two. She needs a place to stay." There it was again — the sugar, the warmth, the compassion for Brianna, and the pain-inducing disappointment in me.

I repressed a sigh. "The *police* are taking her to the hospital so she can be checked for evidence of the assault she claims took place."

"Assault?" There was silence on the other end of the line, then a cautious, "Willow? What have you done?"

Her tone made me feel about five years old, but I defended myself. "Nothing. I was asleep. Brianna went for a walk on the beach in the middle of the night. She accused me of pushing her into the lake. She keeps changing her story. When she resisted being taken to the hospital, it was clear to me and to the police that she was making it all up, and the police don't think it's appropriate for her to continue staying here."

"The police." My mother managed to sound like she was weighing the evidence and managing to remain objective. "I hear it's one policewoman and she's your friend. When are you going to learn to stay out of trouble?"

"I do." Especially when my mother didn't

send me unwanted houseguests. But I didn't dare say that or my mother would be positive I was taking out my frustrations on the unwanted houseguest. "And our chief of police would arrest me or anyone else she thought she should."

"I've told you before not to get involved in murders. Doesn't my career matter to you, if only for the sake of your father, who is as sweet as he can be, but will never earn a penny with those inventions of his?"

I bit back a reminder that my father, her husband, was brilliant. Yes, he might be a bit obsessed with his inventions, and yes, he might never earn anything, and yes, my mother had been supporting him for years. And she'd also supported me and put me through school. She was basically a good person and she loved both my father and me. I said evenly, "I have not been involved in any *murders*."

"Investigations, then. Can't you at least stay out of the newspapers? Unless you're running a fund-raiser or something that could attract voters."

"I'll do my best."

"So, that's settled." Her voice became crisp and optimistic. "Brianna can continue to stay with you."

"That's not up to me. Isn't it against the

law to make false accusations?"

"Only if it's knowingly done. I'm sure she just made a little mistake. Everyone does. Including you. And *you* would want to be forgiven."

"Mother, she's been using my phone to make long-distance calls to Australia that go on for hours."

"I'm sure she has a good reason."

Right. She wanted to hear the weather report for Sydney repeated umpteen times. "She's using it as an alibi, pretending she's inside when she's really outside. She did it Thursday evening while a woman was being murdered nearby."

I heard my mother's sharp intake of breath. "Now who's making wild accusations?" I could almost see her smoothing her forehead with one long and elegant finger. When she finally broke her silence, I again heard her sorrow over my shortcomings. "Try to give that child a break, honey. Todd Shrevedale is an honest, upright man. He's not paving the way for his children with gold. He expects each of them to start a company and make their own way. Don't even think of charging her for those phone calls, honey, or charging her rent, or anything else. She's only *just* finished college with lots of debt and has only *just* started out in this thread business. She'll have barely a cent until she gets established."

*Only two hundred dollars to pay for a curse against me or you . . .*

My mother urged, "I hope you're buying lots of thread from her."

Finally, we were in territory where I should be able to please my mother. "I have. She's representing some wonderful lines. I'll continue to order from her." *If she keeps herself out of trouble.* "But I can't force our police chief to let her stay here."

"Willow, honey, I hope you'll do what you can to help that girl. There's no telling what the police might to do a young and impressionable child once they get her into their clutches. They may *say* they're only taking her to the hospital, but believe me, honey, I've seen some pretty bad abuses of trust. Totally innocent people do their best to cooperate with the police and end up being accused themselves. I'm heading a committee studying such abuses right now. Don't let that happen to our little Brianna. It would be *such* a travesty."

*Our* little Brianna? "Okay, Mother, I'll try." Now what was I getting myself into? Next thing I knew, Brianna would be a permanent resident in my guest suite.

My mother ended the call with her usual

candied grace.

Brianna hadn't touched her tea. I left her mug where it was and went into my guest suite.

Vicki stood, arms folded, watching Brianna heave things toward a suitcase lying open on the floor. At this rate, Brianna wouldn't leave for at least another two weeks.

I beckoned to Vicki. She followed me back to the kitchen.

"Brianna called someone — her father, I guess — and my mother called me. Do you think you can get Brianna to retract her accusation? Then you wouldn't have to take her to the hospital, and I would let her stay for the rest of the weekend so she could attend the craft fair where I promised her she could have a table to sell thread, and you and I can go back to what we were doing."

"Are you sure?" Vicki asked me.

I made a rueful face. "I'm sure I don't want to be disowned."

As if she didn't believe me, Vicki gave me an assessing look. Then she returned to Brianna's suite.

A few minutes later, Vicki was back. "Okay, now she only 'tripped' and fell into the lake, and she agrees that she was mistaken that someone pushed her." Frowning, she tapped her fingernails on my counter-top. "I'm overdue to go off duty, but if you'd like, I'll sleep on your couch tonight."

"I could give you my guest room and she could sleep on the couch."

"Nah. Your guest room is much too messy. You'd have to spend the rest of the night cleaning it up. I'll be fine on your couch."

"Thanks, but you need your rest, too, which is not something you'd get here with weird music and noisy pets and odd comings and goings. I'll be okay. I've got guard dogs and guard cats. And Brianna wouldn't dare do anything to me now that you've been alerted."

"And she'd better hope that no else does anything to you, either, or *she* might be blamed," Vicki said darkly, settling her hat onto her head. "Lock your apartment door *and* your room door."

I grinned. "If she didn't already know how easy it is to open those doors, she knows now."

Vicki pulled her business card out of a pocket, scribbled on it, and handed it to me. "That's my home number. Do not hesitate to call me or 911 if you need any help tonight. And I mean it."

I thanked her, let her out, and locked the patio door behind her. I stared at my own reflection. My hair was a tangled fright and my eyes looked even more tired than Brianna's.

She had friends in high places, but I did also. My mother. But far from protecting me like Todd Shrevedale protected his daughter, my mother could be making certain that I was in danger. *From* Todd Shrevedale's daughter.

And what about Vicki? After threatening to cart Brianna away, Vicki could be in Todd Shrevedale's bad books, also. The man's empire stretched through most of the world. Would he cause trouble for Vicki? Could he?

I locked myself into my room, put on my jammies, and climbed back into bed.

All I could hear was Brianna's music, once again booming from her room. I must have fallen asleep, though. I woke up to silence except for Sally-Forth's rhythmic snoring. That sweet and motherly dog could be comforting even in her sleep. It was still dark outside. I closed my eyes and didn't awaken again until my alarm went off.

No music or other sounds came from the guest suite. I knew it was too much to hope that Brianna had rethought everything and departed, but I made no attempt to be quiet when I took my pets outside for their pre-breakfast tour of my flower beds. If Brianna wanted to make use of the table we were giving her at the craft fair, she needed to be up soon. The Threadville Get Ready for Halloween Craft Fair was scheduled to open at ten.

I fed the animals, ate breakfast, shut the kittens into my bedroom, and took the dogs upstairs. Usually, Ashley, a high school student, helped me in the store on weekends, but I had let her choose between working at In Stitches or at the craft fair, so she was at the fair and I was at In Stitches.

Shortly after I opened the shop, music from downstairs began vibrating my floor. It continued long after Brianna should have left if she was going to join the other crafty salespeople at the fair.

I went out to the front porch. Brianna's car was gone. Maybe she had actually gone to the craft fair.

My regular customers were probably there, also, planning Halloween costumes and decorations and scooping up bargains. Leaving the dogs in the shop to announce any customers' arrival, I ran downstairs to my apartment.

A quick knock on my guest room door got no response. I marched into the suite. It was marginally neater than before Vicki had attempted to help Brianna pack. I had to step over suitcases overflowing with wrinkled garments, but I managed to turn off the music. The sudden silence almost hurt my ears.

I was about halfway up the stairs when the dogs barked and the beach glass chimes on my door jangled. I ran the rest of the way.

Detective Neffting stood just inside the door with his notebook in his hand. "I have a few questions for you," he said. "Ms. — er — Vanderling."

The way he added my last name to his statement didn't make me comfortable, and neither did his cold, bulging eyes.

I made an attempt at a smile. "Okay." Maybe he was going to ask more about Brianna and where she'd been the past couple of nights. Maybe he was about to arrest her for murdering Isis.

He asked, "Why were your fingerprints on the plug of the electrical cord attached to that death con*trap*tion?"

## 29

"Many people's fingerprints were on that plug." It probably wasn't the answer Neffting wanted from me.

"I get that." He sounded miffed. "But why yours, specifically?"

"I unplugged it."

"When?"

Hadn't I already told him? "After I saw the skirt under the water, I ran up to the bandstand to see if anyone was there. No one was, and the skirt was plugged in, so I unplugged it."

"Why?"

"In case the line was still live. I didn't want anyone jumping into the river and electrocuting themselves."

He looked skeptical, so I explained, "I guessed the line would have shorted itself out when the lightbulbs popped, but I needed to be sure."

He said drily, "Electricity doesn't usually

wander around loose. You said lots of people's prints would be on that plug. Who else's?"

"Clay's, because it's his extension cord. And Opal plugged the cord in when we were in the fire station earlier Thursday evening. Naomi and Haylee, too, other nights. We had fun with the music and light display on that thing."

"Death con*trap*tion," he repeated. "Fun for everyone. Who plugged the skirt in before the deceased rolled down the ramp?"

"No one. I mean, when we left the skirt in the bandstand about a half hour earlier, the skirt was plugged in. Clay had plugged it in."

Detective Neffting's hair was brown, with a comb-over that started on both sides of his head above his ears and met at the top, where it had been glued to the middle of his head in a straight line imitating a part. He scratched at the fake part and dislodged the glue from his skin, but the glue still connected those two upward sweeps of hair, and the thing that had resembled a part now looked more like a millipede teetering on thousands — well, maybe hundreds — of hairy legs. "You told me you heard the deceased uttering threats the night before she died. Who were the people she threatened again?"

I tore my attention away from the fascinating "millipede." "Not threats. She appeared to be reciting curses. One was for Gord Wrinklesides to spend his afterlife with her. With Isis, that is. The other seemed to be a spell designed to condemn Edna Battersby to — I'm not sure what — no afterlife at all, I think. And Floyd the zombie accused her of casting spells on him, but I don't know if she did, or if he merely thought the curses I saw her call down on Gord and Edna were actually for him. You can probably learn more about the curses and the afterlives by reading one of Isis's handmade books. Isis brought some of them with her and kept them in Edna's apartment."

Afraid he'd question me about how I knew what was in those books, I held my breath. Had Opal offered her copy to the police yet?

But Detective Neffting had a different agenda. "When did Edna Battersby touch that extension cord's plug?"

I felt the blood drain from my face. I was certain he was bluffing, acting like he had incriminating evidence against Edna in hopes that I would give him more. But he didn't have any, and neither did I. All he had against Edna was a weak motive — jealousy that she didn't even feel — and an alibi that was only from her adoring fiancé. "She didn't. She didn't have a reason to. She first saw the skirt around nine that night, and it was already plugged in. Then she and Gord went to his place."

"How do you know where they went? Did you follow them?"

"No. That's where they said they were going."

"Did you see Gord Wrinklesides touch that plug?"

"No."

"You're sure?"

"Yes."

"About what time did you see Edna and Gord leave the park?"

"Around nine twenty, but I'm not sure. I left shortly after, and took more than the usual time getting home because the trail was dark and foggy. I got home around nine thirty."

"And when did you hear the first scream on Thursday evening?"

"Around nine forty-five. Again, that's a guess."

He closed his notebook. "Okay, that's all I wanted to know. Call if you think of something you haven't told us about that night." After giving me a piercing look from those oversized eyes, he headed for the door. With each step he took, the millipede-like line of glue bobbed up and down on its little hairy legs.

How could he think that either Edna or Gord could be a killer?

I should have stayed up late and re-searched Patricia. I could do that now, before customers arrived.

My dogs showed their wriggly appreciation when I joined them in their pen and sat at my computer. Soon after we'd left her apartment, Naomi had sent me the photos I'd taken with her camera. I saved those to my computer and then, faster than I'd have thought possible, I found the names "Isis Crabbe" and "Patricia Alayna Aiken" together on the website of a high school on the outskirts of Chicago. Isis Crabbe had been a history teacher at that school for many years, including the four when Patricia had been a student there. There were many mentions of them at school plays, debates, and even dances.

And then, in the archive of their community's local newspaper, I read a headline that made my hair stand up almost as much as Detective Neffting's glued-together comb-over had.

*Senior Suspended Over Plagiarism.*

Immediately, I pictured Isis on Thursday

night in the fire station, telling Patricia she was nothing but a copycat. Patricia had kept her anger tamped down, but I'd seen it smoldering beneath the surface.

Patricia Alayna Aiken had been suspended from school for two weeks after it was determined that the essay she'd attached to her admission application to a prestigious East Coast university was identical to the essay a boy from the same high school had sent. The other student's mother had testified that she had read her son's essay before he sent it.

Patricia, who'd said she had not shown her essay to anyone besides that same boy, had withdrawn her application and attended a community college instead.

The boy, whose name wasn't given, had received a substantial scholarship from the East Coast university.

I found an article listing the postsecondary schools that members of Patricia's high school graduating class were planning to attend. Only one of them was going to that prestigious East Coast university, and his or her name was Heru Crabbe.

Heru, not Hero?

I searched for "Heru" in a naming dictionary. It was a boys' name, a variation of

Horus, an ancient Egyptian god, the son of Isis.

I typed "Heru Crabbe" into my search engine and an obituary popped up. Heru Crabbe had attended most of a semester at that East Coast school, but had died suddenly about a year after the plagiarism scandal. He'd been predeceased by his father, and would be greatly missed by his mother, Isis Crabbe.

I phoned Vicki and left her a message that I'd found information linking Isis to someone I'd seen Isis scold.

While I waited to hear from Vicki, I searched for the name Isis Crabbe associated with Madame Juliette. To my surprise, I lucked out again. They were both listed on several sites listing schedules for psychic festivals, craft fairs, and bridal shows.

Bridal shows? How odd.

Isis must have encountered Madame Juliette telling fortunes at these events, and that's why she had accused Juliette of making things up. Would Juliette have murdered because of that accusation? It didn't seem likely, but I wasn't going to discount it.

Vicki came in. The dogs greeted her with kisses, wags, and friendly yips.

I showed her the articles linking Patricia and Isis. After she'd had time to read and absorb them, I reminded her, "Patricia and Isis squabbled almost immediately when they ran into each other at the fire station on Thursday."

Vicki only gave me a blank stare.

I explained, "Like they already knew and disliked each other. Hated each other, in fact."

Vicki darted a glance up toward my bright white cathedral ceiling and then back to me. "Okay, I'll grant you that the two women in these articles probably didn't like each other. But we don't know if they are our Isis and the Patricia who is staying with Opal. And even if we *knew* they were the same two women, what you've found is known as . . ." Watching my face, she tapped the toe of one of her police issue boots on my beautiful black walnut floor.

"Circumstantial evidence," I supplied. "Yes. And here's more circumstantial evidence — the person I saw skulking behind my yard right before Isis was killed was about Patricia's height, and was wearing dark slacks and a dark jacket. Later that night, Patricia was wearing jeans and a matching jean jacket."

Vicki reminded me, "You've been insisting that this skulker was a man. You also guessed it could be a zombie named Floyd or Clay's cousin, Dare Drayton."

"They all had means and opportunity," I pointed out. "Everyone did. Isis got into this big heavy skirt with wheels on it, and anyone could have pushed her down the hill and tied a ribbon from the skirt around her neck. And they had motive, too. Floyd didn't want her cursing him. Maybe Dare killed Isis in order to see what murdering someone was like, so he could add authenticity to his thrillers."

"That's pretty cold-blooded," Vicki observed.

"So is Dare, as far as I can tell. And Floyd is hot-blooded."

"A hot-blooded zombie," Vicki repeated in mock wonder. "That could be one for the record books."

I tapped my computer screen. "*Patricia*, however, had a strong motive."

"Could you e-mail those links to me?" In my humble opinion, Vicki could have sounded more impressed by my deductions about Patricia. "I doubt that they mean anything, but I'll forward them to Detective Neffting." She spouted her e-mail address for me.

As I added the links to the e-mail, I reminded her, "Patricia should be at the Threadville craft show right now."

"Detective Neffting is handling the case. He'll decide what to do with the info. There's not much here, really. Nothing concrete."

"Yes, but —"

She adjusted the heavy belt she wore around her waist. "*Maybe* we'll find something to bolster this evidence about Ms. Aiken that will lead somewhere, but only maybe. 'We' being the police, Willow, not you."

"I wasn't interfering. I just looked on the Internet for a connection between Patricia and Isis based on the way they treated each other." Vicki didn't need to know how I'd learned Patricia's full name.

"But you already told me that Isis yelled at nearly everyone shortly before she was murdered. Who, again?"

"In addition to Patricia? Dare, Floyd, Brianna, and Juliette the fortune-teller."

"And you. She scolded you for trying on Edna's overskirt."

I waved my hand in dismissal. "That woman had a hair-trigger temper."

"I noticed." Usually, Vicki used that dry tone when she was about to say something scathing or funny or both. "She told me off — yelled at me, actually — for pulling her over for speeding."

I gulped down a laugh. "No! Who would do something like that?"

"A very angry person. Maybe someone whose husband and son died young."

"I wonder if Isis or Patricia had anything to do with either of those earlier deaths," I began.

Vicki shook her head. "Don't even start thinking like that, or about how anyone in Elderberry Bay could have been one of their accomplices way back when or *anything*. Leave investigating to the experts."

I confessed, "I found something else."

She demanded, "What did I just tell you?"

"It's only something I discovered on the Internet." I switched to the website of an annual psychic festival. "Someone named Madame Juliette has been telling fortunes at festivals where Isis has been . . . hmm." I read aloud, " 'Exploring ancient Egyptian beliefs.' And I found them both on sites for craft fairs and bridal shows, too, though I'm not sure what those types of shows have to do with ancient Egyptian curses and fortune-telling."

Vicki reminded me that both Isis and Madame Juliette had come to Threadville for our Get Ready for Halloween Craft Fair. "Apparently some people spend almost their entire lives doing these events, one after another, picking up whatever income they can at them. There's a whole circuit of the shows, with the same booths in many of them." She gave me the name of the company that sponsored many of shows. Not ours, though. We'd organized it ourselves.

Excited, I loaded that company's website. "Maybe Patricia's on their list of exhibitors." I ran my finger down their list of regular exhibitors, but had to admit that I didn't see Patricia's name.

"We didn't, either," Vicki said. "As far as we know, this is Patricia's first foray into the craft show world."

"Aha! Because she saw on our website that Isis was coming? And Patricia was planning revenge for the way Isis and her son treated her in high school!"

Vicki shook her head. "Your imagination's running overtime again, Willow. Maybe Patricia signed up for your craft show because it has something to do with her subject?"

"It does, more than Isis or Juliette's, but treadle sewing machines aren't exactly a big thing. She could have come here to track down Isis."

"Anything's possible, but that doesn't make it evidence." Vicki stood still for a second as if listening, then asked me, "Where's your houseguest?"

"Not in my house, thank goodness. She should be at the craft fair. Her stuff's still in my guest room."

"What did you do, go down and turn off her stereo?"

"You got it."

"Maybe you should turn off all the circuit breakers to your guest suite, and she'll give up and leave."

I could tell she was joking, but it wasn't a bad idea. Maybe I could turn off the water to her bathroom, too, but then she might decide to use mine.

Vicki said more seriously, "I have a question for you."

## 30

Vicki flipped pages back in her notebook. "Willow, do you know a Mrs. Battleaxe?"

I burst out laughing. "No, but I know a Mrs. Battersby. Battleaxe might describe her, except that she knits tiny perfect sweaters and caps for premature babies and sends them to hospitals."

"Must be the same person, then. As you know, before Brianna recanted her accusations against you, she called her father. Todd Shrevedale called a bigwig in the Pennsylvania State Police, who sent a couple of troopers out to talk to you. Meanwhile, Brianna told her father she was mistaken, and it wasn't you who had pushed her, but although she wasn't certain about it, she thought someone had."

"Wait," I objected. "Didn't she tell you she must have tripped?"

"Yep. The girl was spinning her story for her father. Those two troopers decided that since Isis was pushed into the water, maybe we were having an epidemic. So they helpfully called Detective Neffting with this new 'evidence' of a serial water-shover and asked him who else Brianna might have seen. He named Haylee."

I covered my mouth to hide a smile. I thought I saw where this was heading.

Vicki had a way of turning the corners of her mouth down when she was trying to hide amusement. "So they went to Haylee's apartment and pounded on the door, and were met by this Mrs. Battleaxe. She was still up and dressed, and she said she'd been knitting in Haylee's living room the entire evening, and that Haylee had not come out of her bedroom. She was quite defensive of Haylee."

My eyebrows shot up all by themselves.

"Does that surprise you?" Vicki asked.

"A little. Mrs. Battersby is a bit of a character. She's Edna's mother, and she complains that Haylee doesn't act like a real granddaughter, all the while pointing out that Haylee is *not* her real granddaughter. Edna's been staying with Haylee, too, until the state police are done with her apartment. They're going to have to let Edna into her apartment by Monday, though, so she can get her wedding dress and everything that goes with it."

"I'll tell them to hurry and release the scene. As I told Brianna early this morning, they've already taken Isis's things away."

I asked, straight-faced, "Did, um, did those two troopers accuse Mrs. Battersby of pushing Brianna into the lake?"

When I'd first met Vicki, I'd have never believed she could have a twinkle in her eye, but she did now. "It must have crossed their minds. They interrogated her about where she'd been all night." She shook her head. "Too bad I was off duty and didn't know they were going there. I'd have loved to have witnessed the discussion. I gather that Mrs. Battersby became quite, um, animated."

"Feisty?"

The twinkle was still there. "They did report that her name was 'Mrs. Battleaxe.' "

I said, "I still believe Brianna immersed herself in the lake and intended to blame me, but I don't know why." I urged Vicki to be careful around Brianna. "If her father's as powerful as we think he is, he could cause you trouble."

"What sort of trouble?"

"I don't know, but he might try to end your career in law enforcement."

"Then I'll take up sewing," she teased.

"Oh, please, and leave Mrs. Battersby to

the tender mercies of earnest state troopers?"

"I'm sure they're trying to do a great job. They don't know her or any of you, though."

I suggested, "And the fact that you *do* can be used against you. Brianna complained about it to you and me last night, and told my mother that you and I were friends."

Vicki gave me one of the icy, stern looks she'd perfected long before I met her. "Don't kid yourself, Willow. I'd arrest you if circumstances warranted it." She pocketed her notebook and pen. "And there have been times when I've wished they did."

I made my grin devilish. "That's why I like you so much. You're not biased toward us or against us. You're good at what you do."

"I'm getting out of here before I puke." She pointed a finger at me. "You be careful. If you really can't upset your mother by sending that girl away, keep her locked out of your room when you're sleeping. And be sure to call me or the state police if you need us." With more admonitions and cautions, she left.

Because my customers were at the craft show and not in my store, I had no problems giving my pets a midday outing and fixing a sandwich to eat in the shop. The afternoon could have dragged, but fortunately, I had plenty of embroidery to design and stitch.

Shortly before closing time, Georgina showed up in a burnt-orange outfit with machine-embroidered pumpkins and vines over most of it. She handed me the receipts from our table at the craft fair.

I praised her for the amount of merchandise she and Ashley had sold. "Was the fair crowded?"

"Was it ever! Zombies were selling costumes and other things I didn't want to know about. Also, that woo-woo woman, Juliette, was offering to use a crystal ball to tell fortunes, and that poor scared mouse of a thing, Patricia, was demonstrating using a treadle sewing machine to make Halloween costumes. Zombies were shopping, too. They loved Edna's spangles and baubles, which are lovely, but don't have much to do with zombies as far as I can tell. Lots of potential customers picked up your brochures and said they wanted to sign up for machine embroidery workshops." Her forehead wrinkled. "And that thriller writer was there."

I said drily, "Not to sign up for Threadville courses, I suspect."

Georgina flicked invisible lint from her burnt-orange top. "He said he was researching characters. He seemed particularly interested in that thread distributor, Brianna, and the shy Patricia with the antique sewing machines." She gazed past me, out toward the trees beyond the back windows. "But you should have seen the way he looked at them, at all of us. Like we were mice in a maze he'd built, with poison hidden in the peanut butter." She shuddered. "He creeps me out, mainly because of that presentation he gave last night. He read from his latest book, and his writing's okay — not my style — but he also talked about committing the perfect crime. I had this strong feeling that he was talking about actually doing it, not only about writing about it. He said . . ." We were alone in the store with my two dogs, but she leaned closer and lowered her voice. "He said that people *often* get away with murder by making the death appear either natural or like an accident."

Isis's death could have looked like an accident if we hadn't found her quickly. If I hadn't been outside at the right moment and heard her scream, the killer could have had time to shove the trailing extension cord under the water, and we might not have guessed that Isis and the skirt were in the river. We might have surmised that she had left Threadville for a few days and that the skirt had been stolen. I'd seen her down by the riverbank earlier that evening, but if no one had figured out for days that she was missing, we might have taken a long time to drag the river, and by then, the ribbon around her neck could have drifted off in the currents, and her death could have possibly been ruled an accident.

Georgina went on, "Dare Drayton also said that if anyone was planning a murder, they should know who to frame as a scapegoat, preferably a person who had means, motive, and *no* alibi." She folded her arms and gave me an expectant look.

A thousand ideas crowded into my head.

She voiced one of them. "It was like he was bragging that he had killed that Isis woman and would get away with it because someone *else* would look guilty." She took a deep breath. "Isn't Dare Drayton your boyfriend's cousin?"

"Clay's only a friend." I'd recited it so many times, mostly to myself, that it sounded rehearsed. "And yes, Dare is his second cousin. He's staying with Clay."

Georgina planted her fists on her hips. "I hope your *friend* Clay sleeps with a hammer, a saw, and five drills underneath his pillow."

I laughed.

She scolded, "And you should, too, Willow. I don't trust that Brianna."

"Sleeping with a bunch of hardware doesn't sound comfortable."

"Being attacked in the night by some sly thread distributor doesn't sound comfortable, either."

"What's she going to do, pelt me with spools of thread?" I waved toward the dogs. "Lucky thing I have my guard dogs." Sally and Tally grinned and wagged their tails.

Georgina called to them, "You hear that, you two fluffy guys? Try to look dangerous." After she left, I locked the front door and swept and tidied the shop. Humming, I took the dogs downstairs, where we had a joyful reunion with Mustache and Bow-Tie. The animals scampered outside. Sally and I managed to keep the kittens from wandering off.

After we were all inside again, I put pieces of chicken in a ginger and lime zest marinade.

Knowing I wouldn't have time to make dessert for tonight's barbecue, I had ordered cupcakes from the bakery. I ran down the street and picked them up. The evening was warm. Haylee, Ben, Clay, and I could spend at least part of the evening outside on the patio. With candles hinting at romance . . .

Back home again, I threw together a couple of large salads and put the cupcakes, decorated with sugary autumn leaves, on a platter.

Setting the picnic table on the patio was fun. I used dishes and real fall flowers that coordinated with the flowers I had embroidered on my napkins and tablecloth.

I was setting the candles on the table when Haylee arrived in my backyard.

With Mrs. Battersby.

## 31

Haylee gave me an apologetic look, but I welcomed Mrs. Battersby with a smile widened by the memory of how Vicki, probably on purpose, had mangled the woman's name. Luckily, I'd prepared more than enough food for the four of us plus Mrs. Battersby, and Brianna, too, if she showed up.

Mrs. Battersby plunked herself into a lawn chair near the grill. "What was going on last night? Why did those state troopers come by in the middle of the night and demand to know where Haylee had been, and then where *I* had been?"

"What?" Haylee asked.

"Calm down," Mrs. Battersby told her. "They didn't have a search warrant and I wouldn't let them into your apartment. The nerve of them! You were sound asleep, and I didn't want to bother you today while you were at work to tell you about it. They claimed they were searching for someone who looked like Willow. Me? Were they having hallucinations?"

I glanced across her head at Haylee. "It was a false alarm." I flicked my eyes toward my suite.

Haylee must have understood that I didn't want to discuss it in front of Mrs. Battersby. She said, "I told Edna's mother you'd be glad to have us both come for dinner."

I smiled again at Mrs. Battersby. "I am."

Mrs. Battersby retrieved a tiny, partially knit sweater from her bag. "I told Haylee I could fend for myself, or go over and bother Edna."

I asked, "Is Edna allowed in her apartment?"

Haylee nodded. "Yes. She has about five thousand more beads to sew on her gown. She was getting nervous about packing for the cruise, too."

Mrs. Battersby growled, "Don't tell me I'm supposed to have one of those heart-to-heart, mother-to-daughter talks with her about the birds and the bees!"

Haylee and I both laughed.

Mrs. Battersby glared at us. "Your generation can probably inform her generation about that, and everything else. Like phones. Whoever said that *phones* needed to be smart? How's anyone supposed to cope with phones that know more than we do? What next?" Her hands moved the yarn and needles with lightning speed. "But don't worry about feeding me, Willow. I don't need to eat."

"I made lots," I said, "and I'm glad you came." I studied her knitting. Each of the sweaters she made was different, but they were beautiful and original, and they combined colors that looked great together. This one reminded me of a misty summer dawn over Lake Erie. "I can use your color sense and ideas for my cottage design."

Mrs. Battersby sat up straighter. "Design?"

"Yes." I explained, "You met Clay when we showed you the wedding skirt —"

"That thing!"

I ignored Mrs. Battersby's outburst. "He built the base and wired it for sound and lights —"

Mrs. Battersby shook her head. "Tsk."

I soldiered on. "Clay and his friend Ben are coming to dinner tonight. Haylee and Clay planned the renovations to Haylee's shop and apartment, and to Opal's, Naomi's, and Edna's shops and apartments." I pointed toward my apartment. "My building, too. And Clay and Ben worked together to restore and renovate Ben's lodge. Haylee and I helped Ben decide which vintage photos to hang, so I've asked all three of them to come tonight and make suggestions about my cottage's design." I nodded to Blueberry Cottage, slightly downhill from my patio.

Mrs. Battersby adjusted her glasses and peered at it. "Ha. It looks like it was designed a long time ago."

"It was," I agreed, "but Clay gutted it, winterized it, and updated the wiring and plumbing."

Mrs. Battersby turned a little sleeve and started a new row. "I wanted to be an architect, but I didn't have the gumption to go for all that schooling. I did interior design, instead. Edna didn't inherit my taste." She shuddered. "Have you seen her apartment? You need welding goggles just to walk through the door. It's all mirrors and crystals and shiny things."

Haylee's smile was nearly as bright as Edna's mirrors. "We've seen it."

I bit back a giggle. "Perfect for a bride on her *weld*ing day."

Haylee groaned.

Mrs. Battersby demanded, "What does she do, stare at herself in those mirrors all day? I didn't intend to raise a vain daughter. Or maybe she believes she's living in Versailles. And Naomi should think beyond quilted things. It's like she has to decorate with rags and tatters. Opal's the only one of the three of them with good, solid, classical taste." Mrs. Battersby looked up at Haylee. "You've got that minimalist style down pat, but it's so hard and cold, I don't know how you can stand it. Sterile."

I told her, "I love the clean lines of Haylee's apartment."

Mrs. Battersby frowned. "I suppose yours is just like it."

"No, Haylee knows my taste — uncluttered, with touches of wood, and matching the Arts and Crafts style of the building's exterior. Haylee got Clay to renovate my apartment and shop the way I would like them before I even saw them or knew they existed."

Mrs. Battersby began casting off. "What a strange thing to do."

"The shop and apartment," I corrected myself. "I knew Haylee existed."

"It worked," Haylee crowed. "Willow came to live and open a shop in Threadville."

Mrs. Battersby harrumphed. "To think I'd end up with a devious granddaughter. Not that she's a *real* granddaughter."

Grinning, Haylee patted her shoulder.

"You should be used to me by now."

Mrs. Battersby offered to go inside with Haylee and me to help retrieve the appetizers, but I told her to stay put and keep knitting.

In the kitchen, I quickly brought Haylee up to date on Brianna's latest antics, which had sent a pair of state troopers scurrying to her door in the wee hours only to be blockaded by Mrs. Battersby. During the dozen years that Haylee and I been friends, I'd confided lots about my mother and my occasionally stormy relationship with her. Haylee understood why I couldn't kick Brianna out, even though I wanted to.

I also told Haylee what I'd learned about Patricia and Isis Crabbe's son, Heru.

"Wow," she said. "False accusations from Brianna, and Patricia must harbor a huge grudge against Isis. We'd better keep our eyes on both of those women."

"And Juliette and Isis have been attending the same shows and fairs for several years, so who knows what run-ins they may have had." I also told Haylee what Georgina had said about Dare's presentation.

"I wouldn't put murder past that man," Haylee said, "even if he is related to Clay."

"The person I saw sneaking around that night could have been Dare, Floyd, Patricia, or Juliette. But if the skulker wasn't the murderer, I hope the *real* investigators have Brianna in their sights."

Haylee and I took platters of veggies, dip, crackers, and cheese to the table. Mrs. Battersby tucked her knitting away, and we all slathered Brie on crackers.

Whistling, Clay appeared around the corner, with Ben right behind him.

Mrs. Battersby's eyes opened wide. "Don't tell me that handsome dark-eyed giant with Clay is the Ben fellow you were talking about."

I bent down and whispered to Mrs. Battersby, "Yep, that's Ben." Imagining her saying something embarrassing, I quickly added, "They're just our friends."

Both men handed me bottles of wine. Clay ruffled my hair.

"Just *friends*," Mrs. Battersby muttered. I was sure Clay heard.

I quickly told Ben, "I'm glad you could get away. The lodge must be busy."

His laugh was warm, and so was his deep voice. "I feel like I've seen enough zombies to last a lifetime."

Haylee clutched at her face and staggered backward. "That doesn't sound quite right."

Ben gave her a huge smile. "I suppose it doesn't."

Haylee didn't seem to know she was blushing.

I asked Clay to light the barbecue. Ben opened both bottles of wine. Wineglasses in hand, he and Clay waved tongs over the chicken on the grill.

As the chicken began sending mouth-watering aromas our way, Brianna straggled down through my side yard. The dogs romped to her. Glaring at them and keeping her hands out of their reach, she asked me, "What's for dinner?"

I told her and offered her a glass of wine. Ungraciously, she accepted.

Mrs. Battersby sat straighter. "Not long ago, young lady, children were taught to say 'thank you' when someone did something for them."

"Yeah." Brianna didn't look at any of us. "Thanks."

Mrs. Battersby stared at Brianna for long moments, then asked me, "Do we have time to tour your cottage before supper? Afterward, it could be too dark to see." She turned her attention to Clay. "Or have you already installed lights inside it, young man?"

He gave her an easy smile, the kind that warmed his eyes and had to make her feel special. "Not the final ones. Willow still has some decisions to make. And the chicken won't be ready for a while. What do you say, Willow?" His gaze landed on me with an amused fondness that made me forget to breathe.

"Sure," I managed. "It won't take long."

Mrs. Battersby stood up. "Let's go."

I was beginning to understand where Edna had inherited her enthusiasm.

We trooped down to the door that faced my apartment. I tended to think of it as the cottage's back door, which meant the back doors of my two buildings faced each other. It seemed confusing until I remembered that the back doors of houses in cities and towns often faced each other. The riverside trail had been a road when Elderberry Bay was first established. Blueberry Cottage's front door faced the former road and the river. My shop faced the next street up the hill, Lake Street.

Brianna hadn't come with us. I didn't see her at the picnic table, either.

Mentally shrugging, I opened the door, and we followed Sally and Tally inside.

The subflooring inside was lower than the doorstep. "Take my arm, Mrs. Battersby," Ben offered.

She complained, "It's too high."

He leaned toward her and lowered his arm.

Mrs. Battersby hooked her arm through his. A look of appreciation flickered across her face. "It has good bones."

Haylee gasped, *"What?"*

Mischief sparked from Mrs. Battersby's eyes. "You thought I meant this giant's arm, didn't you? That, too, but I was looking at his head. Above his head, actually. This cottage, Willow. It has good bones. You can do a lot with it. You and your young man there."

"My contractor," I supplied, ignoring Clay's wink and Haylee and Ben's smiles.

"So," she said, "you've roughed in the kitchen here beside the back door, and a fireplace against that wall." She scanned that half of the cottage. "Which leaves the area overlooking the river as the sitting area?" She turned again, gestured toward the window near the door we'd entered, and spoke rapidly. "An L-shaped kitchen counter there underneath the back and side windows, a dining table in front of the fireplace, and a couch maybe here, where people can sit and look out at the river and your flower border and cedar hedge, and they can also gaze at the fireplace while keeping an eye on the kitchen."

"Works for me," I said.

"And speaking of working, how about a table or desk under this window beside the fireplace? And lots of bookshelves and storage cabinets that you can close to keep dust and moths away from the books and yarn."

*Yarn?*

I hadn't said it aloud, but my eyebrows must have zoomed upward.

Mrs. Battersby waved her arm dismissively. "Or games and jigsaw puzzles. Whatever people keep in their cottages. For me, it would be books and yarn."

She tromped into what used to be the kitchen, with one window overlooking the river and another facing the northern side yard. "Windows on all four sides! Lovely! Lots of natural light." She checked out the back wall. "Aha. I see you've roughed in a bathroom. So that means the rest of this space becomes a bedroom, am I right? With a wall right about here." Standing in approximately the middle of the cottage, she tapped a foot. Tally barked.

Clay gave her a lazy grin. "Um, not quite there. Willow wanted this original feature of the cottage kept, and it is rather necessary." He reached up to the low ceiling and unhooked a latch.

He didn't even have to lower the stairs before Mrs. Battersby clapped her hands. "I see why! That's not your common, everyday attic ladder, either. Those are almost normal stairs. They must be heavy."

"They are," Clay said, "but the original builder counterbalanced them, so they feel lighter than they are." With only one finger underneath them, he let them down.

"Show off," Haylee teased.

Mrs. Battersby peered up the stairs. "What's up there?"

I answered, "Two small bedrooms, each with a closet and two windows. The windows are flush with the floor, which makes the cottage look bigger from outside."

"It's like a doll house." Mrs. Battersby spoke with something like admiration. "Your tenants can fasten those stairs up against the ceiling whenever they don't want to heat the whole place, or lower them if they have overnight guests or want to use the second story themselves. They could use those rooms upstairs as offices or workrooms if they wanted to. Then they wouldn't need a desk by the fireplace. Actually . . ." She looked wistful. "A spinning wheel would go beside the hearth very nicely. And who needs a big dining table? If you had a small one, you could fit a floor loom in front of the fireplace."

She lifted her chin and gazed at Clay. "Do

you have drawings of this place? Could you give me a copy so I can sketch my ideas?"

"Glad to," he said.

Brianna popped her head around the doorjamb. "Yuck. You were right, Willow. This shack's unlivable. Just so you know, the chicken's burning."

Wagging their tails, Sally and Tally bounced toward her.

She shrieked and ran away. Naturally, Sally and Tally followed. I called them, and they came back for praise.

We all left.

Mrs. Battersby watched me lock the door. "You should finish that cottage," she told me. "And rent it out. What're you waiting for?"

"I would . . . um . . . I'd like to see *your* sketches before I make decisions."

"It should be comfy," she went on, "like Opal's apartment, not modern and minimalistic and sterile like Haylee's. It needs to reflect its Victorian roots. I read an article in an architectural magazine about a hotel around here that was recently restored. The writer said the people who restored it did an exceptional job. You should go see it and emulate what they did. Help me up the hill, Ben." She grabbed Ben's arm.

An impish glint in her eyes, Haylee asked,

"The Elderberry Bay Lodge?"

Mrs. Battersby snapped her fingers. "That's it. That's the one."

I couldn't help telling her, "That's where Edna's rehearsal dinner is tomorrow night. And her wedding the following day."

"Ha," Mrs. Battersby said. "That man she's marrying must have drummed some sense into her."

Haylee told her, "And Ben owns the Elderberry Lodge."

Ben smiled down at Mrs. Battersby. "And Clay was my contractor, and my design consultant. He's done most of the new work around Elderberry Bay."

"With a lot of help from my employees," Clay said. "They're the best."

"Well, then," Mrs. Battersby said with satisfaction, "we should be able to do a bang-up job on this cottage, then."

*We?*

## 32

Leaving Ben, Haylee, and Clay to help Mrs. Battersby climb the hill, I charged to the barbecue to rescue the chicken that Brianna had said was burning. Brianna was holding the barbecue lid open and giving the cooking meat a disgusted look.

It wasn't burning. It was perfect and smelled delicious. I thanked her for reminding us. Saying nothing, she turned away.

Haylee, Ben and Clay helped me serve. Mrs. Battersby ended up between Ben and Haylee. Brianna sat between Clay and me. Not quite the romantic seating arrangement I had envisioned.

Worse, Mrs. Battersby watched Brianna's every move and commented whenever Brianna's manners were less than perfect, which was most of the meal. Mrs. Battersby may have thought she was being subtle. Haylee kept putting a cautionary hand on her wrist.

Mrs. Battersby snatched her arm away. "Why are you patting me as if I'm some doddering old auntie? I'm way too young to be your grandmother, anyway."

Haylee looked more amused than contrite. "Sorry."

On the other side of Mrs. Battersby from Haylee, Ben grinned across the table at me.

Brianna didn't stay for dessert. She threw her napkin down on her plate and stalked inside.

"Well," said Mrs. Battersby. "I don't know why you don't try to teach that girl some etiquette, Willow. It's not like you're entirely lacking it yourself."

"Thanks," I managed.

By eight thirty, it was dark and becoming chilly, but we all stubbornly stayed outside with our coffee and cupcakes until Ben and Clay said they'd have to leave soon, and insisted on helping carry our dessert plates and coffee mugs inside.

Her knitting bag in one hand and her mug in the other, Mrs. Battersby came, too. She examined my great room. "Very nice. You do have decent taste." She frowned. "What's that dreadful racket?"

I shrugged. "Brianna likes her music." For once, my phone light wasn't on. Maybe Brianna had heard enough of the weather forecast for Sydney, Australia.

Mrs. Battersby glared at Brianna's door. "Well, if I were you, I'd tell her to turn it off."

My mouth twisted.

Mrs. Battersby conceded, "I suppose that would just make her turn it up louder."

I pointed to my comfy couch. "Turn on the lamp, and you can sit down and knit."

"I'm not as ancient as you two girls seem to think I am." She put her knitting on the couch and then helped with the cleanup.

When the kitchen sparkled again, Ben and Clay headed for the patio door. "Are you folks coming later?" Ben asked us.

"Where?" Mrs. Battersby asked.

Clay answered with a nicely straight face. "The Haunted Graveyard."

Mrs. Battersby demanded, "Why would you want to go to a haunted graveyard? Halloween's over three weeks away. Not that it makes any difference. A graveyard sounds like a perfect way to ruin an otherwise decent evening."

Clay and Ben laughed, and Ben explained, "Tonight's the last big event of the zombie retreat at the Elderberry Bay Lodge, and the public's invited. Clay rigged up a graveyard. It's going to be amazing."

"Clay rigged up a graveyard at *your* lodge,

Ben?" Mrs. Battersby asked.

"Yep."

"And you both seemed like such nice young men!"

They smiled down at her.

"Seemed?" Clay asked.

"There was that foolish wedding skirt rig, too. But Ben almost passes muster." Mrs. Battersby turned to Haylee. "And that's where my daughter is having her wedding? In a haunted graveyard?"

"Not exactly," Haylee began.

"The graveyard's behind the lodge, in the woods," Clay said.

"The wedding will be in front of the lodge, near the beach," Ben added. "Edna chose a beautiful spot."

"Outside?" Mrs. Battersby was very good at subtle or not-so-subtle objections. "What if it rains?"

"It's not supposed to," Ben answered. "But just in case, we've set up a huge white tent on the front lawn. The reception will be in our banquet hall."

"Which is also lovely," I commented, "with a wall of glass doors overlooking the lawns, the beach, and the lake."

Mrs. Battersby grumbled, "Weddings in graveyards, or almost. I always said that daughter of mine lived in a fantasy world.

Take me back to your place, Haylee. We'll need to dress more warmly if we're going to spend half the night outside."

"I'll be along in a minute," I said. "As soon as I settle my pets for the evening."

Mrs. Battersby grabbed her knitting bag. "Put on a sweater, Willow." She latched onto Ben's elbow. "You can help me up Willow's steep hill."

Clay sent me a lopsided grin. "I don't know if I'll see you at the Haunted Graveyard, Willow. Ben and I will be working behind the scenes, but maybe we'll run into you."

Trying not to show my disappointment, I nodded.

Clay and Haylee followed Mrs. Battersby and her conquest out the door.

I changed into warmer clothes, grabbed a jacket, shut my pets into my suite, and left.

Running up through the side yard, I grinned to myself. I was dressed all in black, the way Haylee and I often dressed when we didn't want to be noticed checking on things at night. Subconsciously, I must have felt I'd be safer in a haunted graveyard at a zombie retreat if I could fade into the darkness.

Haylee must have thought the same thing. She had also changed into black slacks and sweater. Mrs. Battersby was beside her, in black jeans and a bulky red and gray Nordic sweater with bright white zigzags around the neck and shoulder.

"Did you make that gorgeous sweater?" I asked her.

"This old thing? A long time ago."

She must have made it before the days of glow-in-the-dark yarn, or the zigzags could have been even more visible at night.

We walked toward my car. I cautioned the other two that we should stay together all evening.

Mrs. Battersby stated, "I'm not walking around any haunted graveyard by myself. But if your two hunks finish whatever they have to do, they can protect us."

Haylee helped Mrs. Battersby into the passenger seat. "Don't go off without one of us or one of them along."

Mrs. Battersby responded, "Tell that to each other!"

Haylee and I clambered into the car.

I'd barely pulled out onto Lake Street when Mrs. Battersby informed Haylee, "If you want that mountain to look at you, you're going to have to stop being so bashful."

*Haylee, bashful?* I turned my face toward the mirror on my side to hide a smile.

Haylee answered gently from the backseat. "Ben was widowed a couple of years ago. I don't think he'll be interested in another woman for a very long time."

"Horse feathers," Mrs. Battersby said. "He can mourn her and still fall for another woman."

Haylee reached over the seat and patted the older woman's shoulder. "You're right. He's already fallen for you."

Mrs. Battersby sniffed. "Horse feathers with apples on top." I could tell by the light of the dash that her smile was quite smug.

I sped the car along Shore Road's dips and curves, and turned down a narrower road sloping toward the lake.

Mrs. Battersby leaned forward and read the sign for the Elderberry Bay Lodge. "So we're really going to wander around in a graveyard with a bunch of zombies, one of whom may have already killed a woman this week?"

"Don't worry," I told her. "Zombies don't need to push someone into a river. They can simply chow down."

Haylee laughed and admitted, "Those zombies can be pretty scary, even though I know they're only people in costumes and makeup."

I teased, "Luckily, we're here to be

scared."

"And not to do any sleuthing," Haylee said.

I agreed, "We would never do such a thing."

"Why not?" Mrs. Battersby asked. "Doesn't either of you have a backbone?"

Uh-oh. We were going to have to keep a close eye on Edna's mother.

I conceded, "We'll tell Vicki if we see or hear anything that would help her solve the case —"

"Vicki?" Mrs. Battersby asked.

"Chief Smallwood," Haylee explained. "But she's not the lead investigator. Detective Neffting is."

"I'd rather help Vicki," I said.

Haylee agreed, "I would, too."

"Is she a state trooper?" Mrs. Battersby asked.

I explained, "She used to be, but now she's the police chief of Elderberry Bay."

"Also known as Threadville." Did I detect pride in Mrs. Battersby's voice? "Then I'd rather help her, too, unless she's the one who sent those two goofs to Haylee's apartment last night."

I assured her that Vicki hadn't even known they were going there.

The lodge parking lot was nearly full. I

pulled into one of the last spaces, next to the tour bus that Rosemary usually drove. She must have brought a load of people from Erie to attend both the craft fair and the Haunted Graveyard.

A sign painted in what looked like dripping blood said *Haunted Graveyard* and pointed toward a fog-shrouded cobblestone pathway. I glanced down beyond the lodge and the big white wedding tent to the lodge's beach. Not even a wisp of mist. The zombies had to be running a fog machine near the path.

Mrs. Battersby unfastened her seat belt. "This will be fun."

I opened the driver's door. "If someone chases us, we'll go hide in the lodge. Together."

From the back seat, Haylee spoke in a voice of doom. "The lodge could be full of ravenous zombies."

Outside the car, we had to run to keep up with Mrs. Battersby.

The rising moon peeked between trees on the hill, but except for creeping fingers of fog, the pathway in front of us was dark. Farther ahead, small lights like red fireflies darted between trees. Unmoving shapes on the wooded hill could have been gravestones or zombies crouching on the ground.

Last I knew, that hillside had been a smooth lawn with trees on it.

A female zombie jumped menacingly out from behind drooping branches.

## 33

The zombie could have been a 1950s house-wife in a prim dress and frilly apron if she hadn't had gobs of fake — I hoped — blood dripping from somewhere beneath her lace-trimmed collar.

She pointed to a table tucked in under the bush's branches. "Take a light," she urged in a raspy voice. "If a zombie aims his teeth at you, shine a red light in his face."

We reached for the small flashlights.

Growling, the zombie lunged toward us. Her open mouth and her dead eyes looked starved.

Mrs. Battersby took a threatening step toward the zombie. Haylee and I picked up the lights, flicked them on, and shined them at the zombie's face, though we avoided her eyes. Baring her teeth and blinking, the zombie backed away.

Still shining my dim red light toward her lower face, I asked "What do you want?"

"How did you know we have to answer honestly when you shine a red light on our teeth? That's supposed to be a secret known only by the brotherhood of zombies. Did someone betray us?"

I played along. "Nope, I just guessed."

She came closer. "You're a zombie."

"No."

"Then in answer to your question, what I want, what we all want, is meat." She gnashed her teeth together. "Fresh, human meat. Why not turn off those lights?" she encouraged in 1950s housewifely tones. "You can be zombies, too." She cocked her ear. "Aha. Go away. You three are too wily for me. I hear another possible meal coming."

Footsteps hit the paved parking lot. The 1950s housewife zombie melted into the bushes.

Laughing, we hurried along the pathway toward the festivities.

Mrs. Battersby reassured us, "It's all harmless."

Staring up the hill, Haylee stopped as if transfixed. "Look at what Clay built! That wasn't there before."

The building was a small, neat rectangle with a peaked roof, double front doors underneath an arched window, and tall windows flanking the doors. The original design could have been based on an ancient Roman or Greek temple. The doors were closed, the windows shuttered.

Mrs. Battersby raised both arms as if to embrace the faraway building. "It's the Evans City Cemetery chapel!" She lowered her arms. "Not really. It must be only a quarter the size of the real one."

"What's the Evans City Cemetery chapel?" Haylee asked.

Mrs. Battersby turned to us and demanded, "Haven't you ever been there? Evans City isn't far from here. It's south of Butler and north of Pittsburgh. The opening scene of *Night of the Living Dead* was filmed in the Evans City Cemetery, near the chapel."

We both merely stared at her.

"You're not horror fans?" she asked.

What other surprising interests did Edna's mother have? I told her, "I know the movie is about zombies, the living dead. I didn't know there was a local connection."

Haylee added, "We'll have to make a trek down there sometime."

I lowered my voice and muttered, "If we survive tonight."

But everything looked innocent. People in street clothes laughed and called to each

other as they wandered through the graveyard shining red flashlights on Clay's replica
chapel and on wood and cardboard painted
to resemble gravestones. We stopped to read
inscriptions. Even Mrs. Battersby chortled
over silly puns the zombies must have created in their spare time.

Suddenly, Haylee grabbed my arm. "I
can't believe it," she whispered. "Dare Drayton is here. I would have thought this
evening's entertainment would have been
beneath him."

Tall and dark in his black slacks, turtleneck, jacket, and loafers, Dare had emerged
from a break in a rhododendron hedge near
the lodge's porte cochere.

"Who's Dare Drayton?" Mrs. Battersby
asked.

"Clay's cousin," I answered.

"Can't be," Mrs. Battersby said. "Clay's a
nice young man. That man is . . . not."

I slanted a glance down at her. "You can
tell from here? In the dark?"

"You bet."

"Who's with him?" I murmured.

Haylee brushed her hair away from her
face, as if that would help her see between
ribbons of fog drifting through the inky
night. "Brianna? I thought she was sulking
in your guest suite."

Dare and Brianna angled away from us, up the hill and out of the fog. Dare casually draped one arm across Brianna's shoulders. I snuffled back a laugh. "I feel like I need to protect one of them from the other, but which one?"

"Neither," Mrs. Battersby decided. "They make a good couple. That way, they can't spoil two couples. But isn't he a little old for her?"

Haylee explained, "Her daddy's wealthy."

I added, "But my mother said that Brianna's daddy doesn't support her, so a bestselling thriller author could be just what she needs."

"Awwww," Mrs. Battersby breathed. "True love."

A form jumped out from behind one of the larger tombstones. "Boo!"

Mrs. Battersby lashed out with one hand and shined her flashlight with the other.

Wearing a flowing red gown trimmed in gold braid and a pair of gold sandals I'd seen on the floor of Naomi's closet, Juliette backed out of Mrs. Battersby's reach. "Oops, sorry, I didn't mean to startle you."

Patricia stepped out from behind the next gravestone and laughed. "Couldn't you foretell the future, Juliette, and *know* you were going to startle them?" Patricia was wearing a dark blue shirt, jeans, matching jacket, and sneakers. Her skulking and murdering outfit?

Juliette scowled. "My crystal ball is too heavy to carry around all night."

Although she sounded annoyed, she wasn't looking at Patricia or at the other three of us. She was watching Dare stroll farther up the hill with Brianna.

Patricia followed her glance. "He likes them young, doesn't he?" Was she disappointed? Disapproving? She was only about ten years older than Brianna, but so was Dare.

And so was Juliette. She looked longingly up the hill and said softly, "Dare Drayton must leave broken hearts wherever he goes."

I was going to say something about Brianna being able to look after herself, but the ground suddenly shook with a low roar.

An earthquake?

Mrs. Battersby jumped and shrieked. I reached for her. A rapt expression on her face, she shook me off and concentrated on the chapel.

Its doors exploded open. Expecting flames at the very least, I jumped, but the chapel was dark inside.

Red beams from a hundred flashlights converged on the open doors.

Floyd stooped to pass underneath the lintel, and started down the hill in his odd stiff-legged gait. Zombies paraded out behind him. I recognized Lenny and other zombies I'd seen around Threadville during the past few days. They snaked down the hill in a line, and then fanned out, heading toward people who, until then, had been cheerfully traipsing through the cemetery and illuminating gravestones with small red lights.

# 34

Okay, I got it. The zombies came out of the chapel because they couldn't arise from fake graves. We'd all be richly entertained.

None of us would be eaten. None of us would become zombies.

When their retreat was over, the zombies would wash off their makeup, pack up their costumes, and go home to their families.

Mrs. Battersby smiled up toward the advancing zombies. She was obviously loving every moment of the haunted graveyard.

I mumbled to her and Haylee, "Stay together."

I didn't mean for Juliette and Patricia to hear me, but they sidled closer to us.

Floyd and Lenny switched direction and lumbered toward us. Those two hadn't scared me before, and they were not going to scare me now. I was more afraid of Patricia and her long-standing grudge against Isis than I was of men playing dress-up.

Perhaps Floyd and Lenny would protect me from her. Floyd shambled too close to me. He stretched his lips in a gruesome grimace. "Did you sic the police on me after that woman was murdered? They interrogated me about where I'd been."

Remembering the 1950s housewife zombie's words, I shined my light toward his mouth. "I hear you have to tell the truth when I shine a red light at your teeth." I wished I could control the shaking of my voice. "Where *had* you been?" Nothing like asking blunt questions.

He answered, though. "At a party, here at the lodge. I went for a walk on the beach. Your police buddies discovered that a lot of zombies saw me at the party, and surfer boy here followed me along the beach."

"I can't help searching for my surfboard whenever I'm near a beach." Lenny crooned like a wistful teen. "I wasn't following anyone."

With a broad smile, Mrs. Battersby turned her head back and forth to follow the exchange. I could have enjoyed her pleasure more if I didn't sense undercurrents of anger between the two zombies.

Floyd growled, "You saw me on the beach, though."

"I didn't really see anyone." Lenny spoke

with care, as if he were making up a story as he went. Or, as Floyd might have put it, as if he were staying in character. "I was scanning the waves."

Floyd pointed one finger at Patricia, "You saw me, though, right? Didn't I walk with you for a while? We talked about treadle sewing machines. I said my mother had used one."

Patricia licked her lips. "Yes," she muttered.

Why did I get the impression she wasn't telling the truth?

For a second, Juliette narrowed her eyes, and I remembered that Patricia and Juliette had been on the trail after the murder, but that had been an hour and a half later. Did Juliette know something about Patricia's whereabouts at the time of the murder?

I asked Patricia, "Did you hear Isis scream?"

She shook her head. "No, I'm afraid I didn't. I . . ." She crossed her arms over her chest in an attitude of awe. "I was *enthralled* by the waves, and that's all I heard."

I turned to Floyd. "But you heard Isis scream."

He showed his teeth. "Yes."

I shined my light toward Lenny's mouth. "And you came running, too."

He pulled his towel up over his shoulder. "Someone yelled, 'Help!' so I did." He turned toward Floyd and added in boyish tones, "I saw you, then." Even his smile seemed tentative.

I stepped closer to Mrs. Battersby in case I needed to guard her from these guys. "I was the one who shouted. Thank you *both* for rushing to my aid."

Lenny only shrugged and glanced longingly toward the beach down the slope, beyond the Elderberry Bay Lodge. "I seem to have this thing for water."

Floyd mumbled, "He has this *thing,* as he calls it, for pretending he's not one of the undead." Snarling, he tottered toward me.

I grinned and shined my light toward his mouth. Mrs. Battersby and Haylee stayed beside me, shining their lights at him.

Floyd turned and made a grabbing motion at Patricia. She shrieked and ran. He chased her.

Lenny feinted toward Juliette. She ran, in a different direction from Patricia. Lenny took off after her.

Acting undead with joints that didn't seem to work well, neither Floyd nor Lenny ran quickly. Unless the two zombies didn't stay in character, Patricia and Juliette would easily outpace them.

I said, "I don't think Patricia was really on the beach that evening with Floyd right before the murder."

Mrs. Battersby stated flatly, "That girl was lying."

Haylee concurred. "Floyd's statement that Patricia was with him did seem to surprise her."

I folded my arms. "It certainly did. And Floyd seemed to think he needed to use Patricia as an alibi, especially after Lenny denied seeing Floyd on the beach after the party and before the murder."

Mrs. Battersby asked, "Where are your two handsome *just friends* who said they'd be here?"

"Maybe some helpful zombies will herd them toward us," I joked.

His towel out like a Superman cape, Lenny was still chasing Juliette. She was almost at the porte cochere.

Floyd lurched up the hill toward a clutch of tourists. Squealing, they ran toward the chapel.

Taking Mrs. Battersby with us, Haylee and I crept down the hill and peeked around a stand of rhododendrons. I wanted to see where Patricia was going. We watched for a few minutes, and then she came into view, pacing back and forth in front of the lodge's front door.

I commented to Haylee, "I already told Vicki about the grudge, and I'll also tell her about the waffling about that seemingly fake alibi. Maybe they'll arrest her."

Mrs. Battersby asked loudly enough for almost everyone on the hill to hear. "Who's going to arrest *who*?"

Behind us, a lazy male voice drawled, "Yes, who will arrest *whom*?"

## 35

I whipped around to see who had been eavesdropping.

Slightly uphill from us, Dare Drayton smirked. We should have checked to see if anyone was following us during our mission to spy on Patricia. We had allowed Dare — and Brianna — to sneak up behind us.

How much of our conversation had they heard?

Mrs. Battersby raised her chin and growled at Dare, "You don't need to give me an English lesson. There are times when 'whom' sounds just plain stilted. You can be stuffy if you want. I choose to be with it."

Dare sneered. "I hope you local yokels don't think you have proof that the mousy treadle sewing machine woman murdered that Egyptian goddess wannabe. I saw that mousy woman sitting in an armchair in someone's window about the time of the murder."

I pounced. "How do you know it was the time of the murder?"

"Someone was screaming bloody murder, which was a pretty good hint. And your police friends asked me where I was at that time."

Brianna clung to his arm. She was sort of smiling, too, and hers wasn't what I'd call a nice smile, either.

Hardly believing my ears, I asked Dare, "You heard someone screaming and you didn't try to help?"

He countered, "No, why would I?"

*Because it would be the right thing to do?* I wasn't about to get into an argument with Dare Drayton about right and wrong, though. His attitudes about them were obviously different from mine. Did that mean he could have killed another human?

Haylee asked him, "Where were you when you saw Patricia and heard screaming?"

Dare backed up the hill a step. He towered over us. "I was just walking around. I was in a parking lot at the back of some stores."

Trying to imagine what he'd meant earlier, I repeated, "An armchair in a *window*?"

"The armchair wasn't *in* the window. Sorry, I guess I have to spell it out for you. I was looking through a window. No, I *glanced.* No, I *happened* to glance through

359

a window. I wasn't a Peeping Tom, in case you're about to run to your police friends with that information."

Mrs. Battersby managed to look impressive in that bulky sweater. "If you weren't a Peeping Tom, then what *were* you?"

He ignored her.

His superior attitude was infuriating me, but I asked as evenly as I could, "Which parking lot?"

"The one behind the post office. In case you can't figure this out for yourselves, I had to be close to the river if I heard screaming. That mousy woman was in what looked like someone's dining room in the back of a store. She was ensconced — is that too big a word for you? — in an armchair. She appeared to be reading. The chair was beside a fireplace."

Mrs. Battersby flashed a message at me from those dark eyes as if she also recognized Opal's dining room from the description.

If Dare was telling the truth, then Patricia and Floyd had been lying. But if Patricia and Floyd had told the truth, which hadn't seemed likely based on Patricia's demeanor at the time, then Dare was lying now.

On the other hand, it was entirely possible that all three of them were making up stories to provide themselves with alibis.

I half expected Mrs. Battersby to inform Dare that Patricia had said she was on the beach with Floyd at the time of the murder, but she only pursed her lips in disapproval, and Haylee and I didn't say anything, either.

Dare heaved a fake sigh. "I hope you rustics don't manage to get your friends to arrest an innocent person."

I snapped, "We have no control over the police."

"Ha," Brianna said. "She nearly had that policewoman kick me out of my room."

Mrs. Battersby's eyes gleamed. She shook a finger at Brianna. "You sent those troopers to interrogate me in the middle of the night."

Brianna only smiled up toward Dare. "And where would I have stayed if she'd kicked me out?"

Mrs. Battersby inhaled loudly. "Tsk," she added.

I thought of about a million responses to Brianna's allegations about me — like it wasn't *her* room, and maybe guests shouldn't accuse their hostesses of murder and attempted murder — but I was too interested in Dare's response to her flirting.

He didn't answer her. He looked out over our heads and said in a weary voice, "Uh-oh, looks like it's time to flee from zombies again." Arm in arm, Dare and Brianna sauntered toward the parking lot.

"You're right, Willow," Mrs. Battersby concluded loudly. "Those two deserve each other. And there are no zombies anywhere near us. That man is incapable of telling the truth." She looked up the hill. "Let's go see that chapel. It looks like an excellent replica."

Zombies were still staggering around, chasing Rosemary and other Threadville tourists, who ran away shrieking in gleeful terror.

Mrs. Battersby, Haylee, and I climbed the hill. Mrs. Battersby showed no sign of flagging. Was this the same woman who had complained about a shorter slope on Thursday evening?

The front doors of the chapel were still open.

Mrs. Battersby admired the exterior, then aimed her little red beam around the interior. No zombies seemed to be hiding inside.

"The outside looks like stone or concrete," Mrs. Battersby commented, "but the inside is plywood."

"Clay's clever with a paintbrush," Haylee answered. "He probably faux-finished the outside to look like that."

"Talented," Mrs. Battersby said. "One of you should grab him before someone else does."

"Willow has dibs on him," Haylee told her.

I merely spluttered and changed the subject. "The floor slopes rather drastically." Actually, it wasn't a floor. It was grassy ground. A door was built into the lower part of one of the side walls.

Mrs. Battersby explained, "They made it look like the original chapel in Evans City, which has a side door like that. I think the Evans City chapel has a partial basement or crawl space."

I guessed, "Maybe this chapel was too small for the number of zombies it needed to accommodate, so while some of them lurched out the front doors, others were coming in through that lower door."

"One of them lost his jacket," Haylee said. She picked up a black garment, which turned out to be a cloak, slashed and gory with fake blood. "Ugh." She dropped it where she'd found it.

We could see the entire interior of the chapel, but Mrs. Battersby called Ben and Clay's names anyway. No one answered. She poked her head outside. "They've stopped shrieking. Either all the humans have been turned to zombies or the Haunted

Graveyard is over. Let's go back to your place, Haylee. I need to make more sweaters and caps tonight."

Haylee offered Mrs. Battersby an arm. "Yes, let's. Even though this chapel is new, it freaks me out."

Mrs. Battersby grasped Haylee's arm. "I never expected to have a wimpy granddaughter."

I'd have liked to have seen Clay again, but after a late night followed by an interrupted one, and both of them accompanied by loud music, I was stifling yawns. We headed for the path to the parking lot.

I wasn't sure I believed Dare's alibi for Patricia. He could have fabricated it because he had no way to prove he was somewhere besides the riverbank when someone — Patricia, probably — pushed Isis in.

The possible good news was that if Patricia had killed Isis, then Brianna had not.

That didn't mean that Brianna wasn't a threat to me, but perhaps the most harm she could do was cause my mother to scold me. In any case, I was going home to sleep. In a locked bedroom.

I drove home and parked near In Stitches. We got out.

Haylee asked me, "Is Brianna's car here? I don't see it."

I didn't either. Last we knew, Brianna had been with Dare. What — or who — was about to welcome Clay home?

Haylee and Mrs. Battersby said good-bye and headed toward The Stash. I went down the hill through my side yard to the patio door. My pets were very happy to be let outside, and just as happy to be let in again.

No music came from Brianna's room. I texted Clay that I had no houseguests and he might have two.

Singing under my breath, I began emptying the dishwasher.

First, I thought that the scratching at the patio door was only the kittens.

Glowering at nothing and at everything, Brianna unlocked the patio door, stormed in, and slammed herself into her bedroom.

My pets stared at Brianna's closed door as if bereft, but they must have figured out that Brianna never paid them attention. Brianna had acted angry, which seemed to be her usual state. Didn't she know that sweet, furry animals could make her feel better about whatever was bothering her?

Music blared from her suite. Sooner or later, I'd learn to sleep soundly through it.

I finished putting the dishes away, ushered my pets into my suite, and locked us all in.

My smartphone rang. It was Clay. "I

looked for you," he murmured, "but it was late and I missed you. Thanks for the warning about the potential houseguest. Only my usual one arrived here."

"You did a great job on the graveyard, and especially the chapel. Mrs. Battersby loved it. Too bad we didn't see you and tell you in person. How did you create that flash of light and the rumble when the doors burst open? The ground shook."

He laughed. "We did some fun pyrotechnics and had speakers all over the place. You may have only felt shock waves."

"It was effective, whatever it was. Meanwhile, I was just about to text you again to tell you that my houseguest returned. Does yours seem angry?"

"No. Bored. Same as always."

"Mine seems to be in a rage."

"Is that unusual for her?" he asked.

I laughed, "No, but she seems more furious than ever."

"Is that her music I hear?"

"You can hear it?"

"I'll probably hear it after we hang up."

He was joking. He lived miles away.

"Yes, it's hers."

"Be careful. Lock your bedroom door, and call me if you need help."

That made me almost teary. I was tired.

Maybe trying to learn to sleep through loud music was not a great idea. After telling me he'd pick me up the next night at seven for the rehearsal dinner, Clay ended the too-short call. I crawled into bed.

The phone rang again.

It was Haylee. "I just talked to Opal. Patricia arrived in her apartment a few minutes ago. Opal asked how her evening was, and she said it was okay, but Opal thought she looked worried, so she called me to find out what I knew."

"Which was?"

"I told her that Patricia seemed to be fabricating an alibi without apparently knowing that Dare already had one for her."

"And you have only Mrs. Battersby as a houseguest?"

"Yes. I think she's planning to knit half the night and sleep all morning again. I told Opal to come sleep here, but she said a good hostess wouldn't abandon her guest, and Opal wants to believe the best of everyone, so she's accepting Dare's alibi for Patricia. How about you? How many house-guests do you have?"

"I have one, and Clay says he has one. Mine's not happy. *Definitely* not happy."

"Lock your bedroom."

"I did."

"Better yet, leave her to her own devices and come over here. Edna's mother is definitely not dangerous."

I laughed. "Certainly not! She even used the word 'granddaughter' without reminding everyone around that you aren't a *real* one."

"Apparently I'm 'wimpy,' though."

I smiled. "I like her."

"So do I. So, are you coming over?"

"Thanks, but I'll be safe here with my guard dogs and guard kittens."

"You can bring them, too, you know."

"If I have to, I will. Vicki would come in an instant, and Clay said to call him if I needed help."

"In that case, tell him you need him right now!"

I grinned in the darkness. "Maybe another time, when I don't have an enraged guest."

"I suppose that could put a damper on anything resembling romance."

"Definitely."

"When's she leaving Threadville?"

"I don't know. After the craft show ends tomorrow afternoon, there's nothing to keep her here."

"Dream on. She thinks she lives at your place. Before long, she'll decide that *you're* the interloper."

I was afraid Haylee could be right. "And Mrs. Battersby is going to take over Blueberry Cottage. If all that happens, I'm moving in with you or Opal or Naomi."

Haylee laughed and said good night.

Brianna's music was still booming when I drifted off.

## 36

The next morning was one of those warm October days when it feels like summer might go on forever. Brianna's music had ended during the night. I took all four animals outside for a few minutes, and then, because the morning was so glorious, put the kittens inside and leashed the dogs for a jog. We trotted along the beach to the cottage colony and back.

Outside Buttons and Bows, Edna was sweeping her sidewalk. Leashes in hand, I wished her a happy day-before-her-wedding.

She beamed. "And it's supposed to be beautiful tomorrow, too, and even warmer."

"All packed for your honeymoon cruise?"

"Almost! And I can't fit one more bead or spangle onto my wedding gown, so I guess it's finished." She turned serious. "Thanks for helping keep my mother out of trouble."

I grinned. "I've enjoyed it. She's a character."

Edna made a show of staring up toward the sky. "She certainly is. I hope she's not going to find a way of disrupting the rehearsal dinner tonight or the wedding tomorrow."

I hugged her. "She seems to have mellowed since she arrived in Threadville."

She tilted her head up to look at me. "I was thinking the same thing, and hoping I wasn't imagining it." She shook her broom at an imaginary adversary. "She could always regress. She'll be beside me at the head table at both dinners, but can you try to keep her from going overboard during the actual wedding, when Opal, Naomi, Haylee, and I might be too occupied?"

I laughed. "I'll be glad to. But don't worry. Even if she gets into mischief, tomorrow will be your big day. Yours and Gord's."

Edna went back to beaming. "I know. Gord's a wonderful man."

I left her with her broom and anticipation and hurried back to my apartment. Nothing should mar Edna's happiness, I thought, but a needle of worry pricked at my optimism. What if Neffting decided to arrest her?

To my surprise, Brianna was up and dressed when the dogs and I returned home, but she grabbed her mug, turned abruptly, and shut herself into her suite as if she feared I might grab the coffee away from her. I had made it *for* her.

Ashley and Georgina were working at the Get Ready for Halloween Craft Fair during the morning, leaving me in charge of In Stitches until after lunch, but most of my customers were at the craft fair again.

Still worrying that Neffting might arrest the wrong person for Isis's murder, I called Vicki. Her phone went to messages. I quickly rattled off that during the previous night's Haunted Graveyard, Patricia and Floyd had agreed on an alibi for each other that they'd appeared to be making up, and that Dare had later told us that he'd seen Patricia in Opal's dining room when Isis was screaming.

Vicki didn't call me back, and I had a quiet morning.

Around one, Rosemary arrived from Naomi's quilting shop to take over during my lunch hour. A frown creased her forehead. "Naomi wants you to go talk to her at Batty About Quilts."

"Is something wrong?"

"She didn't say, but she was hoping you could come right away."

I thanked Rosemary and rushed across the street.

Haylee was already there. Naomi took us into her back room, where sounds were deadened by huge rolls of quilt batting hanging from rods. She spoke even more softly than usual, as if she didn't want customers in the front rooms to hear her. "You two know more about police and their investigations than I do. I found something in my wastebasket. That detective said to call if I learned anything, but I'm not sure this is important." She waved a fistful of paper triangles at us. "Do you understand how quilters do paper piecing?"

Haylee nodded, and I looked confused.

Naomi smiled. "Okay, as fascinating as quilting is, I'll keep my explanation short. Basically, in paper piecing, we sew fabric onto paper to make our quilt blocks. It's sort of like paint-by-number. We print or photocopy exact replicas of the blocks on paper, one for each block in the quilt. Then, using a piece of fabric that allows at least a quarter-inch seam allowance around the number one shape on the paper, we pin our number one piece of fabric to the paper, wrong sides together, pins on the paper side." She picked up a piece of paper with shapes drawn and numbered on it, and demonstrated with a scrap of fabric, smoothing the cloth against the paper.

She picked up another scrap of fabric. "Next, we pin on the number two piece, again larger than the finished result should be, with the right sides of the two *fabrics* together. We then turn the whole thing over so that the paper is on top, and stitch along the line on the paper, creating a seam connecting the two pieces of fabric. We trim the seam to a quarter inch, press the seam, then flip the fabric so that the wrong side of both pieces of fabric are against the wrong side of the paper, the number one fabric against the wrong side of the number one on the paper, and the number two fabric against the wrong side of the number two, and then we pin the right side of our number three fabric, bigger than the number three shape with a quarter-inch seam allowance around it, to the right side of the number two fabric, stitch that seam, trim it, and fold it back to cover the number three shape."

I asked, "Do you mean the pieces aren't cut to the right size until after they're stitched?"

Naomi nodded. "You got it. And we stitch with the paper on top so we can see the lines and stitch exactly on them. Then we do the fourth piece, then the fifth. We keep doing that until the block is complete. Then we tear the paper off — it will be in numbered bits — and throw it out. Some of my quilters won't quilt any other way, while others prefer to cut the pieces to the exact dimensions first, including the quarter-inch seam allowance, and stitch carefully. Either way, we square up the blocks afterward."

I stared at the paper triangles in her hand. "Don't you waste a lot of paper?"

Naomi frowned. "I suppose, but it's a clever way of putting our seams where we want them, over the lines we drew, and if we do it correctly, our squares are exact. If I come upon a sheet of paper that's good on one side, I pile it near my photocopier, and we recycle it for the blocks. So . . ." She arranged the paper triangles on the shelf beside her. "I found these in the wastebasket. Because of what happened to Isis, the word 'curse' jumped out at me."

She stood back.

The words weren't entirely clear because of the perforations the sewing machine's needle had made and some random tears, but I made out something like instructions: *To break the curse, encircle the intended victim in light.*

Haylee turned to Naomi. "Who wrote this?"

"I don't know. I don't recognize the handwriting, and I don't remember ever seeing the words before. Someone else must have added it to my pile of scrap paper." She showed us the number six on the other side of one of the triangles.

"Could Isis have written this?" I asked Naomi.

"She could have. She was in my store at least once, fingering fabrics and yelling at me because I sold cottons besides Egyptian cotton."

I patted Naomi's arm. "She was angry at everyone."

Naomi smiled, but she still looked sad, as if she couldn't understand why everyone couldn't just get along.

"A circle of light," I said slowly. "Someone left glow-in-the-dark thread along the riverside trail. Could that have been the beginning of someone's attempt to place the intended victim — of a curse — inside a circle of light?"

"That sounds like a big circle," Haylee commented. "Did it go all around Thread-ville?"

Naomi grabbed her arm, obviously excited. "It would have to be a big circle, wouldn't it? If you didn't know who the intended victim was, or if you did know who the victim was to be, but didn't know where he or she was?"

Haylee nodded. "Or if you didn't feel quite right about going up to someone and asking, 'Mind if I tie you up in glow-in-the-dark thread?' "

Naomi chuckled. "Who would feel quite right about that?"

I ran my thumb along the bumpy perforations. "The thread went from the bridge, along the trail, and up to the bandstand. I think the person who left the thread got sidetracked then, and found another way to break the curse." I snapped the piece of paper down onto the shelf and glared at it. "By murdering the person who had uttered the curse."

Naomi shuddered. "Horrible. Who would do such a thing? Who was the intended victim of Isis's curses?"

I began, "Floyd the zombie claimed he was, but the names I heard Isis call out when she was casting her spells were Gord and Edna."

Naomi covered her mouth with one hand, then dropped the hand and stood straighter. "Gord and Edna would never hurt anyone."

We agreed with her. But did the police agree with us?

Naomi gathered the ragged-edged paper triangles. "I think I answered my own question. I'm not giving these paper scraps to that spindly-necked detective to use against Gord or Edna unless he produces a search warrant or a subpoena."

I asked, "How long had that sheet of paper been in the stack next to your photocopier?"

Naomi slid the paper triangles into an envelope. "It could have there for months before any of us ever heard of Isis and her curses."

Haylee and I told her not to worry. We returned to our shops.

Rosemary had everything under control in mine, so I ran downstairs to give my pets a trip outside and myself some lunch. Brianna's room was quiet. I double-checked that the patio door was locked, ran upstairs, and told Rosemary I'd send Ashley back soon.

Brianna's car was not parked on Lake Street, but as soon as I pulled into the community center parking lot, I saw it. I also saw Vicki's cruiser, off in a corner. Head down as if she were writing in a notebook, she sat in the driver's seat.

Floyd was in her passenger seat, chopping at the air with his hands as if talking. He must have been mortified at being in his zombie persona in a vehicle produced after 1934.

Inside the community center, the Threadville Get Ready for Halloween Craft Fair was crowded. Patricia and Juliette stood on one side of the hall and stared at Dare on the other.

Why was he here again? He wasn't one of our vendors. He was walking from table to table, picking things up and putting them down again. Listening to others' conversations? Gathering local color for his Lake Erie thriller?

Sitting at her table, Brianna glowered at Patricia and Juliette.

Georgina and Ashley told me we wouldn't have much left unsold to pack when the fair ended. Georgina drove Ashley back to In Stitches to relieve Rosemary.

Floyd strode into the hall, changed his stride to a stomp, then seemed to remember to stay in character as a zombie and went into his hobbling, living-dead stagger.

Patricia scurried away from Juliette, sat down at her table, which was next to my In Stitches table, and bent to peer down toward the foot pedal of one of her sewing machines.

Floyd shambled to Patricia's display of treadle sewing machines, manuals, and accessories and slapped one hand on her table. "Thanks for nothing," he barked.

## 37

Patricia straightened, place a hand over her heart, and looked timidly back at Floyd. "What? What did I do?"

Floyd growled, "Reported me to the police. Just what I do not need."

She shook her head. "I didn't."

Juliette glided in her long red gown to Patricia's side.

"You didn't?" Floyd repeated. "That's not how I see it. First, that policewoman came in here a little while ago, and you agreed with me that when that Egyptian goddess babe was murdered, you and I were together on the beach, then this thriller writer went and talked to the policewoman, and she marched you outside, and the next thing I know, you're back in here, and *I'm* outside in the front seat of a squad car, and the policewoman is interrogating me because you went and changed your story. Why?"

Patricia's eyes widened until she resembled a rabbit caught in the headlights. "I . . . I didn't. Dare Drayton told her he saw me in Opal's dining room, reading, when Isis was screaming, and when the police chief told me that, I remembered that's where I was, not on the beach with you."

On the other side of me, a scornful male voice said, "How could you remember being on a beach and then remember *not* being on a beach?" Dare had managed to insinuate himself into the discussion. "Listen, Pretty Boy, or whoever's long-dead remains you're pretending to be, I'm known for my skills at observation. Why wouldn't the police believe *me* about when and where I saw this treadle machine woman?"

Floyd stood straighter. "When given a choice of two possible alibis, this dame chose the famous man to support." Under the fluorescent lights, the fake blood on his chin gleamed like thick, oozy pudding. "And the police are in awe of the famous thriller writer, too." He scowled. "This treadle sewing machine woman probably lied about being where *you* claimed to have seen her, too."

Juliette stepped into the argument. "I saw Patricia at the park. Remember, Willow? We saw you, too."

I agreed. "You'd both been on the trail along the river. But that was about an hour and a half after Isis . . . fell in."

Patricia nodded eagerly. Even her teeth looked rabbity. "Dare must have peeked in at me while I was reading in Opal's dining room. Later, I went for a walk, and caught up with Juliette on the trail. And then we saw Willow, and we witnessed the whole . . ." She heaved a tremulous breath. "The whole *tragedy* going on at the park, and then Dare came along. From the trail we'd just been on."

Why had she chosen the word "tragedy" so carefully, and emphasized it, also? Was the death of her old foe anything *but* a tragedy, as far as she was concerned?

Juliette's eyes narrowed as if she were wondering something similar, or maybe imagining gazing into the crystal ball she'd left behind on her craft sale table. "Tell this zombie what time you left Opal's and went for a walk on the trail."

"It must have been after eleven . . ." Patricia's voice diminished. "I wasn't paying attention, really, and don't remember."

Floyd scoffed, "There's a lot that you don't remember."

She pushed her thick glasses up her nose. "I do remember that I wasn't with you on the beach. I was never with you on the beach. I was never with you that night, period."

"Then why did you say you were?" he exploded.

"I thought you wanted me to."

If Vicki wasn't going to arrest Patricia for murder, she might consider arresting her for impersonating a doormat.

Floyd seemed to stop breathing. Maybe he really was a member of the undead. "Lucky thing I was able to give that police-woman names of people who saw me at the party at the lodge that night. They'll confirm I was there."

"One wonders," Dare drawled, "why you didn't use that alibi to start with instead of making this treadle-woman think she needed to lie for you." He raised one eyebrow.

Dare was obnoxious, but his point was a good one.

Floyd glared at him. "And where were you when that Egyptian goddess babe went underwater?"

"Simple." I wasn't sure if Dare was talking about the people around him or about the truth — or about his version of the truth. "I had been waiting for my cousin, who didn't show up, so I strolled to the beach, then wandered through the parking lot, and I saw this treadle-woman reading. Lucky thing for her I'm so observant and have a good memory, or she could be languishing in a jail cell right this very minute." He skewered me with an amused look. "One wonders where my esteemed cousin was at that moment. *He* could be the villain who pushed the woman in."

Everyone seemed to know — or think they knew — that Isis had been pushed. I answered hotly, "Clay was sitting in his truck waiting for you. He'd promised to drive you home, but you disappeared."

Dare shrugged. "We don't know if what he said is true, do we? And we probably never will."

I retorted, "Clay is a good person —"

Dare interrupted me. "So I've heard, from my mother, all the time I was growing up. 'Why can't you be more like Clay?' " he mimicked in a shrill, quavering voice. " 'Clay's such a *good* boy.' Sickening, isn't it?"

It was, but Dare didn't wait for any of us to answer. He marched out of the community center without saying another word to anyone.

Obviously seething, Brianna watched Dare leave. What was wrong with her? Her fury seemed to center on Dare. A woman scorned?

Juliette went back to preside over her crystal ball. Neither she nor Patricia seemed to be bringing in much business, though for the rest of the afternoon, Floyd and Lenny had people at their table, where they were selling makeup, slashed and bullet-riddled costumes, and horrendously realistic stick-on wounds with the jagged ends of fake bones poking out of them. Brianna stayed occupied, also, until four, when she closed her display cases and lugged them out. The fair wasn't officially over for another hour. Maybe she was in a hurry to drive all the way home to South Carolina? I could hope.

Juliette yawned and beckoned to me. I went over to her table.

"Do I have to stay until the bitter end?" she asked. "I thought this would be my clientele, but I've hardly booked any events. Want me to tell your fortune?"

"I'd just as soon not know." I smiled to soften my words, then bent to peer more closely at her crystal ball. "You really can see things in it."

She stroked its smooth, gleaming surface. "That's because it's made of polished rock — quartz, actually. People expect them to be made of molten glass, and many are, but this one is special. It's been passed down through my mother's family, mother to daughter, for generations. We all have what they call 'the sight.' "

"It's quite an heirloom," I agreed. "A family treasure." Actually, up close, the darkness inside the sphere of rock seemed to negate the cheerful reflections of the ceiling lights, and the thing gave me the creeps. I could barely restrain a shudder, as if Juliette had actually foretold a drastic future for me.

Fortunately, she didn't seem to notice. She pulled a vinyl bowling bag from underneath her table. It was two-toned, brown and mottled beige, with matching brown piping — a real vintage piece. Juliette smiled with pride and ran a finger along the stitches attaching one of the handles to the body of the bag. "This bag is a family treasure, too," she told me. "It was my grandfather's. He bowled all the time. It's the perfect way to carry my crystal ball."

Lovingly, she lowered the crystal ball into the bag, then went around to all the tables and said good-bye to everyone. Except for the long gown, she looked ready for a 1960s bowling tournament.

By five o'clock, I was nearly out of brochures, course calendars, stabilizer, and

CDs of embroidery designs. I did have a fair amount of embroidery thread, even though my thread sales had picked up after Brianna departed.

Carrying my mostly empty plastic bins outside, I passed Lenny coming in for another load of zombie clothing and accessories. "You'll need a fur-lined towel when the weather gets colder," I joked.

He grinned.

Floyd stumbled past us with his ever-changing but crooked limp. Although he grunted, he couldn't quite stay in character while pulling a wheeled trolley full of merchandise. The trolley was definitely post-1934, which undoubtedly bothered him.

I stowed my bins in my car, then drove home

Brianna's car was outside my shop. So much for hoping she had packed up and left town.

# 38

I carried everything into In Stitches, chatted with the day's last customers, said good night to Ashley, and closed the shop for the night, and for the next day, too. Tonight was the rehearsal dinner and tomorrow was the wedding. I spun around in an impromptu pirouette. We were all going to forget the sordid events from Thursday night, or at least put them in the backs of our minds. Instead, we would celebrate with Edna and Gord, who deserved our best wishes and good cheer.

Downstairs, Brianna was listening to music and spreading peanut butter on toast, but she rushed toward her room with her snack.

I called to her, "Wait! We need to talk."

She said over her shoulder, "No, we don't."

"Yes, we do. Why did you accuse me of shoving you into the lake?"

She only half turned toward me. "I thought it was you."

"You made it up," I accused. "No one pushed you."

She shrugged. "So? I made a mistake. Everyone makes mistakes."

Despite what my mother would say, I was tempted to toss the wretch out. "I don't have to keep letting you stay here, you know."

"You owe me!" she snapped. "You and your mother both owe me. I don't get a cent from my father. He gives it all to your mother. The least you can do is give me a place to stay, feed me, and pay for my phone calls."

"He gives *all* of his money to my mother?" I repeated. "He must keep some for himself and his . . ." I paused, then made a wild guess. ". . . his current wife and her kids."

She bit into her toast. "That doesn't count. You get more than I do."

"I do not! Where did you get that idea?"

She turned toward me then, but made a sulky face at my great room. "Look at this place. My father gives your mother money, and she gives it to you."

"Wrong on all counts. Your father donates to my mother's *campaigns*. My mother supported me up to and through college, but I paid back my tuition before she ever ran for office, before your father ever donated to one of her campaigns, and I've worked very hard to buy this place by myself and build up a business."

She didn't look convinced.

I suggested, "You should double-check with your father about the reason he donates to my mother's campaigns. He knows how she votes, so he wants to help keep her in office."

"Your mother accepts *bribes.*" She went into her room and slammed the door.

I toyed with the idea of calling my mother and telling her what I thought of Brianna Shrevedale, but all I would receive in return would be a lecture about Southern hospitality and not sabotaging her political career.

Besides, a morsel of compassion for Brianna welled up in my insides. The girl apparently felt like her father had discarded her in favor of, I guessed, a bunch of half siblings.

But that didn't mean she could stay with me forever. I went upstairs to my computer and made a quick list of sewing and quilting shops that she might visit on her way back to South Carolina. I left the list in the middle of the kitchen counter where Brianna would see it the moment she left her

— my — guest suite.

My pets deserved an outing. Mustache and Bow-Tie quickly returned, as if Sally had been telling them stories about trolls lurking in flower beds. The kittens watched from inside while Sally and Tally tore all over the yard, gnashing their teeth, crashing into each other, and growling in mock ferocity. Tongues lolling, the dogs trotted inside, and I shut all four pets into my suite with me so I could spend a luxuriously long time getting ready for Edna and Gord's rehearsal dinner.

Bass thumped from Brianna's room. She was leaving soon, I reminded myself. Maybe even that night.

I polished my nails, all twenty of them, and enjoyed a relaxing soak in a bathtub piled high with bubbles. I dried my hair and coaxed it into long, shining curls.

I'd made a dress for the rehearsal dinner, and another for the wedding. I removed the pale teal linen one from its hanger, slipped it on, and checked the mirror.

It fit perfectly. I'd decorated the hem with a narrow band of hardanger embroidery, but I had left the neckline unadorned so I could show off the necklace of silver and teal beads that Edna had made for me. I fastened it around my neck, put in the matching earrings, and grabbed a silver cuff bracelet.

Knowing I might be away from my apartment for a long time during the evening, I put on sneakers and took the pets out one more time.

Back in my room again, I slid my feet into black patent high-heeled sandals. A gossamer shawl that Opal had knit from fine silk yarn the color of my dress and a silver beaded evening bag completed the outfit. The bag was adorable, and almost too small for my phone. Why would I need a phone? I'd be with Clay, and almost everyone else who might call me would also be at the lodge. And even if my mother tried to reach me, I wasn't about to answer calls or look at texts during dinner. I crammed the phone into the bag, anyway.

After checking that the door to my room and the door to the patio were locked, I climbed the stairs to In Stitches so I could watch for Clay.

He was already on the porch. Even from the back, he looked yummy in his navy suit. He turned around the moment I opened the door. His smile and eyes warmed me so much I was tempted to simply walk into his arms. Flustered, I locked the door.

When I looked up again, he smiled and

held out his arm. I happily grasped it. My heels were a little high for negotiating the stairs by myself.

"I'm afraid I still don't have a vehicle besides my pickup," he apologized.

I grinned up at him. "I'd have preferred a bulldozer, but your truck will have to do." The two of us were almost never alone together — the cab of a pickup would be an improvement.

Clay opened his passenger door. I climbed in quickly so he wouldn't feel the need to give me a helpful push from behind.

He got in, gave me another wonderful smile, and headed toward the Elderberry Bay Lodge.

I asked him, "How did the rehearsal go?"

"Fine. The wedding will be perfect, as long as no one minds that the bride and groom may break into unplanned songs and dances."

"No one will mind." I thought about it a second. "Except maybe Edna's mother."

"I hope she won't. I've brought copies of the sketches of Blueberry Cottage for her," he said. "Do you think she was serious about helping with the interior design?"

"Definitely! And maybe about renting the cottage after it's finished, too."

"I thought so, too. It might be fun to have

her around."

"Maybe. But I'm reconsidering winter- izing the cottage. Maybe I don't want a year-round tenant after all."

He laughed.

During the rest of the way to the rehearsal dinner, we discussed flooring materials. Maybe not terribly romantic, but I enjoyed it, and Clay seemed to know everything.

He parked next to Naomi's SUV. Naomi, Opal, Haylee, and Mrs. Battersby were get- ting out of it.

I was all set to link my arm in Clay's for the walk to the inn, but Mrs. Battersby took one look at me, pointed down at her royal blue lace dress and matching jacket, and stated, "You and Haylee both have to stay away from me. We clash. Haylee, you and Willow walk together. I'll walk with your *friend,* Willow. He and I don't clash."

Haylee was in a perfectly tailored hunter green dress and jacket that she'd made. I didn't think her green went terribly well with my teal, or that Clay's navy really set off Mrs. Battersby's royal blue, but I didn't say anything. Naomi was in a goldenrod silk dress that Haylee had made for her, and Opal wore a hand-crocheted persimmon gown. Mrs. Battersby directed them to walk together. They led the procession, with Clay and Mrs. Battersby in the middle, and Hay-lee and me trailing behind.

No zombies were in sight, but lots of people in dressy outfits milled around the lodge's lobby.

I was surprised at the number of tables in the banquet hall. They were decorated with white linen, silver candles, gardenia plants with big white flowers, gleaming china, crystal stemware, and sterling cutlery. Everything sparkled, including Edna, in yet another glittery silver dress. Throwing us kisses, she stood at a table on a temporary dais at the far end of the room. She pointed toward the wall behind her, bowed toward us, mouthed, "I love it," and threw more kisses.

In all its glory, the wedding quilt that Threadville had made for her covered a large amount of the wall behind her. The quilt was, to put it mildly, stunning. And probably too big for any bed. The embroidered lace bride and groom dolls in their garden were in the place of honor in the center square, but because the quilt was hanging on a wall, they seemed to be gazing up at the ceiling, which was better than staring down at the floor, maybe.

Looking quite formal except for the twinkles in his eyes, Gord strode toward us and pried Clay from Mrs. Battersby's grip. "You're at the head table," he told her. "Clay, do you mind escorting Opal and Naomi to the head table to join us?"

Clay winked at me and offered Opal and Naomi each an arm.

In a well-tailored black suit and smiling broadly, Ben showed up beside us. He must have followed us from his office across the lobby. "You two are at a table with me," he said. "May I show you to your table?"

Of course we accepted. We each took one of his arms.

"Good bones," I said seriously.

Haylee burst out laughing, and Ben grinned. The ice, if any, was definitely broken.

Edna had created the place cards, with names in silver calligraphy on white and a spray of rhinestones and glitter decorating each one. Ben led us to a table.

As we rounded it, I read the names.

Cards for Patricia, Juliette, Dare, and Brianna were also on our table.

## 39

In their excitement, Gord and Edna must have invited almost all of Elderberry Bay, plus our houseguests, to their rehearsal dinner. The evening might not turn out to be as much fun as I'd hoped. Although disappointed, I reminded myself not to let the presence of relative strangers, including my nemesis, Brianna, spoil my evening with friends. Including Clay . . .

He was devastatingly attractive. He was also charming and a gentleman. From my seat, I watched him hand Opal and Naomi to Gord, who seated them and then put an arm around Edna's shoulders and pulled her to him. Happiness shone from both their faces.

Haylee had quailed at asking Ben to be her date, but Edna and Gord must have conspired in a little matchmaking, and had seated them side by side.

I caught Edna's eye and winked. Her big

grin told me she knew exactly why I'd winked. But as soon as Clay joined us at his place between Haylee and me, Ben excused himself. "I'll have to check on things from time to time, so I won't be able to sit with you three as much as I'd like."

I'd have to tease Haylee later about her revealing blushes.

I hoped that Brianna wouldn't show up, but she did, wearing black leggings and a matching turtleneck, which she'd dressed up with heavy chains that looked like real gold. Scowling, she sat at her place, right beside me.

Patricia and Juliette arrived together. Juliette wore a floor-length white velvet gown. A rainbow of ribbons of different widths and lengths, each of them attached at only one end, dangled and floated from the dress. As if determined to resemble a rodent, Patricia wore a brown faux suede dress that was too loose. She sat beside Ben's empty place, and Juliette sat beside her.

That left one seat at our table — Dare's, between Brianna and Juliette.

I didn't recognize a man at the next table until he smiled at me.

Lenny.

Gord and Edna had invited zombies, too.

Lenny was now a real man, with no makeup. He'd lost that wandering undead look of puzzlement, and his blond hair looked dry instead of wet. The suit he wore was for business or dinners out, and he looked great. Next to him, a tall but nondescript man gave me a tentative wave. Floyd. The fake blood and the black slicked-down hair were gone. His hair was a nice shade of light brown, and his suit was from today, not from the 1930s, but he still wore a dissatisfied expression, maybe because Edna had seated him next to Vicki Small-wood.

Apparently, Vicki wasn't on duty. I'd never seen her in frothy chiffon before. The tangerine color suited her. She looked great, but not particularly happy. And no wonder. Toby Gartener, her favorite detective, must have had to work that night, and she was beside Detective Neffting and his glued-down comb-over instead.

Detective Neffting stared at Edna as if expecting her to march to the podium and confess that she'd murdered Isis.

Waiters began serving amuse-bouches. Gord went to the microphone and welcomed us.

Wearing his signature black slacks, turtle-neck, blazer, and loafers, Dare sauntered in while Gord was talking. Juliette stood and waved him to the empty seat between her and Brianna.

The people at our table were an odd group. Ben, Haylee, Clay, and I were happy to laugh and chat together during all the delicious courses, but Ben had to leave the table frequently, and he tried to pay some attention to Patricia, who was on his other side and being ignored by Juliette. Patricia blushed and answered Ben's questions, but didn't seem to ask any of her own.

Beside Patricia, Juliette flirted with Dare and laughed at everything he said, most of which seemed to be nasty comments about other dinner guests and the locals in general.

Brianna didn't speak to Dare, me, or anyone else. Staring at her plate, she made angry-sounding sighs between bites.

As the day outside turned to dusk, the candles inside provided most of the light.

Edna and Gord contributed light of their own. Beaming and probably missing some of the wonderful food, they visited every table.

"You're radiant," I told Edna.

"Add bling to your dress and you'll radiate, too," she answered. "I hope I don't wear out my smiler before tomorrow, but I just can't help it."

Juliette beckoned to Gord. He bent to listen to her. She seemed to be asking him a quiet question. He asked her to repeat. She glanced nervously toward us, then asked if anyone would be making speeches later. He nodded. She pointed to herself and murmured something to him, and I thought she said something about making a speech herself. After a tiny delay, he nodded.

Everyone loved Gord. He probably shouldn't have been surprised that if he invited mere acquaintances to his rehearsal dinner, some of them might want to give the couple their best wishes publicly.

Looking concerned, Ben emerged from the kitchen and asked Clay to go with him to check on one of the refrigerators. "I'm not sure the thermostat's working, and we need to keep everything cool for tomorrow night's dinner."

Clay apologized, patted my shoulder, and headed off with Ben.

Juliette went back to chattering to Dare. I overheard her tell him where she'd gone to college.

It was the school where Isis's son, Heru, had died in his freshman year.

I froze with a forkful of roasted eggplant halfway to my mouth.

Juliette was approximately Patricia's age

and therefore would have been close to Heru's age, also. Juliette could have been a student at Heru's school during his short time there.

Reminding myself that it was a huge school and Juliette might never have met Heru or even heard of him, I forced myself to continue eating as if nothing had happened.

Dare seemed bored by the conversation, but Patricia seemed to shrink away from Juliette. Was Patricia afraid that Juliette had ferreted out her past battles with Isis Crabbe and Isis's son, Heru?

I'd have to find a way of suggesting to Vicki that even the alibi that Dare had given Patricia was flimsy. Times weren't precise, and Patricia had been eager, it seemed, to accept a possible alibi from Floyd, and then, later, a contradictory one from Dare.

Dare could have lied about seeing Patricia in Opal's dining room, either to provide an alibi for himself, or to stir things up for the sake of pure devilment.

During dessert, various people toasted Gord and Edna. I thought that Gord might forget about Juliette's request, or that maybe I'd misunderstood what she wanted, but he did call on her to come to the microphone.

Juliette set her inherited two-tone brown vinyl bowling bag on the table, unzipped it, and lifted out her crystal ball. She carried the sphere of rock to the podium. Multicolored ribbons fluttered from her gown. Adjusting the mini light beside the microphone this way and that, she gazed into the ball.

The banquet hall was almost dark except for flickering candles and a strange glow that seemed to come from inside that polished ball of quartz. As Juliette probably expected, everyone quieted.

Juliette frowned and bit her lip. She moved the light again. Finally, she looked at the audience and gave us a huge smile. "I see a wonderful future for Gord Wrinklesides and Edna Battersby," she announced in a drama-filled voice.

Everyone clapped.

After the applause subsided, Juliette continued telling Gord and Edna's fortune. "Gord and Edna will spend many years of beauteous happiness, encircled in light."

Juliette's words chimed through my brain. *Beauteous happiness, encircled in light.*

Haylee and I had found the words "beauteous happiness" hand-printed on a piece of paper in Juliette's room and we'd commented that people don't use the word "beauteous."

We'd also seen "encircled in light," written out longhand on one of the torn pages that Naomi had found in her wastebasket. We'd assumed that Juliette had printed the fortunes we'd found in her room. Had she also written the light-encircling method of breaking a curse? On a piece of paper that a quilter had found in Naomi's recycling?

I shivered. What had caused that sudden draft, like a door opening to a real graveyard? The glass doors leading out to the porch were all closed.

Barely aware of Gord's voice thanking Juliette for her good wishes and thanking all

of us for attending the dinner, I looked across Clay's empty seat at Haylee. She stared back at me with her eyes wide open.

*Encircled in light . . .*

I had guessed that whoever had written about breaking a curse by encircling some-one in light could have been the person who had "stapled" thread to the ground with my thread nippers near the bridge, and had then unspooled it all the way down the trail past my place and into the park. I had also theorized that the person had seen Isis put-ting on the wedding skirt and had thought of a more certain method of putting a stop to Isis's curses.

The person I'd seen on the trail could have been Juliette. It was easy to believe, based on the mud on her jeans and the way I'd seen her tuck that tag in, that she had changed out of her flowing peasant outfit into dark slacks and jacket, and then back into the peasant outfit.

The person who didn't stop running away from the scene of the crime when I yelled for help had been wearing hard-soled shoes that had slapped loudly on the concrete sidewalk. When we saw Juliette that night, she'd been wearing pale satin party shoes embellished with sequins.

Cradling her crystal ball against her,

Juliette started toward our table, but stopped when a woman reached out to touch the crystal ball.

Juliette was close enough that I could tell she was again wearing those sequin-covered shoes.

I leaned toward Haylee. She scooted her chair closer.

"We need to find a way to take a good look at the soles of her shoes," I murmured, "to see if the soles are hard enough to make the footsteps I heard after Isis went into the water."

Haylee nodded.

Gord told us all good night and turned off the microphone. Lights came on.

Chairs scraped against the floor. Patricia stood quickly, gathered her dull brown evening bag, and almost raced out of the hall.

With a sardonic nod at Haylee and me, Dare left our table. Brianna followed him.

Juliette returned and eased the crystal ball into its bag.

"Great speech, Juliette," I told her.

Zipping the bag, she smiled. "I always do that. It's my little gift to the couple. It helps them get started on the right track."

"I love your dress," Haylee said. "Did you make it?"

"No, but I added the ribbons for a festive touch. I got them from Edna's shop. Another way of helping make the evening special for her."

I asked, "Did you buy the sequins for your shoes from her, also?"

She obligingly lifted the hem of her dress a little to show off the shoes. "Aren't they cute? They came like this."

*I bet they didn't come with water stains on the toes, and* only *on the toes . . .* I could hardly breathe. "Where did you get them?" I asked.

"Who makes them?" Haylee added.

Juliette frowned. "I forget." She reached down, slipped one off and tilted it, peering into the inside of the heel.

The soles were hard leather.

They could have made those footsteps I'd heard shortly after Isis was pushed into the water.

A sequin fell off Juliette's shoe and clinked down onto my dessert plate.

With an apologetic smile, Juliette said, "They weren't expensive. I guess that's why the sequins are falling off."

Haylee peered closer at the sequin on my plate. "Those shoes really are cute. They must be for meditation. The sequin has OM written on it."

Juliette nodded. "They're my special fortune-telling shoes. I find that reflective surfaces help me see into the future. See you two at the wedding tomorrow, if not before." She picked up her bowling bag and headed for the door.

As soon as she was out of earshot, I whispered to Haylee, "OM?"

"I wanted to make sure you noticed."

"I did. And that this so-called sequin has no hole for sewing it on."

"It's not 'OM.'" She tilted her head, waiting for me to finish the sentence.

I did. "If we read it upside down, it's 'zero double-u,' part of the printing on a lightbulb. It once said '20W' and the lightbulb was on the flashy skirt we made for Edna. Those bulbs had been lit for a while, so they were hot when they hit the cold water. I heard them shatter. And a piece of one of them must have landed among the sequins and gotten stuck on the wet toe of a satin shoe."

Haylee clutched my wrist. "And the wearer of the shoe had to be very, very close to those lightbulbs when they shattered. The pieces were small and lightweight and couldn't have flown far."

I craned my neck to search among the people milling around saying their goodbyes. Detective Neffting and Vicki had left their table.

I caught a glimpse of tangerine-colored chiffon near the door leading into the lobby. "Wait here," I told Haylee. "Don't let anyone take my plate away. I'll bring Vicki back to see this."

"Did you bring your phone?" Haylee asked. "I didn't bring mine."

I pulled it out of my evening bag and handed it to her. "Vicki's on speed dial. I'll probably catch up with her, but if I don't bring her back here in ten minutes, call her and tell her what we found."

I draped my shawl over the back of my chair and left it and my phone and evening bag at the table with Haylee, my dessert plate, and the incriminating glass fragment.

Wishing I'd chosen more comfortable shoes than these high-heeled sandals, I headed toward the doorway leading from the dining hall into the lobby. A group of chattering people clogged it. I peeked over and between heads.

Juliette was in another bottleneck at the lodge's front door.

Neffting and Vicki were in the crowd behind her. I didn't want to shout or whistle, and possibly alert Juliette, who was on her way outside. Should I run back across the dining room and leave via the wide porch facing the lake? I'd be able to teeter around to the front of the lodge with hopes of intercepting Vicki and Detective Neffting.

Even if I'd worn sneakers, I'd never make it. People were waiting there to go outside, also. The lobby would be faster. I tried not to show my impatience. Ducking, I peered out the front windows.

Juliette disappeared behind rhododendrons lining the path to the parking lot. What if she chose this moment to leave Elderberry Bay?

Vicki and Neffting had made it through the doorway and were underneath the roof of the porte cochere. They were behind Juliette, but they couldn't know what I knew, and they didn't seem to be in a particular hurry. I was certain they weren't following Juliette on purpose.

They were, however, getting away from me rapidly, and the people between me and the door seemed reluctant to end their enjoyable evening.

Finally, I was outside, clopping across the pavement under the porte cochere. People dawdled along the path to the parking lot. In my heels, I wouldn't be able to race past them on the grass, either.

Behind me, someone whispered, "Willow!"

## 41

I whipped around. No one was on the path behind me.

Who had whispered my name? Haylee?

Or was I hearing things? The haunting of the graveyard on the hill above me was seeming all too real.

Something rustled in the rhododendrons beside me.

I could run back to the lobby if I had to. I could scream.

I could hurry to the parking lot. Maybe Vicki and Neffting would still be there.

But maybe they wouldn't be.

I took a half step toward the lodge.

"Willow!" The whisper came from the rhododendrons. "Don't go away. Wait. I need help."

I wasn't about to wait. Was Juliette ambushing me?

I eased away.

Clawing strands of hair from her eyes, Patricia staggered out of the rhododendrons. "Is she gone?" Her voice trembled.

"Who?" Was Patricia hiding from Vicki, or from . . .

"Juliette." She pulled a twig out of her hair.

I backed out of her reach. "I thought you two were friends."

"I thought so, too, but now I'm not so sure. Are you on your way to the parking lot? Can I walk with you?" She twisted her hands in the skirt of her faux suede dress.

She was as tall as I was, and wearing flats. I wouldn't be able to outrun her unless I kicked off my heels, and I couldn't simply kick them off. They were buckled on. But I also wasn't going to stay here, out of sight of everyone else, with a woman who, for all I knew, was a murderer. What if Patricia had borrowed Juliette's shoes long enough to push Isis into the water that fateful night, and had given the shoes back to Juliette before I saw the two tall women emerge from the trail? "Okay." I didn't sound very gracious. "Why?"

"I'm afraid of Juliette. I think she pushed that woman into the water to drown." Her voice dwindled until I could hardly hear her. "On purpose."

I started toward the parking lot again.

"Why do you think that?"

She kept up. "It goes back a long time, and is a long story. I went out with a boy in high school once or twice. I decided for lots of reasons that I didn't like him. We went to different colleges, and he died in his freshman year. The police came questioning me at my school about where I'd been and who his friends were. That was really scary for a seventeen-year-old. Luckily, lots of people had seen me in the town far away from him when he died."

I was almost positive she was talking about Isis's son, Heru Crabbe, but I wasn't about to suggest it. I reminded myself that she could be making up stories to hide the fact that she'd murdered Heru. And had murdered his mother, too.

However, the details seemed real enough, and talking about it seemed to boost Patricia's confidence. Her words tumbled out. "Fast-forward to this week. Juliette acted strange the evening that Isis was murdered. I went outside for a walk before bedtime, and saw her ahead of me on the trail. She kept stooping over as if putting things down or picking things up. She had a flashlight, and I didn't. I was behind her, but staying back because the ending of the book I'd been reading had gotten to me, and I didn't

414

feel sociable. And then I sneezed. She quickly bent down as if shoving something underneath the fence beside her, and then she stood again and came back toward me. She asked what I was doing out there in the dark without a light, and I made some dopey reply like I just got there and was thinking I should turn back. She said she would come with me to light the way, and . . ." Patricia stopped walking and bit her lip.

"And?" I prodded.

"Do you ever get stubborn and want to do something because someone expects you to do the opposite?"

I muffled a laugh. "Um, lots of times . . ."

"So do I, that time, anyway. I said I would keep going because there should be lights in the park, and I'd get to that lit area sooner than I would if I retraced my steps to the street near the bridge. But get this — she stood in my way. The trail is wide, but whenever I tried to go around her, she seemed to step to the side and block me. She was making suggestions like the trail was more interesting the way I'd come because wildlife might be coming to the river for a drink. But that didn't make sense. Wildlife would be as likely to come from the park as from people's backyards."

Mine, for instance. "I don't understand why that would make you afraid of her."

"It didn't, at first. It was only tonight. She said something that made everything fall into place. Two things. The first was during dinner. She said that she'd gone to the same college where the boy I'd dated had died. And I might as well tell you, he was Isis's son. So I had to wonder if Juliette had played a part in his death, and maybe she was afraid that Isis knew that, or would figure it out."

I mumbled something agreeable. I recognized this reasoning, having used it myself when I theorized that Patricia could have been the double murderer. Ahead, lights flickered between trees. We were almost at the parking lot. And I still wasn't positive that Patricia hadn't killed Isis, and maybe her son, also.

Patricia went on, "I'm not sure, but I think that Juliette and Isis have been going to the same craft shows and psychic fairs for years. So I started wondering if, you know, they could have been stalking each other to find out what the other one knew about Isis's son's death? Like, if one of them killed him, was the other one trying to find evidence? Did Juliette think Isis was about to kill her, so she struck first?"

It all made sense. We didn't know which of the two might have killed Heru Crabbe, but I was guessing it would be a girl his age, not his mother. And we certainly knew that Isis, and not Juliette, had been murdered. It was all circumstantial, though, except for that piece of glass on my dessert plate. I hoped Haylee was guarding it well.

I suggested, "You said that Juliette said something else that made everything fall into place for you?"

"Yes. When she was up at the microphone with her crystal ball, she said something about Gord and Edna being circled by light, and I understood what she'd been doing on the trail, and I guessed that she had also killed Isis."

I stayed silent.

As I'd hoped, Patricia kept talking. "And I remembered the way she'd blocked the trail and she'd thought up reasons for me not to go to the park, but in the end, she decided to go with me. At the time, I thought it was strange that she shined her light to the left of the trail, not right on it. And I still didn't figure it out when she kept asking me if I'd seen any of your glow-in-the-dark thread. Except she didn't call it that, she called it bright thread or light thread or thread that shines like the sun."

"And that's frightening?" I pressed. *Shines like the sun?*

"Not on its own, but in addition to craft shows and psychic fairs, Juliette takes that crystal ball to bridal shows. Brides actually hire her to come to their receptions and tell fortunes. I think it's creepy, but maybe that's just me."

"I agree with you."

"Juliette had already told me something about someone ruining one of the predictions she'd made at a wedding reception. Juliette had told a fortune of great fame and beauteous happiness — I picked up on the word 'beauteous' because it's so old-fashioned — and that night, this *person* had stood on a riverbank below the banquet hall, and had cast a spell on the bride. The marriage hadn't lasted, and word somehow — courtesy of the person who had cast the spells, I guess — went around the bridal show circuit that Juliette was a fake, and Juliette wasn't hired for as many weddings."

My giggle was more from nerves than from amusement. "Don't tell me that all of the other couples Juliette made those predictions for lived happily ever after!"

"Makes you wonder, doesn't it? But she seemed really angry about this *person* — I'm guessing the person was Isis because of what Opal read aloud from Isis's book — who had ruined her reputation."

"Why would Isis try to ruin Juliette's reputation? It seems to me that casting spells on brides would do more harm to the person casting the spells than to the person telling good fortunes."

"I don't know, but it fits my theory of the two of them following each other around, going to these shows, and trying to make trouble for each other. Maybe Isis thought she could force Juliette to admit to murdering Heru? Or maybe she couldn't prove that Juliette killed him, so she was getting revenge. Maybe she had more planned."

And that's why she had brought her craft of handmade books and her spell-casting skills to Threadville? She'd known Juliette was coming to our Get Ready for Halloween Craft Fair, and Isis planned to exact more revenge?

"Meanwhile," Patricia continued, "Juliette had learned somewhere that she could circle a couple with light and prevent that person's curses from working. And I thought she meant thinking good thoughts that would send virtual beams of light to people, you know?"

My nod in the darkness was enough to keep Patricia talking. "She seems caught up in believing in her powers and wanting others to believe in them, also. Last night, when we were talking to her here at the Haunted Graveyard, I joked that she could have predicted that jumping out from behind tombstones at people would startle them. I didn't mean to upset her, but she seemed angry."

I nodded. "I thought so, too, but I wasn't sure if your suggestions set her off or if seeing Dare and Brianna together did it. However, this afternoon at the craft fair, she asked Dare when he'd seen you, and she asked you when you'd gone for your walk. Maybe she was trying to figure out how much you saw of what she was doing on that trail."

"All she was doing was walking and stooping and walking and stooping. I never would have concluded from that alone that she'd murdered Isis. She could have been gathering dewdrops, for all I knew. But just now when Juliette said that thing about encircling someone with light, I thought about her obsession with your glow-in-the-dark thread on the night Isis was murdered, and I remembered that she'd helped sew some of that thread to the big wedding skirt that was supposed to be Edna's. I wasn't sure what it all meant, but I was afraid she would guess how much I'd figured out about her. I probably should have stayed inside with the rest of you — safety in numbers and all that, but I got scared and ran out of the lodge."

"You had a good head start. Why didn't you just get into your car and drive away?"

"I was afraid that Juliette might be right behind me, so I decided to hide in the bushes. I drove her here, but I don't want to drive her home. I guess that's rude, but . . ."

"Under the circumstances," I said. "Understandable." I hid a smile at the idea of Patricia worrying about offending a murderer by fleeing from her. "I've walked from downtown Threadville to the Elderberry Bay Lodge and back many times. It's not far, and Juliette's wearing flats." I wouldn't want to try it in the heels I was wearing.

"I could be totally wrong about her. I can have a wild imagination."

I knew what that was like. "You could have talked to our police chief. She was in the banquet hall."

"She was? I didn't see any police officers."

"Chief Smallwood and Detective Neffting came as dinner guests. Last I knew, they were heading toward the parking lot, too. I hope we can catch them before they leave."

"I'm scared. If Juliette killed Heru and Isis, and guesses that I suspect her . . ."

I knew *that* feeling, too, and I still wasn't comfortable being alone with Patricia. High-heeled sandals and all, I sped my pace. We came out into the parking lot.

Most of the cars had already left. Juliette and Dare stood chatting near an expensive sports car. Dare's hand was on the roof. I checked and checked again. No police cars, no Vicki, and no Detective Neffting.

# 42

In the distance, I heard a siren. Had Haylee called the police?

The sound became quieter.

Juliette turned her face toward us.

Whimpering like a scared rabbit, Patricia took off. Sandals pattering on the cobblestones, she dashed down toward the lodge.

I backed behind rhododendrons and whispered to her to wait, but she kept going.

I peeked out. Juliette was talking to Dare. Maybe she hadn't recognized us.

If Haylee had not yet called Vicki, she would soon. Maybe Patricia would tell Haylee what she'd just told me.

Meanwhile, I could hide from Juliette and watch to see where she went. But I didn't dare stay where I was in case she'd seen me peeking out at her. All I had to do was climb the hill between fake gravestones and peer down on the parking lot from the shelter of the woods above it.

All?

I pushed through a break in the hedge. Brushing bits of foliage out of my eyes, I started up the sloping lawn through the haunted graveyard. I had to lean forward as I climbed, or my heels would have sunk into the ground.

Clay and his crew had not put any gravestones in the woods above the parking lot. Very few leaves had fallen so far this year, but last year's leaves and a few twigs made sneaking quietly impossible.

Below me, I heard Dare's bored rumble, and then Juliette's laugh.

I peeked around a fat tree trunk.

Dare's back was toward me, but Juliette was facing me. Was it my imagination, or did she look up toward me? I ducked behind the tree.

A car door slammed. I edged around the tree trunk again. Dare was talking to Brianna between his car and hers, and Juliette was leaning against another one. Patricia's?

Carrying her bowling ball bag, Juliette strolled to the edge of the parking lot nearest me, at the foot of a steep embankment. She wasn't going to climb it in her long white velvet gown and party shoes, was she?

I heard Brianna's sardonic laugh, then

Dare's lazy drawl. "Juliette, what are you doing?"

"I think I saw Patricia. I'll go tell her not to wait for me."

Brianna was becoming a regular laugh machine.

But I didn't have time to wonder about her sudden tendency toward merriment. Below me, I heard a stone roll down the embankment.

Again, I was at a disadvantage in my shoes. Running down the hill to the lodge would be nearly impossible. The replica of the Evans City Cemetery chapel was much closer, and I could dodge from tombstone to tombstone on the way.

Knowing that Juliette had a steep climb to reach the top of the hill, I sprinted on tiptoe past two tall gravestones before ducking behind a shorter one.

I couldn't see Juliette, but I heard her thrashing through underbrush. I dashed to the nearer of the chapel's doors, the side one.

It was locked.

I turned around. In her long white gown, Juliette had reached the edge of the woods, and was gazing down toward the lodge. I zipped around the back of the chapel, past the side farthest from Juliette, and crept into the front doors, still open all the way since last night's haunted graveyard extravaganza.

Struggling to control my ragged breathing, I stood where I could watch for Juliette to go on down the hill toward the lodge. The doorway was wide. If she ran into the chapel through it, I could easily avoid her and run out.

Minutes passed, and she didn't show up. I was about to trot down through the fake graveyard toward the lodge when I heard someone try the chapel's side door.

Had she seen me come this way?

Maybe the locked door would make her go back to the parking lot or to the lodge. By now, Haylee should have reached Vicki and told her to come back from wherever she'd been heading. That siren I'd heard, though — would Vicki need to attend another call before returning to the Elderberry Bay Lodge?

With only the slightest creak, the side door behind me swung open. At the same time, the doors in front of me closed.

Clay must have built in switches to operate the doors, and Juliette must have found one.

Even with the side door open, the chapel was almost completely dark inside. Trying to keep my bearings and plan an escape route, I stared down toward that doorway.

What was I seeing? Not fireflies in October. Probably not glowworms, either. These glowing spots were so small that I had trouble convincing myself I was actually seeing them. But I was. They moved, all at the same time.

Juliette had sewn many different ribbons to her dress, and she'd apparently stitched them on with glow-in-the-dark thread. After losing the spool of it she'd taken from the fire station, she must have bought more from Brianna.

Juliette had encircled herself in light.

I could see her, but could she see me?

"Patricia?" she whispered.

I said nothing.

"Willow?"

Again I stayed quiet.

"I know you're in here," she said. "And I want to know why you're chasing me and spying on me."

I still didn't answer. She obviously didn't have a light or she'd be shining it around in an attempt to locate me. Did she have a weapon?

Maybe she would decide I wasn't in here and that I hadn't been spying on her after all, and she'd leave.

The glowing stitches on her gown stopped

swaying. She was standing very still. She'd stopped talking. Was she listening for me?

I didn't move. I barely breathed.

Finally, the glowing stitches undulated toward the side door and disappeared.

The door creaked shut. A latch clicked.

## 43

If Juliette had any sense, she would cut through the woods behind the chapel, go all the way up to Shore Road, walk back to Naomi's place, pack, get into her own car, and drive home.

I did not know how to open the doors of this replica chapel, but I would not be trapped long. Haylee would find me. Or Clay would. And when he did, I might even indulge in a tiny bit of damsel-in-distress histrionics.

For the moment, though, I didn't move. I hoped to hear Juliette crunching on leaves uphill from the chapel, which could mean she was heading for Shore Road and away from all my friends in the lodge. All I heard, though, was a loud bump and a bitten-off curse spoken in her voice. Juliette was downhill from the chapel.

Was Juliette heading to the lodge? Would she harm my friends? Wouldn't a murderer be continually on the lookout for people who might figure out her guilty secrets? If Juliette had noticed Patricia and me peeking at her, she may have gotten an inkling that we suspected her of murdering Isis.

Juliette might guess that my friends also suspected her. I couldn't wait here for my friends to find me. I needed to warn them.

I needed to find a way out of this chapel.

The previous night, the front doors had slammed open, and zombies had poured from it. Clay and Ben had been working behind the scenes. Did that mean that they opened the doors remotely? Juliette had found a switch on the outside of the chapel. Were there also switches on the inside?

It was inky black inside the chapel. I patted the left side of the double doors as high as I could reach. Nothing. I felt my way along the door to the left jamb and rubbed my hands up and down the wood. Finally to the right, about elbow height, I found a switch and flicked it.

With a roar that resounded all over the hillside, the doors flew open and slammed back against the walls. No pyrotechnics this time, but the building shook. And so did I.

My foot snagged something. That zombie cloak. The color of my dress was too light. I threw the musty-smelling thing around my shoulders. Wonder of wonders, it even had a hood.

Way below me, at the foot of the hill, lights were on inside the lodge, and through the lobby windows, I could see the legs of people, men in pants and women in dresses, running through the lobby to the front door. Maybe they thought a real zombie invasion was about to occur.

Halfway down the hill, Juliette was squatting behind a tombstone and peering over it at the lodge below her.

Unbuckling those sandals seemed to take forever, but finally, I was barefoot. Leaving the shoes behind, I pulled up the hood of the cloak and slunk downhill to the nearest fake tombstone.

Juliette still seemed intent on the people streaming out of the lodge. Afraid she might turn around and see me, I zigzagged from monument to monument.

Calling, "Willow!" Haylee, Clay, and Ben strode up the hill.

Juliette was lower on the hill, and couldn't see them over the hedges, but she could hear them. In a weird sort of crouch, she ran across the hill toward the parking lot.

Cloak flying, I took off after her. I stepped on a pebble and, without trying to, started limping like a zombie. I dropped one shoulder, raised the other, held my head at a strange tilt, and kept going.

Juliette must have seen me. She stopped and gestured urgently. "Help!" she whispered.

I caught up. "What's wrong?"

She stared at my face for a shocked second. "Willow? I thought you were a zombie."

I couldn't help smiling. "Sorry to disappoint you." Apparently, she didn't know for sure that I'd been inside the chapel with her, and she was going to play innocent. Fine. To save my skin, I'd play along and try to hide my suspicions.

She clutched her bowling ball bag to her chest. "The people who murdered Isis are after me!"

"I doubt that. I heard them call me."

"Yes, but . . ."

"Let's go see what they want, okay?"

"I don't know . . ."

Below us on the pathway, a man laughed, a cruel, sardonic laugh.

"It's Dare," Juliette crowed. "We'll be safe with him."

I wasn't sure about that, but Dare could be an improvement over being alone on this unlit hill with Juliette. Mentally apologizing to Ben and his gardeners, I shoved rhododendron branches aside for her, and she struggled to the cobblestones where Dare was.

I followed her out of the shrubbery. The hood of the cloak nearly stayed behind, but eventually the cloak and I pulled it out with us.

Before Dare could make one of his sarcastic remarks, I said quickly, "Dare, there's something inside the lodge that you may want to see for your research."

Dare eyed my zombie cloak. "What have you rurals cooked up for me this time? A vampire reenactment? International spies?"

Juliette tugged at Dare. "Weren't you going to take me home?"

Behind me, Brianna snorted. The way she crept up behind me, Dare didn't have to look far for a spy.

Juliette corrected herself. "I meant back to Naomi's so I can pack?"

"I thought you said you came with your friend, the treadle-woman, and that's why you went crashing up into the woods."

Juliette hugged her bowling bag. "I couldn't find her."

"I think she's in the lodge," I said helpfully. "Let's go see." I turned toward Dare. "And we could use your expert opinion."

He started toward the front door. "Okay,

and maybe we'll find your ride, Juliette."

We came out from behind the hedge. Haylee, Ben, and Clay were halfway up the hill. Clay turned around, and I beckoned to him. He must have recognized me despite the flapping cloak. He grabbed Ben and pointed down the hill toward me. I beckoned again. Haylee, Ben, and Clay started running down the hill.

I led Dare, with Juliette in lockstep beside him, into the brightly lit lobby and from there, into the dining room. I turned to give the other two, and Brianna, straggling behind them, an encouraging look. Beyond them, Clay, Haylee, and Ben entered the lobby. Her finger to her lips, Haylee raised her eyebrows. She was telling me she'd already warned Clay and Ben not to spook Juliette.

Gord, Edna, Mrs. Battersby, Naomi, and Opal stood beside our table. They appeared to be merely planning the next day's wedding celebration.

That table was the only one with its tablecloth still on. The candlesticks and bouquet were still on the table, along with my evening bag, my phone, and one dessert plate bearing the vestiges of fudge frosting. And one small and slightly curved piece of glass.

My shawl was still draped across the back of my chair.

Before I could point out the broken glass, Dare announced in a sarcastic voice, "Lake Erie thrills at their best! A bunch of people dressed up around a white tablecloth, and everyone else departed! Maybe the zombies got them." He glanced at me and my hideous cloak. "They got one of them already."

"Come see," I urged him.

"What did you find, a horrible, terrible, scary spider intent on destroying all of humanity?"

But he came with me, and Juliette did, too.

People whispered behind us in the dining hall doorway. Clay, Ben, and Haylee stood aside to let Neffting and Vicki into the dining room, then closed ranks behind them. We all gathered around the table. Juliette paled and moved closer to Dare.

On Dare's other side, Neffting carefully watched Edna and Gord, not Juliette, as if he expected to connect the evidence Haylee must have told him about to Edna. Vicki inserted herself between Juliette and me.

I pointed at the tiny fragment of glass in the dessert plate.

Dare raised one finger in the air. "Aha! They fed us ground glass tonight. We must find someone to save us. My cousin can finally be a hero!"

Ben looked pained. Haylee spoke up, "Actually, that piece of glass fell off Juliette's shoe."

Dare placed one hand dramatically over his heart. "They fed us food cooked in *shoes*?"

Vicki ignored his antics. Neffting continued eyeing Edna.

Vicki asked Haylee, "Did you see that piece of glass actually on the shoe?"

Haylee shook her head. "If I did, I thought it was only one of the sequins. But I saw it fall, and it had to have come from the shoe."

Dare stared at the fragment. "Now I see the fascination. They fed us bits of glass with mantras printed on them. The plot is unfolding — evil spiders try to take over the world by forcing everyone to meditate." He closed his eyes and intoned, *"OM-MMMMMMM."*

Juliette turned as if to go. "You're joking. I think we've seen enough. Coming, Dare?"

Smiling, Neffting turned to Dare. "And there will be this one state trooper who sees the whole plan and attempts to stop it."

Vicki asked Juliette, "Can you explain how that piece of glass got on your shoe?"

Juliette heaved a sigh. "I guess it happened

when I was changing a lightbulb at home before I came to Threadville. It broke. Maybe a piece of it got wedged in with the sequins." She glared at Dare. "Let's *go*."

Dare didn't seem to hear her. "A state trooper?" he repeated to Neffting.

Neffting puffed out his chest, which looked strange considering his paunch, stem of a neck, and bulbous head. "A detective, perhaps. For instance, I'm a detective with the Pennsylvania State Police, which means I'm also a state trooper. A proud one, I might add."

Vicki asked Juliette quietly, "May I see your shoes?"

Juliette scowled.

Neffting was still lecturing Dare. "You can call me Trooper Neffting." He wagged a finger. "But it wouldn't do to forget that I'm also a detective."

Vicki reminded Juliette, "Your shoes."

In one smooth movement, Juliette stepped back, lifted that vinyl bowling bag by its handles and swung it toward Vicki's head.

Neffting and Dare were still not paying attention to the rest of us.

I reached behind Vicki and grabbed for the bag. The fingers of my left hand closed around one of the handles.

I'm right-handed, and that horrible cloak

hampered me. Clumsily, I slowed the bag down slightly, maybe, but with a sickening thud, the crystal ball, still inside the bag, slammed into the side of Vicki's head.

Vicki slumped to the floor.

# 44

Juliette let go of the bag, but I was still hanging on to it, and the momentum of the crystal ball inside it sent me flying, cloak and all, backward into Clay.

Juliette ran away, across the dining hall. The soles of her shoes slapped against the oak floor in a rhythm that I remembered from the night of Isis's murder, when Juliette, wearing the same shoes, had fled up Lake Street.

Ben and Haylee surged after her.

Clay lowered me into a chair, then took off after the others, while Gord and all three of Haylee's mothers knelt beside Vicki.

His mouth a round O, Neffting tore his attention away from Dare and turned toward me.

There I was, with that bowling bag still dangling from my left hand. I couldn't seem to think of anything to do besides shake my head.

Yipping and yelling to the point that he was practically yodeling, Dare pelted out of the dining hall behind Clay.

Neffting shouted into his radio for backup and an ambulance.

Juliette had disappeared into the lobby.

Neffting touched the top of Gord's head. "Look after her, Doc, help's on its way." Bellowing, "Stop!" he dashed away with surprising grace and disappeared into the lobby behind the others.

As if fearing she'd faint, Patricia folded her arms on the table and rested her head on them.

Mrs. Battersby sat beside me and patted my arm. "Oh, my," she said. "Oh, my. Oh, my. Oh, my. The poor thing. And such a lovely dress, too. That orange suits her. Or it *did* when she still had some color in her face. Is she still breathing?"

Baffled, sickened, and afraid for Vicki, I lifted my shoulders in a helpless shrug. I felt like I'd also been clobbered. I whispered, "She has to be." That bowling bag weighed a ton. I let it drop the last three inches to the floor, then I more or less slid down to the floor to kneel beside Opal.

"Vicki?" I asked. "Are you okay?"

Obviously she wasn't, but she was breathing. I nearly sobbed with relief.

Gord brushed her hair away from her temple. "She's going to have a lump and a bruise."

Vicki opened her eyes. "Where's my bag?" She sounded panicky.

"On the table," I answered.

"Give it to me." She struggled as if about to sit up.

Edna pulled my shawl off the chair, folded it into a neat bundle and eased Vicki's head down onto it. "There, there," Edna cooed. "Lie still."

Opal spread her own wrap over Vicki.

Gord cautioned Vicki, "Don't move. Your head's been hit, hard. An ambulance is on its way."

With great care, I picked up Vicki's bag and handed it to her. It weighed almost as much as that crystal ball had. Vicki thanked me and wrapped both arms around it.

Gord turned to me and raised an eyebrow. I explained, "A police officer never loses track of her weapon."

"Great," he retorted. "A likely concussion, and we give her a gun."

"I'm okay," Vicki claimed. "Just dizzy. Help me up. I need to join the other officer until backup arrives."

"Don't worry," I said. "Clay, Ben, Dare, and Haylee chased after Juliette while

Detective Neffting radioed for help for you. They'll catch her."

Vicki tried to prop herself up on her elbows, grimaced, and let Edna help her down again. "Civilians. That's just super. All they'll do is get in the way. That woman could be armed, besides."

"She was," I said, chagrinned at not having stopped that bowling bag before it collided with Vicki's head. "But she's not now." I glared at the bag. "Maybe I'll take her weapon — her crystal ball in its bag — and go outside to help hunt her down."

Vicki and Haylee's three mothers yelped in unison, "Don't you dare!"

Vicki mumbled to the mothers, "I've been around you three too much."

"Don't worry," I told them. "I don't feel like lugging that heavy thing around. And you'll want it as evidence, Vicki. I hope I didn't wipe off all of Juliette's fingerprints. I'm afraid Detective Neffting thinks I attacked you with it."

"He went after *her*," she pointed out.

I tried to control a doubtful expression. "Maybe he just wanted to talk to Dare some more."

She didn't take the bait, didn't criticize her colleague for his momentary lapse of attention. But to be fair, Juliette had attacked viciously and quickly. Vicki said, "I saw that bag in Juliette's hands. He must have, also. And I saw you, Willow, trying to deflect the thing. I owe you." She winced. "Again."

Behind me, a female voice said, "Yuck." I turned around. Brianna scowled at me. "You people make me *sick.*"

I said evenly, "Then you'd better go home. But before you do, put your card on my kitchen counter so I can order more thread."

Brianna slouched toward the doors leading out to the porch, but Vicki called to her. "Don't go now, though. Don't *any* of you go outside. That woman could be armed with something else, and even if she's not, Detective Neffting may be forced to fire his weapon. Stay inside and away from windows. And that's an order."

With an exaggerated groan, Brianna plunked herself into a chair close to the door.

Patricia raised her head. Pale and shivering, she gazed into the distance. Slowly, she lost the shocked expression, but she moved cautiously as if she feared being attacked. She eased out of her chair and pointed at something on the floor underneath the table just beyond Vicki. "What's *that*?"

# 45

Patricia tiptoed to the table beyond Vicki, peered underneath it, turned to face us, and ran her palms down the skirt of her brown faux suede dress. "Juliette's wallet must have come out of her bowling bag when she swung it at Chief Smallwood."

"Don't touch it," Vicki ordered. I had to admire the authority she exerted despite being injured and stretched out on the floor.

Patricia absently brushed at the streaks her hands had made on her skirt. "Pictures spilled out of it. The one on top is of . . ." She swallowed, then spoke quickly, as if the words might burn her tongue. "It's a picture of Isis's son, Heru Crabbe. I knew him in high school. Juliette went to the college he attended. He died there."

Vicki and I exchanged glances. I patted her shoulder and struggled up from my kneeling position, which wasn't easy in that voluminous cape.

Haylee, Ben, and Clay trooped back into the banquet hall. Ben and Haylee gave each other a high five.

Haylee sang out to the rest of us, "Juliette's handcuffed and locked in the back of Detective Neffting's unmarked cruiser."

"Where's Dare?" I asked.

Haylee pulled her hair back into a hand-held ponytail. "Detective Neffting asked him if he'd like to sit in the front seat and continue their conversation. Dare accepted."

Still prone, with my lovely shawl as a pillow and Opal's as a blanket, Vicki groaned, pulled a radio out of her evening bag, pressed buttons, and said into it, "Detective Neffting, would you please bring that woman back into the banquet hall? There's something here that we need to question her about."

Clay and Ben looked at each other and rushed toward the lobby. Haylee sprinted to catch up.

Vicki objected, "Stay here, you three."

"We'll be right back," Ben answered.

Vicki closed her eyes. "They'll just get in the way." I knelt beside her again.

Minutes later, Neffting led Juliette, hand-cuffed and barefoot, into the dining hall. Looking like he thought he had accomplished an extremely important task, Dare swaggered in on Juliette's other side. Their faces serious and determined, Ben, Haylee, and Clay walked tightly behind the other three. Juliette didn't have a hope of escaping.

Vicki demanded, "Help me sit up."

Gord agreed with obvious reluctance. "Okay, but lean on us."

Opal, Edna, Naomi, Gord, and I all helped prop Vicki up, and she held court from the floor. "Where's your wallet, Juliette?" she asked.

Juliette lifted her head. Her eye makeup had run. "I must have lost it."

Vicki demanded, "Is that it, underneath the table?"

Neffting took Juliette where Vicki was pointing.

"I guess so," Juliette said.

"Give me a break," Vicki scolded. "You should recognize your own wallet."

"It's mine," Juliette mumbled.

"And how did it get there?" Vicki demanded.

Neffting looked unhappy about letting Vicki ask all the questions, but since he couldn't know what direction Vicki's interrogation might take, he didn't have a choice.

Juliette answered, "Beats me."

Vicki persisted, "Could it have fallen out

when you swung your bowling bag around?"

"I didn't." Juliette eyed me. "Willow's the one who swung that bag at you. I was just . . . lifting it."

That prompted a loud chorus of "We saw you!" and "Willow didn't do it!"

Vicki pleaded with everyone to be quiet. "You're hurting my head." A twitch of her mouth reminded me that she often hid her sense of humor. "Whose picture spilled out of your wallet, Juliette?"

"Lots of things spilled out."

Vicki asked, "Patricia, can you point to the picture you told me about? Sorry I can't get up and do it myself."

Warily keeping her distance from Juliette, Patricia pointed.

Juliette shrugged. "Just some guy."

"Work with me, here, Juliette," Vicki said. "No one carries pictures of strangers in their wallets."

"I didn't say he was a stranger," Juliette shot back.

"So who is he?" Vicki probed.

"Some guy I knew in college."

"Name?" Vicki asked.

Juliette hesitated. "I think it was Hero."

"Her*u*," Patricia corrected her. "Heru Crabbe."

Juliette's head shot up. "How would you

know that?" Her words were as ferocious as her eyes.

Patricia backed farther away from her. "I knew him in high school. His mother was my history teacher."

Juliette continued glaring at Patricia. "His *mother* was to blame for his death."

My resolve about letting the police handle their own inquiries suffered a temporary lapse. "How?" I demanded.

Vicki frowned at me and framed the question her way. "What do you mean his mother was to blame for his death?"

"The way she brought him up to lie, cheat, steal other people's term papers, and everything else. Like get in with the crowd that supplied the drugs that eventually killed him."

Vicki sat up straighter. "How do you know what killed him?"

Head lowered again, Juliette spoke from behind a curtain of her own hair. "That's what everyone said, and I believed it. And then I met Isis here in Threadville and . . ." She shrugged. "Other places. Other craft shows and fairs. After she found out where I went to school, she asked me if I was the tall girl named Juliette who had dated her son in college and had given him a drug overdose."

Neffting finally found his voice. "And were you?"

"Of course not," Juliette said. "I barely knew him."

Vicki's injury hadn't damaged her sarcasm. "So that's why you carry his picture in your wallet."

"It was a reminder to myself about what can happen to people who get in with the wrong crowd." Instead of the self-righteous smirk I'd have expected from someone delivering that statement, she continued gazing down toward her bare feet.

Neffting warned her, "We're going to have another look at all of the people who were at the party the night he died."

Juliette shot back, "If Isis told anyone I slipped those drugs into his drink, she was lying. He took them himself."

"So you *were* there," Vicki accused.

Juliette shook her head. "You didn't have to be at those frat parties to know what happened at them." The ribbons dangling from her white velvet gown were now creased and bedraggled, transforming the dress from cheerful to pathetic. "I didn't contribute to Heru's death, and I didn't kill his mother."

Dare widened his stance. "Ha! Detective Neffting allowed me to have a close look at your shoes before he loaded them into an evidence bag." He gave me a smug smile. "You all think you're such great sleuths, but *I* detected at least two other bits of light-bulb caught among the sparkly things originally attached to those shoes. The lab is sure to find more."

Juliette flushed. "So?"

"So, those little bits of lightbulb aren't heavy enough to travel very far, even if the bulb shattered. The only person who would have gotten those on her shoes had to be the person who was next to Isis when the lightbulbs hit the water. And that would be . . ." He raised one finger dramatically in the air. "The person who pushed her in."

"I wasn't wearing those shoes that night." Juliette looked wildly around at other people's feet. "I lent them to Haylee. She's your murderer."

Mrs. Battersby stood up and raised herself to her full height, all of about four-eight. "No she's not." Did I detect a note of pride in Mrs. Battersby's voice? "I was with Haylee that entire evening until she ran off to answer the fire siren and try to rescue that woman that someone had *already* pushed into the river."

"Willow, then. I get those two mixed up." Juliette's voice had become thin and nasal.

I defended myself. "I never wore your

shoes. Besides, when the lab looks at the outfit you were wearing that night, they could find bits of glass in it."

Puckers in Juliette's forehead relaxed slightly. "And maybe they won't." Her voice became almost strident again.

"I wasn't talking about the long skirt and peasant blouse," I told her. "I was talking about the dark jeans and matching jacket that you changed into and quickly changed out of after you pushed Isis into the river."

Juliette's bare toes curled against Ben's lovely dark oak floor. "That's nonsense."

Neffting took out his notebook and nodded at me. "Why do you say that, Willow?"

"Her blouse was on backward after Isis was pushed in. I saw her tuck in the tag."

Neffting took notes, probably about what to ask Juliette — and me — later.

"So?" Juliette asked. "I must have put the blouse on backward and worn it that way all day and all evening, too. That tag pops out all the time."

I accused, "I didn't see you tuck it in earlier, in the fire station."

She backpedaled. "Well, not *all* the time. And I did tuck it in, several times."

I asked the group, "Did anyone else who was there that night see the tag hanging out or see her tucking it in? Opal and Naomi?

You were working with her on the skirt."

Everyone said they hadn't seen her tuck the tag into the front of her blouse in the fire station.

Juliette's toes uncurled. She'd painted her toenails different colors, matching the ribbons she'd sewn to her gown. She pointed out, "So? I tucked in the tag without anyone noticing."

Although pale, Vicki's face showed her usual tough determination. "Maybe when we search the room where you've been staying we'll find the jeans and jacket."

I carefully did not look at Haylee. Vicki would never need to know we'd snooped among Juliette's things.

As if her brain felt like it was sloshing around inside her head, Vicki slowly turned toward Naomi. "Juliette has been staying with you, right?"

Naomi nodded. "Yes, Chief Smallwood."

Neffting took over. "You'll have to stay out of your apartment until it's searched."

"Okay." Naomi didn't look happy about it, and who could blame her? Edna's wedding was the next day, and like the rest of us, Naomi would want to get ready in her own apartment. But ever helpful, she told him and Vicki, "I found scraps of paper in my shop. Someone had written something about breaking a curse by encircling the victim with light. And that's like what Juliette said about Gord and Edna."

Juliette shrugged, "What bearing does that have on anything?"

I answered her. "You were trying to break Isis's curse on Edna. Isis has been following you around from show to fair to show, trying to ruin your reputation as a fortune-teller, hasn't she? You either had to stop her or find another way of earning a living. I saw you on the trail that night, before Isis was murdered."

Vicki frowned. I guessed I wasn't supposed to admit that, but I went on, "And we found the thread you were unwinding from the spool of glow-in-the-dark thread that we'd been using in the fire station. That thread was to be your circle of light, wasn't it?"

I could tell I'd rattled Juliette. Her breathing choppy, she stammered, "That was later, right before Patricia came along. I'd seen Isis at the river the night before, casting spells on Edna and Gord, and I knew I could counteract those spells by encircling Threadville and everyone in it with light. But that's all I did. I wouldn't have harmed Isis. Or her son." She added belatedly and untruthfully, "Or anyone."

453

I asked, "Did you cut a frill off the over-skirt we made?"

"Isis did that."

"How do you know?" Vicki asked.

"I saw her. She was attacking that over-skirt with scissors. I didn't stick around, though. I ran off to get help. She was ruining that skirt, and I knew that you people had put a lot of time and effort into it."

"Who did you ask to help you?" I demanded.

Vicki glared at me.

Juliette merely shrugged. "I couldn't find anyone. But I didn't harm Isis. I wasn't there."

I snapped my fingers. Juliette jumped and stared at me.

"It's obvious that you can hear perfectly well," I pointed out. "I heard you running up Lake Street *after* Isis was pushed in. I yelled at you to come help, but you kept going."

"I didn't hear you," she insisted. "The person you heard running couldn't have been me. I was probably knocking on your door or Haylee's to tell you about the damage Isis had done to the overskirt. I did no harm to Isis. I suspect she harmed herself."

Her excuses were a little late. She had attacked Vicki after the glass fragment had been identified. Vicki had only asked to see Juliette's shoes.

Neffting must have agreed. He said evenly, "None of this really matters at this moment. As I told you before, you're under arrest for assaulting a police officer, which is a serious offense. No other arrests yet, but we're also going search your car, your home, and the room where you've been staying here in Threadville. I mean Elderberry Bay. We're going to question you more about the night that Isis Crabbe died, and we're going to take statements from all these witnesses."

Dare tossed his hair back. "Those light-bulb fragments from her shoes should be enough, though it's lucky they stayed on her shoes for so long."

I took some pleasure in explaining it to the man who knew it all. "The shoes are fabric. Satin. The tiny piece of glass could have gotten stuck on the satin if the fabric was wet. The water stains on the toes of Juliette's shoes are subtle, but I was looking for them."

Dare gave me a gotcha look. "Why didn't the pieces of glass fall off after the shoes dried?"

Vicki smirked. She probably knew I was about to lecture Dare on fabrics or fashion.

I explained, "Fabrics are often stiffened

455

with a kind of starch called sizing. Starch can become sticky when wet, and then act like glue after it dries. In addition, when the bulbs exploded, pieces of glass would have shot out from them. Some of them could have slipped sort of sideways between sequins." I swooped my hand, palm flat and fingers straight, through the air like a fragment of glass being propelled sideways. "They could have become wedged underneath the edges of sequins."

As if I hadn't spoken, Dare turned to Detective Neffting. "Be sure to check for similar pieces of glass in the jeans and jacket she says she wasn't wearing. Your lab can put them together with any lightbulb fragments found at the scene. You *did* retrieve them all, I hope?"

Apparently not minding Dare's patronizing tone, Neffting gave Dare an appreciative nod. "We'll also look into the death of Hero Crabbe."

"Her*u*," Patricia muttered.

"You're making a mistake," Juliette complained. "These are all false charges."

*Sure, including assaulting Vicki, to which there were about a dozen witnesses.* I asked Juliette, "Couldn't you have looked into your crystal ball and predicted all this would happen? And prevented it?"

Vicki cautioned, "Willow . . ."

Cursing and staring daggers at me, Juliette wrenched her upper body forward, obviously trying to break free from Neffting.

## 46

It turned out I could rise to my feet in that cloak very quickly after all.

Clay and Ben were even faster. They put themselves between Juliette and the rest of us.

But Neffting had a viselike grip on her arm. He marched her outside.

Clay and Dare shadowed them. Ben stayed behind, still guarding Vicki sitting on the floor and all of the people around her. I could have hugged him. Haylee stared at his back with admiration.

Mrs. Battersby reached for my hand and held on. She may have been small, but she was mighty. I squeezed back.

Slowly, my breathing returned to normal. Vicki's face was greenish, but she hadn't let herself lie down again. She must have been feeling terrible. Ordinarily, she would have gone outside to help Detective Neffting, but she hadn't even attempted to get up and sit in a chair. Maybe she'd guessed that Gord would overrule her if she tried.

The state trooper who had collected Isis's little boats from the beach strode into the room with another state trooper. They rushed toward Vicki.

She cried out, "Stop! I'm not the one who needs help. Detective Neffting is outside with the woman who assaulted me and who I suspect murdered Isis Crabbe."

"It's okay," the cute boat-collector told her. "Two other troopers are out there with him and will help transport her for booking and questioning. He said you could show us evidence that he wanted us to collect."

Ben led them to the bowling bag containing the crystal ball and to the wallet and the photos and cards that had spilled from it. With a small camera, a trooper snapped pictures.

Mrs. Battersby let go of my hand. "Too much excitement," she announced. "A real granddaughter would not have gone tearing around in that unladylike way. Take me home, Haylee." She brushed at her royal blue lace dress. "Oh, that's right. We came in Naomi's car." She went over to Ben and tapped his arm. "Young man, you can help me out to the front of the hotel and wait with me while Naomi gets her car."

Vicki said, "Please, no one leave before you give these troopers your names and how to reach you."

Mrs. Battersby muttered, "As long as I don't have to answer any more questions from those other two who came barging in and thought I could be mistaken for Willow or Haylee."

The troopers circled the room, taking our names and addresses. The boat-collector asked me, "Do you need medical care, also?"

I'd merely stepped on a pebble. I shook my head, then saw him gazing in awestruck amazement at my knifed and red-smeared cloak.

"Oh, this old thing!" I gave a careless shrug. "I borrowed it."

He grinned and went on to Patricia.

Mrs. Battersby told me, "That thing is dreadful and not really your style. I thought you had better taste."

I made a horrible face and lurched toward her in my uneven-shouldered, loose-necked gait.

She batted at me. "Stop that. You're as bad as everyone else, after all."

Smiling, I removed the hooded cloak and draped it over a chair. Ben would undoubtedly help its rightful owner find it.

Mrs. Battersby stroked the cloak's scarlet lining. "Real silk. Too bad someone slashed a vintage piece like that and dabbed horrid red stuff all over it." She shuddered.

A siren blared. Ambulance attendants dashed into the dining room. They apologized for being delayed by an earlier call, examined Vicki quickly, agreed with Gord that she should be thoroughly checked out at the hospital, and went outside for their gurney.

Vicki had managed to pack a lot into her oversized evening bag. I'd guessed she had a weapon in it, and I'd seen her radio. Now she pulled out a phone and told the person on the other end that she was fine, but could he — I was pretty sure she was talking to Toby Gartener, her favorite detective — please meet her at the hospital.

I helped her make certain that she had control of her heavy evening bag even after she was underneath a blanket on the stretcher.

"See you at the wedding tomorrow," she called as they wheeled her out of the dining room.

For some reason, that made me teary. Maybe you were supposed to cry at weddings, but really, the night before, also?

I wiped my eyes before Brianna might

notice and announce again that we were all too disgustingly sappy, but Brianna was gone. She must have slipped out when we weren't looking.

She was on her way to my place to pack and leave, I hoped.

I also hoped that she'd already be gone when Clay took me home.

I put on my shawl and handed Opal hers, and then Haylee, her three mothers, Gord, Patricia, and I followed Ben and Mrs. Battersby outside.

Patricia looked at her feet as she walked.

I tapped her elbow. "Are you okay?"

She pushed her glasses up her nose and gave me a watered-down smile. "I feel terrible, like I betrayed Juliette's friendship. In a way, we were both victims of Isis Crabbe and her son. They were horrible people, but Juliette shouldn't have taken anyone's life. If I'd known what she was planning, I might have been able to stop her. Now Isis has ruined Juliette's life, too."

I shook my head. "Juliette murdered Isis and possibly Isis's son, too. You should be proud of yourself for helping catch her."

"I suppose." She said good-bye and stumbled, head down, toward the parking lot.

Gord and Naomi, who also needed to

fetch their vehicles, gave each other looks and sped their pace. They'd catch up with her, no doubt, and chat with her on the way to their cars, and maybe Patricia could stop blaming herself for writing a college application essay that Heru stole and then used to get himself into a school where he could, as Juliette had put it, "get in with the wrong crowd" — a crowd that must have included Juliette.

Mrs. Battersby settled herself on a Victorian bench. "Sit beside me, Willow, while your escort brings his chariot around. You shouldn't have to walk another inch. Where are your shoes?"

I sank down beside her and glanced up the hill. "In the chapel. I'll get them sometime."

Ben dashed up the hill.

Clay gave Mrs. Battersby a big smile. "My pickup truck? A chariot?"

Mrs. Battersby scowled. "Very romantic." She shook her head. "I don't know what's wrong with you young folks. Haylee, too. Driving a truck!"

Edna sat on the other side of Mrs. Battersby. "Life is short. I'm glad Haylee's enjoying it with that truck of hers."

Clay sent me a special smile, then loped up the pathway that led to the parking lot.

Gord was the first to return. He helped Edna into his car, made certain that Mrs. Battersby had a ride, and drove off with his bride-to-be.

Naomi came next. Opal slid in behind Naomi. Ben raced to the porte cochere, handed me my shoes, helped Mrs. Battersby into the passenger seat, closed the door, and opened the one behind it for Haylee. After she was seated, he leaned over the top of the door. I overheard his gentle, "See you tomorrow." He shut her door.

Clay arrived in his chariot, hopped out, and opened the passenger door for me. I tossed my shoes and evening bag in first, then, clutching my shawl around my shoulders, I managed to clamber in without stumbling over my feet or anything else.

Clay eased out of the circular driveway. "Is Edna okay? The disruption wasn't until after dinner, but it must have put a blight on her evening anyway." Concern etched lines on his forehead.

I turned quickly toward him. "Edna's nearly *always* okay. She always makes the best of everything."

He laughed. "She must have learned that as a defense mechanism against her mother."

"What a character! I'm supposed to keep

Mrs. Battersby out of mischief at the wedding tomorrow. Haylee, Naomi, and Opal are in the wedding party and won't be able to."

"I might be able to help a little between ushering people up the aisle. I get a kick out of her. What about the reception? Who's going to keep her out of trouble then? You'll be dancing. With me, I hope."

I managed to answer calmly, "Opal, Naomi, and Haylee will keep an eye on her. And you know Gord will dance at least once with her."

"And Ben had better be available for a few dances with Haylee," he said.

I sighed. "She was afraid to invite him to the wedding and reception as her date."

"Edna and Gord invited him. He'll be an usher tomorrow."

I grinned. "And Haylee's a bridesmaid. Perfect!"

"Gord and Edna invited nearly everyone, including Dare. He's going." Clay didn't sound terribly happy about it.

I suggested, "So he can make more fun of our rustic ways?"

"He joined our rustic ways tonight. He became the Great Detective."

I laughed. "The next thing you know, he'll move here."

Clay gripped the steering wheel and stared straight ahead.

I put a hand on his arm. "Don't tell me he's moving in with you!"

"He says his research in the area could take the rest of autumn, and winter, too."

I made appropriately sympathetic — and perhaps rude — noises. "I made a list of sewing and quilting shops for Brianna to visit on her way home."

"Good luck." He parked the truck next to the curb. Right behind Brianna's car. "I'll come around and open that door for you," he said, "so I can catch you when you tumble off your seat."

Until that moment, falling down into his arms hadn't occurred to me. I'd done it once already that evening, and he had unceremoniously plunked me into a chair and run off in pursuit of a murderer.

But this was different. It was around eleven at night on a street lit only by streetlights, and I didn't see anyone else around.

Smiling, Clay opened the truck door.

I fell out of his passenger seat and into his arms.

He gazed down into my face. "What an evening," he whispered.

I checked. My bare feet were on terra firma. Although my hands were full of shoes and my bag, I put my arms around his neck.

He lowered his head.

"Clay and Willow!"

I pulled out of Clay's arms and turned to see who was shouting.

Outside Naomi's shop, Opal and Naomi waved madly at us.

Two state police cars drove slowly up Lake Street toward them.

Naomi beckoned to the cruisers. She would take the investigators through her shop and up to her apartment, where they could search through everything Juliette had left there, and then she would go off to spend the night with Opal or Haylee.

I grabbed Clay's hand and pulled him toward the front porch of In Stitches. I didn't have to pull hard.

As always, a night-light burned inside my shop. Our silhouettes would be easily seen among the shadows on the porch. Naomi and Opal were probably distracted by the investigators, but if anything was going to happen between Clay and me, I wanted it to be private.

I unlocked the shop's front door.

Clay stroked my upper arm with the lightest of touches.

I opened the door, glanced up into his eyes, and murmured, "Come downstairs

467

with me?"

No music boomed from my apartment. Brianna's car was outside, but maybe by some miracle she'd fallen asleep without turning on her music.

I left my shoes near the cash desk and tiptoed across the shop.

At the door leading down to my apartment, Clay was right behind me, his breath warm on the back of my head. I again considered turning around, throwing my arms around him, and clinging, but that night-light seemed altogether too bright.

I quietly opened the door.

Gesturing to him to follow, I started down the stairs.

I didn't turn on a light. He placed a hand on my shoulder.

With one of my hands covering his, I guided him the rest of the way down the almost-dark stairway to my apartment.

The only light in my great room was the one over the wall oven.

At the foot of the stairs, I took a deep breath and turned toward Clay.

Smiling, he pulled me to him.

Brianna's door banged open. We jumped away from it. And from each other.

Light poured from Brianna's room. She stomped out, turned on the overhead lights, and said loudly into the phone, "She just came sneaking in with her boyfriend. Here she is."

## 47

Brianna thrust my phone toward me. "Your mother needs to talk to you."

"Sneaking in?" my mother said into my ear. I couldn't be sure if her amusement was real.

"Not exactly." My voice didn't work.

"Boyfriend?"

"Not really." Did Clay know what I was denying? Knowing Brianna was probably in my apartment, I shouldn't have invited him inside.

Clay must have thought the same thing. He waved and let himself out the patio door.

Brianna plopped down on my couch, hugged one of my sofa pillows, and sneered at me.

"A big, lavish wedding down here would help erase your reputation," my mother suggested.

"My w*hat*?"

My mother let out one of her glassy

laughs. "Oh, not your reputation with men, Willow, honey, but Todd Shrevedale called me just now with a tale about you interfering with the police." She became very serious. "You do realize that if you injured a policewoman you could end my career? I might not even be able to return to being a physician."

"I didn't! I prevented an attack from being worse than it was."

"Brianna warned me you'd say something like that."

"That's not true."

"Yes it is. You *did* say what she told me you'd say."

"Mother, I think you should get some sleep. And maybe talk to someone else who was there."

"Like the boyfriend?"

"And about ten other witnesses."

"Why would Brianna make things up?"

*To discredit me and therefore you.* But I wasn't going to explain that in front of Brianna. "I have some theories. I'll e-mail them to you."

Brianna glowered at me. She must have understood that my "theories" were about her. She threw the pillow down, padded into her room, and slammed the door.

I asked my mother, "When's she leaving?"

"Leaving? Not until after the wedding she's helping you with."

I nearly choked.

My mother went on, "And I've told her she can use your home as a base while she tours that part of the country."

This time, I did choke. "No," I stated firmly. "Absolutely not. This is my home, and I do not want her here."

"You've often told me your guest suite was for your father and me. I'm just giving her our share until we can come up and visit." Her voice took on those syrupy tones that should frighten me. "Now don't disappoint me by being ungracious to the child, honey. I know you can be hospitable if you really, really try."

*"No,"* I said again, with even more force. "The whole time she's been here, she's tried to make trouble in an attempt to discredit both you and me so that her father will stop supporting you. We wouldn't want her damaging your campaign any more than she already has, would we." It wasn't a question. "As I said, I'll e-mail you the details. But it's late, and I have a busy day ahead of me tomorrow. Good *night,* Mother." I hung up.

I sounded so much like my mother that I scared myself.

■ ■ ■ ■

The sky was that painful, pure blue of October. The temperature was perfect for an outdoor wedding. Lake Erie rippled and danced in the sunshine.

Mrs. Battersby insisted on passing up the other ushers and waiting until Ben and Clay were free to usher us to our front row seats, and then she took Ben's arm. I looped my hand into the crook of Clay's elbow. He placed his hand over mine for a moment and smiled down at me, and then we slowly walked up the aisle behind Ben and Mrs. Battersby.

True to her word, Vicki was among the congregation sitting in chairs facing the flower-covered archway. She looked fine, and why wouldn't she, with Toby Gartener at her side? With a jaunty grin, she gave the thumbs-up sign and beckoned me closer.

I bent toward her.

She whispered, "They found enough to charge Juliette with Isis's murder."

Gartener put a protective arm around her. I smiled at them both. I was getting teary again.

Clay ushered me to the front. I slipped into my seat beside Mrs. Battersby, and

Clay joined the other groomsmen facing the congregation.

I half expected Gord to hum the "Wedding March," but a string quartet played it instead. I turned to watch the bridal procession.

Her cheeks flushed with excitement, Haylee came down the aisle first. Looking every bit as happy, Naomi and Opal followed her in their elegant sea foam silk gowns.

Behind them, Edna marched by herself with suitable drama and a huge bouquet. The dress she had beaded was stunning, and she had wound bling-embellished white velvet ribbons through her glittering silver hair.

Beaming, Gord stepped forward to join her.

Edna's dress was as pretty in the back as it was in the front. No one would be able to detect the teensy lights she'd embedded between beads. She planned to turn them on at the reception.

Mrs. Battersby leaned toward me and said, "Her dress isn't *that* bad, Willow. At least it doesn't look like it was dredged out of a mummy's tomb." She probably hadn't expected the music to end the second she began speaking.

Opal frowned. Naomi looked pained. Haylee smiled.

Standing in front with Ben and the other groomsmen, Clay smiled at me.

I forgot all about Edna, Gord, the sparkling lake, and the blue, blue sky.

# WILLOW'S EMBROIDERED
# WEDDING CARD

When friends or family have special occasions that call for cards, how about making your own? And how about making them really special with your own embroidery designs?

**Materials:**

1. Fabric:

Your embroidered designs and message will show up best on plain colors. Use matching or contrasting fabrics, whichever you prefer. I used the sea foam silk from Edna's bridesmaid's dresses for the outside of my card, and the white silk that Edna used for her dress (before she stitched on about a million beads!) for the inside.

Each of the two pieces of fabric must be larger than the machine embroidery hoop you plan to use, and be sure to leave room for a seam allowance all around the size the card will be when opened flat. I made a rectangular card, but you can be creative.

2. Stabilizer:
Use the appropriate weight for the fabric you've chosen. It doesn't need to be water-soluble or tear-away.

3. Thread:
Use as many colors of embroidery thread as you'll need for your design — this could be a fun time to experiment with metallic or glow-in-the-dark threads.

You'll also need thread that is strong enough for sewing the card together. Choose a color that blends with your fabric(s).

4. Interfacing:
Use a heavy interfacing, sturdy enough to make your finished card crisp.

**Construction:**
1. Hoop the fabric for the outside of the card with the part of the fabric that will be the front of the card (the half of the rectangle that is to your right) centered in the hoop.

2. Stitch the design you've chosen. I stitched

"Best Wishes" surrounded by tiny hearts. Knowing Edna's love of everything that sparkles, I used glittery silver thread.

3. Unhoop that fabric and set aside.

4. Hoop the fabric for the inside of the card with the part of the fabric that will be the inner message (again, it will be the half of the rectangle that is to your right) centered in the hoop.

5. Stitch your message — and your signature, if you'd like.

I used the same glittery thread that I'd used for the outside. On the inside, I stitched Edna and Gord's names, the location of the wedding (okay, I said it was Threadville instead of stitching the proper name of the village . . .), and the wedding date.

6. Unhoop that fabric.

7. Cut both pieces of the fabric and the interfacing to the size of the finished card plus sufficient seam allowance (5/8″ is the norm).

8. Baste interfacing to the wrong side of

one of the pieces of fabric.

9. Making certain that both of your designs will be right side up when the card is turned right side out, pin the two pieces of fabric right sides together.

10. Stitch around the rectangle, leaving the seam allowance you've chosen and a gap in the stitching large enough to turn the card through the gap — a longer gap for heavier fabrics and bigger cards, a shorter gap for lighter fabrics and smaller cards.

11. Trim interfacing close to the stitching and trim the two pieces of fabric in layers (hint: leaving the fabric next to the gap untrimmed will make it easier for you to tuck that fabric in — see next step). Trim corners.

12. Turn card right side out and press, folding the fabric in neatly at the gap.

13. Stitch close to sewn edge all around (hint: for precise edge stitching, use a presser foot especially designed for it).

14. Fold card in half and press fold.

Please send photos of your finished projects

to Willow@ThreadvilleMysteries.com and let me know what the recipient said about the card!

Happy celebrations!

# WILLOW'S TIPS

1. Before stitching pieces that you can join as a 3-D freestanding machine embroidery lace figure or structure, note the finished size and draw a copy (template) of each element on a piece of lightweight cardboard.

2. When creating 3-D freestanding machine embroidery lace, don't rinse out all of the water-soluble stabilizer you used. Some of the residue will serve as starch.

3. Press your lace pieces while still damp and pin to fit your template (see tip #1 above) to dry completely. This will help you fit the pieces together after they're dry.

4. Use a pressing cloth to keep the starch off your iron's sole plate. What, you don't own a pressing cloth? Use pinking shears to cut a square, about a foot on each side, from unbleached muslin. Wash and dry the mus-

lin to remove the sizing (starch) from it before using it as a pressing cloth.

5. Always use a pressing cloth when pressing your embroidery and use a low setting on your iron — you don't want to melt your design.

## HAVE FUN! THAT'S WHAT IT'S ALL ABOUT, RIGHT?